Just like going to sleep . . .

"Susan didn't suffer, Daddy," said Hester. "She went quickly and quietly. Just like going to sleep. You see how beautiful and still she is, with her cheeks glowing red through the makeup. That's what happens when you get the carbon monoxide quickly."

As the lift reached the van's open side door and turned so she could wheel him inside, Lester made a guttural sound.

"Oh, no, Daddy," Hester said, "Dr. Broward won't get it quickly. That wouldn't be fair at all. Not to either of us, Daddy. It wouldn't even be fair to Susan. Dr. Broward will have to suffer as much as you did from the poison in her blood."

A POISON IN THE BLOOD

A POISON IN THE BLOOD

FAY ZACHARY

J

JOVE BOOKS, NEW YORK

A POISON IN THE BLOOD

A Jove Book / published by arrangement with
the author

PRINTING HISTORY
Jove edition / October 1994

ISBN: 0-515-11472-3

A JOVE BOOK®
Jove Books are published by The Berkley Publishing Group,
200 Madison Avenue, New York, New York 10016.
JOVE and the "J" design are trademarks
belonging to Jove Publications, Inc.

PRINTED IN THE UNITED STATES OF AMERICA

10 9 8 7 6 5 4 3 2 1

DEDICATION

In memory of my aunt, Jean Gropper,
who gave me the courage to try.

ACKNOWLEDGMENTS

My heartfelt thanks to the following:

Donna Shea Newman, for the inspiring idea behind the plot.

Cynthia A. Fissel, for technical help on the courtroom scene.

Lee Goodwin, who taught me how to murder by Mercedes.

Gary Hoff, M.D., for technical help on poisons.

John L. Myers, for critical comment on the manuscript.

Alex Krislov and Janet McConnaughey, CompuServe Litforum Sysops, who run the friendliest cybersalon in the world for writers.

All my online friends on CompuServe and GEnie, who support and encourage me in my literary efforts.

Joe, my husband, Karen, Janet, and Michael, my children, for showing their pride in my accomplishments.

My mother, Rose Bortz, for bragging about me to all who'll listen.

My brother, Fred Bortz, for sharing my literary sufferings.

My cousin, Barbara Krueger, for throwing wonderful parties to celebrate my successes.

Judith Anderson, road buddy on my Arizona adventures.

Norine Dresser, for unfailing support and friendship.

PROLOGUE

PHILADELPHIA—EARLY SEPTEMBER

"We're going to the funeral home," said Hester Jones to what remained of her father. Her voice at thirty-five had not lost its little-girl lisp and light tenor, though her body was large and muscular—like a man's except for her overflowing bosom. Both qualities suited her for the cross she bore—the lifelong care of the limbless blind man on the hospital bed sharing her room. They suited her for her profession, too. Till she gave up her job to care for him full-time, she'd been a rehabilitation nurse in a hospital that treated brain- and spine-damaged people. There she'd helped *them* bear their crosses.

"What would you like to wear, Daddy?" Like a mother preparing an excited child to visit Great Adventure park, she held out two outfits draped on wire hangers. In her right hand she displayed olive-green Bermuda shorts, matching vest, striped short-sleeved olive and gray shirt, and gold tie. In the left, she presented his charcoal dress suit—pants legs pinned up to the thigh and coat sleeves pinned up to the elbow—and the light gray shirt, and the tie with quiet black and white houndstooth pattern. She herself wore a gray faille tentlike shift, bow-tied at the neck, and low-heeled black walking shoes with laces.

He turned his face toward her, and his head lolled slightly. He made a guttural sound.

1

"Yes, you're right," said Hester. "The gray would be more appropriate, but she always thought you so handsome in the shorts. She'd love to have you come in them, I'm sure. And they're so much more comfortable, don't you think?" She gestured to her right hand with her head. "It's decided!"

He grunted and drooled a little.

She put the suit down on the blanket where his legs would have been, grabbed some tissues from the nightstand, and dabbed his mouth. Then, after returning the charcoal outfit to the closet, she took off his pajamas, irrigated his colostomy, cleaned its bag, and replaced it. Then she pulled his shorts on over his lower stumps and his shirt and vest on over his upper ones, which looked like little levers meant for operating him.

When she'd spit-combed his short brown hair spikes into place, and lotioned his face till it shone, she looked at him and laughed and clapped her hands. "What a dear Tweedledum you are, Daddy! I'd put a hat on you if only it wouldn't fall off when I picked you up."

With that she said "Upsy-daisy!" and she threw her massive arms about his torso and locked her thick fingers like bolts; then, barely straining, she hoisted him, the 100 pounds remaining of the 220, the three feet left of the six that he once had been. It was when she moved him from his bed to his wheelchair that she knew he was still alive inside the lump that most people thought him. He sprang into her arms and lightened himself as if of his own volition; he seemed to help propel her across the few feet to the chair. Then he caught the chair arms with his stumps as she lowered him into it, making it easier for her to sit him there without dropping him like a stone.

Then his round face split into a smile reminiscent of the one he'd smiled when his face had been firm and craggy. On that face of just a few years ago, three days' growth of beard often had darkened the hollows of his cheeks. He had frequently let himself go that way after her mother had died, not shaving for half a week, not bathing for an entire five days, not sticking to his diet but gorging on sugary and fatty foods, drinking beer when he knew he shouldn't have.

Now, of course, she kept him scrupulously clean, shaved him daily, fed him strictly according to American Diabetic Association protocols, and checked his urine and dosed him with his insulin rigorously. She also took him out for their daily walks in nearby Rittenhouse Square, took him grocery shopping, even to movies, which he couldn't see, but which he seemed to enjoy for their background music and sounds. They went to special places, too, like the one they were going to today. Today she would place him in the van and drive him across town to the Morningside Glen Mortuary in Glenside, where Susan Freiden lay in state.

The rude ones stared, open-mouthed, as she wheeled him to the Tudor-style funeral home's ramp entrance. The others turned away and pretended not to see, though their eyes did strange acrobatic twists as she passed.

Inside the main foyer, she signed the visitor's book: Hester and Lester Jones, of Pine Street, Philadelphia. She looked forward to the thank-you note she'd get from Susan Freiden's husband and children. She'd put it into her scrapbook with the newspaper article about Susan's suicide. There, she'd already mounted pictures and articles about the product liability trial, and a newspaper story about how Dr. Liz Broward had received a local medical society award for humanitarian acts, how she'd brought more honor to the prominent Main Line family name. *Soon she'd have more articles about Dr. Broward for her scrapbook.*

After signing the "Friends" book, Hester wheeled her father into the chapel where Susan reposed. Susan had been very popular, especially with her patients; and though today was a workday and it was only a little past one, knots of people milled about and buzzed to one another.

Hester wheeled her father among the knots to the one nearest the casket. Suddenly, that group broke up, recoiled. Hester and her father had Susan's body to themselves.

"Oh, Daddy! Look at her. Isn't she beautiful?" Shining through the mortician's makeup artistry, the vermilion face glowed lifelike. The undertaker couldn't have pulled that off if she'd died any other way. Hester admired him for using what nature had provided, instead of trying to cover it. She moved the wheelchair as close as she could.

Her father moved his right arm stump and rested it on the casket. A tear from the corner of his eye ran fat and hot down his cheek.

Once more Hester knew he was alive and feeling. He missed Susan. Despite her betrayal.

A blond woman about Hester's age came up behind her. "She was always a beautiful woman—inside and out. Death couldn't change that," she said. "She did so much for so many. Was . . . he . . . ah . . . a patient of hers?"

Turning, Hester said, "Yes. She was his nurse for years. And my friend and colleague."

"She cared for my mother till she died," said the woman. "A wonderful human being." Tears burst from her reddened eyes, and she turned her head away and scrambled through her handbag and got a tissue. After blowing her nose, she cleared her throat and said, squeaky voiced, "What could have made her do such a thing? It doesn't make sense."

But it did make sense! Susan Freiden had paid for her sins—for her treachery! She'd died perfectly logically, because of what she'd done . . .

Susan Freiden had destroyed Lester Jones. Lester's lawyer had called her to testify *against* the company that had built the defective car. But trust the car company to hire Paul Broward to defend them. Yes, and trust that fancy lawyer to turn even Susan Freiden against Hester's father. With her help, he had converted a multimillion-dollar claim into a farcical $500,000 award. An award that turned out to be less than $200,000, once the Joneses' lawyer got her cut, once the expert witnesses were paid for proving that the car's defect *could* have cost Lester Jones his limbs and sight, *could* have rotted his lower bowel, vitiated his brain.

Susan had meant to testify *for* the plaintiff, her diabetic home care patient. But it didn't come out that way.

"You'd been visiting Lester Jones for how many years?" Rosemary Jenkins, Lester's diminutive, red-haired attorney asked Susan.

"Six. Since his wife died." Susan ran a hand nervously through her long black hair and blew a clinging wisp from her damp brow.

"How often?"

"Monthly, till the changes. Then more often."

Lawyer Jenkins said, "Often enough to monitor his condition closely?"

"Yes."

"Did there come a time when you noticed a change in his condition?"

"Yes, it began to deteriorate in August, the year before last."

"Two months after he bought his new car?"

"Well, I don't know exactly when he bought the car. He didn't tell me about that." Susan glanced uneasily toward the plaintiff's table where Lester sat in his wheelchair, head lolling, next to Hester.

Jenkins smiled reassuringly at her witness. "Try to remember when he said he bought the car, Mrs. Freiden."

"Well, I think it was in June—two months before I saw the changes."

Looking at the plaintiff, his lawyer then looked at the jury box and back at the man, the half-person who was left of the man. He couldn't speak, but his condition spoke eloquently for him. The jurors could barely stand to look at him. Jenkins steeled herself and looked at him intently.

"The changes that led to what we see?" She glanced at the defense lawyer, a lean gray-haired man in his sixties, who'd practiced law longer than the forty years she had been alive. She knew well of his canniness. He sat back in his chair, aristocratic and cool in his navy blue three-piece suit, his icy blue eyes unrevealing, a smile curling his thin lips. She'd expected him to object that the condition of the plaintiff was not relevant to the date on which Lester had bought his car, and she was ready to argue its pertinence. He said nothing, did not even shift his position in his chair or his unnerving gaze.

Did the jury notice her momentary discomfort? Probably not, for they were too intent on looking down at their laps to avoid seeing Lester's condition. So she quickly recovered what she deemed her advantage and turned to question Susan again.

"What were the changes you saw?"

"Reduced circulation in his extremities."

"His hands and feet?"

"Yes. Suddenly, his toes became gangrenous. And cuts on his fingers wouldn't heal."

"And what did you do about that?"

"Well, Dr. Thomas had him admitted to the hospital, where we could monitor his care."

"Did the cuts begin to heal?"

"Yes. After a few weeks. But he lost a few toes."

"And then he was sent home?"

"Yes. He was well enough to go back to work as a handyman. The toe loss didn't bother him much."

"So he went back to driving to jobs?"

"I assume he drove. I know he always had work and supported himself."

Rosemary Jenkins glanced at the defense attorney again. She was certain he'd object to a witness's assumptions. He didn't even raise that steel gray brow. What surprises was he holding aside? Or did he hope that by not challenging this sympathetic witness he'd avoid antagonizing the jury, turning them against his client? That must have been it.

Jenkins went on, "And how did he progress after that?"

"All right for about a month. Then the same thing started again."

"The same thing?"

"He got cuts on his hands and they wouldn't heal."

"And his feet?"

"He wouldn't let me look at his feet. Not for several months." She looked at Lester and shook her head.

Jenkins looked surprised. She turned to look at the plaintiff in his wheelchair, then turned again to the witness. "Do you know why he wouldn't let you examine his feet?"

Looking at her former patient, her eyes glistening with tears, she said, "He was—is—a very proud man. He didn't want to give up his work. He never complained about the pain."

"Go on."

"He didn't want me to see that his feet were becoming gangrenous again. We'd have put him back in the hospital and he wouldn't have been able to work. But I knew what was happening . . . because . . . because I could smell it. And I was helpless. Even Hester—his daughter—couldn't convince him. He got up every morning and laced on tall work boots, which made things even worse because they rubbed him and made pressure sores, and he drove to his calls, all over the city, till, at last, he couldn't do it one morning. Partly because his eyes were going, too, and he just couldn't see well enough to drive."

The attorney for the auto company crossed his arms across his chest and nodded.

"And do you think that was what finally made him seek treatment?" asked Jenkins.

"Yes. He finally agreed to be hospitalized. And when Dr. Thomas put him in again, they found out his digestive system was riddled with lesions, and his kidneys weren't functioning as they should."

The defense attorney stood up and objected in a soft, aristocratic lisp, shooshing between his back teeth. "This nurse isn't qualified to diagnose the patient's condition. That's up to the doctors on the case."

"Sustained," said the judge. "The witness should stick to her own observations."

Jenkins said, "The exhibits of medical records will support her," then returned to her questioning. "And what happened when he was discharged from the hospital?"

"The home nursing department dispatched me again to see him regularly. I had a good relationship with him and could help him deal with his emotional response to his condition."

"And what *was* his condition at that time?"

"He'd had both legs amputated just below the knees, and had lost his left hand and forearm."

"How often did you call on him after discharge?"

"Three times a week. He had custodial care round the clock. Hester took care of him weekends, too."

"So he needed twenty-four-hour care. At that point, did you hope to rehabilitate him?"

"Yes. Once the limbs had a chance to heal and the ostomy was working well, we felt he could be at least able to take care of most activities of daily living. He wouldn't be able to return to work, though."

"And how did the rehabilitation go?"

"His limbs never healed. Eventually he lost his legs halfway up the thighs, and the other arm. His diabetes seemed to be under control. We couldn't figure out why the condition should worsen, until his daughter, Hester, read in the paper about the—"

"Objection!" The defense attorney shot out of his chair. "Again, this nurse is beyond her expertise."

The judge sustained the objection.

Jenkins said, "No further questions," and, nodding to the defense attorney, said, "Your witness."

The auto company's lawyer nodded and rose again. An imposing man more than six feet tall, Paul Broward towered over the witness. Jenkins was smaller and less threatening than anyone else on the case. Her opponent, as befit his giant of a client, was larger than any witness on either side; larger than even the judge. And his reputation for ruthlessness on his clients' behalf was even larger than his physical size.

Rosemary Jenkins told Hester that in this case, ruthlessness was a disadvantage. How would it look to be ruthless toward someone who'd suffered the pain and loss Lester had? The car had all but killed this man. The blind, crippled man need only appear in court every day to convince the jury he needed ten million dollars for his lifelong care, for his agony. The agony wouldn't go away, but it could be eased if his daughter could quit her gainful employment and nurse him. The auto giant's slovenly assembly practice, their shoddy design, had cost two lives, not just one! How could the ruthless defense lawyer prevail against that? The jury would recoil from his usual tactics, just as they recoiled from the man in the wheelchair.

But it was obvious the moment the imperious old man leaned toward the frightened home care nurse in the witness stand that ruthlessness was his favorite sword, and he meant to thrust it home.

Jenkins smiled, leaned sideways and whispered to Hester: "He's dead!"

"Six years?" the man asked the witness, his lisp shearing off the consonants. "You made home visits to Lester Jones for *shixsh yearsh*?"

Susan shifted and seemed to cower. "I . . . ah . . . yes, sir."

"Why?"

"Well, he's a diabetic, you know."

"Yes. And for how long has he been diabetic?"

"It was diagnosed when he was a teenager."

"He's fifty-eight now. And you've only been visiting him for six years. Didn't he get home visits before?"

"Well, no. He never had to have home visits. He was under control. His wife was a nurse. A licensed practical nurse, that is. She always made sure he followed his diet and checked his urine. She gave him his insulin."

"And she died, you say, just before you began the home visits at Dr. Thomas's request, I believe. Or so earlier testimony indicated."

"Yes. That is, I was sent out by the home nursing service at the hospital to evaluate his condition a couple of months after she died. Dr. Thomas's office ordered it."

"Is an evaluation like that usually called for?"

Susan's eyes darted, imploringly, to the plaintiff's table. Lawyer Jenkins stood up. "Your honor, now the defense attorney is asking Mrs. Freiden to go beyond her nursing judgment and read the mind of the doctor."

"Not at all, Judge," said lawyer Broward. "A home health nurse would certainly know how often such cases required evaluation. After all, it's her business to make such calls."

The judge said, "The plaintiff's counsel has a point. The nurse would know what kind of calls she usually made, but not how usual certain kinds of requests are in general. I sustain the objection."

Jenkins sighed and sat down. Susan looked relieved.

Shrugging and curling his lip, the man again turned his lean tense face to the witness. "So, Mrs. Freiden, you made your evaluation. Did you report your findings to Dr. Thomas?"

"Yes. My findings and my care recommendations."

"And those were . . . ?"

"That without having Mrs. Jones there anymore to make meals and, well, more or less monitor his medication and so forth, a monthly visit would help make sure he kept his condition under control."

"I see. You say that Mr. Jones went out to work regularly. Because, as you put it, he was a proud man."

"Yes. He was always a good provider."

"And physically, there was no reason for him not to work, at that time."

"Oh, no. He was pretty healthy. Controlled diabetics can live fairly normal lives."

"Yes. I believe there are some sports heroes who are diabetics."

Susan nodded vigorously. "Yes. That's right."

"*Controlled* diabetics."

"Yes. Naturally."

"They can hold down jobs, provide for their families?"

"Many do."

"And go see their doctors regularly to monitor their condition."

Susan started to say "Yes," then her eyes widened.

The defense attorney smiled. "And did Mr. Jones go to see his doctor regularly?"

Jenkins objected, "Your Honor, that's hardly relevant." But she could see from the expression on Susan's face that Susan thought it was.

"Your Honor," intoned the auto maker's lawyer, "if you'll allow me to continue my questioning along this line, the court will find this matter to be relevant."

"Overruled. You may continue the questioning. Please answer, Mrs. Freiden."

Biting her lip, Susan shook her head.

"Please answer aloud, so the court recorder can hear," said the judge.

"I . . . no."

"No what?" the lawyer pressed her.

"No, he didn't go to the doctor regularly. That is, not after his wife died. Before that, she made sure he did."

"So, before she died, he took care of himself, and afterward he didn't."

Rosemary Jenkins said, "My colleague is twisting the witness's words, Your Honor. And, I still don't see the relevance of his questioning."

"Please don't interpret what the witness says," said the judge to the defender. To Jenkins he said, "We'll let him develop his line of questioning."

"Shorry, Your Honor. Now, Mishuszh Freiden, let me ask you this way: How often did Mr. Jones go to his doctor for diabetic monitoring after his wife passed away?"

"Up until the time I saw him the first time?"

"Yes."

"He didn't go at all."

"Are you sure of that?"

"Yes. Dr. Thomas called the home care service because Mr. Jones had missed three appointments. Knowing about Mrs. Jones's death, and of how dependent Mr. Jones was on her to keep him under treatment, he was afraid he'd slip in his self-care."

The steel gray brows rose above the lawyer's haughty, hooded eyes. "And had he slipped?"

"I couldn't tell for sure. His urine tested negative for glucose. And he showed no signs that he was out of control."

"Oh? But you recommended monthly visits anyway? Why?"

Jenkins shot up from her chair. "Please, Your Honor. Mrs. Freiden said her patient's diabetes was under control. My colleague has no right to question her nursing judgment under those circumstances."

"I'm not questioning her judgment, Judge Stern. I'm asking her to explain what she based it on. Furthermore, she said that even though the disease appeared to be under control, she wasn't sure the patient hadn't 'slipped' in caring for himself."

"Hmmn, yes she *did* say that. Recorder, please read back the witness's last answer."

The gray-haired court recorder adjusted her steel-rimmed glasses and read from the transcript in front of her exactly what Susan had said.

"You're right, Counselor. All right, Mrs. Freiden, please answer the last question."

Susan looked confused.

The defender said, "Let me ask *my* question more clearly. Why were you unsure that he hadn't slipped, even though his diabetes seemed to be still under control?"

"It . . . it was other things besides his physical condition."

"What other things?"

"Well, the evaluation includes things like the way he ate, and if he was getting enough sleep, and just the general appearance of the house. And his personal hygiene."

"Did something about any of those things bother you?"

"A . . . a little."

"Specifically, what bothered you 'a little'?"

"I deliberately came at mealtime, so I could observe what he made himself to eat. He'd stopped at a fast-food place on his way home and bought something for dinner." She looked at Hester with apology. Obviously she knew what the lawyer was getting at, and so did Rosemary Jenkins.

Hester glowered.

The defender smirked at the plaintiff's table, and raised his eyebrows again. "Fast food? What specifically had he bought for his dinner?"

"A double cheeseburger with everything, and French fries."

"And something to drink?"

"Yes. A couple of beers."

The jury appeared bewildered; the judge, nonplussed. The defender, aware of this reaction, said, "Are any of these things recommended for a diabetic to eat?"

"No. He shouldn't have been eating any of them."

"Why not? Briefly, please."

"A diabetic's body doesn't make enough insulin to handle foods like these, which are high in carbohydrates and fats."

"And if they do eat them, what happens? Again, be brief."

"Well, their blood sugar goes up."

"But taking insulin would help keep it down."

"Well, yes. And he didn't have sugar in his urine, which was a good sign. So I just scolded him gently and told him his wife would never have let him eat that way."

"What other things did you see on that first visit that worried you 'a little'?"

"Well, the house was dirty, and he was unshaven and not very clean. I'd never seen the place before, though, and he had just come home from working as a handyman. But that bothered me enough to want to come back over a period of time, just to see how he'd progressed."

"And how did he progress?"

"Well, as I said, I'd never visited him before, and I really didn't know very much about his habits, so . . ."

"So? Go on."

"So I'm not sure if he'd always let himself go that way."

"What way?"

Jenkins jumped up again and said, "Your Honor, the witness has said she didn't know about her patient's previous habits. So the question of his personal hygiene and housekeeping is irrelevant."

The judge nodded and sustained the objection.

"Very well, Mrs. Freiden," the defender continued, "was Mr. Jones your only diabetic patient?"

"No."

"How many others like him did you call on?"

"Most of my clients are diabetics. I'm a diabetic nurse clinician."

"Aha! Then you must know a great deal about the progress of the disease."

"Objection!" Rosemary called out as she rose. "We are talking about one patient, not a whole class of people."

"Overruled. The progress of the disease in most patients is certainly relevant to its progress in this one. The witness may answer."

The defender of the auto-making giant said, "Thank you, Your Honor." He leaned forward toward Susan and asked, "Do you know a great deal about the progress of the disease?"

"Yes."

"Tell me then, have you ever had any other patient who's developed gangrene?"

"Yes."

"Many?"

"Well, no. Any are too many, of course."

He turned and stared at Lester Jones. "Of course. Even just one is too many." He shook his head and asked the witness, "Of those, have some lost their limbs?"

"Yes . . . usually legs."

"How unfortunate. And have any lost their eyesight?"

"Yes."

"And when diabetics develop pressure sores, how well do they usually heal?"

"Sometimes, not always, they don't heal as well as nondiabetics do. But most well-controlled diabetics do very well." She looked at the jury with passion and hope on her face when she said this.

"Those that don't let themselves slip? Those that don't let themselves go?"

"Objection!" cried Rosemary Jenkins, her face perfectly matching her red hair.

"Overruled. Mrs. Freiden may answer."

Susan answered calmly, "It may have nothing to do with a patient's self-care. Even compliant patients sometimes develop complications."

Rosemary Jenkins turned white. The defendant's attorney smiled. Susan Freiden had obviously given him even more than he'd hoped for.

"But," Susan added without being asked, "I've never seen complications like these develop as fast. When the blood sugar seems to be under control. And I've never had a patient lose all four of his limbs in such a short time."

The defender could have requested the judge to strike that last comment from the record, but he simply continued smiling and said, "No more questions, Your Honor."

And so the jury said that because part of Lester's condition was due to his own personal negligence, a $10,000,000 award would be overkill. They agreed that the carbon monoxide that had leaked into his new minivan's cabin had made his condition worse, but not enough to punish the automaker so harshly. They had, after all, recalled the defective model when they learned about the problem. They'd paid for studies on the healthy drivers of the car, who suffered vague, bothersome fatigue, dizziness, constipation or diarrhea their doctors couldn't diagnose or help. They'd fixed all the cars, then settled quickly out of court with those whose ailments made them miss work or be hospitalized.

The car company hadn't *deliberately* hurt anyone. They hadn't *deliberately* crippled Lester Jones, the jury decided. Lester had been careless, noncompliant with his medical regimen. They felt sorry for him, of course. Who wouldn't? And they felt sorry for his daughter, who had to give up her paying work to care for him. So they awarded them half a million dollars. On top of his Social Security disability and Medicare, that should guarantee his decent lifelong maintenance.

But the truth was that after the attorney and expert witnesses took their fees, Hester and Lester Jones just got by on the award's income. And it was Susan Freiden's fault. She'd betrayed them. That was why it was necessary for her to die in her own car of carbon monoxide poisoning.

And it was the carmaker's lawyer's fault, too: that proud and arrogant man who made more from his client than Hester and Lester and their attorney and the expert witnesses' incomes combined, that wealthy Main Line attorney whose daughter would inherit that fee, along with the rest of the old man's fortune. She would never have to spend *her* life taking care of a basket case of a father, whatever might happen to him.

How proud he must be of her, his only child! What a grand lady she might someday be, to carry on his family name, maybe to give him a grandson to join his law firm. He must be waiting for her to get married, looking forward to the day he could give her a society wedding that cost more than Lester and Hester's award.

Hester had read a couple of years ago that Dr. Broward was getting married. But that wedding had fallen through, and the man she'd been engaged to had married another heiress.

"I hope she cried and cried!" said Hester as she wheeled Lester from the funeral home to her van. She activated the lift and set his wheelchair into it. "I hope she still cries every night."

She switched on the lift and as it raised her father into the van, she said, "Susan didn't suffer, Daddy. She went quickly and quietly. Just like going to sleep. You see how beautiful she still is, with her red cheeks glowing through the makeup. That's what happens when you get the CO quickly."

As the lift reached the van's open side door and turned so she could wheel him inside, Lester made a guttural sound.

"Oh, no, Daddy," Hester said, "Dr. Broward won't get it quickly. That wouldn't be fair at all. Not to either of us, Daddy. It wouldn't even be fair to Susan. Dr. Broward will have to suffer as much as you did from the poison in her blood."

CHAPTER
▪▪ ONE

A WEEK LATER
THE PATIENT ON PINE STREET

I don't want to be here! thought Dr. Liz Broward as she turned her medical van onto Pine Street on a late September Friday afternoon. *I really don't.*

She wasn't *afraid* here. She felt safe in this neighborhood, even at dusk. The old brick row homes, rising up two or three stories from concrete stoops, housed many up-and-coming professionals, some living above first-floor offices. They lived here to be near, but not in, Central Philadelphia, with its museums, theaters, specialty restaurants, and shops. They could walk to these and to nearby Rittenhouse Square, where local artists sometimes displayed their wares beneath pink and white spring blossoms, tree-shaded summer sun, or gold and red fall foliage. Dr. Broward lived in a Society Hill high-rise overlooking a section of Delaware River not marred by oil storage tanks. She practiced family medicine with partners in a University City office. But she could imagine herself living and practicing here. It appealed to what her father—from his upperclass station with his dim view of her ways—called her bourgeois tastes. Paul Broward's view of her never, in her forty years, had kept her from living her own life, going where she wanted—even here to make what he disdained as unprofitable house calls on unworthy people. People like the Joneses of Pine Street, whom he'd *proven* unworthy.

Liz didn't need her father's approval. His strong disapproval, even his shock, hadn't kept her from deliberately embarking on unmarried motherhood. In fact, the grandson she'd given him eighteen months ago had brought them together over what once seemed an unbridgeable chasm of conflicting values. Her mother, Grace Ellen Stanford Broward, had taught her how to deflect his bigotry and turn aside his mean personal jabs with humor. He was, after all, her father, a valuable commodity in itself. And Jimmy, her son, needed roots. All children needed roots.

Oh, Jimmy had roots on Zack's side. Liz and Zack, an amateur genealogist, would go to Arizona next February to explore them. But he needed *her* roots, too, right *here*, right *now*. She had to help him develop and strengthen his ties to the Browards, whose surname he carried, because sooner or later her father would have to learn about Zack James and *his* roots. Paul Broward would find them despicable. As despicable as he'd found her Pine Street patient. Yes, only God knew what Paul Broward would do if he learned about Zack too soon, before his bonds with Jimmy were too precious for even Paul to shatter. The Pine Street patient was living proof of his power to dispossess, to ruin and make ruining seem right and just. What Paul had done was the reason Liz had to be here tonight, and also the reason she didn't want to be here.

Though Hester Jones probably didn't know that Paul Broward was Liz's father, Liz did. She'd come here not just because Hester had called requesting a house call; she'd also come to atone—anonymously she hoped—for her own father's sins against Hester's father.

Liz left her mobile medical van rumbling by the curb outside the three-story red brick row house. Using the wooden wheelchair ramp that slanted down over the steep concrete stairs, she mounted the stoop. Though what happened to Lester Jones had taken place years ago, the horror of the condition it left him in hung over this spot. She'd never

seen more than his newspaper picture when the trial was
in the news, yet knowing her father had defamed him,
Liz cringed every time she thought of him. True, she
seldom thought of him, hadn't for a year or more. Her
full-time practice, single motherhood, and her trysts with
Zack filled her days and nights, her mind and heart. Now,
suddenly, Lester's daughter Hester had called her office for
the medical van call. She *had* to think of him now, had to
look at and acknowledge what her father and his clients had
done to the Joneses of Pine Street.

So she took a deep breath of chill autumn air, shivered,
and approached the door. She knocked and waited.

After a few moments, in which she longed to turn and
run, she heard some scratchy sounds near the peephole
and imagined one wary eye pressed against its indoor lens.
Then came a deadbolt's clack, followed by the doorknob's
rattle. The door swung inward, and a gargantuan woman
loomed in the opening, a gaping smile splitting her flat,
round face.

Feeling about to be eaten for dinner, Liz stepped backward to the stoop's edge. Just in time to keep from pitching
backward down the wheelchair ramp into the early evening
gloom, she caught—along with her breath—the wrought
iron railing.

Hester seemed pleased she'd rattled her. Her eyes grew
wide with malicious mirth. In the moment before regaining
her composure, the doctor forgot why she'd come. *Dear
God, I'd really rather be* anywhere *but here!*

Then the woman said, "Hi, Dr. Broward. Remember
me?"

"I . . . ah . . ."

"I used to work in neurology and rehab at UMC. You
sometimes came in to see patients."

"Ah, yes. How could I forget?" Indeed, how could *anyone* forget this woman, once having seen her? Her height
and girth were like a very large man's, and her over-ample
bosom, as well as the muscles of her arms, could well
have been pumped up with steroids. Only the light, giggly

quality of her voice and the oddly feminine-looking ankles protruding below the hem of a blue denim tent dress were clues to her true gender. Liz now recalled seeing this woman, wearing a mammoth white uniform, lifting a 220-pound paraplegic like a doll and placing him in his wheelchair for a ride to physical therapy.

"I always wished you were Daddy's doctor. Everyone knows what a good diagnostician you are for rare conditions like his. I bet if you were, he'd never've got so bad." Hester stepped aside as she said this, and motioned Liz inside. She took the doctor's lightweight tan trench coat and hung it on a wall hook near the door.

A surprisingly bright and clean crystal light fixture filled the small entry hall with an unexpected gaiety. In here, Hester seemed more a clown than the demonic character that had encountered Liz outside. Of course! She *was* a clown: a poor, sad buffoon with a gaping smile, her pale coarse-fleshed face set with round, dark eyes and framed by a fluffed brown hoop of hair. The demon had been Liz's irrational sense of inherited guilt. And the malevolent smile had been turned on Liz by her fear she'd be found out as Paul Edward Broward's daughter.

But Hester couldn't know who Liz's father was. Liz didn't look anything like him. She resembled her mother, whose honeyed hair she'd inherited along with the high cheekbones and high-bridged nose. Her tallness—she was five-foot-nine—came from both parents. And she had her mother's calm, not the tension that strapped her father's muscles to his jaws and toned the sandy-colored skin that overlayed them. Even in this moment of nervousness, Liz knew she *looked* composed, serene. She seldom revealed her inner feelings. Her violet eyes remained cool as she smoothed the skirt of her wool knit chemise, which matched them.

As to her name, she knew the phone book contained a long list of Browards, Brourds, Braurds and others who might or might not be related to (or want to claim or deny relationships with) the old Main Line family. One thing she'd learned about genealogy from Zack was that surnames in themselves told little or nothing. So why worry? Obviously, Hester had formed her opinion of Liz during professional contact.

Liz thanked her for the compliment, then said, "I doubt I could've done more than Dr. Thomas, Hester. He's the best in his business. Probably no doctor could've helped your father. Slow CO poisoning symptoms are so vague. They could've been caused by so many things. You'd've had to know about the car defect."

"You'd've figured it out. I know."

"Well, let's see what I can do for him now. Where is he?"

Hester turned and motioned to an open door at the entry hall's rear. On the door's left, a stairway led up to the second story. "In our bedroom, there, next to the stairs."

"Let's go see him."

"Sure." Hester, her denim tent hem brushing the yellow papered walls, ushered Liz along the hallway.

The bedroom was bright and cheerful. Again confounding Liz's expectations, it felt welcoming and fresh, spruced with light floral curtains on the pair of double-hung windows, fluffed with thick flowery comforters and pillow shams on the beds. Between a double bed and a hospital twin, Lester sat in his wheelchair, looking roly-poly and cute, more like a polished-up child than the remnants of an old, sick man.

"Daddy, Dr. Broward's here to see you. She wants to make sure I'm taking good care of you."

"Hello, Lester. Looks like she takes fine care of you." Liz smelled no colostomy odors, saw no stains on his clothes or bed.

Lester grunted and smiled in Liz's direction.

"He's glad to see you. Doesn't get many visitors. We go out for walks to get company. Shopping and to the park."

Liz tried to imagine the giant woman pushing her truncated father along in his wheelchair and wondered how much company passersby would be when they saw them. Most would probably withdraw from the bizarre pair in disgust, despite their polished appearance.

Hester stepped around the wheelchair and picked up something from the dressing table behind him. "I try to be a good nurse," she said, and handed Liz an aluminum-encased hospital chart. "I keep good records for Dr. Thomas's home care nurse."

Liz opened the chart to the top page, which had scrupulous notes, signed off by Hester and occasionally by the home care nurse. Morning and evening baths were noted, the treatment of any incipient pressure sores, the administration of insulin, the checking of urine drawn from the in-dwelling catheter, the care of both bowel and bladder stomas, oral care, ear care, eye care, care of every crevice, pore, and follicle, every hair and lash.

A separate page graphically charted urine test results—always negative for sugar—along with insulin dosage; another page graphed daily fluid intake and urine output; another diagram showed vital signs and noted that Lester's pulse was taken over his carotid artery.

"Hmmmn," said Liz, "I'd say your care is impeccable." She looked up at Hester. "With this and the nursing visits, a monthly doctor's visit seems almost unnecessary."

Her face clouding, Hester said, "Dr. Thomas thinks a doctor should see him, too."

"I guess," Liz said, reflecting, "with what happened—"

"It wasn't Daddy's fault!"

"Of course not." Suddenly Liz realized the tough spot she might be in. She knew why Warren Thomas would have to take extra care. Whatever the merits of the previous case, Hester would be apt to sue again. Having had her father made a scapegoat by the auto company, she'd be looking for a scapegoat for him and herself. Seen this way, her meticulous record keeping took on an ominous aura. Should Warren Thomas—or, for that matter, Liz Broward—refuse to deliver requested care, and should Lester develop complications, insulin overdose, diabetic coma, *anything,* the doctor had better get a lawyer in a hurry. Each act of care, *each lapse,* would be documented. Was Hester setting

Liz up? Wouldn't the Joneses' lawyer love to take on Paul Broward's daughter!

So, the malice in Hester's welcoming grin may not have been all in Liz's mind, after all. "Well," Liz said, nodding and hoping the woman could not see the hair rise on her arms, "I'll check him over, then. Can you give me a hand with him?"

With Lester's short-sleeved plaid sport shirt off, Liz could examine his chest. Hester tipped him forward so Liz could listen over his back to his lungs and heart. She asked him to take a deep breath, and his quick obedience surprised her. He may have been nearly blind and unable to speak, but he still had his other senses and responded eagerly. He coughed on command, and made sounds that Hester replied to.

"Well, his lungs and heart seem fine," Liz said. "I'll need to have you put him on his back to check his abdomen."

"OK, Daddy, one, two, three, and upsy-daisy!" she said, and hugged the man around the chest as she lifted him easily to his bed. The move, with its slight bounce on the top of the puffy print coverlet, made them both seem joyful, and Liz saw a mother-child bond between them. Oddly, the tragedy that brought them together had let them fulfill each other. Liz didn't know about the man's childhood or his past relationships with women, but a woman as grotesque as Hester wouldn't likely get to mother children, if fate hadn't dropped her childlike father in her lap.

Liz quickly finished the exam. Lester was able to hold his breath long enough for her to feel that his liver was not palpable. His bowel sounds were normal. His penis responded normally to her scrotal exam, confirming, as ever, the persistence of sexual desire under the worst conditions.

"Oh, Daddy, be good, now," Hester admonished.

That would be hard, Liz thought, with her still probing his groin for pulses and masses.

"It just shows he's healthy," she said as she finished the exam and covered his genitals. "Right, Lester?" She smiled at him, and he blushed as if he could see her.

And healthy was the right word for him, despite his missing limbs, his blindness, his partial loss of bowel, and his diabetes. He must have been a horse of a man before slow carbon monoxide poisoning had combined with his high blood sugar to damage his brain, rot his arms and legs, and ulcerate his gut.

This thought hit Liz in her own gut, and she drew a sharp breath and turned her head aside for a moment. Then she looked at Hester and said, "You can dress him now, and put him back in his chair if he's staying up."

As Hester obeyed, Liz wrote her findings on her own chart, and reached for the one Hester kept. "I'll start doctor's notes in your records, if that's all right. Then we'll both have an account."

Grunting as she moved her father into his chair, Hester nodded. Liz sat on Lester's bed, wrote detailed exam notes, and handed the chart back to Hester. She stood. "He's doing well, Hester. I'll tell Dr. Thomas how well. I'm sure he'll agree that monthly visits aren't needed. Maybe just every six—"

"No! That's not enough."

"Well, then, why don't I come just every other month—"

"I want you *every month*. Daddy deserves it. *And you should do it!*" She placed two pink, bloated bladders of hands on her hips. "You give a better exam than the nurse. And you can weigh him."

Liz, feeling blamed and uneasy, looked from Hester to her father. "I'll be glad to weigh him. But he looks neither starved nor fat. Once every few months would be enough for that, too."

"You don't want to take care of him, do you?"

"Of course I do."

"Then come every month, because I want to have him weighed every month. If there's a change, then I'll know. He hasn't been weighed since he was in the hospital."

"I guess we should set up a baseline," Liz said. She should also squelch any possibility of being accused of negligence or malpractice. Well, she might as well do what she had to. "All right, wheel him outside, and we'll put him on the lift," she said.

Hester put her chart under one arm and pushed her father outside through the chilly, darkening evening to the van, which hummed at curbside beneath a streetlight. When he'd been mechanically lifted into the van and manually deposited onto the scale, Liz shifted the weights along the bars. "A hundred and two pounds. Is that what it was in the hospital?"

Hester didn't answer. Liz looked up. The woman was maneuvering her bulk through the narrow spaces between medical paraphernalia, inspecting the setup.

"Hester?"

She turned. "Yeah? This is quite a getup, Dr. Broward. A real clinic on wheels."

"Yes. I'm proud of it. Your father weighs a hundred and two. That about right?"

"Mmmm." She continued inspecting the equipment, having difficulty squeezing between some of it. "Fantastic. Boy, I'd like to have something like this. I could put Daddy in it and make house calls like you. And they'd pay me. I could be a visiting nurse."

"Well, yes."

"Could sure use the extra money."

"Quite honestly, Hester, vans like this are too expensive. They don't pay for themselves. That's why you don't see very many around. My partners and I run this as a public service."

"But insurance pays for it."

"Well, yes, just barely."

"And it brings you publicity. You got that medical society award and there was that article in the paper."

"So *that's* where you heard about it." She laughed at Hester's brazenness. "Then you know the whole idea is to bring medical service to people who can't go out after it. It's a small part of our practice, and we have to turn people down. And limit the number of calls—"

Hester would have none of Liz's implications. "Wow, Daddy!" she interjected. "Did you ever see a place like this?" Lester, still standing on his stumps on the scale made one of his sounds. He was obviously unimpressed. Hester seemed to realize this and returned to his side and lifted him into his wheelchair. The two women lowered him to the street and wheeled him up the ramp and into the house.

"Oh!" said Hester as they pushed him through the door. "My chart! I left it in the van."

"I'll get it for you," said Liz.

"Oh, no. I remember just where I set it when I was looking around. It'll just take me a minute. It's chilly out here. You take Daddy to our room."

"All right." Liz wanted to leave and get to her secret weekend with Zack, but some time alone with her patient could be useful. Only a two-way relationship would let her see him objectively, free of Hester's influence. He could, as it were, speak for himself, respond to Liz without arousing Hester's judgment or wrath. *"Oh, Daddy, be good, now."* How embarrassed he must have been, having an erection while his daughter looked on! As if he didn't have enough to bear!

She wheeled him into the bedroom. "Where would you like to sit?"

A flipper of an arm pointed generally to the spot where she'd first seen him, between the two flowery beds, closer to his own, the hospital twin. The long table between the heads of the beds, lit by an old-fashioned floor lamp behind it, bore a pitcher and glasses, some books, and a portable stereo next to a stack of audiotapes. Liz wheeled him there and turned him to face the door.

Lester grunted and lifted his flipper toward his ear.

"I'm sorry, Lester. I don't know what you mean."

He waved his flipper and growled and whined.

"You want something from the table?"

He nodded and continued his growling and whining sounds.

"Ah," she said, "I'll move you so you can touch what you want." She did. Still growling, he ran the end of his flipper along the table to the stereo. Then he waved to his ear again.

"Music!" she said. "You're singing! You want me to play a tape."

He smiled and made more sounds, whines and growls interspersed to make a song of rising and falling pitches. *Wonderful! I'm learning your language!* Liz flipped open the tape player door and read to him, one by one, the titles from the stacked tapes. He shook his head till she named some big band music. Then he nodded and started keening again.

"Terrific!" she said. She clicked in the tape and started it. Sound blasted through small, tinny speakers and rose from Lester's throat.

He's happy! Liz thought. She hadn't thought such a person could be. He and his freaky daughter had a happy life together, incredible as it seemed. Hester had brought Liz here for only one reason: She wanted to give her father extra care and some company. Being that company, delivering that extra care was little for a doctor to do, thought Liz. She was lucky that Hester had chosen her, for what doctor needed to do it more for this particular patient?

Still, having made her contribution today, Liz grew as anxious about staying as she'd been about coming before. The music had the sharp edge of old forties' recordings, worsened by poor quality tape and a cheap player. Liz was late for dinner at Zack's house. Occasional secret weekends were their only family times together with Jimmy and Zack's teenage daughter, Poke. *What is taking Hester so long!*

Well, Liz didn't *have* to stay with Lester. She bade him good-bye and gathered up her bag, strode down the hallway, got her trench coat from the hook, and donned it as she ran outside.

As she hurried toward the van, she grew worried. Hester wasn't in sight. The side gate and driver's door were closed.

She ran and slid open the gate. "Hester?" she said, as the light poured out onto the shadowed curb.

Over the generator's rumble, she heard a metallic clunk at the van's rear.

"Hester! What's going on?"

The woman, great buttocks first, struggled up from the floor. Thick legs ground against a portable electrocardiograph machine, unmooring it from beside a gurney near the tailgate, knocking it against a side panel.

"Hester! What are you doing? I thought you were getting your chart."

A muscular arm raised the metal chart like a flag. The woman scrambled noisily to full standing, and unwedged herself from the cold, hard-edged embrace of a medicine cabinet and a built-in chair. "How did you get stuck in there? What were you doing on the floor?"

"I was going after the chart. I knocked it down, and it slid underneath the gurney. When I went after it, I kind of got stuck. I'm sorry, Dr. Broward. I hope I didn't break anything." She looked chagrined and frightened. One of her denim tent dress sleeves was torn. The skirt, hiked up in front, revealed hose torn at the knee. She followed Liz's downward glance, and quickly pushed the skirt back in place, trying to smooth it.

Liz drew a breath. "I think you've cut your knee."

"It's OK. I bumped it on something. I'll fix it when I get in the house." The hand with the chart waved Liz away. The other tried to tame Hester's disarrayed tangle of hair. She worked her way up the narrow aisle, forcing Liz to retreat to let her out of the van.

Snapping her satchel open, Liz dug in and pulled out some foil-wrapped alcohol pads. "Here. Take these, then."

Hester snatched them. "I don't want to leave Daddy alone." She moved, tanklike, up the walk and onto the stoop, then vanished into the house.

Liz breathed deeply, shook her head, and shrugged off her vexation. Family doctors met lots of strange people, saw lots of strange things. But Hester and Lester Jones topped any she'd met before. Still, as she got into her van and drove off, she smiled to herself. She knew there were compensations: She'd met Zack through her practice, too. And it was the only way she *could* have met him.

A little over two years ago she had been engaged to Eric Storrey, her father's junior law partner. The wedding had been just a month off, and Liz, unknown to Eric and her parents, had cooled to the idea of marrying. An argument had broken out—the usual argument, about how Liz ran her life and her practice and how, in her father's view, it reflected poorly on her family name. Eric had taken her father's side, hardening Liz's doubts about marrying him. She'd bolted from the house, jumped into her car, and begun driving. A couple of hours later she'd suddenly realized that she wasn't simply running *from* Eric, she was running *to* someone else—a man she had, without even knowing it, fallen in love with: Zack James, a long-haired, self-educated computer graphics artist of mixed Scotch-Irish and Amerindian blood who hated to shave and always wore jeans, plaid shirts, and a hunting vest.

Zack fit Paul Broward's picture of what all Liz's patients must look like—like someone come in off the streets. And Liz knew Zack would never have come to her—from the streets or anywhere else—if his wife, Maryellen, had not been her patient before dying of leukemia a few years ago. Nor would Liz have fallen in love with him if he hadn't, just one week before the family fight, unabashedly told her, "*You, dear person, are full of shit!*"

The comment had been provoked by her ignorance of genealogy. He revealed his passion for it that day, nearly three years ago, when he came to Liz's office with a double pneumonia that would have brought a weaker man to his knees. "So you're a genealogist," she said at his revelation. "I'm surprised."

"What's so surprising?"

She looked at his uneven features, at what her father would call his bastard appearance. Zack would have to be a cast-off, a by-the-way cutting from a well-pruned family tree that he couldn't possibly trace. "Well, frankly," she said, "I never thought much of genealogy. It turns me off."

"How come?" He got down from the examining table and took his shirt and vest from the coat tree.

His energy stunned her. Despite his high fever and congestion, his face and voice had grown animated and strong when he'd told her about some genealogical detective work he was doing for the police.

"I don't like the way people use it."

He put on his omnipresent plaid flannel shirt. "What's wrong with how people use it?"

"They use it to exclude."

That's when he told her she was full of shit. *Her* family, the Browards and Stanfords, he told her, may have used it to exclude. The so-called family history in her church genealogy library had surely been carefully culled of misfits and family skeletons. But real genealogists used it to *include*—to find the truth that tied the present to the past.

Liz was not then interested in finding such truths. They had nothing to do with her, and she told him so.

He challenged her: "Tell me something, Doc."

Unnerved by his growing familiarity, she tensed. "What?"

"Aren't you even curious?"

She swallowed, trying to moisten her throat to keep her voice from cracking. "About what?"

"About your family history and how far it goes and what it excludes and why. It's all there, bound in leather on a shelf in your church genealogy library."

"No. I'm really not the least interested. What may have been excluded doesn't affect me in the least. But I am curious about one thing, and that's why you're so interested in *my* family that you'd bother to go to my church's library. You certainly don't belong to my church and I don't think it's any of your business."

"Why not? You know a lot about my family history. Especially you know all about Maryellen's. You came right out and asked when you were treating her, and you wrote it all down on that fat record. I got a right to know where my doc comes from and how it makes her feel about patients like me."

She flinched. "The family history in your record is vital to the care I give you. I don't see how—"

"I'll put it to you this way, dear person. Don't you think a family doc like you would be an even better family doc than you already are if she knew as much as there was to know about her *own* family and where she came from?"

Then, her anger flared again, and she said, "I know all I need to know about where I came from."

His brashness had set her afire and forced her to look at herself, to ask herself: *Why am I marrying Eric?* It was not because of passion. Never had her loins burned for Eric as they had begun to burn for Zack. Then she knew: *She didn't want to marry* anyone; *she only wanted a child. And at thirty-eight, she had little time.* Eric, a decent, hardworking lawyer, had fallen in love with her. Well, why not marry him? Passion, being in love, were nice if you had them; but she'd never had them. Sex was pleasant, enjoyable even without them. It was with Eric. And he, unlike other men she'd known, was not put off by her family name and money, her being a doctor, or her tallness.

Suddenly, though, she'd found passion and tasted its joys with Zack, and suddenly she had wanted her child to be born of joy, of passion. So she'd conceived. Then, sure she was pregnant, and in love as never before, she'd known she did *not* want to marry. Zack had wanted to, still did. And she, very much in love to this day, still didn't. Not yet. Maybe someday.

Meanwhile, she'd told no one who Jimmy's father was; she did not even record Zack's name on the birth certificate. Why upset her father with the truth? It would only estrange him from his grandson, deprive his grandson of his affection. And never had she known her father capable of such affection, such pride over a child. One born out of wedlock, to boot. She knew, of course, why Paul Broward had gone far beyond forgiving her such a shocking indiscretion: He thought that Eric, who'd married on the rebound after Liz had jilted him, was Jimmy's father; and he thought that Liz had not recorded Eric's paternity out of deference to him and his wife, who herself soon presented him with a son. Paul seemed almost proud of her for doing it. Having him proud of her for anything felt good for a change. So why ruin it? Jimmy knew who his father was; he knew his grandparents, too. He would neither ask questions nor tell tales for at least a couple of years. Meanwhile his bonds with Paul Broward would become unbreakable.

And Liz's forbidden romance with Zack would remain forever sweet.

She could taste the sweetness now as she parked her van in its slot in her office parking garage, turned off the generator, and hooked it up to the electrical power so its refrigerator would keep running. She could smell desire's aroma on her own breath. It permeated the cockpit of her iridescent gold Mercedes-Benz as she drove across Philadelphia and up North Broad Street to Glenside. Rebreathed, it built on itself, making the forty-minute drive to Zack's small house seem interminable.

The cold air shocked her hot cheeks as she got out of her car and mounted the flagstone walk to his front porch. She gulped a breath of it as she jangled through her keys and felt out his door key. Before she could use it, the door opened.

"You're late," he said, seeming neither worried nor angry as he stepped back to allow her through the door.

"I know. As usual." She stepped into the small foyer. As she pecked his cheek, she looked to her left past him into the cluttered family room and beyond it into the small, bright kitchen. "Where's Jimmy?"

"In bed."

"Oh, damn!" She tossed her tote bag and coat onto the entryway table and went through the living room on the right to the small guest room at the back where Jimmy always slept in his "Daddy's house crib."

"It's kind of more than 'as usual,' " Zack said in hushed tones as he followed her.

"I guess it is. Damn! I hate to miss him." She tiptoed into the tiny room and bent over the crib rail. She ran her fingers lightly over her son's small head.

Jimmy lifted his head, barely opened his eyes, and laid his head down again. He inched his thumb into his mouth, and smiled around it as he began sucking lightly. His eyes closed.

"Hi, sweetie," she whispered. She lowered the rail softly and bent and kissed him. Sniffing him, she marveled at how much the scent of one's just bathed little boy resembled the scent of sex. Was it just her own little boy she smelled that on? Or was it still her own breath she smelled? "Mommy missed you."

Zack, his shoulder brushing hers, bent over and kissed him, too. When he straightened, he raised the crib rail and the two left the room.

A few moments later in the family room, Zack said, "He didn't miss *you* one bit."

"He never does when Poke's around," she said of Zack's sixteen-year-old daughter, whose nickname—short for Pocahontas—referred to her Amerindian heritage.

"Right."

Liz went into the kitchen. She saw that the gold melamine tabletop had been cleared except for one place setting. "Good!" she said. "You ate without me. Poke in her room?"

He grinned. His eyes switched from green to brown. They often did that in an instant, triggered, she now knew, by an emotional switch. "She's sleeping over at Christy's."

She smiled and raised her brow. "We're alone?"

"Right. She left something for you to heat in the microwave." He opened the refrigerator door and reached in.

"Never mind." She took his arm, then shut the refrigerator.

"Not hungry?" He grinned again.

"Only starved. It's been two weeks." She touched his face. "You shaved, damn you! You know I like you all scratchy. I hope you didn't shower and scrub away all those pheromones," she said, sniffing behind his ear.

"Since when have you needed pheromones to turn you on?"

"Since the first time I smelled you. The more you stink, the more turned on I get. You know that."

"Well, I shaved so I could nuzzle Jimmy. *He* doesn't like me scratchy and stinky."

"Fatherhood's made you soft," she said, her tongue seeking out errant stubble, salty sweat, on his chin, underneath it.

"Not where it counts." He ground his groin against her.

"Mmmmm. Tell me about where it counts."

"That's your line, dear person. I'm the one that has to *smell* dirty in bed. You're the one that has to *talk* dirty in bed."

She laughed. "We're made for each other, aren't we, Zack?"

"Convince me."

She did. In the very colorful language that she saved for special occasions like this. She smiled as she fell asleep in his arms, remembering their last trip to Arizona, envisioning the one coming up. What special occasions they were! How their secret adventures kept love young, ever sweet, ever delicious! Some day the world would know Liz Broward led a double life. But why change things now? Having things both ways made everyone happy.

CHAPTER
▪▪ TWO

A FEW MONTHS LATER—
THE SUNDAY AFTER CHRISTMAS

"Call her again, Pop," said Poke. "Everything's going to dry out. Dinner'll be ruined." She crooked her slim arm over her heat-flushed face and wiped sweat from her nose. Then she pushed the turkey back into the oven to keep warm. In the incandescent glow of the kitchen, Poke looked more like a woman in her twenties than a sixteen-year-old girl, despite the long black plaits, girlishly beribboned, falling forward over her narrow shoulders. As she turned toward Zack, she tossed the plaits back into place between her shoulder blades, in another womanly gesture. The ribbons, red like her sweater, touched the inward curve of her waist. More and more, she reminded him of her mother, whose petite features and light coloring contrasted with Zack's rough appearance.

And this gesture, of a woman straightening up from over her cooking, called up from within him that usually dormant pang of grief. That she was cooking his last spring's hunting trophy, a cagey old Tom who'd led him a merry chase through the northeastern Pennsylvania woods, deepened and sharpened his grief. Notwithstanding that he'd won this Tom for Liz, his wife Maryellen was never entirely out of his thoughts on the times he sat in the misty chill of predawn, his back stuck up against an ancient oak, waiting for the wild turkey hens he'd scouted out the previous day to come down from their roosts and begin their feeding.

Maryellen had been dead more than three years and it was Liz and Jimmy he and Poke were awaiting. Liz was late and hadn't called. Still, his anxiety over her was suddenly submerged by this old, familiar poignancy. After all, he had been happily married to Maryellen for eighteen years. He and Liz, on the other hand, had never truly lived together at all, except for brief weekends and holidays. And the holidays were celebrated late so she could spend the actual day with her parents.

Zack didn't like that arrangement, but he knew why he must accept it. Paul Broward *was* Jimmy's grandfather and Liz was right to want them to be close. And he knew that nasty man could never accept his unmarried daughter's child if he knew that Zack was his father. The old bigot couldn't have stood the thought of his mixed blood. Especially the twelve and a half percent Amerindian expressed in Zack's broad, ruddy face and black hair. Zack loved Jimmy and Liz too much to stand between the boy and a loving, accepting grandfather, even a grandfather like Paul Broward. A joyful relationship with a little boy, Liz hoped and continually asserted, might be the very thing to melt the ice encasing Paul Broward's soul, so that one day he'd love Jimmy even *knowing* Zack was his father.

Maybe, Zack thought. But from what he knew of Paul Broward, probably nothing would. Ice didn't just *encase* Paul's soul, it *formed* it—if he had one. Zack hadn't met him personally, but his personality was etched in the public mind, and his calumnies against the innocent on behalf of his wealthy, powerful clients were infamous. How Liz had evolved from under his influence into the humanistic doctor Zack dearly loved must be a testament to her mother. Zack knew nothing about Grace Broward except that Liz admired her.

"Pop?" Poke tilted a worried brow toward him.

"Yeah, Poke. I heard you. She's probably on her way. Stuck in traffic."

"On a Sunday?"

"Well, you know the weekend after Christmas. Everyone's returning stuff. And it snowed last night."

She wiped her forehead with her arm again, then said, "I'm calling her, Pop, if you don't. You know shopping won't tie up traffic between Society Hill and Glenside. And the snow didn't stick."

The chrome legs of the kitchen chair scraped the yellow vinyl tile floor as he shoved it back from under him and turned toward the adjacent family room. There a fluorescent lamp shone on the telephone, a personal computer, a fax machine, and a modem that shared a cluttered desk. Great gobs of his life were centered on that desk, in a few square yards carved out of the furniture-crowded room. He hadn't always spent so many hours here. A few years ago, before Liz, he'd burned up all his energy in his office at Squire Technical Publishers, where he'd often worked seven days a week. Back then, he'd used his home computer strictly for networking with genealogy buffs like himself. He'd kept his barbells, exercise bench, and punching bag at Squire, so his sedentary work there, also at a computer, wouldn't turn his 175 pounds to flab on his compact five-foot-nine frame. And his sometimes frantic exercise breaks kept his mind from clogging during sixteen-hour workdays.

Back then, when he wasn't pulling his lat bar, sweat trickling down his arms and over strong, broad hands, he was coolly directing his precise, restrained fingers over the computer keyboard and mouse to create graphic designs for Squire's publications. People would see his designs emerge on the computer screen, and they'd look from the screen to him, at his long, uneven black hair, at his eyes, which might change from green to brown in seconds for no reason, at the perpetual shadow of beard lurking in the shallow hollow below high Amerindian cheekbones. Then they'd look at his green-and-brown camouflage hunting vest over his red-and-black plaid shirt and again at the computer screen and the proofs coming off the image printer, and they'd shake their heads. They couldn't believe that someone who looked like *him* could turn out something that looked like *art*. That someone who kept his shotgun in a corner behind his office door—an office thrown out of kilter by heavy gym equipment—could create such incredibly delicate, well-balanced designs on paper. And they wondered how Squire's polished executives, in their blue vested suits, white shirts, striped ties, and shiny black shoes could tolerate him and his office. Then they looked back at the screen and the proofs, at the finished work samples in their brochures and books, and they knew that Squire couldn't find anyone better than Zack to create the artwork and execute the designs he explained to amazed clients. Called a supervisor, he was, in truth, Squire's one-man art department, grossly underpaid at $45,000 a year. So they humored him and ignored his idiosyncrasies.

But they didn't have to humor him now—at least not about his exercise gear. He'd moved it home to a basement corner. He kept his shotgun at home now, too, still always polished and ready to grab up and toss into his van when spring and fall turkey seasons opened. He wasn't running away anymore, as he'd been before; running to work seven days a week so he wouldn't remember that Maryellen was dead; running to the lat bar, grabbing it, and pulling it because he'd started remembering again; grabbing up his camo-taped Winston 870 and running from his office late on a Friday evening, then driving half the night to the Delaware State Forest, so he'd be too exhausted to do anything but fall asleep by the time he got to his camping spot.

He had run himself ragged, run his health into the ground, and ended up with a case of pneumonia that would have killed him if Poke hadn't made him go to Dr. Liz Broward about it. Liz had changed his life—saved it, in fact—helped him stop running away, and given him something to run *to* again. He now did about half his computer design work at home in the family room and transmitted his graphics to the office by modem and fax. That left him plenty of exercise time, but now he used that time to think, not to drive thoughts out with each pump of every aching muscle. Two or three days a week he went into the office to take care of details he could do only there, and to talk to clients.

He still refused to shave more than twice a week, usually on office days, and he still wore his hunting vest, plaid shirt, and jeans. He wore them *everywhere*. He was wearing them now, though he'd shaved this morning for Jimmy's sake, or for his own, as he loved to rub the boy's soft cheek against his. "OK," he said to Poke, "I'll try again. But if her machine answers again, what'll we know that we didn't know before—that she's on her way and got held up somewhere?"

He lifted the receiver and punched the redial button. Liz's answering machine picked up the call again.

Poke had followed him from the kitchen and stood, close behind him, anxiously wringing a dishtowel. "That's not all we know, Pop. What else we know is she felt sick on and off the last couple months. And a couple of times she forgot to come when she was supposed to."

That had worried him, too, but he didn't want to admit it, even to himself. He hung up the phone, cutting off Liz's recorded message. "If she forgot, she'd have answered the last time and I'd've reminded her. Probably just got a late start. Be here any minute."

Poke crossed through the family room to the small entry foyer between family and living rooms. Gray light slashed in as she opened the front door. Beneath her sneakers, a thin, nubby layer of frost on the small wooden porch crunched softly as she stepped down. Hugging herself to keep the chill breeze from cutting through her red sweater's loose weave, she leaned over the railing and scanned the narrow residential street. Mature evergreen shrubs lent the neighborhood quiet and privacy. No traffic broke the ominous quiet.

Zack followed her onto the porch. "Poke . . ."

She turned, her oval face mottled with cold and tension.

"She's not here. Something's wrong, Daddy." Poke called him Daddy only when she was afraid.

"Look, honey, Liz can take care of herself. Besides, what could have happened?"

"She's got Jimmy with her. Something's happened to them both. Oh, Daddy, it's that turkey. Everytime you bring a turkey home and want us to have it together, something awful happens to us." She ran to him and threw her arms around him. Clearly too upset to cry, she hugged him tightly around his neck and took deep, audible gulps of air.

He held her tightly, feeling her frosty breath on his ear, understanding her chilly words. Whenever he'd brought home quarry the last few years, something had happened to them—some of the worst things that *could* happen. Four springs ago, he'd missed the old gobbler he'd gone for, but brought down a younger one who'd practically jumped into his arms. He and Poke had dressed and cooked it for Maryellen's birthday. Though feeling lousy, Maryellen had put up a show of gaiety while eating it. A few weeks later, she was too sick to put up a show. A few months later, she'd died of leukemia. Not until the following spring did he finally bag the old Tom he'd promised Maryellen for the Thanksgiving she'd never lived to see. At the moment he bent to pick up the bird, he'd felt the worst of his grief drain away, but while taking the Tom to his van, he'd stumbled on a partly buried body in the woods. When four more bodies were found at the site, amateur genealogist Zack suddenly had turned amateur detective. He helped the police chase down a maniacal killer. But before he and Liz trapped the killer, the lunatic had kidnapped Poke and almost killed Liz. It was months before the hard-won Tom landed on Zack's dining room table. Though they shared it with Liz, they ate with little gusto. No wonder Poke thought his turkey shoots brought bad luck. No wonder she sometimes panicked about Liz.

Now she broke from his arms and ran into the house and jerked the phone from its cradle. She hit the redial button, listened a second, then slammed the receiver down. "The line's busy. She's talking to someone."

"Nah, someone else called and got the machine."

She tried again, several times. After ten minutes, the line was still busy.

"Maybe she's trying to call us," Zack said. "Let's stay off awhile."

They did. Five endless minutes later, the telephone hadn't rung, and when Zack tried Liz's line again, a dry rapid busy signal buzzed like a pesky insect in his ear.

His worry turned to anger. *Why would she talk so long to someone else, when she hadn't even phoned him to say she was coming late?*

Poke must have read his thoughts. "She's not talking to someone. Her phone's off the hook," she said.

"Our ringing and hangups were bothering her! Cheeze, she could've just—"

"No. It's Jimmy. He knocked it off."

"She'd've seen it by now. She doesn't just let him wander around the apartment, Poke."

"That's just it. Something's happened to her, and he's wandering around. Go there, Daddy. Hurry." Her face was livid, her eyes wide with fear. She *knew*. She had that scary kind of intuition that Zack knew he'd better not question.

He couldn't leave her there waiting and scared. "You're coming with me," he said.

From outside Liz's apartment door they could hear Jimmy crying and running back and forth through the large, high-ceilinged condominium. Zack threw open the door and the boy went dashing by in damp blue flannelette pajamas, whimpering stertorously, face dirt-streaked. Plainly, he'd been crying a long time. Instead of quieting when he saw his father and sister, he continued running, occasionally tripping over his pajama feet, as if he'd been programmed to take the same path over and over, to fall and get up again. Poke had to stand directly in front of him and stop him with her body.

"Jimmy! Oh, baby, where's your mommy?" She bent and lifted him.

Zack didn't wait for the boy to calm down and answer; he left his children in the marble-floored foyer and ran to the large master bedroom at the back of the the apartment. The tall white double doors were open, exposing Liz's king-size bed, its fluffy white comforter crumpled, drawn unevenly up over a mound, and covering one humped up pillow. "Liz!"

He sprang to the bed and pulled the comforter off the heap on the pillow, which turned out to be her balled flannel nightgown and underwear, and tore it off the mound on the bed, which turned out to be mashed and crumpled bedclothes.

"Liz!" He wheeled around.

"Daddy, where is she?" Poke stood in the doorway, hugging Jimmy to her chest. Jimmy was still crying and gulping, and rubbing his eyes on her shoulder.

"Where's Mommy, Jimmy?" Zack cried, running past them through a door that joined this room to a smaller one, Jimmy's nursery. His railed youth bed was piled with toys, and his clothes were scattered over the floor, with several stuffed animals. He looked behind him through the master bedroom door. "Poke! Someone's ransacked this place! Jimmy! Who came into your room?" He ran and took his son from Poke's arms. "Tell Daddy, who's been here? What's happened to Mommy?"

The boy kept on crying and shaking his head. "Oh, son, please don't cry. Daddy's here. He wants to find Mommy. Did someone come and take her away?"

"Daddy . . ." Jimmy stopped crying.

"Daddy!" Poke called from deep in the master bedroom. "She's in the bathroom. The shower's running."

"Jesus!"

"I didn't hear it before with Jimmy crying."

"Oh, Poke." He ran to her. "Here! Take your brother.

Oh, Jesus God, she's all right. She's just been taking a shower . . . cheesus . . ." He plunked the little boy into her arms again.

Jimmy had stopped crying. "Mommy, sower," he said. "Dimmy hungy."

"Hungry?" said Zack. "You bet. Thanks to your mommy, you're already an hour late for dinner. I have to have a talk with her about that." His relief over learning that Liz was safe was followed by irritation over her lateness and lack of consideration.

"Oh, Pop, can't you see, he hasn't even had *breakfast* yet."

"Sure he has, Poke. Liz wouldn't let him go without breakfast."

"Look at him, Pop! He's still in his pajamas. And they're soaked. He's been running around here like that all day, I bet. Something's wrong with Liz. Something's wrong!" She hugged the boy to her again and began running toward the bath in the master suite. She pushed open the bathroom door. "Liz! Are you here?"

The water continued to pound against the shower stall door.

"Mommy sower," said Jimmy, holding out one hand toward the shower stall.

Zack dashed past Poke and began to pound on the corrugated sliding glass doors. "Liz? Are you in there?"

Amid the splashes and gurgles he heard a soft human sound, somewhere between a word and a moan. He could see a rounded shadow through the lower left corner of the door.

"Jesus!" He grasped the brass door handle and slid the panel back. Icy cold water splashed onto him. "Oh, Jesus, Liz!"

"Mommy sower."

"Oh, Daddy, is she all right?"

He reached in and pushed the faucet off. Liz sat naked, legs extended and spread, her back supported against the wall, her tawny hair soaked and flattened, her skin bluishly mottled and pimpled like a freshly plucked bird's. Her mouth drooped at the corners, and her eyes, though open and looking at him, held little expression. Her tongue reached out of her mouth and gathered the water drops from around her lips. One arm rose weakly toward him, then fell back to her thigh where it had been resting.

"I . . . I think she's OK, Poke. I mean, she's alive, anyway. Go get Jimmy his breakfast. I'll take care of her." He knew she was very, very weak and sick, and his heart felt as waterlogged as her skin, and his own skin was chilled at the sight of her.

"I'll help you, Pop . . ."

"No! Get Jimmy his breakfast and clean him up. Then pack up some of his clothes and toys. We'll take him to our place."

"But what about her?"

"I'll get her dried and dressed and take her to the hospital."

Liz said, "Zack, I'm tired. Just get me to bed." Had her words not been amplified in the echo chamber of the tile and glass shower stall, they would have been barely audible.

"Oh, Liz, dear person, I'll get you to bed."

Her eyes closed, and she nodded. "Time is it?" she slurred.

"Don't worry about that now. Poke's taking care of Jimmy." He pulled her body sheet from the towel rack next to the shower, thankful for its thirsty thick pile, and raised her head and shoulders from where they leaned against the wall. Slipping the towel behind her, he made a hood of part of it and a shawl of the rest, and gently rubbed her dry, first her hair, then her shoulders and arms and torso; then he wrapped it around her and lifted her out of the stall.

She shivered as he carried her to the bed, then became almost deadweight. Her heaviness, her flaccidity, frightened him. This was Liz Broward, tall, confident, physically and emotionally strong, a woman who strode, not walked, toward her destinations. This was Liz Broward, who always faced life head-on. When he'd run away from life three years ago, she'd grasped him by the shoulders and straightened him up and made him take charge again. When Poke had been in danger, she'd risked her own life to rescue her, then fought back from the brink of death against terrible odds.

But now her fighting spirit seemed to have fled. Her skin, before taut and golden, was turgid, mottled in unnatural hues of blue, pasty white, and fevery red, as if icy cold water from without and superheated blood from within were fighting for possession of her body. And as she lolled listless in his arms, he saw that she didn't seem to care if she froze or burned up. He'd never known Liz not to care.

"Dear person, I love you. Oh, Liz!" He laid her down on the bed, and unwound the damp towel from around her, then used a drier corner of it to sop up some drops from her creases and dry her icy feet. The beds of her toenails, which he'd expected to be blue, were rosy, like the early flush of a bruise. Had something fallen on her toes? Had she tripped over something and fallen, maybe hurt her head, and had a concussion before or after going into the shower?

"What happened, Liz?"

"Tired, tha's all." Her eyes remained closed as she pulled the words painfully out.

"Did you fall in the shower?"

"Uh-huh. Needed cold shower. Please . . . want to sleep."

He thought he was figuring things out. She'd gotten up, how long ago he wasn't sure, and probably she wasn't, either. She'd taken off her gown while still in bed and left it crumpled on the pillow, then she'd crawled out of bed, thinking a cold shower would wake her up, and walked or crawled to the shower. Able to turn the knob to cold and start the water, she was not able to remain standing, so she'd slid down to the stall floor and couldn't get up again. Whether she'd dozed on and off, he'd no idea.

In any case, he knew such pernicious tiredness wasn't normal.

Something more must have happened. She must have tripped over something and fallen and hurt herself. He hadn't seen anything she might have tripped over. But he'd run into the bathroom so fast, there was no way he would have seen everything.

He unwrapped the towel from around her and slipped the gown over her head, then helped her settle beneath the down comforter. As sleepy as she was, he felt she was probably in no present danger. She had to be warmed up first of all. He pulled a cedar-smelling blanket from the chest at the foot of the bed and added it to her covers.

Then he went back into the bathroom with the body sheet and hung it over the rack.

That was when he noticed the blood on the towel, and the drops of blood leading from the shower stall across the white tile bathroom floor and across the blue carpet to the bed.

Bleeding! Oh, God, that was it—she was bleeding!

He ran back to her bed and tore off the covers and checked the sheet beneath her. Yes, there it was, bright red blood under her hips. Now he knew what had happened—her not feeling well the last couple of months— the bone achy tiredness she'd described the last time they'd been together. He'd heard all that before, from Maryellen, when she had been pregnant with Poke. He'd practically had to drag her out of bed in the mornings during those first months. It had passed, of course, and after the fourth month she'd been her usual vigorous self again.

When Liz was pregnant with Jimmy, Zack hadn't even known for a couple of months. They weren't living together and barely had seen each other until the day she'd called him into her office and announced she was carrying his baby. By then, probably the worst had been over.

That she hadn't told him this time, either, didn't surprise him. She hadn't planned to have another child at age forty. Too many complications, she'd said. Too many things could go wrong.

Now something had! She was miscarrying. He had to get her to the hospital.

He'd called ahead and told the emergency room triage nurse that he was on his way with Dr. Liz Broward, who seemed to be having a miscarriage. They were waiting with an IV trolley when he drove up to the emergency vehicle curb and threw open his van's side gate. Before he had parked and returned, they had her in the operating room, and had blood of her type already withdrawn from the hospital bank.

He caught an elevator to the waiting room and waited, still scared, but confident that he had acted wisely and in time to save her. After twenty minutes, a green-gowned middle-aged surgeon with a paper mask drooping under his chin pushed through the surgery wing's double doors and approached him, head shaking, brow furrowed.

"Zack James?"

He rose uncertainly from the blue upholstered chair. "Right. How is she, Doc?"

"You brought her in?"

"Yeah. Is the operation over?"

"She didn't need surgery, sir."

"What?"

"Did she tell you she was miscarrying?"

"Ah . . . well . . . I saw the blood, and . . ."

"She's menstruating. Didn't she tell you that?" The surgeon reached up and took off his paper cap and loosened the strings of his mask. He seemed to be struggling with his temper. His green eyes looked frosty.

Zack took a deep breath, grasped the chair arms, and lowered himself into the chair again. He trembled. "Then she's OK . . ." Nothing else mattered, his mistaken diagnosis, the panic he'd stirred among the emergency room and operating room staffs of the hospital where Liz was known and loved.

"Whatever made you jump to the conclusion that she was miscarrying? Didn't she even object to your crazy idea to bring her here?"

"Doctor, she was almost unconscious when I found her. When I saw the blood I . . ."

The surgeon looked puzzled. He stopped his irritated fiddling with his mask ties. "Found her? What do you mean?"

Shaking his head, Zack explained what had brought him to Liz's apartment, and what he'd discovered there. As he spoke, the surgeon's features softened, and he nodded.

"I guess if I'd been in your place, I might've drawn the same conclusions. The ER staff should've checked her out before sending her up."

Zack stood up. "Excuse me, Doc, but the triage nurse, Jennie, knows me. I guess the last time Liz came to ER and I was involved—well, it's a long story—anyway, I guess she must have thought I knew what I was talking about, that, like you thought, Liz had told me she was miscarrying."

"Well, that doesn't matter." He'd finally worked his mask ties loose and pulled it off. His face creased now with concern. He took Zack by the elbow. "Look, can we go to my office? I want to call a colleague of mine in and let you tell him what happened."

"Is Liz going to be OK, Doc?"

"Well, I guess as soon as what she must have taken to get to sleep last night is out of her system—"

Throwing the doctor's hand off his arm, he said, "Liz would never take anything to get to sleep. She doesn't believe in it."

"Well, maybe that's so. But you said you don't live with her, so I guess it's hard to be sure. People don't always behave like they tell you they do. Sometimes you don't know the truth, even if you live with them, sleep in the same bed with them every night."

"I *know* Liz," said Zack.

"Sure. Anyway, now that she's here, we'd better keep her a day or so. We'll run some tests. And when she comes out of it, we'll see what she has to say for herself."

CHAPTER
▪▪ THREE

ONE WEEK LATER

Liz Broward sat in the deep floral print armchair by the window of her Gold Coast hospital room. She watched for Zack, hoping with all the strength she had left that he wouldn't come too soon. Her parents had come unexpectedly on this morning she was being discharged.

"Maybe now you'll drop the altruism." Her father's affected, bitten-off lisp made the last word come out as "awl-tru-izhm." After a lifetime's exposure, she was so used to his lisp that she seldom noticed how much it added to his autocratic manner and lent him a guileful air. Now it was clear, for he'd spoken the word with a mean, sarcastic twist. He plainly meant to chastise her for making herself unnecessarily ill with deeds he considered beneath her. Deeds like her mobile house calls. He blamed them for the fatigue that had dogged her the past two months. He seemed almost gleeful when she'd nearly passed out before Christmas dinner with her parents. It served her right. Should teach her not to waste her time at parking lot holiday health fairs, examining the riffraff that trailed snot-nosed waifs through her van. Two weeks of that were all it took to bring her down. He wasn't surprised.

She continued to look out the window. Along with her physical strength, her emotional fortitude had slipped. She hadn't recovered enough yet to endure his nastiness and come up loving him. Later she'd face him and smile, counter his sarcasm with humor, deflect his arrogance with self-confidence, as her mother had taught her.

"Paul," said her mother, her voice as soft as the folds in her peach silk dress, "Liz always worked hard. Bob Ryan thinks it's chronic fatigue syndrome. Probably caused by a virus."

In the window, which the winter-chilled silvery sun had glazed with a mirror finish, she could see her parents' reflected profiles as they faced each other, her mother's face calm as usual, her father's hard, strapped with tension. She hoped her mother's soft voice would deflect her father's next sarcastic barb.

"She wouldn't be so prone to viruses if she worked with a better class of patients." The shushing of the esses heightened their cruel shearing power.

Had he come here today to kick her when she was down? She hadn't wanted him to know she was down. When she'd called her mother Wednesday to say she was too tired to come to her parents' Bryn Mawr home with Jimmy for their usual dinner, she hadn't said she was phoning from a hospital bed, but after what happened on Christmas, Grace had been so alarmed by her daughter's persistent fatigue that she'd immediately phoned Liz's office and learned the truth from one of her partners. Grace had visited that very night, and she had grown alarmed at Liz's utter weakness. Anticipating Paul's response, Grace, in her "handler" role—she was "handler" *par excellence*—held off telling him about Liz's condition for a few days. By the time she told him, Liz had improved enough to stay awake during visits, to walk without help to the bathroom, and to shower and dress herself in clean nightclothes. Handler Grace stayed every evening, though, to make certain Liz got safely back to bed.

Grace brought Paul this morning because she saw Liz had almost recovered, though Liz hadn't told her she was being sent home. Grace also felt Liz should know her father cared about her. Whatever the strains between father and daughter, Grace, with intuitive wisdom, felt that was important. She'd always taken risks to promote and cement family relationships. This time she'd risked that his disdain for his daughter's lifestyle wouldn't overrule his concern for her well-being.

Disdain had won. What a wonderful chance he had to bully her—weak as she was—into being a proper Broward and stop fooling around with the poor, the unworthy, the irresponsible.

"Paul! Any family doctor is exposed to viruses. Even *you* pick one up now and then," said Grace, as Liz watched her parents' reflections in her hospital room window. The tawny eyebrows knit with displeasure above the high-bridged nose.

"One can locate one's office to avoid the kind of patients she gets." He turned his head to stare at the back of Liz's, and she felt the heat of his scrutiny. "She could at least wait for them to come into her office."

At this, Liz turned from the window. "Please, Dad. Some other time. I have to get dressed to go home." She had meant to show some mettle, and her flaccid voice frightened her. She sighed, then swallowed, as her fingers dug into the arms of her chair.

He stretched his long neck and dug a finger beneath his collar and tie. "It seems," he shushed between his teeth, "my warning's already too late. Look what you've done to yourself!"

"Your warnings are always timely." She mustered her full, rich voice this time. "My heeding them's what's too late."

A twitch of a smile curled Grace's full lips. "Well, you needn't worry, Paul. She's still a match for you, dear."

"Without you, she wouldn't be," said Paul. But, as always, he seemed to mellow a bit and give in to his wife's good-humored chiding. He began to put on his overcoat. Liz felt a wash of relief. Too little to flush the distaste for him from her mouth.

And too late, for after a rap on the door, a young, dark head with long braided hair peeked in. "Hi, Liz!" The girl pushed the door open and came in, carrying a small suitcase. "Oh!" She looked awkwardly at Grace and Paul, who stared back in shocked unison.

Liz started up out of her chair. "Poke . . ."

"I got your clothes to wear home. Pop got them out of your closet. He'll be up soon. The nurses downstairs all stopped him to get a good look at Jimmy."

"Oh," said Liz. "Poke, these are my parents, Mr. and Mrs. Broward. Poke is the, ah, the baby-sitter who's been taking care of Jimmy while I've been in the hospital."

"Baby-sitter?" said Grace. "I thought Joyce Price was taking care of him."

Poke knit her face into a puzzled knot.

"Well, she couldn't take him twenty-four hours a day, and Poke is out of school on Christmas break, so—"

"Liz, you should have told us. You know your father and I'd've been happy to care for him."

Poke looked from one woman to the other, then hazarded a glance at Paul, who was glaring at her.

"Your father came to Dr. Broward's apartment to get her clothes?" Then he looked at Liz. "Was it necessary to have her father come to your apartment? Your mother could have brought you your clothes, if you'd asked. It's enough you let a child stay there overnight with the boy for a week, let alone have her father come in and root through your closets."

Poke jumped to her own defense. "But Jimmy was staying at our house, Mr. Broward. And Pop's Jimmy's—"

"Poke!" Liz said quickly, swaying a bit as she spoke, "Don't mind my father's concern. He's upset that I've been sick. Like your father would be if you were. Bring my things here, and I'll take them out of the suitcase. I want to be dressed when your dad gets here, so we can go home right away."

Grace put her hand to her mouth, eyes widening, face paling. *She knows! Nothing gets by her.*

Paul glowered at Poke. "What were you saying, young lady?"

"Please, Dad. Leave her alone. She's Jimmy's baby-sitter and she's done a fine job." She was getting weak, clammy handed.

Grace put a staying hand on Paul's arm. "Yes, dear. Liz wouldn't have hired someone incompetent. Now, let's go and let Liz get dressed and back to her apartment." She motioned Poke to put the suitcase on the foot of the bed, and the girl did so, hurriedly glancing at Liz.

"*We'll* take her to her apartment, and *you'll* stay with her and the boy there, Grace. As long as necessary."

"No," said Liz. "I won't have it."

"You're in no condition to decide what you'll have and won't! This child doesn't have the breeding to address you as Dr. Broward. How can you let her call you by your first name? You're not thinking straight." He turned to his wife. "Until her judgment's improved, *we'll* handle her affairs, Grace."

Liz opened her mouth to protest, but her mother cried out softly and looked up at the door. Paul's eyes followed hers, then narrowed, as Zack James entered the room, a squirming Jimmy in his arms. "See Mommy," the boy said, and scrambled down from Zack's arms and toddled headlong into Liz's knees, knocking her back into her chair. She clutched the chair arms for a moment before grasping Jimmy's head in both hands and leaning to kiss his tousled head. "Jimmy, baby. Mommy missed you."

Clamping his hands at his sides and opening his mouth, Paul stood stock-still. He stared at Zack, taking in the wildly mismatched outfit of blue jeans, camouflage hunting vest, and plaid shirt, the long black hair pulled back into a ponytail, the broad jaws and flaring nostrils, the eyes—brown when he entered the room, flashing green as they met the older man's, as if Paul's icy glance had penetrated and chilled them.

Zack looked at Liz, a question in the knitting of his brow, the answer following quickly upon it in the widening of his eyes and mouth. His face darkened with realization.

"Zack," Liz said, "these are my parents, Paul and Grace Broward. Mother and Dad, this is Zack James, Poke's father."

Zack moved toward Paul, hand extended. Rebuffed, his hand seemed to wither and dropped, though the momentum carried Zack forward an extra step.

Paul shrank back. "Yes, the relationship's clear. And now that you're here, you may take your daughter home. Her services are no longer needed. Nor are yours." His voice crackled with disdain.

Liz pushed Jimmy toward Poke, gesturing that she should take him. She rose from her chair, finding more bone in her legs than she'd thought was there. She looked at Zack, who clearly was reading her intent and steeling himself, shoulders drawn up and back, face twitching with resolve, hands flexing at his sides, legs set firmly.

"Zack is taking us home, Dad."

At this, Grace took a step backward and nodded. Softly she said to her husband, "Come on, Paul. We're not needed here."

He turned on her angrily. "Enough, Grace! Stop telling me what to do."

She flinched, then turned and shook her head. She'd run out of ways to manipulate, soften, direct the course of events, Liz knew. Events would take care of themselves, had already begun to spiral out of anyone's hands. The charade that Liz had constructed had started to fray. This meeting, so long eluded, had been bound to occur.

Jimmy's father and her own had met, and they must now acknowledge each other and their ties to Liz and the boy.

"No! Your mother and I will take you to your apartment. She'll stay with you and the boy."

"She doesn't have to. Zack and Poke will help me take care of Jimmy till I can go back to work."

Paul stiffened, the tension that clamped his jaws threatening to rupture their tendons, so his face would surely explode. Though no sound came from his throat, his face seemed to twist and roar like a surreal lion's. When he found his voice at last, it was cracked. "Who is this man?"

Poke hugged Jimmy, who'd begun to cry and reach out for Liz.

Grace walked to the window, and stared out at the sky, which had begun to gray as clouds moved over the sun.

Liz looked at Zack, suddenly overwhelmed by what she had allowed to happen, had *guaranteed* would happen, the moment she'd decided to tell no one who Jimmy's father was. A secret like that could not be kept forever. It might have been kept, she'd hoped, long enough to make telling it to her parents easier. Now she realized that keeping it even a year and a half had defied all odds.

She knelt next to her son and gathered him to her, without taking her eyes off Zack.

He responded as she'd expected, for he was no coward, and he'd never been cowed by men like her father.

"I'm Jimmy's father, sir."

Grace stood by the window, nodding.

"Liar!" breathed Paul.

"No, Paul," said Grace, turning to face him.

"Liar! Eric's his father. Even he knows it. But he has the good grace to say nothing. He's got too much character to go around ruining lives." He was referring to the wife Eric had taken on the rebound from Liz, and the child born just weeks after Jimmy. "And so does Liz. She could have pinned him with Jimmy to keep Eric from leaving her if she had less character than she did."

Yes, as Liz had known all along, that was the tale he'd woven for himself and her. She'd been jilted by her fiancé and kept a stiff upper lip; she'd accepted her punishment and borne her cross like a trooper, enabling her father to forgive if not condone her misbehavior. Liz simply shook her head.

"It's the truth, sir," said Zack.

"Dad—"

"Shut up! Both of you. I don't know what's possessing you to feed this . . . this person's fantasy, Liz. Can't you see he's after your money—*my* money? What makes you think he'll ever see a penny of it? What makes you think I'll allow you to claim my grandson as yours, so you can strip him of his inheritance? What makes you . . ." He trembled and shook his fists.

Jimmy began to cry and cling harder to Liz, who could no longer maintain her half kneeling position and didn't have the strength to pick him up. She looked to Zack, who strode over and gathered the child into his arms.

"Put the boy down! Give him to me!" Paul advanced toward the man and boy. The child bawled louder and Poke put her fists to her mouth and cried out, "Daddy!"

"No! Paul! Can't you see the boy's scared of you? He thinks you're angry with him." Grace ran to her husband and caught his arms. "Please, let's go. You can work this out some other time with Zack and Liz. When the boy's not here in the middle."

He flung off her hands, but he stopped. After a moment in which he continued to tremble with rage, he said, "I won't speak to this man ever again. I'll work it out, all right, but not with him." He turned and glared at Liz. "This man is not Jimmy's father. I'll never accept him into our family, and I'll never let Jimmy go. Mark my words." Then he wheeled and marched from the room.

"He'll calm down, Liz," her mother said. "I'll talk sense to him when he does." She looked at Zack with dismay and hurt in her eyes. "Where can I call you, Liz?" she said, without taking her eyes off Zack.

"I'll call you when I'm up to it, Mother."

"Of course." Grace quickly left the room.

CHAPTER
▪▪ FOUR

THE NEXT WEEK

Liz woke to the redolence of bacon and eggs. The fragrance seeped under the Jameses' downstairs guest room door and teased her from her morning torpor. Suddenly she sat up in the narrow guest bed.

No more charades! That part of my life is over!

The thought, from inside a dream, jolted her awake.

She heard Jimmy's small voice bouncing atop the padding sounds of his footed pajamas as he followed Zack around the house. From the clatters and scrapes and occasional deep-voiced curses in the kitchen, she guessed that Zack, not Poke, was this morning's cook. Of course! Poke's winter vacation had ended and she'd returned to high school, where she was entering her final semester.

Until today the morning noises from the living quarters just outside the tiny bedroom's door had barely penetrated Liz's consciousness. Poke had had to knock loudly several times, and had come in to shake her awake at least once. If she would fall back to sleep, the orders—*Zack's* orders—were to forcibly get her up and moving. He would stride into the room, snap up the window blind so sunlight stabbed through the double-hung window. He would pull her from bed by her arms. Without this bodily mustering— and left to Poke's soft heart and her own lassitude—Liz would have slept the day away.

Now the truth, tougher and more ruthless than her lover's yank, shocked her awake, wrenched her head from the pillow: The charade, the lies she'd told herself all her life, no longer worked. *If ever they had.*

Her father had known all along that her mother was "handling" him. He'd let Grace manipulate him. Her manipulations had gotten him what he'd wanted—a wife and daughter who thought they were getting what *they* wanted out of him. They all—yes, Liz, too—needed the same facade behind which to exist: the Broward and Stanford names and all they had meant from generations back, *black sheep excluded.* Liz had found Zack unworthy of her, a Broward woman, his name unworthy of a Broward son.

She and Zack both had been blinded by passion. Oh, he'd seen clearly at first that she was full of shit about who she was, where she'd come from. But she, sly and manipulative like her mother, deluded them both into thinking she was not. She'd needed him, yes, but only on her own terms. Those terms were to let her continue to live her lies and to teach her son the same lies. Zack would be excluded, a black sheep neatly bracketed out of the lineage—as Paul Broward himself might have done it—by tampering with official records through omission. *And, dear God, Zack had accepted those terms! How much he must need her and love her and their son!*

In her hospital room, the lies had come out. Surely he saw them for what they were. Did he still trust her? Was it too late for her to put the lies behind her, for them to start over again as a family?

On that thought, she sat up straight. She reached to the window on the wall adjacent to her bed and raised the blind. As the eastern light filled yet barely warmed the tiny room, she shivered. Yes, he *must* trust her. Look what he'd done to get her on her feet again. He'd thrown himself into her care, as she'd thrown herself into his when he'd had pneumonia. He'd put her on a regimen of outdoor walks on crisp, cold afternoons. When she'd looked in the foyer wall mirror on returning to the snug, warm house, she'd noticed her eyes had regained their amethyst sparkle. In the mornings, and when sleet and icy sidewalks had precluded outdoor exercise, he'd dragged her downstairs to the gray painted concrete block basement and supervised her on his cross-country skiing machine. As the hot, raspy breath of the oil-fueled furnace hissed in her ear and brought a dry flush to the high arched ridges of her nose and cheekbones, he'd insisted she keep going till her muscles ached. She'd gasped for breath, and cried out, "No! No more, please!"

And tears had washed over his eyes, which switched from slate green to warm brown, deepening beneath the shadows of his concern. *He loved her in spite of her lies, trusted her to tell the truth from now on. Surely he must!*

And she would fulfill his trust. She would acknowledge the lies. Their planned trip to Arizona would be a honeymoon. She would put all the records in order. Zack would adopt Jimmy, give both of them his name, officially.

That would rid her of the true black sheep in her family, *her father.* No . . . the mythical creature she'd needed her father to be so she and Jimmy could love him.

The man who'd stood in her hospital room wasn't lovable. He was a bigot who hated people like Zack; a ruthless lawyer who twisted the truth for powerful clients that wronged people like Lester Jones; a wealthy, powerful manipulator who owned newspaper reporters, politicians, racketeers, even a judge or two, and never hesitated to use them. Her father was in all ways a truly evil man. As an adolescent, she'd defied him and gone her own way even when he'd threatened to disinherit her. She continued to defy him, still as an adolescent would, with half an eye on his hoped-for approval. Now, as a full-grown woman, she must shun him and his approval. Why should she need approval from such a man?

She didn't. And it was not too late. Thank God for whatever virus had brought her down, brought out the truth, made her face it at last. Without it, she would not be here now, fully awake for the first time in weeks—*for the first time in her life.*

With conviction, she got out of bed and reached for her purple velour robe, which hung over a mahogany spindled bedpost.

"Liz?" A knock on the bedroom door accompanied the voice. The door opened a crack, and blue-pajamad Jimmy pushed it wider and came padding in across the floral carpet.

"Mommy up."

Zack, in striped pajamas and slippers but as usual wearing no robe, though the morning chill still gripped the house, leaned against the doorjamb. His fingers rasped on his whiskers as he rubbed his chin. His eyes widened; his face creased with pleasure. "I thought I heard you talking. Ready to eat?"

"Did I say it out loud? Did you hear me?"

"Your voice. Not what you said. Breakfast's ready."

"I said, 'No more charades,' Zack. No more lies. I'm not full of shit anymore. I want to be part of your family. I need you—and Jimmy and Poke—to be part of mine. On the record. In the family history."

Jimmy ran toward her, squealing.

She grabbed the robe and wrapped its thick sash around her waist as Jimmy threw himself at her legs. Entangled in her flannel nightshirt, he chortled. She fell back into a sitting position on the bed. He wound himself tighter in her clothing, and hid his head between her knees.

"Hey, kid! Let your mommy get up."

Jimmy peeked at Zack from behind the robe, which had fallen slightly aside, revealing Liz's flannel-covered leg. As Zack came forward, the boy laughed and hid his face again. Zack gently pulled him away.

"He wants to play hide-and-seek," said Liz.

Zack lifted his son, then pulled Liz to her feet and hugged Jimmy between them. "Yeah, I know. And it's OK, I guess. As long as we go into it with our eyes wide open from now on."

■ ■ ■

When she opened her eyes late the next morning, confusion beset her. She was in Zack's bed but couldn't recall going upstairs with him. She saw Jimmy's empty crib against the wall. Where was he? Where was Zack? Where was *she*? How had she gotten here?

She leapt from the bed and ran to the closed bedroom door, pushed it open and ran toward the stairs. From below she heard Jimmy's chortling, his father's humming. She stopped and looked down at her body. She was wearing only panties and a bra.

"Zack!" she cried out. "Zack! What happened?"

Quickly, he appeared at the foot of the stairs. "Liz . . . ?" He ran up to her and clasped her in his arms.

"Oh, Zack," she said, "I'm so frightened. My dreams . . . I don't remember . . ."

"Liz," he said, holding her tightly. "Nothing bad happened. You fell asleep is all, while we were trying to get Jimmy to bed. Don't you remember? It was Poke's idea. We took the crib downstairs, but he refused to sleep there in the guest room. So we moved it back here and he wouldn't let us out of his sight."

"Poke's idea? To move him so I could sleep up here with you?"

"She's not fourteen anymore, Liz. She got past seeing you taking Maryellen's place or hers. She got past her grief, like all of us did."

Something fleeting raced across Liz's consciousness. Then she shook her head and began to cry. As he held her, shushing her, Jimmy came up the stairs and put his head against her naked thigh and began to suck his thumb.

"Mommy kye. Poor Mommy." He planted a kiss on her thigh. Then he reached up and tugged at Zack. "Daddy tiss, too."

"Sure thing," said Zack. He kissed Liz lightly on her cheek.

"No! Daddy tiss egg. Mommy hoot egg."

Zack pulled back. "What's he saying?"

A surge of warmth dried her tears. She smiled and stooped to hug her son. "He wants you to kiss my leg. He thinks I hurt it."

"Sure thing," said Zack. He pulled her to her feet, then knelt and kissed her thigh. Then he rubbed his stubbly face against it. "Feel better, now, Mommy?"

"Ummm," she said. "Better than I've felt in a long, long time."

"Should I do it again?"

"Oh, Zack! I love you so much." Her fear had fled in the flush of sexual reawakening.

But the uneasiness remained, for she still could not remember something that she thought must be important.

Her first memory of yesterday emerged when she went downstairs to the guest room to fetch her robe and prepare to wash up for breakfast. Jimmy came into the room and grabbed her legs as she'd sat on the edge of the guest bed, buried his head in her lap.

"Hide-and-seek, again?" Zack said.

"Ah, yes! I remember. We weren't going to play it any-more!" Relief poured over her.

"Well, we both have our eyes open now," he said.

"Right!" Liz grasped the skirt of her robe and hugged Jimmy against her with it. She kissed the covered back of the toddler's head, laughed aloud at having remembered at least part of yesterday, and cast a catch-him-if-you-can dare at Zack. The boy's gleeful giggles puffed against her thighs, which still remembered the earlier touches.

Zack took her challenge. He skulked toward Liz, growl-ing softly, eyes twinkling. Jimmy tightened himself against the bed. Zack dove and captured his shoulders, only one of which stuck out from the velour robe's purple pile.

Jimmy squealed and struggled, as a child often does when what was a game becomes suddenly serious, and someone is about to lose face. He began to cry.

Zack persisted, though Liz tried to signal that Jimmy's mood had turned. "Come on, guy! Grrr . . . grrr . . ."

"No! Daddy bad!"

"Zack. Stop now. He's not playing anymore. He's scared." She hugged Jimmy tightly. "Daddy's letting go," she said.

Pain flooded Zack's eyes. He stood up, took a few steps backward in obvious puzzlement. The shadows in his jowls darkened.

"Oh, Zack. It's not you. Hide-and-seek's serious business to little kids. He just wants to prove you won't disappear. But he didn't expect you to turn into a tiger." Now she slowly uncovered Jimmy's head, kissed it again and said, "Where's Daddy?"

The boy continued to cling to her, shaking his head against her lap, though no longer crying.

"I see Daddy," she said. "Don't you want to go to him?"

More head shaking. A lap-muffled "No."

"Aw, Jimmy," said Zack. "Daddy wants to see you."

Liz gestured him closer with a toss of her head, then lifted her hands from Jimmy's head; Zack approached and leaned down and kissed the spot where her hands had been. "Daddy tiss Dimmy," Jimmy said. "Peek-a-boo, Daddy." He grew suddenly giggly again, pulled himself free from between Liz's knees, and scrambled out from under Zack's descending kiss and ran out of the bedroom.

Zack's kiss landed on Liz's well-kissed right thigh. She captured his head with tingling fingers, and held it there for several moments. When she finally let him go, he grasped her hips and pulled her pelvis against his lips. "Oh, God, Zack," she whispered. "Oh, God."

His answering exclamations, blowing warm and moist against her body, were muffled in her dampening panties.

"Peek-a-boo, Daddy," yipped Jimmy, who'd run back into the room and begun smacking his father's head.

Zack caught his little hands and sat back on the floor next to the boy. "Hey! You're hurting Daddy. More than he knows," he groaned to Liz under his breath.

"I love you so much, Zack."

He picked up the boy and swung him around to sit on his legs. "Play horsie with Daddy." He leaned back, his large arms and hands supporting his muscular upper body as he stretched out his legs full length and lifted his straddling son about a foot from the floor. The loose fitting pajama bottoms tightened around his thighs, accenting the rise of his groin. "Giddayap!"

"Tell him to give me a turn," said Liz. She laughed at his quick double arching of his brow and rose, walked around the bonded pair, stooping shortly to pat each of them on the head, and went through the living room to the downstairs bathroom off the foyer and emptied her bladder and brushed her teeth. The former did nothing to dissipate the pang that his kiss had set off in her pelvis; the latter did little to relieve the thickness of her tongue in her mouth.

Through the day, there was little Zack and Liz could do about their mutual longing. With a little boy sitting in his high chair, his greasy hands pushing crumbled bacon into his mouth, more than occasional brief semi-deep kisses between his parents was impossible. Hands that could have stroked each other's were kept busy picking up sticky spoons, wiping up crumbs and trails of spilled milk from the floor tile. Her bending to these tasks placed her rump at Zack's disposal from time to time, causing her to linger in that position long enough to allow a tantalizing caress, the slipping of one hand between her legs. Jimmy rewarded her for one of these moments by tossing his oatmeal, bowl and all, onto her head, cutting short both her hope for release and her breakfast.

In the funny, frustrating hours that followed, they learned, as Zack put it, "Foreplay and child's play don't mix so well!"

"When he takes his afternoon nap," she said with a hopeful laugh and a sigh. But that fervent wish, too, was dashed when Poke arrived home from school five minutes after Jimmy went down for his brief sleep.

At the front door's slam, Liz whispered, "So much for married bliss," as she brushed by his ear while breaking an interrupted embrace in the family room.

Poke rushed in with a cheerful cold gust and red cheeks. "Hi!" She whipped off her red scarf, tossed her books on the table by the computer, and slid her plaid wool coat off, but for one sleeve. "Did she read it?"

"Read it . . . ahh . . ." Zack's embarrassment found a new focus.

"Did I read what?" said Liz, puzzled, a bit worried. Had she forgotten something else from yesterday?

"The book with Great-Great Gramp's notes! Pop promised he'd show it to you." She slipped her arm out of her coat sleeve and tossed the coat on the back of the swivel chair, cutting off all possibility of the hoped-for romantic interlude.

"Oh, Poke, I'm sorry. It's been a crazy day. I just forgot," said Zack.

"Will somebody just fill me in?"

Poke shook her head, clearly exasperated with her father. "Not now. I have homework to do. I'll explain after dinner."

Then she sat at the family room desk and booted up the computer.

Liz turned to Zack. "I guess family life means I just have to wait my turn in line."

"Right," he said. And he grinned.

When Jimmy woke from his nap an hour later, Poke took immediate charge of him, saying that from the looks of the house, Liz and Zack had much to learn about running a household. They could pick up the toys he'd scattered about, while she and Jimmy got dinner ready. He would "help" her set the table while she made the spaghetti and meatballs. "It's a good thing I'll be here till next August," she said. "By the time I take off for school in Arizona, you might get the hang of things." She whisked Jimmy off to the kitchen.

"I hope so," said Liz, laughing, as she started to pick up scattered toys from the family room floor. She'd never pretended to love this part of running a household. The thought of it took her aback for a minute. Then she remembered that things would get back to normal in a week or so. Jimmy would go back to Joyce Price for day care.

She'd get back to her office. Until they would leave for their honeymoon, she'd remain in her apartment, coming here only for weekends. When she'd done that before, parenthood had not interfered with her sex life. Desire had built up during the week, only to be fulfilled with gusto on Friday and Saturday nights.

She bent to pick up a small plastic truck at the same moment Zack did. They bumped, then took each other's hands and stood up together. He looked at her, grasped her shoulders, his eyes dancing as they met hers. She touched his face, rasped her fingernails lightly over his emerging beard, combed her fingers through his silken hair, separated out a thick strand of it and pulled it to her lips, brushed her face with it.

A crash followed by hollering from the kitchen broke the spell. Jimmy scrambled in, crying loudly. Zack dropped Liz's shoulders. Poke burst into the room, looking cross. Amorous thoughts evaporated again under the stress of family exigencies.

Liz looked at Zack and said from behind her hand, "When do married people with children get to do it?"

He said, "You'll learn soon enough, dear person."

After dinner, she sat across the gold-topped, chrome-trimmed kitchen table from Zack while Poke told Liz of her plans to go to Arizona State University and study anthropology.

"I *know* they'll accept me. You have to write an essay about why you want to study there. Bet no one beats my essay." She got up from the table and began to clear it.

"Right," said Zack. "It's about Iliad. A real good writing job. 'Course, I helped her."

"Iliad? Well, I guess mythology does have something to do with anthropology," said Liz. She rose to help Poke, who motioned her to sit again. Liz obeyed. Not without some gratitude. The fatigue was settling in again.

"It's not that Iliad. It was Great-Great Gramps. He carried the book around with him. He wrote stuff in it."

"Oh. The book you were talking about. That I was supposed to read."

"Right," said Zack. "My grandmother inherited it from her Apache mother."

Poke nodded as she turned from the dishwasher to look over her slim shoulder.

"Zack," Liz said, "you never told me your tribe was Apache."

Thick black eyebrows raised, an ironic smile on his beard-shadowed face, he said, "Liz, this is the first time we've lived together for more than a few days since Phoenix. When did I have a chance to tell you? Besides, you never asked me what tribe it was. You found a generic type Indian sexy enough. Especially mixed with Scotch-Irish."

"I want you to put your sweet Scotch-Irish–Indian cock inside me." And she'd gone to him, and parted her thighs.

"You sure don't mince your words, Doc," he'd said as he'd entered her. Standing . . . And Jimmy had come from that night in Phoenix.

The memory flooded and stirred her, banished the encroaching fatigue.

"Yeah, we're part Apache," Poke said, not seeming to notice the flush that crept up Liz's throat and face. "My great-great-grandfather wasn't. He was white. He fell in love with my great-great-grandmother when he was working on The Trail."

"The trail?"

"The Apache Trail," said Zack. "In east central Arizona. They had to build a trail so they could bring in equipment and dig out the Tonto Basin and build the Roosevelt Dam. It was right in Apache territory. At least it had been Apache on and off. Part of the San Carlos Reservation. The white man had given it to them when they thought it was worthless, then driven them off the most valuable part when they found a big globe of silver there."

"Globe, Arizona," said Liz. "I've heard of it. And The Apache Trail."

"Later," Poke said, brown eyes flashing to green as she shoved in the dishwasher racks and pushed the door shut with a thud, "the Apache massacred all the whites. As usual, *they* were the ones who were called savages. Just for fighting *back!*" She latched the machine with a fierce thrust. "We've even been blamed for raiding the Salados and chasing them out of their settlements in the 1400s. *That* turned out to be a crock. We weren't even around there for another hundred years after that."

The legs of Zack's chair scraped on the vinyl floor as he pushed back from the table. He mocked his daughter with a gentle grin as he stood up. "Which 'we,' Poke? The Scotch-Irish or the Apache?"

"Oh, Pop! You know what I mean!" She tossed her black braids and lifted her chin. She dried long-fingered, delicate hands on a striped linen towel, which she returned to its rod with a snap.

"You'll have to excuse Poke's schizophrenia, Liz. She's carrying burdens from all sides. Her mother was part Jewish, but we haven't got to exploring that part of the family yet. Maryellen kind of just put up with my little hobby. But we owe her a good search one day. Meanwhile, we got a neat mystery to work on in Arizona. It's a natural adventure for Poke—a search for some of her roots as she works on her future." He motioned Liz to get up and follow him into the family room, where he sat on his brown vinyl recliner, swung up his legs, and raised its foot.

Sitting on the sofa across from him, Liz said, "Hey! Let me in on the mystery, too. Sounds like a great way to spend a honeymoon. That's where we're going, isn't it?" She pulled her legs up under her and sat forward.

"Sure. Great-Great Grandpa was killed in an accident on The Trail. Before Great-Grandma was born. She never even knew him, or what his real name was. Just knew what her aunt that raised her told her." Poke rolled down her red sweater sleeves and swiveled the chair by the desk with a creak, so she could sit facing Liz.

"But you know he was Scotch-Irish," said Liz.

Zack shook his head. "Nope. That was the next generation. My grandmother married Jamie James, and moved with him to Chicago, where Dad, their only child, was born. Mom met Dad when he came to her parents' house to fix their refrigerator. And the rest," he said, with a crooked grin, "is history."

"Your dad was a refrigerator serviceman?"

"Still is. Sixty-six and still keeps working."

"Still in Chicago?"

"Right. Doesn't know any better."

"She wants to know about Great-Great Gramps, Pop," Poke interjected impatiently. She spilled out, "All we know about him is he was killed in a construction accident on The Apache Trail two years before they started digging for the dam. That's what the mystery's about. After Great-Great Grandma died, Great-Grandma tried to find out more about him. But nobody seemed to know anything, not even where he was taken and buried. And people from the project all denied there was an accident at the time her mom said he worked there. They said they never even heard of a man with a nickname of Iliad. He got it from reading Homer and carrying the book around and quoting from it."

Zack added, "That's how my great-grandmother knew him. Just Iliad. Unusual enough a name for folks to remember. But after the accident, everyone forgot so fast, it seemed suspicious. Great-Grannie never even saw his body. That wasn't unusual, 'cause the Apache don't like to deal with dead bodies. Part of their superstitions about death. But, she found his book in the entry of her wickiup a day or so after she heard about the accident. That was it. A classic kind of cover-up followed. Might call it Apache Trailgate, today."

"But," said Liz, warming to the excitement as she recalled her first trip to Arizona to solve a more recent mystery with Zack, "how could we learn anything about him now, Poke? That happened how long ago?"

"Eighty-some years."

"And what you do know was all passed on by word of mouth. It's more like a legend, isn't it? Embellished the way those things are. Maybe—"

"There are clues in his book. His copy of the *Iliad*. He wrote stuff in the margins. There are dates and stuff, and notes in the back. It was a scholar's edition, and they used to have blank pages in the back. Great-Great Gramps used them to write about his own adventures on The Trail. It's got names—at least every name but his, his initials, though—places, lots of stuff, in a kind of shorthand code."

"Neat heirloom, to be passed from eldest daughter to eldest daughter—an Apache custom," said Zack. "Since the last two generations just had boys, and I was the first in my family, Poke got it. Couldn't've fallen into better hands."

"I'm taking it with me to ASU. They have contracts for all sorts of archeology projects. They're digging in the Roosevelt Lake area now. I can't wait. Want to see the book?"

"You bet I do. Oh, Zack, I can't wait for that trip!"

"Well, we'd better get cracking on planning. You and Jimmy and me in the van on a cross-country trip. That question you asked when we were picking up toys before? Well, you ain't seen nothing yet."

Liz flushed again.

"What question?" Poke asked, brow knit.

"Just between Liz and me," Zack said.

"And Jimmy," Liz added.

"Oh," said Poke. "Well, at least you won't have me to contend with."

Zack said, "Who said anything about you?"

Poke rose from the swivel chair and started to the kitchen. "I'm not the one that falls asleep on the kitchen floor after dinner," she said, speaking of Jimmy, who had done just that. "I'll get him his bath again, tonight."

When she returned with the boy against her shoulder, she looked from her father to Liz and said, "I'm not some dumb kid, you know. I'm going to be seventeen soon. Pop doesn't seem to know much about girls like me. He always let Momma handle that. You ought to have a talk with him about that." Then she went upstairs. A few moments later they heard the rumble of water running through the plumbing.

Liz rose from the sofa and crossed the room to Zack, who'd pulled the recliner back forward and now sat, elbows on knees, chin propped on curled fists, a chagrined look on his face. "You never talked to her about sex?"

"You heard what she said. Who needs to talk to a girl her age? Cheeze, Liz!"

She laughed. "Oh, Zack!"

"You just cross your fingers, that's all. Her mom prepared her. I never could've. Not the way things are now. I just hope she . . ." He stood up and shook his head. His face ruddied beneath his beard.

"That she's still a virgin? I think she is, Zack. She's too smart to take chances."

"That's not exactly what I mean. I mean, well, if she isn't, I mean, ahh, if she really likes some guy and something happens—"

"That she uses protection? Look, if you want me to have a talk with her before she leaves for school—"

"Oh, shit, Liz! That's not it." He looked into her eyes, and his flush darkened. Then he said, "I just hope she doesn't . . . doesn't talk like you."

"What! Oh, for God's sake, Zack!" She burst into laughter and bent double. "I p-p-p-promise, I'll never breathe a word."

She was still giggling as they got into bed and he reached for her. "Jimmy's listening," she whispered, and grabbed his hand, stopping it in its frank explorations, then kissing each finger, sucking each, one at a time, kissing his palm, the back of his hand, chortling softly as she did so.

"Aw, Liz." He freed his hand, then silenced her laughter with his mouth. It spilled out from between their lips till the stirrings of his tongue brought hers into play.

"Zack, Zack. How can I fight those words?"

He chuckled and ran his freed hand up under her night-gown. "Right. Don't want to teach *him* your colorful expressions."

As his fingers found their mark and parted her aching flesh she said, "Oh!" loud enough to cause Jimmy to stir in his crib.

"Nice start. I should have known better than to bring a woman with a mouth like yours into my house," Zack said.

"What was colorful about that . . . ooh, uhmm . . . ?" She set her own hands to undressing him, her mouth to sucking his face, his neck, his chest.

"I interpreted it colorful."

"How did you interpret it?"

"It meant, put it in deeper, Zack. Like this?"

"Like that, oh that's right," she said into his mouth.

"What else?" he said.

"You know what else. Don't dare me to say it. You don't like it."

"Say it. Like you always do. I won't breathe a word. I promise."

"I never should have said it in the first place. Nice girls don't talk that way."

"What shouldn't you have said? What don't nice girls say?" He was over her now, his powerful hips between her parted thighs.

She looked down, then up at his eyes, ambered in the glow from the night light by Jimmy's crib, his ironic, teasing grin revealing squared teeth.

She spread her legs wider and whispered, "I want you to put your sweet, Scotch-Irish–*Apache* cock inside me."

He laughed aloud. "You got it, baby."

"Shhhh!" she said, placing two fingers across his lips. "I thought Apaches knew how to move silently."

"Yeah. Like this." Then he entered her. "Now let's see how quiet you can be, lover." He again covered her mouth with his own, drew up her hips with his hands.

The night light burnished the opposite wall with its amber glow, casting their dancing shadows upon it. Containing her cries, keeping to a whisper her vivid instructions to him, biting off the yesses that came spilling from her tongue, she watched their merged silhouettes flame at the edges as the pace of their movements increased.

But her love, in its climax, never could, and could not tonight, keep silent like its burning shadow.

"Aw, Zack," she murmured before falling asleep, "I never said things like that to anyone but you."

He squeezed her hand, lifted it to his lips, and sighed, and she felt him smile.

CHAPTER
▪▪ FIVE

**TWO WEEKS LATER—
LIZ BROWARD'S OFFICE**

"Who?" Liz rose from her swivel chair with an irritated sigh and shoved aside her half-eaten tuna salad sandwich. It was supposed to have been her lunch, but, as usual, it had sat in the utility room refrigerator all the busy afternoon. Both her stomach and head had been paining for that and the accompanying apple, which rolled off her desk and bounced to the side at her sudden motion. "Damn!"

"I don't know her name. But she really looks terrible, Liz," said her tall blond receptionist, Claire. "Jim and Elsie just left. I was on my way out, too, and she just burst in—"

"In trouble, you think?" She bent and scooped up the apple, rubbed it with a paper napkin, and took a bite out of it. "Wish I'd gone, too. But I'm famished. Should have stopped for lunch. All right, send her back. Then you'd better leave, too, before somebody else shows up sick and dying on our doorstep." Such were the perils of the small family practice. She took another bite of the apple and, in three huge gulps, drained her red and white Coke can. The sugar and caffeine should take the edge off her headache, though she would need more than that to slake her appetite, which had returned with a vengeance two weeks after she'd left the hospital. The colas, quick and easy to toss down between patients, had become her drug of choice, and she kept a case in her closet and a six-pack in the refrigerator. They also seemed to help the recurrent fatigue and occasional brief memory lapses that dogged her still, only a couple of weeks before her planned honeymoon trip.

As Claire ran out, Liz swept the rest of her lunch into a deep desk drawer, allowing herself an extra bite of the apple before tossing it in after the sandwich. Though anyone barging in like this after office hours should be glad to be seen in any setting, she didn't want her office to reek of tuna.

"Dr. Broward, I'm sick. I feel like I'm going to die."

For a moment, Liz stood frozen behind her desk, staring at the massive woman in the doorway.

"Hester—?"

The woman took three steps forward, then collapsed in the crumpled mass of her stiff denim tent dress. Her legs' and buttocks' sheer size kept her from keeling over completely; she sat, her enormous handbag against her thighs, heaving and sweating in her own bulk. Liz ran to her and lifted a flaccid, clammy arm. As she counted the thready beats in the wrists, she looked into Hester's pale face and glazing eyes. The pupils were wide—with fear?—or with some other kind of reaction?

"When did this start? Has it ever happened before?"

"T-ten min . . ."

Liz dropped the arm. She counted the heaves of Hester's chest. She whipped her stethoscope from her pocket and called for Claire. When she didn't come, Liz cursed her silently for leaving as she'd been told. "Can you move to where you can lie down?" The woman simply shook her head weakly. She was too heavy for Liz—a tall, strong, usually vigorous woman herself—to move, and too weak to move herself a few feet from the spot where she sat with insufficient space for her to lie back and get her blood flowing brainward.

Liz wanted to check Hester's blood pressure, which she guessed might be dangerously low, but didn't have handy

an oversize blood pressure cuff. She would have to get one
from an examining room, and with Claire gone, she'd have
to leave Hester alone. She decided that the worst that could
happen was that Hester would pass out completely, still
sitting. Supported by her lower bulk, she was unlikely to
fall and hurt herself. "Then put your head down on your
lap. I'll be right back," she said, and ran to fetch the extra-
large cuff.

When she returned, a familiar but elusive odor hung in
the air around Hester. It piqued Liz's hunger again for the
moment before she wrapped the cuff around the woman's
arm. Then Hester raised her head and belched some of the
odor into Liz's face, killing her appetite. When Hester
sighed and belched again, Liz turned her head, as much
to escape the smell of her patient's breath as to see the
sphygmomanometer's mercury column.

"Is your stomach upset?" She watched the beat of the
mercury column as it fell. The blood pressure was 95 over
60, on its way to being dangerously low, even if Hester's
thick arms made the reading misleadingly low.

After wafting another deep belch in Liz's direction, Hester
answered, "Yeah." Her voice seemed slightly stronger.

"Ah!" said Liz, nodding. "When did you eat last?"

"Last night. Supper upset me, so I was afraid to eat
today." Another long bellow traveled up her esophagus.

"But you came downtown."

"Yeah. A friend promised to stay with Daddy, and I
needed to get out for a change."

"That makes sense. I hope you do it regularly. But not
on an empty stomach." Liz went to the utility room and
got a Coke from the refrigerator. "You're suffering from
the same thing I am at this moment," she said when she
returned. "Hypoglycemia." With a quick, practiced thumb
she popped the can open, then held it to Hester's lips with
one hand and tilted back her head with the other. "Drink
this. You should feel better in just a few minutes."

Hester's eyes widened and she drank. Ten minutes later,
Liz rechecked her blood pressure and found it near normal.

Hester's color had returned, presumably ratcheted up by
the series of burps and sighs that followed the drink. Her
muscle tone also had improved. She was able to grasp and
drink the second cola Liz gave her.

"I'll join you in your therapy, if you don't mind," said
Liz, opening her desk drawer and retrieving her sandwich
and apple. "As I said, my sugar's a bit low, too." She ate her
food and washed it down with another Coke she'd brought
from the refrigerator for herself.

When she'd finished and sent the trash clunking into the
metal trash can and stored the empty cans for recycling, she
asked the still somewhat caved in Hester, "Better now?"

She shifted and stared wide-eyed at Liz. "I knew you
would know what was wrong. You always know what's
wrong, Dr. Broward."

"I try to keep on top of things. I'm surprised you didn't
know, what with your background and experience with your
father. You've got to be on the alert for insulin reactions."

Hester giggled and tried to stand up.

"Did I say something funny? Here, let me help you
up." She stooped and offered her patient a firm arm to
lean on.

"I guess I feel kind of giddy. That's part of it, too." With
Liz's help, she got to her feet. Then she waddled to the gray
armchair beside Liz's desk and let herself heavily down into
it. Air hissed from its leather seat. "Can I rest for a while? I
still feel weak."

"Ten minutes more. Then I'm getting you a cab and
sending you on your way. I've got to get home, too."

Hester nodded. "I guess you're feeling better from when
you were sick."

Sitting behind her gray oak desk, Liz knit her broad
tawny brow and studied Hester a moment. "You knew I
was ill?"

"Yeah. Your office called to say you couldn't come to
see Daddy this month."

"Oh, of course. I'm sorry about that. I'm the only one
here who does the house calls. So we had to discontinue

that service for a while. Probably till the end of March or
the middle of April, now."

"What did you have?"

"I . . . I'm the doctor, not the patient, Hester. I don't like
to discuss my health with people outside my family."

"Well, it's nothing contagious, is it? A patient should
know about that."

Liz laughed. "No, they didn't find anything contagious.
Or I wouldn't have come back to work. You don't have to
worry about that." *Was the woman inferring that Liz might
have AIDS? Something else she might sue for? Remind me
not to stick her with a needle, or cough in her direction,*
Liz thought.

"But they did find out what was the matter. So you won't
get sick again. Why will it take you so long to start the
house calls again?"

Perplexed and disturbed by this grilling, Liz sighed. She
picked up the phone. "I'll call you a cab, Hester." She
punched in the taxi service number and held out the receiver
to her.

"No!" Hester reached across the desk for the phone.
"Please don't make me take a cab. I hate cabs." Liz hung
up.

"How did you get downtown?"

"By bus."

"Well, maybe you can catch one home, then. You're
feeling well enough, aren't you?"

"No. I feel bad again. Sick to the stomach again." She
pressed her arms, clasped, across her abdomen and pushed
up a belch. "Like before."

"Well, you have to get home somehow, Hester."

"You take me."

"Hester, I—"

"You can stop in and see Daddy. You haven't checked
him in nearly two months. You said you're not coming for
maybe three more."

"I really can't—"

"He has to be weighed."

"Well, I can't do that, Hester. I'm not even driving the van."

"Well, you can look and see if he looks like he's losing weight. He's been sick at the stomach, too. Like me."

Taking a deep breath and slowly letting it go to purge out an uneasy, trapped feeling, Liz said, "I'm sorry, Hester, that he's not feeling well. You should call the visiting nurse."

"What can she do? She's not a doctor. At least you can stop in and see him. He hasn't been able to eat, and you know that's bad for a diabetic."

After another sigh and a helpless clenching of her hands, Liz asked, "How long has he been feeling this way?"

"About three or four days."

"I wish you'd called me sooner."

"I didn't want to bother you in case you were still sick. You're the only doctor I trust with him."

Liz stood up and shook her head. "I'm complimented, Hester. But you know I can't be everywhere, and Dr. Thomas and his nurse really know your father best. They've been treating him since long before I came on the scene."

Raising her round, fat face and frowning, Hester said, in a slow, drawn-out, angry tone, "One of his nurses turned against Daddy."

Liz caught her breath. "Why would a nurse do that? I'm sure—"

"She said he didn't take care of himself. That's why they didn't give him the money he deserved."

Liz hadn't followed the trial in detail. She knew nothing about specific testimony and who gave it, but she imagined quite easily how Paul Broward might intimidate a witness into saying things she'd never intended. "Oh. I'm sorry that happened," was all she could say. *Paul Broward's daughter, still, even though she was taking the final steps to break the relationship. She and Zack would be married next week. They would begin proceedings for Zack's adoption of Jimmy when they came home from their trip. Paul would disinherit her and that would be that. Still, she was trapped again.*

"You should stop in and see him. You should take me home, and not make me call someone else."

Liz nodded slowly. All right, then, what would be so horrible about driving Hester home? It was barely out of her way to Joyce's house to pick Jimmy up before returning to her own apartment, where they still slept weeknights. And she could discharge in some small manner a guilt debt her father had once more brought on her. The visiting sins of her father left her little wiggling room in this case. "Well, I'll stop in long enough to make sure he's in no immediate danger. Come on. My car's parked not far from here."

She supported Hester's arm as she ushered her out of the office, a few yards down the fourth floor corridor and through the steel door to the enclosed parking lot. Her gold Mercedes-Benz, just a few slots away from the door, was the only car left in the doctors' parking section.

"Nice car," Hester said, studying it inside and out. "Looks and smells new."

Liz's irritation at the woman's forwardness passed quickly this time. She laughed. "Actually it's five years old. With nearly a hundred thousand miles on it. I'm not in any hurry to trade it. With good care, it'll outlast me."

Hester, settling her bulk into the complaining beige leather backseat, seemed to find that funny. She giggled and chortled as Liz drove down the spiral parking lot ramp into the gray, chilly night. In her rearview mirror, Liz saw the face of Hester the clown. Then, after a silent ride to the Joneses' home, just as Liz was about to turn off the engine, Hester said, to Liz's surprise, "You don't have to come in and see Daddy if you don't want to, Dr. Broward. I'll bring him to your office next week." She opened the door and slid easily out onto the curb, apparently fully recovered.

Powering down her window as the rear door slammed, Liz said, "You're sure? Now that I'm here—"

"It's late. And your office is so easy to get to from the parking lot. I can park our van in that handicapped spot near the door, practically next to your car, and just wheel Daddy right in. You make things so easy for us." Then she grinned as she had the first time Liz had come to this house. But this time her icy breath formed a wreath about her head . . .

SEVERAL DAYS LATER

"Just sit here, Daddy. I won't be long." Hester strapped Lester into his seat and secured the wheelchair in the van.

He whined a bit, and some tears appeared in the corners of both eyes.

"Yes, I know you like her. She's nice. And it's a shame. But Susan was nice, too. That doesn't mean she shouldn't have been punished, does it? She did a bad thing to us. And Dr. Broward may be an innocent victim, but so were we, Daddy. And the lawyer has to be punished, and this is the only way to do it. She's his last living heir. He'll never be able to have grandchildren now." She patted his shoulder and kissed him on his shiny, damp cheek. "It'll all be all right in the long run, you'll see. I couldn't keep her coming to visit you much longer. She'd soon get too sick to drive the van, so she'd stop getting the poison altogether, and she'd start getting better, like she did this time. So we've got to finish the punishment. Make it quick and sure this time. Then I'll have so much more time for you. You don't need her. You need me." She smiled broadly, and his lips crooked in a trembling smile.

She backed herself out of the van side gate, closed it, and went to the tailgate and opened it. From it she removed a nine-inch-long two-by-four board; a large gauge steel cannula and trocar she'd taken from an operating room at UMC Hospital years ago, without then having in mind a use for it; a roll of duct tape; and a tube of muffler epoxy. She placed the epoxy and the surgical instrument in the large pocket of her denim skirt. A crackling sound, as if someone had come up and stepped on a piece of gravel, startled her. She whirled.

No one was there. She sighed with relief as she realized that she'd jammed the cannula and trocar into the fold-ed diagram in her pocket. Why she'd brought the greasy paper the Mercedes-Benz serviceman had drawn the diagram on for her, she didn't know. She remembered the details explicitly: the position of the exhaust pipe as it ran beneath the chassis, the location of the exhaust system vent flap. She'd practiced on an abandoned car in the alley that ran behind her row house the maneuvers she'd need to execute. True, it wasn't a Mercedes, but it was almost as heavy—a 1955 Chevy—and had a suspension taller than most late-model cars.

As a few cars passed, heading up the spiral ramp from below, she closed the tailgate and walked casually past three cars to Dr. Broward's. When the second of the three newly parking drivers slammed his car door, she dropped the two-by-four to the cement floor behind the left rear tire. Its clatter was lost in the noise of resounding slams. Hester kept on walking as a small pickup truck came from below. Its driver braked as he noticed a parking spot, then bucked the truck forward with a loud engine surge as he noticed the space was reserved for a physician. His brakes squealed as he reached the last slot on the level—the topmost tier of the indoor lot—and found access precluded by the crookedly parked car in the neighboring slot. His echoing angry turnaround maneuvers filled the garage with screeches. They'd have been a perfect cover for the noises she'd be making soon, but their timing was premature.

Hester sighed and turned and walked back past her van toward the end of the tier as the pickup sped past her. It stopped suddenly, and backed up, then stopped beside her.

"You parked back there, lady?" the driver shouted.

"I thought I was," she said. "But I think I'm on the wrong floor."

"This is four," he said.

"Oh," she said. "I thought it was two. I must have got off the elevator at the wrong floor."

"Two! That's where my doctor is, and I'm late. Hop in and I'll take you down so I can get your spot."

After a brief hesitation, Hester shook her head. "No. I'll take the elevator down. I don't get in trucks with strange men."

"Shit! I don't know why you'd have to worry about strange men. OK then, tell me what kind of car you have and I'll wait till you come down."

Genuinely angry, she said, "No! You'll have to find a spot for yourself." She turned toward the fourth-floor office wing door.

"Shit! Up yours, cunt-face!" He gunned his truck forward and the sounds of his receding screeches ricocheted off the orange-painted concrete walls.

For a moment Hester stood clenching her fists, but as the pickup's noises subsided, she recalled her mission and returned to her van, opened the tailgate, and removed the small cordless electric drill that she'd given a full charge last night. She tucked it under her arm and hurried back to the doctor's car. Hearing someone coming through the door from the offices, she leaned back against the car and waited. An old man walked slowly to his car, searched through his keys several times until he found the one he was looking for, got with difficulty into his seat, took minutes to fasten his seat belt and start his engine, then made a false start while backing out of his slot. At last, he re-maneuvered his car into the correct turning position and drove out. His engine stalled twice before he managed to turn down the ramp and putt-putt to a lower level.

By the time he had gone, two other people had come for their cars and were driving by. Hester sighed heavily when the last one disappeared from the tier. Though she heard another car coming up from below, she stooped quickly and pushed the drill underneath Dr. Broward's car. After the new arrival had found her parking space and run into the office wing, Hester kicked the two-by-four between the Benz and the car to its left. Then she sat on her back under the car with her butt up against the rear tire, tensed her muscular thighs, and straining her legs, which were encased in heavy tall Western boots, she slowly lifted the rear left corner of the car. Holding it in that position with trembling muscles, she grabbed the two-by-four at her side, stood it on edge, and set it beneath the rear axle jack point. Grunting and panting, she counted to ten as she brought her aching legs down. The tire still rested tentatively on the ground, but, once recovered from her exertions, she was able to fit her full mass beneath the slightly suspended chassis.

No one would notice the car had been slightly jacked up. No one would guess this 220-pound woman was under the gold Mercedes-Benz, arranging its owner's painful demise.

Now the comings and goings through the garage helped her through her plan. The screech of starting engines and turning wheels masked the sound of her drill as she bored through the exhaust pipe and into the metal chassis. She heard a ripping sound as the drill bit encountered the beige carpet inside the passenger compartment. She knew from her diagram that at this point the tear would show from inside the car only on close inspection. Her arms ached as she held the drill at the right angle for several minutes. At last she was satisfied with the caliber of the bore, which was just slightly less than that of the cannula, so the tube would fit snugly when she reamed it through with the trocar.

She laid down the drill and wiped her sweaty, soiled hands on her skirt. Then she took her trocar and cannula, assembled them so the point of the trocar extended through the cannula tube.

Damn! She'd left her sledgehammer in the van! There was no way to ream the instrument through the drill bore without it.

She rested a few moments while people and cars came and went on their noisy reverberating ways. As the time passed, the garage became busier, her times for action briefer and more tenuous. Dr. Broward was unlikely to come to her car. She brown-bagged her lunch and ate in her office, Hester knew. From the red nose and sniffling she'd seen during her father's visit, the doctor seemed to be catching a cold. She'd be unlikely to go out unnecessarily in today's chilly weather. And though Hester's father's appointment had been the doctor's first of the day, not a single chair in the waiting room had remained unoccupied by the time Hester had wheeled him out of the office.

But other doctors in the building might not have the same habits. They might come and go at any time. If one parked at either side of the jacked-up car should drive off now, that would leave her exposed to other passersby. Someone might notice the slight upward tilt of the car's rear left corner. Someone might look underneath and discover her. She hadn't come up with a story to explain her presence, her drill and the metal shavings it had created, the makeshift jack. As good as she was with pretexts, she couldn't think of one for this occasion.

She'd known how to handle the doctor last week. That had been easy. She'd injected herself with Lester's insulin just a few minutes before barging into the waiting room that day. She'd secreted a sugary chocolate drink in her voluminous handbag, and drunk it when Dr. Broward had left her alone for a moment. Though she'd had little doubt that the doctor would immediately spot the hypoglycemic reaction to the insulin (without dreaming it was caused by insulin), the drink provided insurance against Hester's going into shock. Even without the Cokes Dr. Broward had given her, she would have begun to recover. As for wangling a ride home, she'd played on the guilt she knew the doctor felt. For though she'd never admitted her father was the lawyer who'd screwed the Joneses, the look in her eyes whenever Hester mentioned the case spoke clearly enough. Guilt, which Dr. Liz Broward's father never felt for even a moment, lay heavy on her shoulders. For she was a good human being. She *cared*. And that was why she was so easy to fool. What a shame that she should have to suffer not only the guilt of her father, but the punishment for his acts as well. But that was the only way to punish *him*. The only way to show him how it felt when someone you cared for—probably the only one *he* cared for—was slowly poisoned into oblivion and uselessness.

As she thought these things, Hester waited for a moment when no cars were coming or going; then, leaving behind her tools, she slid out from beneath the Mercedes and stood up. Seconds later, as she leaned over the opened tailgate of her van, a woman came through the door and high heels clacked to the far end of the garage. Hester ducked her head and searched for the sledgehammer.

Lester whined for her attention.

"Daddy, I'm almost done. It'll just take another five minutes, and I'll take you home." She groped around the storage area and finally found the hammer where she had hidden it, jammed in beside the spare tire. "Oh, Daddy! How wonderful! I just got the best idea."

He moaned his "I'm uncomfortable" moan.

"Just a minute," she said. Then she unclamped the spare tire and lifted it out and leaned it against the van's rear bumper. As soon as the woman passerby had driven away, she pulled out the sledgehammer, supported it out of sight behind the spare wheel, then slammed the tailgate and went to tend to her father.

She kissed and fondled him for a moment, rearranged the padding around him, and said, "Only a few minutes more, I promise." With another kiss, she left him.

The spare would give her the pretext she'd need if someone should find her working under the car. She laid it between the car and its neighbor to the left and slid the sledgehammer beneath the chassis. Soon, with a few hard clunks masked in ambient garage noises, she had augered the cannula through the exhaust pipe and into the passenger compartment. The length of the tube was perfect! Just as the serviceman's diagram had predicted. What a help he had been! Ask an expert a question in that dumb little girl innocent voice and you'll get more answers than you'd ever dreamed of. He would never guess that you weren't really a murder mystery writer wanting to get your facts straight about murder by Mercedes-Benz exhaust system. You were too little girl and dumb to dream of pulling off such a scheme by yourself! He'd never notice your muscles, which he'd think were flab collected around your bones as you spent your days in sedentary work at a typewriter.

She chortled now as she pulled out the trocar, leaving the tube in place. She giggled her little-girl laugh as she applied the muffler epoxy to seal the tube and hold it in place. And, as she taped the exhaust vent flap closed, to make certain none of the deadly carbon monoxide would escape the passenger compartment, she sang to herself in her surprisingly light little-girl soprano.

CHAPTER
▪▪ SIX

THE NEXT DAY, AT DUSK

"Thank God it's Friday, eh, Liz?" said redheaded, freckled Joyce Price, Jimmy's fifty-two-year-old nanny, as she nudged a reluctant Jimmy out the door of her brick one-story house. The yellow porch lamp turned her hair brassy, hard, belying her true warm personality. She pried Jimmy's snowjacketed arms from around her slim slack-encased legs and laughed. "All right, fella," she said, "time to go home with Mommy."

"That's no big treat, is it, Jimmy?" Liz ducked to kiss her son on the head. As he twisted his head away, she tugged up his jacket hood. "What is a big treat is that we're going to see Daddy and Poke."

Jimmy let go of Joyce's legs and squealed, "Po, Po, Po!" He headed immediately down the portico stairs to his mother's car in the floodlighted driveway.

Joyce grinned at Liz. "Looks like you've said the magic word. I'm jealous. I've spent my last year and a half with that kid, given him the best hours of every weekday, and then Poke comes along, takes care of him for a few weeks, and wins him away."

Laughing, Liz said, "There's just no justice, Joyce. How did it go today?" The two women followed the toddler to the driveway.

Joyce raised the garage door and went with Liz to retrieve

the child car seat. Jimmy was banging on the rear auto door. "Looks like he's got his energy back now, but this morning after you dropped him off, he was hardly himself, Liz. Did he have a bad night?" She was hugging herself against the cold. Her breath froze as it rose around her head.

Liz heaved the car seat up and carried it to the car. Opening the door, she started to secure it in place. Joyce caught Jimmy by his legs, as he tried to get into the seat before it was secured. As she fastened the seat belt around the child seat, Liz knit her brow. "No. As far as I know he slept well. As a matter of fact, when I got him home last night, he was unusually bushed. Conked out right after dinner. So did I, as a matter of fact. But that's not unusual for me. This morning he seemed as chipper as ever. What happened today?"

"You're OK, Liz?" Joyce shot her a worried glance. "You sound a little stuffed up."

Liz sighed and shrugged. "I think I've shaken the virus that hit me last month. It does seem to come back in waves, like cramps. One kicked me just as I was on my way here. But it was a horribly busy day and, as you noticed, I seem to have caught a cold." She sneezed and blew her nose as if to demonstrate. "What happened with Jimmy?"

Jimmy climbed into his seat. As Joyce fastened him in, she said, "Maybe he's catching something, too. He fell asleep in my car on the way to the library for story hour. He slept through the whole story time. Through Dr. Seuss, mind you. Right on the floor."

"Story hour? That *is* strange. It's his favorite thing next to the Franklin Institute."

Kicking both feet against the seat, Jimmy said, "Po! Po!"

Joyce laughed. "He's fully recovered from whatever it was, anyway. Didn't notice any sniffles, either. My guess is he didn't sleep well last night, but you did and didn't hear him." She kissed her small charge and hugging her shirt-sleeved arms around her chest, stepped back from the car so Liz could close the door. "Now you take care of

yourself, Liz, with that cold. You're supposed to be the
doctor, you know. That wave passed, I hope."

"Oh, yes. Must've been the car was stuffy. I opened up a
window and the sunroof. This weather's a bit bracing. But
it's a bit more than that for you. You better get back inside
before I have to doctor you for frostbite."

"Right, Doc! Take care!" Still hugging herself, she waved
the fingers of one hand and turned and ran into her house
through the garage, just before the snow that had been
threatening all day began to fall in large, fat flakes.

Liz started the engine, and powered the window and
sunroof aperture closed. She hoped the snow wouldn't get
so deep as to tie up the remainder of Friday evening rush
hour. Going up Broad Street to Glenside at this time of day
was bad enough without a snowfall.

Broad Street to Glenside! Oh, shit! she thought. *I forgot
to bring our suitcases. Another damn memory lapse!* Last
weekend she had brought all of Jimmy's and her clothes
home to her apartment to launder them and prepare for
their trip next week. He wouldn't have a single pair of
pajamas for tonight, or be able to sleep without his favorite teddy. To go back to the apartment with him now
would make him late for dinner, which would put him in
a terrible mood that could last the whole weekend. Not a
good idea, with a month-long RV trip in the offing. She
turned off the engine, undid her son from his car seat,
and sent him toddling in front of her, back to Joyce's
front door.

"I'd better call Zack to come get him," she told Joyce,
explaining the situation. "My memory's slipping. I wonder
what else I forgot."

"You've been under too much pressure, Liz. Maybe you
shouldn't have gone back to work so soon."

"Well, I can't just walk out on my partners, then run
away for a month. Anyway, luckily Zack went to Squire's
downtown office today. He can be here in fifteen minutes."

"Sure. You know where the phone is."

"I'm terribly sorry. On a Friday. You've had your hands full all week."

"Really, Liz. No problem." Joyce knit her brow.

"You've been a treasure," Liz said to Joyce as she dialed.

Zack, who had been just about to leave, said he'd be right there. Liz left Jimmy with Joyce, ran to the car, once more turned on the engine, and pulled out of the driveway.

The snow-slicked, traffic-clogged streets, obscured by thick, flying flakes, demanded Liz's full concentration. Somehow she managed to muster enough to get her to her Society Hill apartment. Usually fifteen minutes got her there, even during rush hours; this time it took a full forty-five. A half hour into the trip she was growing irritable and weary. She could not get around the bus ahead of her, and it seemed to stop at each corner to load and discharge passengers who took longer than usual to mount or dismount the stairs as they shook thick snow off of buckling umbrellas. She yawned, almost gasped on the lungful of air she took in, forgot for a moment where she was going. Her eyes teared and burned. Excruciating aches gripped her muscles. Her vision blurred as one swell of fatigue followed another.

She didn't recall getting around the bus at last. Or had it turned off somewhere? She knew the bus route pretty well, was usually adept at avoiding the wrong lane, at maneuvering her car around traffic. Now the steering wheel reacted slowly to her adjustments. A few times she nearly scraped the rear fender of a car she was trying to pass. The driver of one opened his window and shouted at her as she passed. Something in her felt it should be reacting to this; something else blunted and delayed her response for several minutes. Then that feeling was gone, and she was fumbling with her apartment parking garage key card, missing the slot entirely several times while someone's horn blared behind her, then putting it in backward, then finally getting it right. The steel door clattered, rolled up. Its noise nauseated her, hurt her head.

At last she parked in her berth, bumping the concrete wall slightly, and later found herself in her apartment, though she didn't recall going in or picking up the mail she had in her hand.

She put the mail down on the foyer table, picked up the teddy bear from on top of Jimmy's suitcase, which she'd left near the door this morning, meaning to take it with her then.

Hugging it to her, she collapsed on top of it.

Four hours later, Zack found her crumpled there, took her to the hospital emergency room, whence she was whisked to the intensive care unit. They would do all they could for her, do all they could to find out what was behind this mysterious ailment. She'd awakened only momentarily, they said, asked where the teddy bear was, then sighed and lost consciousness again when they told her Zack had it. He might as well go home. There was nothing he could do by staying.

Liz's mind clawed at the edge of consciousness as she heard from far away a familiar, disturbing voice.

"Surely . . . know what . . . has . . ."

The words in between were missing, unrecoverable. She knew the lisp. He was angry. At her? At whom? Was he talking to Zack? Where was she?

"Someone else . . . lousy hospital . . . rate doctors."

"Paul . . . Ryan . . . what he's . . . Gary Hoffman . . . not heart . . ." Grace was pleading someone's case.

Formidable lawyer . . . he'd win whatever it was.

She sensed she'd opened her eyes, saw formlessness, light without shadows.

"Liz . . . ? Waking up . . . all right."

". . . seem to see . . . coma . . ."

". . . out of here!"

". . . ever you say . . . Broward . . ."

"Paul . . . sure?"

Nothing for a long time or short time. A moment. Feelings of moving. Familiar voices. Someone crying. More moving. Nothing. Unfamiliar voices. Nothing. A light she was moving toward. Light bursting over her. Fear melting into it, becoming glorious joy. She moved toward it, gave herself up to it.

"I'm sorry, Zack. We couldn't stop him. He came in early this morning, just after you called in to see how she was doing, and had her transferred to a private facility upstate. He's a lawyer, you know. Threatened us with a malpractice suit," Jennie, the emergency room triage nurse, said. She looked a little like Liz, with blue eyes instead of violet, hair a bit blonder and shorter. Using this resemblance, she'd once risked her life for Liz. She would do it again if it was necessary.

"Where? I have to go see her."

"I don't know. He sent a private ambulance for her."

"Does he have the right . . . ?"

"Zack, he knows how to get the right. You don't argue with Paul Broward."

"Oh, God!"

"Look," said Jennie, laying her hand on his arm, "he wouldn't send her someplace they couldn't care for her. He'd buy her the best doctors he could. She'll probably be fine. She came out of it last time. She'll come out of it this time. She opened her eyes a few times and seemed to hear me talk to her."

He tried to believe that. At least, thank God, Jimmy was with him and Poke. He wasn't wandering alone and crying around the apartment, hungry, scared, in soaked pajamas.

"But," he said, remembering that it had taken several days before Liz's parents learned of her illness before, "how did they find out she was in here again?"

"He made sure that he'd be notified first if she should ever be admitted again and unable to sign herself in. He is her closest relative, you know."

"No! We're going to be married next week."

"I'm sorry, Zack. What can I do? She's still a Broward till then."

"He's got no right. I'm the father of her child. We're going to be married."

"Oh, Zack, I'm so sorry! But you know she's going to be OK. You'll get married then, and all this will be behind you."

TWO DAYS LATER, AT DUSK

"I've come to pick up the boy for Dr. Broward. I'm her father."

Joyce stood framed in the front door of her house, light behind her, yellow mist cast around her by the porch light, turning her blue eyes green, her red hair to kinky brass. She stepped back, put a freckled hand to her mouth. "She didn't bring him in this morning," she finally managed to say.

"I realize she didn't. Surely someone did. Who else would care for him?"

"His father."

"I work with his father."

"At Squire?"

"At what?"

"Squire Publishers. That's where he works when he can't work from home. He stayed home today, with Jimmy. He said he'll keep him there till Liz is better."

He pulled himself stiff. "You mean Dr. Broward. Is it possible she allowed you to call her by her first name?"

"We're friends."

"Another sign of her poorly developed judgment. At any rate, due to such poor judgment, *Dr. Broward* is not getting better this time. As her parents, her mother and I are claiming custody of Jimmy. So, I'd appreciate your telling me where this man you claim is his father lives, so I can get him."

Joyce blanched, stumbled back. "Not getting better? What—?"

"Dr. Broward did not regain consciousness this time. In spite of the best care I could get for her. As you can imagine, this pains me very much. To find that my grandson is in a stranger's hands makes it even more painful." His eyes, also green-tinged by the light, glittered like barely melting ice.

"Zack isn't a stranger. He's Jimmy's father."

"That's what Dr. Broward would have had you believe. But she was only shielding his real father, who's married to someone else. Legally, he has no father. Now, sadly, he has no mother, either. So, if you'll tell me where this man lives, I'll go get the child and bring him home."

"Poor Liz! Poor Zack! Oh, my God!" she whispered.

"Shouldn't your sympathies lie with the motherless child? And his bereaved grandparents? She was our only child. He's all that remains of her for us." A tear escaped from his eye and ran along his quirking cheekbone.

"Of course I ache for Jimmy. I love him! I practically raised him. And I know this must hurt you terribly. Liz treasured Wednesday evenings when she and Jimmy had time with you. She used to tell me—"

"Apparently she revealed more to you than might have been wise. But that should convince you of our sincerity in wanting the best for him." Paul knew when to soften his stance. "So, if you would, Mrs. Price, give me this . . . Zack's . . . address and let us get on with providing for our grandson as his mother would want."

"Of course." She gave him the address and he thanked her. As he left she called out, "Mr. Broward."

He turned. "Yes?"

"Will I get to take care of Jimmy sometimes?"

"We prefer having a governess at home. Someone who can teach him the social graces. But Mrs. Broward, for some reason, seems to have a soft spot for you. Maybe, from time to time . . ." He shrugged and went to his black Lincoln Town Car.

"Liz dead?" Zack's voice cracked on the question. He held the phone in his hand and stared at it. It was real. Solid. The voice at the other end—Joyce's—had been less stable, but equally real.

Now it became firm. "Zack, her father's on the way to your house. He's claiming custody of Jimmy. I know about this man. He's evil. Powerful. He's got powerful people in his pocket. He'll stop at nothing. He's going to take him from you. Liz wouldn't want it that way. You'll have to stop him."

"Dead? Oh, Jesus Christ!"

"Zack! Listen to me. You can't let Paul Broward take Jimmy from you. You'll never get him back."

The voice, the meaning, sank in. "I don't know what to do, Joyce."

"I do. Possession is nine-tenths of the law. He's got to get him from you legally. That means he'll have to serve papers on you. Even he will have to take time to do that. In the meantime, if Jimmy's not there when he comes, there'll be nothing he can do tonight."

"Joyce, say Liz isn't dead. Please say it."

Poke, who had come into the family room let out a cry and covered her mouth with her hand. "Oh, Daddy. Who is it? What are they saying?"

"Joyce says Liz is dead."

Joyce continued, "Get Jimmy over here tonight. You and Poke come along with him. Get your thoughts together. Liz is gone. There's nothing we can do about that. But we can keep Paul Broward from taking Jimmy from you."

"He can't have Jimmy. He's my son."

"He said legally Jimmy doesn't have a father. I don't know what he meant by that, but it must be true."

"I'm his father. Just 'cause my name's not on his birth certificate doesn't change it. I can prove it. With a blood test or something. He can't take him away from me."

"Daddy! Is that awful man from the hospital going to take Jimmy?" She began to cry. "Don't let him, Daddy. Don't let him."

His daughter's terror-filled entreaty struck him as Joyce's controlled injunctions had failed to. "We'll be there as soon as we can," he said.

They whisked Jimmy away from his dinner and into the

van and Zack drove through the twists and turns of Route 309 and North Broad Street. Ten minutes into the trip, a black Lincoln Town Car slid past them, going in the opposite direction, unremarkable, unnoticed in the rush hour traffic surges. Its driver, intent on finding his destination in a neighborhood he disdained to set foot in, paid the van no notice as it approached and passed on. He would have been appalled to see his grandson fussing in his car seat in the seven-year-old van driven by a whiskered, long-haired, red-eyed man wearing the same plaid shirt and jeans he had worn the day they'd met in Liz's hospital room. He *was* appalled three hours later, when the man and his daughter had not arrived at the house where he waited. Why were they not home caring for his grandchild at this hour? They were irresponsible, as he'd feared, keeping the child up at all hours while they drifted around whatever haunts such people roamed. Bowling was a favorite sport of such people, he knew. They'd never miss a bowling evening with their beer-drinking cronies for anything. They'd keep their screaming children in a poorly watched nursery room, the children sucking on one another's filthy toys or blankets they rubbed their noses on.

At ten o'clock he decided to wait no longer. He would come back in two or three days with a marshal and the necessary papers. But, before he left, he went to the sides and back of the house and looked through the double-hung windows. His worst fears were realized when he looked into the kitchen: the place was in disarray, with food on the floor and milk spilled on the high chair tray, a plastic gallon of milk, uncovered leftovers and dirty dishes on the cheap table, a towel on the floor by the sink. *This is the way they live—like the vermin they are! This is the way his daughter had chosen to live! What must the bedrooms be like, the bed she slept in with that hideous, unkempt man? God help me,* Paul thought, *but she's better off where she is! If Grace could see this, she'd understand his reasoning, his zeal in this ugly matter.* As sick at heart as he was angry, he left and drove home.

By that time, Joyce and Poke had fed and quieted Jimmy and gotten him to bed in the neat, familiar room off the basement playroom, where he'd often napped and sometimes slept overnight during his mother's illness last December. In the small, bright kitchen decorated with blue-and-red Pennsylvania Dutch motifs on white painted wood cabinets, they sat numbly in a dining booth trying to turn grief and pain into action.

Disbelief shackled Zack's creativity. Liz couldn't be dead. No, no! Just could not be. She wouldn't die in some cold faraway bed, away from him and his love, without saying good-bye. Maryellen had said good-bye, had died in his arms at home. She'd insisted on it when she'd known that death had to be, that it would be painful, but it need not be lonely.

They'd given her strong painkillers and she'd asked Zack to administer them—enough and a little more—and he had, and he'd held her in his arms as she'd whispered her final good-byes to him and Poke, then closed her eyes and grown still and heavy.

He'd seen her later in her casket and, still not wanting to let her go, he'd touched her face and kissed her forehead. Its coldness had rebuffed his touch, his kiss. *Stone cold dead— now he knew what that meant. He wished he had not done that, but had let her last living good-bye suffice. Maybe losing her would not have hurt so much, for so long.*

Liz never uttered a living good-bye when he'd carried her from her apartment to his van, from his van to the emergency room. She would have insisted on saying good-bye to him. *Stone cold dead, rebuffing his kiss, his touch! He couldn't imagine it!* Involuntarily he cried out, "No! We're getting married in a few days. We're going on that trip with Jimmy."

"Daddy!" Poke cried out.

Joyce said, "A trip? Where?"

"To Arizona," said Poke. "To where my great grandmother was born."

"You have reservations?"

Poke shook her head. "They were going in Daddy's—Pop's—van. Making overnight stops at RV campgrounds. This time of year they're not overcrowded, so they don't have to reserve ahead more than a day. We plotted out tentative stops on the road atlas."

Joyce jumped up, went for a second pot of coffee, poured some for each of them. "Is the van set up for the trip?"

"Almost. The main things, anyway."

"Does anybody know your plans?"

"I don't think so. Liz's parents wouldn't know. She didn't even tell them we were getting married." Zack saw what she was getting at.

Joyce nodded. "She didn't even tell me. Just said she was planning a vacation to help get back her energy. She might have told someone at her office the same thing. Enough to let them plan around her, but nothing more."

"Probably. She did that the first time we went to Phoenix. It's the way she is . . . she . . ."

"Then take Jimmy and go, Zack. As soon as you can get things together. It's got to take a couple of days for Paul Broward to get his ducks in a row and serve you with papers. You can get things ready and be gone by then."

"Not without Liz. How can I . . . ?"

"Pop. She's right. You can't let them take Jimmy away." As usual, Poke saw his needs more clearly than he did. This was a womanly talent, full-grown in the girl before its time. She'd learned to deal with her losses and move on, do what was necessary.

He slid out of the booth and stood up and started across the small room to the basement door, feeling the women's eyes on him. He descended into the colorful, now dimly lit playroom, past toys neatly arranged in bins along one wall, past a wooden playpen with Disney characters bedecking its plastic floor pad, to the open door of the room where Jimmy slept, clutching his teddy. The boy's thumb rested half in, half out of his mouth on the flannel crib sheet. His mouth made vague sucking motions. Zack stared at his features. Not one of them reminded him of himself; all of

them reminded him of Liz, the honey hair, the tawny-rose
color of the skin, the wide-set eyes with long curled lashes.
Even the still babyish hands were more like his mother's,
long fingered and delicate, than like his father's, short and
compact, but broad and strong.

*Not without Liz! That couldn't happen. Wherever he
would go with Jimmy, she would forever be. He had made
sure of that over two years ago, when he'd etched her features in light and stored them in his computer.* He touched
his son's face gently with his knuckles, drew them across
his soft, warm cheek and then away. "We'll take Mommy
with us," he whispered. Then he leaned his head down on
the crib rail and cried for the first time since getting Joyce's
phone call.

Upstairs they all cried together, gathering their grief as
they held one another. Then they put it aside for a while
and made plans.

How long would he have to be away? The answer stunned
him, for it could be years, long enough for Paul Broward to
give up on finding him; maybe as long as Paul lived; maybe
as long as Zack lived. No. Surely a blood test would prove
his paternity. A matching of the DNA. But would that be
enough? He could have the tests done, and still Paul could
contest giving him custody on grounds that Zack was an unfit
parent, couldn't give him the kind of life Paul could. Hadn't
really been a parent, in fact. Had Zack lived with Liz? Why
not? Had she recorded his paternity? Why not? Obviously
she hadn't wanted him to be the father. Her apparent neglect
to record had been an expression of will, a documentation
of her wishes: *While I live, he belongs to me alone. When I
die, I bequeath him to my blood relatives only.* Zack wasn't
named as beneficiary on her life insurance policies, either.
Jimmy was the primary beneficiary, with the death benefits,
along with all her other property to go into a trust for him, a
trust to be handled by her father's law firm, who had drawn
up the documents.

It would be quite clear to anyone who examined the
papers what her wishes were: She wanted Zack to have

questions, making threats. You aren't going to be able to run and hide, like I can."

"Yes, I am, Pop," she said. "I'm part Apache, like you. Blood counts for something, you know."

CHAPTER
▪▪ SEVEN

THE FOLLOWING WEEK

Coming home to the empty house after school terrified Poke. There was always a strange car parked by the curb as, books hugged to her chest, key at the ready, she ran up the porch stairs and pulled the storm door open. By the time she'd unbolted the front door, she could hear unfamiliar footfalls scraping on the stairs behind her. The first person to follow her had been a man, tall, lanky, and dark blond, who'd tried to make her think that the gray streaks of age in his hair meant he was kind. After that they'd sent a motherly woman. That didn't fool her, either. She'd known two real mothers. A couple of men had brought a warrant and searched the house for her father and Jimmy the day after Pop left with Jimmy. After that, no one came in, as she wouldn't let them; but they tried to question her out on the porch. She knew she didn't have to answer them, and she didn't. Her father wasn't a kidnapper like the newspaper article claimed; he had a right to go somewhere with his own son and not tell where it was, not tell her or his bosses at Squire or anyone.

All Poke told anyone was that he was overcome with grief and had gone away to get over it. She didn't even know where he was going. Yes, he'd gone in his van; hadn't three neighbors told detectives they'd seen him drive off? He hadn't tried to hide it. He'd gone in broad daylight. He wasn't *running* away, just *getting* away. He wasn't *hiding*. Just wanted privacy. Look, his license plate was registered. They could trace it. How could she stop them? But, she said over and over again, she didn't know where they should look. Please! Just leave her alone!

After a few days they did. They just parked there until after she was home for a while, and then drove away. It was spooky. There was no way she could keep in touch with her father. They'd probably put a bug on the phone line. They'd probably put a trace on the mail. She knew they even looked through the garbage for clues. They could check on his bank accounts, knew he'd already withdrawn $10,000, said that was suspicious, asked her how she was going to get along without money. If they were so smart, didn't they know she had her own checking account? And a joint money market account, too, with her father, with money in it for school?

Yes, they said, that was suspicious, too. She could live for a long long time without her father sending her money. It looked planned.

"Please! Just leave me alone! Pop taught me to care for myself in case anything happened to him. Like it did to Momma! Like it almost did when he got double pneumonia a few years ago, and Liz saved his life! Like it did to Liz! Can't you understand? Please, leave me alone."

They finally did. At least they stopped trying to make her answer questions. They just parked outside by the curb so she'd know they were going to keep looking for her father, so she might as well make it easier on everyone and talk. Well, she wouldn't. She couldn't tell anyone what she knew and how she felt, not even her best friend Christy, who was scared to be her best friend anymore because so many people believed Pop really was a kidnapper like Mr. Broward said. At best they thought he was a gold digger or fornicator who had no right to a child he had taken no part in raising. *They didn't know! They just didn't know!*

They didn't know what being kidnapped was like. Kidnapping wasn't what happened to Jimmy. It was what had happened to Poke a few years ago when a crazy man took her from her own house and kept her prisoner and would have killed her if Liz and Pop hadn't saved her. Liz knew what kidnapping was, and she'd have wanted Pop to keep Jimmy. If Liz had wanted her father to have him, she'd have said so. And she'd told Poke that Pop was going to adopt him and they were all going to live together as a family after they got back from their trip. Poke couldn't even tell them that now, or they might figure out where Pop was going. Poke couldn't say anything to anybody about that, about the way she felt—scared, beleaguered, alone— because they didn't know all those things. They couldn't; the things hadn't happened to them.

As she came home today, she saw another strange vehicle parked out front—a gray Chevy van this time with two people sitting inside it behind a sun-glazed windshield. She ran past it and up the driveway to the flagstone walk curving up the slight terrace to the porch. She heard the clunk of the vehicle door closing as she hurried up the stairs. The creaking of the cold aluminum storm door, the clink of its closing mechanism, the clack of the inner door deadbolt, the slam of the door itself, cloaked any noises the van driver made in following her. She leaned against the door as she locked it, then stood gasping, leaning against it. She didn't have to open it for anyone. She wouldn't. No matter what they said.

For a few minutes, she heard no sounds of anyone coming up onto the porch. She drew a deep breath, then dumped her books onto the foyer table and took off her red scarf and the navy blue peacoat that Liz had given her for Christmas and hung them on the entry coat rack. As she did so, a new sound approached the porch, like somebody pulling a wagon bumpily over the driveway and front walk flagstones.

Running into the family room, she pulled aside the corner of a window drape and peeked out over the porch. A soft thud at the foot of the porch stairs drew her eyes to that spot. She gasped at the sight of a monstrous woman wearing a navy blue cape and nurse's cap, parking a wheelchair just short of the bottom step. Before lumbering up the stairs, the woman leaned over and kissed the chair's occupant, who was dressed in a long quilted storm jacket with its hood drawn tightly around the face and no sign of hands protruding from sleeves or legs hanging down on the leg rests. On the person's lap sat a large basket covered with yellow cellophane.

At first, Poke could not take her eyes off the person in the chair, until the woman's unexpectedly gentle knock tattooed on the door several times. Poke dropped the corner of the drapery, and, drawn by intense curiosity, quickly went back to the door. "Who is it?"

"Miss James?"

"Yes, it's me. What do you want?"

"My father wants to give you something," said the woman, voice tinkling.

"You can't come in. Just leave it on the porch."

"Oh, please, Miss James. He wants to give it to you himself. He loved her so, and he's been so sad. Please just open the door so you can see."

Did this woman mean that the person in the wheelchair was her father? Was the basket in his lap for Poke?

"Who did your father love? What's he so sad about? I don't even know him."

"How do you know if you know him if you don't open the door and see?"

"Because I . . ."

The woman giggled. "I saw you peeking at us. You're just like all the others. Ashamed to look at people like him."

Chagrined, Poke said, "I'm not. I just don't know why he'd bring me a present."

"It's a condolence present. Because of Dr. Broward. She was his doctor, and he loved her, and we know she loved your father and you, so we wanted you to have the present, 'cause there's no one else to give it to."

Swallowing, Poke opened the door a crack and looked out. The woman's round pasty face split in a gaping grin.

"Why, aren't you a pretty girl!" the woman said in her improbable light, girlish voice. "No wonder she liked you so much. You're just like she described you, with those long black braids, and the bright, pretty face." The grin collapsed and the eyes splashed out tears.

Poke's mouth rounded as she pushed the door wider. "She told you about me? She never told me about you. I . . . I don't think."

"Oh," said the woman, "that's because she was Daddy's doctor, and it was a medical thing and private. And because she was ashamed."

"Ashamed?"

"Look," said the woman, "it's cold out here. Especially for Daddy, 'cause he can't move around down there. How about holding the storm door for us, and I'll bring him up and set him inside. Then Daddy can give you your present, and I'll tell you what made Dr. Broward ashamed."

Poke hesitated. She knew that Paul Broward had hired special agents of all kinds, as Joyce had warned. Could these people be an attempt to get by her? Her glance alternated between the bizarre-looking woman and her grotesque father, who had a vacant grin on his cocooned face.

"He can't see you. The poison in his blood made him almost blind."

The woman's suddenly reedy tone and words made Poke shudder. She pushed the wooden door wide behind her and tentatively opened the storm door a crack.

"Then her father said it was all Daddy's fault, so we didn't get enough money." Her face grew angry. "So she had a poison in her blood, too. She got it from him." Her eyes grew beady and mean. Then suddenly she changed her demeanor. "But I'll go get Daddy and bring him up." And she turned with a sweep of her nurse's cape, clumped down the stairs, slipped one huge arm beneath the basket handle, and clasped both arms about her father, the basket against his back. She lifted the man with a hardly grunting "Upsy-daisy," and clumped up the stairs with only somewhat more laboring treads.

Poke, unnerved and astonished, pushed the storm door wide and held it as the weird pair went through. To the woman's question, "Where should I sit him?" she pointed vaguely toward the family room.

The woman reconnoitered the room, and chose the sofa to set the man down on. Then, after disengaging the basket, she rolled him onto his back and removed his jacket and hood and slipped them from around him as she would undress a snowsuited baby. She kissed him loudly on his cold-reddened face and then set him up in the corner of the sofa and set pillows around him for support. She stood back then, and clapped her hands. Grinning broadly, she looked at Poke, saying, "Isn't he such a dear! Doesn't that gray suit and bow tie set him off beautifully?"

Stunned by this strange display, Poke stood by with her mouth partly open and stared at the man. With his spit-combed hair, bow tie, and suspenders, he looked more like a roly-poly balloon toy sans cardboard feet than a man. After a few seconds she nodded her head.

"You left the front door open," the woman reminded her.

"Yeah," said Poke, and went to close it, glancing over her shoulder as she proceeded, though reason told her this woman and her father couldn't very well threaten her well-being or hurt her house.

When she returned to the family room, the woman had taken off her wool cape and plopped her white-tented body in Pop's brown recliner chair. She had lifted her white-stockinged legs and set white-oxford–shod feet on the foot-rest. The basket sat next to the man on the sofa. One flipper of an arm rested on it.

"Here she is, Daddy. It's time to give it to her."

The yellow cellophane crackled as he rubbed his flipper over it and grunted and turned his face toward Poke.

The woman urged Poke, "Go ahead. He wants you to have it."

"How . . . how does he know me? He can't see me."

"He heard you come back in the room. And he knows all about you. Dr. Broward told us all about you. She described

you to us. I'd have recognized you anywhere. I'd recognize
your father, too. He's five foot nine, has long black hair,
sometimes tied back in a ponytail, and weighs about 180
pounds."

"Why, yes. That's right."

"And ruddy."

"That's right. She told you all that?"

"Oh, how she loved him! And that dear little baby!"
Both the woman and the truncated man fell to weeping,
the woman sobbing and sniffing, the man moaning and
whining.

Poke cried too, thinking of Pop and Jimmy crammed into
that van as they traversed sometimes snowy rural roads. She
thought of Liz, lying dead somewhere. Shuddering, she
pulled a tissue from her pocket, blew her nose gently and
watched her freakish guests, her alarm mixed with wonder.
Could Liz really have told these people so much about her
and her father and half-brother, yet never mentioned these
monstrosities to her and Pop?

"Oh, get us some Kleenex, too. Poor Daddy! His nose
is running."

Poke ran to the computer desk and got a box of tissues.
The woman came up quickly behind her and snatched a few
tissues from the box. She blew her own nose on one, then
ran and gently wiped her father's tears with the others. "It's
all right, Daddy. It's good to cry. Poor Dr. Broward. Her
father's poison was in her blood."

Stiffening, Poke said, "What do you mean by that? Liz
was nothing like her father!"

The woman turned and smiled sadly at her. "Of course
not. She was a wonderful doctor. That's why it's all so
sad."

"Then why did you say that?"

"Because she was so ashamed about what he did to my
father. She tried to make up for it, of course. But nothing
she did would help."

"But why was she ashamed? What did her father do to
yours?"

The woman wiped her father's nose a second time, then crossed the room and tossed the tissues in the wastebasket next to the desk. Shaking her head, she returned to the recliner and raised the foot again. She sighed. "It's a long story."

"Well, *tell me!*" This all seemed so weird. This woman was acting as if she owned this house. Treating Poke like a servant, leaving her no place to sit except the swivel chair in front of the computer, making her feel somehow guilty about the half-man in the corner of the sofa. Poke didn't know quite how to handle it. She made fists at her sides in frustration. Then, realizing the woman was about to begin a narrative, she got the swivel chair and sat down catercorner to both of them. "Please, tell me."

"Oh, I'm going to," said the woman. And she began.

By the time she finished the story of how Paul Broward had turned a jury against the old crippled man and condemned him and his daughter to spend their lives struggling to make ends meet, Poke was in tears. *She understood! Yes, she understood.*

And she felt so close to this suffering pair, because her father, too, had been hurt by Liz's horrible father. Now she and her father were separated, for who knew how long. Her dear little half-brother Jimmy was somewhere between here and Arizona, having to live cooped up most of the day in the van, eat there, have his diapers changed there, get his bath in the tiny square shower stall, if they were able to hook up to utilities at an RV park. And Pop had to worry all the time that someone might be following him, though he didn't even know that he'd been charged with kidnapping. He did know that Paul Broward was capable of anything, would stop at nothing to get his grandson away from Pop.

In fact, he didn't know just how far the lawyer would go to get what he wanted, as Poke now did. How horrible he would feel if he knew what Liz's father had done to these poor people. How awful Liz must have felt! How sick with guilt it must have made her! Now Poke knew what this woman meant when she said that Liz had her

father's poison in her blood. Well, Liz couldn't help these
people anymore. But now they wanted to share their grief
over losing her. It touched Poke deeply. Warmth and pity
surged through her.

"Oh, I'm so sorry," she said.

The woman let the footrest down and leaned forward.
"Yes, I knew you would be. She told me what you were
like."

Poke looked into the woman's damp eyes. "But she never
told us anything about you. I . . . I don't even know your
name."

"Oh, dear!" She giggled. "I didn't tell you, did I? It's
Hester. Hester Jones. And Daddy's name is Lester."

"Hester and Lester," said Poke. "That's easy to remember."

Hester giggled again. Then she stood up. "Oh, my, Daddy, we didn't even give her the present, did we?"

Embarrassed, Poke jumped up from the swivel chair.
"It's my fault. I wasn't polite enough to take it." She
crossed to Lester and smiled at him. "Thank you so much,
Lester. It was nice of you to think of me with this." Gingerly, she touched the man's flipper, which still rested on
the yellow cellophane.

He smiled and made a soft sound, and lifted the stump
against her hand. She took it and shook it, feeling good that
she'd overcome her aversion to the man. She realized for
the first time that he had a kind, handsome face, and that
underneath all the agony he presented to the world at first
glance, he had a heart capable of pleasure. She released the
stump gently, and patted it before taking the basket from
beside him. She saw it was filled with fruit.

Uncovering the fruit and smelling its rich, full aroma, she
looked up at Hester. "It's a lovely basket. And you were so
nice to bring it. Do you want some?"

"Oh, no, Jill dear. We really can't stay. Daddy has to get
home for supper."

Poke knit her brow. "Everyone calls me Poke. Didn't Liz
tell you?"

Hester frowned. "She told me both your names. But I didn't think I should call you by your nickname the first time I saw you. I'm a nurse, you know, and have been taught to be very respectful about people's names. You notice I never referred to Dr. Broward as Liz, as you do. Nurses never call doctors by their first name."

"Oh," said Poke. She knew that the nurses at the hospital called Liz Liz; but then, they knew her personally, not just as a doctor. "Well, I wish you could stay here for supper. I'll never be able to finish all that fruit." She picked up a large brown-skinned pear. "Here," she said, pushing it into Hester's hand. "Please at least take it."

Hester looked surprised, then pleased. "That's awfully nice." She took the pear and slipped it into her uniform pocket. "Isn't it nice, Daddy? Isn't Poke just as nice as Dr. Broward said?"

Lester made some agreeable noises, then began to writhe a bit.

"He's getting uncomfortable, Poke. I have to get him dressed and take him home. But thanks for your hospitality. Can we have a rain check on supper? Daddy doesn't have the chance to eat out very often."

"Oh, yes," said Poke, daunted by the thought that when her first company in a week would leave she'd be alone again. For the first time since Pop and Jimmy had driven off, Poke had talked to someone who wasn't accusing her of obstructing justice. "I'd feel good if I could give you something back for the fruit."

Hester crushed her in an unexpected hug. "Why, isn't that the nicest thing I've ever heard of! Daddy would love to come, wouldn't you, Daddy?"

Lester grunted and writhed. Poke said, "Oh, but you have to dress him. Let me help." She retrieved the storm jacket and helped Hester put her father into it. It reminded her of helping Liz dress a squirming Jimmy for a romp in the snow. Lester didn't squirm, but he was heavy and unwieldy and couldn't do much to help. This helplessness stirred Poke's maternal instincts, and when he was dressed, she laughed, and patted him on the head and cheeks.

"You see what a dear thing he is," said his daughter.

When they left, Poke's terror and loneliness came back. How she wished there were someone to talk to!

Her wish came true the next day after school, when she came home and found the van once more parked outside in her driveway. This time she helped Hester lower the wheelchair to the pavement, and, after Hester had put Lester in it, Poke pushed him to the foot of the porch stairs, allowing Hester to carry her books. Once inside the again warm and welcoming house, Poke set about making the first hot dinner in nearly two weeks, as Hester explained how to make a meal suitable for her father's restricted diet. Their conversation this afternoon was filled with laughter as a new kind of friendship was born between the young woman and her guests.

Sadness entered the room after dinner, as both women spoke of Liz, of their love for her. Poke recalled her first realization that Liz was more than just a doctor when Poke's mother got leukemia and died, and Liz helped Pop and her deal with their grief. She recalled how she'd always believed that her mother's ghost was somehow at work in sending her to cure Pop of his double pneumonia, and how she eventually came to see that her mother, who'd been Liz's friend for years, had sent her to fill in Pop's loneliness and be a friend and sort of a mother to Poke.

"What a lovely thought!" Hester said, as she sat on the sofa next to her father and idly stroked his head.

"You don't think it's dumb to believe in ghosts?" Poke said.

"Of course not."

"Christy doesn't, either. She's—she was my best friend."

"Isn't she anymore?"

Poke shook her head and bit her lip. "She tries to be. But she won't walk home from school with me anymore. Her mother's afraid the FBI and those other agents will bother them. She doesn't believe about Pop being a kidnapper, though. It's just that, well, everyone knows the Browards are important, and if Mr. Broward says he is, then they all better stay out of it."

"You see!" said Hester, her voice shrill as a scream. "You see how evil he is!"

"Oh, Hester," said Poke. The woman's face contorted, frightening her.

"He's cut off your father's legs, too, Poke. He's poisoned your father's blood."

"No! What are you saying!"

Hester rose from the sofa and walked to Poke, who rose from the recliner as the woman approached with an agonized look on her face. "He's crippled your father the way he crippled mine, Poke. Soon, he'll cut his arms off, too. Don't you see? He's turned the whole world against him and you so he can't run away, so he can't reach out and touch you anymore." With that Hester took Poke in her arms and hugged her. "We're like sisters, aren't we, Poke?"

Stiffly, Poke said, "I . . . I guess maybe. Sort of."

Hester released her. "Oh, I guess I'm coming on strongly, aren't I? I'm so moved by what's happening to you. Forgive me. Daddy and I have suffered so much at Paul Broward's hands that I look for comfort wherever I can get it. And you've been so kind to us . . ." She turned toward her father. "You understand, don't you, Daddy?"

"I didn't mean to . . ." said Poke, feeling guilty that her stiffness might have come across as revulsion.

"No, don't feel bad, dear. We understand. You've been through so much. But, we've overstayed our welcome tonight." She went to the sofa and started to dress her father.

Poke felt that maybe she should help again, but the tension Hester had stirred in her held her back. Yet after they left, she regretted her feelings. They hadn't made freaks of themselves, and she'd no right to reject them. To do so was terribly unkind, especially since Hester was right; Paul Broward had in a sense cut off Pop's legs and arms, keeping him from ever running freely again with his son, keeping him from reaching out and touching his daughter without risking the loss of his son.

And that night she dreamed that Hester had come back again with her father, and set him on the sofa and unwrapped him, and Poke saw Pop propped up with pillows on the sofa, a flipper resting on a basket. And when she removed the yellow cellophane from the basket, she saw it contained what looked like a large yellow melon, and Pop touched the melon with his flipper and the melon was Jimmy and it fell out of the basket and rolled across the floor to the foyer and out the door and bounced down the stairs, bounce, bounce, bounce, and rolled out into the street and a car ran over it, smashing it. And she woke up screaming, in a sweat, alone in the night-chilled house.

She spent the next day, a cold sleeting Saturday beneath a slate sky, alone behind frosted windows. Two telephone calls came in, one from a charity, the other from Joyce Price, calling from a pay phone and saying she was Louise, a friend of Pop's from Winchester, Virginia, just passing through town and wanting to visit.

"He's not here." Her heart pounded furiously. Winchester, Virginia, wasn't just next door, but it was only a day away. Even going slow, it wouldn't have taken Pop over a week to get there. Yet this is what Joyce's message meant; she had heard from Pop, and he was in Winchester, Virginia.

"Out of town?" Joyce asked.

"Just not here. I'll tell him you called. He'll be glad to know you keep in touch."

"Oh, we always keep in touch. Either by mail or phone."

Either by mail or phone. Of course. He'd written her rather than called her when he was there. By now he'd be halfway across the country. "Is the weather bad where you live?"

Joyce laughed. "Well, you know those rural roads. The plows take their time in getting there. You'll tell your father I called, then?"

"Oh, yes. Have a good trip." Poke sighed as she looked at the phone in her hand, and, for the first time since Pop left, grinned briefly. "I told you our Apache blood would help, Pop," she said. "Keep sending me those smoke signals."

They'd worked out this way of communicating through Joyce so that no one could trace the messages. Pop wrote or called Joyce to let her know where he was, then Joyce called Poke from the pay phone and passed on as much as she could without giving clues to his whereabouts or her own identity.

"He's turned the whole world against him and you so he can't run away, so he can't reach out and touch you anymore."

Not quite, thought Poke. Thanks to Joyce, they'd worked out a way to touch.

But after Joyce had hung up and Poke stayed on the line to hold on to the feeling of touching, the dial tone with its terrible grating wrenched them apart again. She had no one to talk to openly and honestly. No one. And she was afraid that Hester and Lester would never come back again. They were the only friends she had left, and she'd chased them away.

So the next day when the door chimes sounded, she ran to the door and flung it open.

"Collecting for the *Inquirer*."

"Oh." She invited the young delivery girl in to wait while she got the money for the paper.

The girl stepped into the foyer, and stood there, eyes downcast into her bright red plaid muffler while Poke got the exact change from the money box they kept in the kitchen. When she returned, she tried to engage the girl in conversation to keep her there as long as possible. "It's nicer out today," she offered.

"Mhm," into the windings of scarf beneath her chin.

"I forgot you usually come on Sundays."

"Yah." She stomped black-booted feet impatiently against the foyer tile.

"Well, I hope you have a nice day."

The girl nodded. She jammed the money in her leather pouch and went out.

"Well, bye," said Poke. "See you next month, OK?"

The girl suddenly turned flashing eyes toward her and spat out, "Why don't you tell them where your father is? He's a kidnapper! I read it in the paper."

"No! The paper's lying. It's a lying paper! I don't want to read it at all anymore. It's a bunch of lies is all it is. Cancel it. Who needs to read that crock, anyway?"

The girl laughed. "Good! Then I won't have to come here anymore. My mom told me not to. If he's a kidnapper, he might kidnap me, too. And make my parents pay randsim to get me back. All he wants is the money." She stuck out her tongue at Poke and stomped away.

Poke let the storm door slam and then slammed the inside door, too. Fury rose in her chest, choking her, making her cough. She felt she could grab the snotty little papergirl's scarf and tighten it around her neck and strangle her as she felt strangled by her. Poke hated her, hated the newspaper, hated her neighbors who would no longer talk to her, who turned their eyes away when she passed them, yet sneaked peeks around the edges of their drapes each afternoon when she came home from school. She could feel her face grow hot and her hands grow cold and her knees begin to tremble. She hadn't felt such anger and despair since Momma died four years ago.

For the first time since Pop had driven away nearly two weeks ago, she allowed her jaw to tremble, allowed her knees to give way, allowed herself to crumple and cry. Then weakness overcame her and she dragged herself to the sofa where she soon fell asleep.

She pulled her face free of the damp pillow when she became aware of a tapping on the family room window. "Unhh," she grunted, as she shook the torpor from her limbs and slowly sat up.

The tapping repeated, louder, more insistent.

Aching head against her palm, she rose and went to the window, pulled aside the drapes. The intense early afternoon light hurt her eyes. She'd slept about four hours, she reckoned.

The fat fist rapped the glass before her face, jarring her fully awake. She nodded at Hester, dropped the drape, then, rubbing her eyes, went to the door and opened it. Hester stood at the door, her father hugged against her chest.

"I'm sorry we couldn't come yesterday, dear. It was nasty and cold, and the streets were so icy." She pressed past Poke into the family room where she took over the sofa for her father. While fluffing up a pillow support for him, she stopped suddenly and looked at Poke. "Oh, you've been crying."

Poke nodded and sniffed and smoothed her purple sweater and jeans.

"I should have seen by your face. It's all red and creased."

"That's OK. I'm glad you came. I thought it was you this morning."

"Did someone come and say something? On a Sunday? They just don't think!"

"It was just a dumb papergirl. She was awful." She ran and threw her arms around Hester. "I'm so glad you're here. Oh, Hester, why does everybody believe Mr. Broward?"

The woman put her arms around Poke and said, "Tsk, tsk," and held her and rocked her like a baby. Then she kissed her and returned to settling her father. "It's awful. No one will believe you. And there's nothing you can do to prove it. You can't tell them where your father is, which would prove he wasn't a kidnapper, because they'd take the baby away from him. Poor little baby. His grandfather's poisoned his blood."

"No! He won't be anything like his grandfather! Any more than Liz was. How can his blood be poisoned?"

Hester, huge face pinched up in the center, said, "It's just an expression I use. I guess it sounds awful to you. I won't use it anymore."

"It scares me. I don't want to be scared about you, too, Hester. You're the only friend I have. The only one I can talk to."

"You can talk to Daddy, too. But, I promise, I won't say it anymore." She returned to firming her father in his seat. When he was settled, she turned to Poke again and said, "I hope we can stay for Sunday dinner. I was looking forward to it."

"Oh, yes," said Poke. "Oh, yes!"

Once again, her friends' presence comforted Poke. They stayed after dinner and talked until after dark. When Lester became fidgety, Hester suggested they take him into the living room where he could listen to the stereo. His tastes in music seemed to run in line with Momma's, whose collection lined the cabinet shelf. Poke had her own collection, mostly hard rock, in her room. Pop called it noise and made her listen to it on the headphones while he was at home. Since he'd been away, she still listened through headphones. She felt less alone inside a music cocoon.

While Lester enjoyed the music and keened along with it, Hester and Poke talked on in the family room late into the evening. Suddenly Hester looked up. "Oh, dear. Daddy's stopped singing. I bet he's asleep."

He was, cuddled in the overstuffed chair near the stereo, his head lolling against the thick maroon mohair arm.

Hester crossed the room to him. "What a dear thing Daddy is, Poke. Oh, my, I hate to wake him to go home." She turned to Poke with a plea in her eyes.

"Oh no, you don't have to. You can stay overnight with him." She surveyed Hester's oversize form. "I, ah, don't have any PJ's to lend you, though."

Hester said, "That's all right. I'm a nurse. I'll just make do. But I'd like to give Daddy a bed to lie down in. He'll be in such a bad mood when he wakes up if he has to sleep sitting all night." She turned and gently stroked his messy brown hair. "He's an awful lot like a baby, that way. Change what he's used to, and he fusses and whines."

"Oh, Hester," said Poke, "I have an idea." She crossed the living room to the guest room door, and reached in and switched on the light. "Come here."

Hester followed her into the small guest room, with its narrow bed on one wall and Jimmy's crib on the other. Pop had moved the crib downstairs in the last two weeks before the planned vacation, when Liz and Jimmy stayed just for the weekends. The boy finally had accepted the idea of having a separate room here at Daddy's house, like he did at Mommy's. His parents had yearned for just a little privacy before setting off on vacation in the van, where only a thin curtain would separate his parents' bed from his.

"You can put your father in the crib, and you can sleep in the bed," Poke said to Hester.

"Oh, Poke, I love that idea!" Hester walked to the crib and gave it a couple of hard shakes. She lowered the side all the way and rested her hip tentatively on the mattress. It creaked, as the casters on her side dug into the berber rug, but seemed to hold, so she let out a cry of delight. "It's a good sturdy crib, all right. The kind Dr. Broward would buy."

Pop had bought it. Poke had gone with him to choose it, and he'd tested the store model just as Hester had tested this one.

Hester now went to the bed and sat on it, and bounced it a little. "Good," she said, with a nod.

"It's already made."

"It's perfect for us. Daddy and I share a room at home. So when he wakes up in the morning, he'll see me there and be fine. Oh," she said, "I do have to go out to the van and bring in his ostomy care kit."

Poke knit her brow.

"Daddy has a colostomy and an indwelling catheter. The poison did it to him."

Having heard the terms before from Momma, who'd been a public health nurse, Poke knew what they meant. The thought of what had happened to Lester horrified her all over again. So, as Hester fetched the kit from her van, she stood trembling in the front doorway, hugging herself.

Hester returned with a stainless-steel bedpan and a covered tray. She carried them into the bedroom and set them down on top of the small mahogany dresser. "They'll be right here in the morning. All I'll need from you is some water."

"I can get it now," said Poke, starting to the kitchen for a pitcherful.

"Not tonight, dear. It'll get too cold. It's got to be about body temperature. Don't worry, I'll get it first thing, and have everything done before you even wake up, I bet."

Relieved Hester wouldn't be asking her to help or witness the procedure, Poke sighed. Always squeamish about things like that, she could never have been a doctor or a nurse. How different she was from Momma! And yet, she, not Momma, had been the one to clean and dress the turkeys Pop brought home from hunts. The insides of freshly killed turkeys didn't elicit in Poke the same dread the insides of living people did.

"What's this, Poke?" said Hester, as she turned from the dresser. She held out a worn, leather-bound book.

Poke jumped forward and grabbed it from her hand. "Great-Great Gramps's book! I forgot it was here. Liz was going to read it."

Following the snatched volume with a long-necked look, Hester said, "It's old. It must be very precious. What kind of book is it?"

"The *Iliad*. That was Great-Great Gramps's name. He wrote in it." Realizing she must seem impolite to have grabbed the book from Hester, she extended her arm so the woman got a better look. She opened the book and displayed the notes at the back.

Hester craned her neck and focused on the scrawled handwriting. "It's awfully hard to read."

"Yeah, and it's in code, too. Pop used his computer to decode it. But it's still a mystery." She explained how an accident had killed the old man (who wasn't old then, though Poke had a hard time thinking of a man who was born more than a hundred years ago as young), and how her great-grandmother, an Apache, had received the book from her widowed mother's sister, who raised her because her mother had disappeared, too.

"What a sad and beautiful story," said Hester.

"Nobody knows what happened to Great-Great Gramps. Or even what his real name is. But I'm going to find out." She explained her plans for college in Arizona, how she would search out her roots. "They're digging in Roosevelt Lake, and the secret's underneath there. In a town called Roosevelt, where Great-Great Gramps worked. When Roosevelt Dam was built, they flooded the town. On the very day Great Grandma was born."

"And you're going to try to find out who your great-great grandfather was! You've got very strong family feelings, don't you?"

"Doesn't everybody? Don't you want to know where you came from?"

Hester's face and eyes grew round. "I hadn't thought a lot about it. My grandparents died before I was born, and my parents didn't talk about their childhood. Their present life was always such a struggle. And now . . ."

"That's sad, for the present to be so hard to get through that you don't have time to think about the past. Pop always thought about the past and tried to find out more about it. He's a genealogist."

Hester pricked an ear toward the living room. "That's interesting, Poke. I'd like to hear more. But I've got to get my daddy into bed, so he won't wake up grumpy."

After she'd gotten her father to bed, she asked Poke where she could go to ready herself. Poke supplied her with a new toothbrush and directed her to the upstairs main bathroom for her shower. Then, stanching her curiosity about what Hester looked like in her underclothes, she closed herself in her room until the bathroom was empty and she could take care of her own bedtime needs.

The presence of others in the house comforted her, and her earlier depression melted away. As she drifted off to sleep, knowing that Pop and Jimmy were probably well on their way to their Tonto Basin destination, she allowed herself to dwell on the mystery there and how she would uncover it one day.

In the morning Hester was up before Poke, as she had promised, and had cared for her father's ostomy and fed and medicated him by the time Poke came down for breakfast. Early herself, as she hoped to talk with Hester during a meal that had become dreadfully lonely, she discussed her school program and studies with the woman. In the background, Lester made singsong noises and grunts, so he seemed almost part of the conversation.

"He likes it here," said Hester. "He wasn't even a little grumpy this morning."

"Oh, Hester, would it be too hard for you to come back again this afternoon? I like it, too, with you and him here."

The woman crunched up her face. "Well, I'll try. But I'm never sure. It's really a very long ride."

"Where do you live?"

"Oh, way down near Rittenhouse Square. On nice days, I go for walks with Daddy, and he has some friends there. Don't give up the old friends for new," she said.

That made Poke feel that she was asking too much, too early in a friendship. "Oh. Well, I understand that. I know how I feel about Christy."

"Oh, Poke, I know she'll come back. And then you'll want us to stop coming to see you at all. We're your weird friends in need, aren't we? Not people you're proud to have here."

The truth of that stung Poke, but she denied it. As the two got ready to go to their van, she hugged each of them and said she would miss them if they didn't show up later that day.

She did miss them when they didn't come Monday or Tuesday. The feeling grew worse on Wednesday afternoon with another call from Joyce.

"Hi, Poke. This is your Aunt Diane in Squirrel Springs, West Virginia."

West Virginia! Is that all the farther they've gotten?

"I'm taking off from work at the hospital in the children's wing."

Something was wrong with Jimmy! It couldn't be anything else. Poke tried to be calm. "Why?" she said.

It was the right question. Joyce answered, "Well, the worst is over there for a while, so I thought I'd take off when I could. Besides, I wanted to let you folks know that Uncle Jim's getting over his pneumonia, and should be up and running in just a few days. I knew your dad was worried about him. Can I talk to him?"

"Oh, he's out of town, Aunt Diane. I don't know when he'll be back. But I'm glad you called. You're sure J— Uncle Jim is going to be OK?"

"Of course. He's young, and he's a lot like your dad. Nothing'll keep him down for long. But under the circumstances, the doctors are keeping an eye on him for another couple of days. So, please, dear, don't worry."

She said she wouldn't; but after hanging up, she sank further into fear again. Jimmy would be so upset, in a strange bed again, surrounded by uniformed strangers giving him shots and maybe worse. And Pop must be torn to little pieces. He'd be scared of losing Jimmy the way he'd lost Liz and Momma. Why was so much bad stuff happening?

Hester's knock came moments after Joyce's phone call. Poke greeted her and her father with tears.

"I didn't mean to stay away so long," said Hester, mistaking the reason for Poke's emotional outburst. "I'd almost forgotten how much work there was to do at home. Why, Daddy and I barely had time to go out at all and—"

"Jimmy's sick!" Poke blurted. "In a hospital in West Virginia."

Hester's eyes widened. "Your little brother? Oh, dear. Now your father will have to come home."

"No. He's almost better, and Joyce said they'll be on their way in a few days."

"Hmmm," said Hester as she undid her father's storm coat and set him in what had become his favorite spot on the sofa. That done, she turned and asked Poke, "Who's Joyce?

I thought no one but you knew where your father was. You said you couldn't talk to anyone at all about him."

Poke explained the relationship with Joyce, and how they communicated.

"She must be a very nice woman. And smart."

"Oh, yes. She was the one that convinced Pop to go on the trip to Arizona, even though Liz—couldn't go with them. It was supposed to be their honeymoon."

"Their honeymoon? Oh, how sad she can't be with them! Oh, Daddy"—she glanced at her father—"what an awful thing that man did. How terribly wicked he is!"

Wicked! Yes, that was what Liz's father was—wicked! Poke gasped at the thought, and turned away from her friends, covering her mouth with her hands. Hester came up behind her and grasped her shoulders. She jumped.

"Poor Poke. You must be terribly upset. I wish we could help. But what can we do? We're victims, just like you are."

Touching the hand on her right shoulder, Poke nodded and said in a choked voice, "I don't know what I'd've done without you. What you said the other day about going back to Christy when this was all over, and not being your friend anymore, well, then I thought you were right, but now I know you're not. You and Joyce are my only really true friends."

Hester turned Poke around so they faced each other, and drew her into her arms, held and rocked her. "We'll always be friends, whatever happens. You can turn to us when you need to. And we'll turn to you, dear Poke. I feel as though I've found the sister I never had."

Poke gained strength from the long embrace. When it ended, she drew a deep breath. She crossed the family room and opened the draperies to welcome the late slanting sun. With the days growing longer, the sun would help warm the room, its dwindling rays briefly interlocking with the first tendrils of warmth that rose from the kitchen range, as she cooked for herself and her strange adopted family. Pop might be far away, almost out of touch, Jimmy might be sick, confused by his surroundings, but Poke was no longer entirely alone, afraid, ostracized.

She looked at her new friends and knew that ostracism shared was ostracism defeated. "What would you like for dessert?" she asked.

After the meal, the women talked again while Lester crooned along with the stereo in the living room. How free Poke felt when the conversation turned to her father and brother. She spelled out the story of how she and Liz had planned the honeymoon trip. "It looks like Pop started out following that route," she said as she pointed out RV stops and campgrounds between Maryland and West Virginia. "He's been held up by Jimmy getting sick, but I'm sure he'll continue along it. So I'll almost always be sure of where he is along the way, figuring from three days from now."

"You can be there in your mind. That's lovely."

"We don't know how long he'll have to be away. But at least he won't have to keep running. Once he stops up in the Tonto Basin, he'll settle with the archaeology team, and work as a volunteer. They'll be there for a few years. Then next September, whatever happens, I'll be with him—at least near him, when I start at ASU. And, sooner or later, they'll have to stop looking for him. He can change his name and start over again."

"You've thought it all out. Very clever."

"And I'll never tell anyone, Hester. No one will ever get a word out of me. And nobody knows about Joyce. And she won't tell."

Hester grinned broadly. "You've all been wonderfully clever to think all this out so thoroughly. Somebody'd have to be even more clever than you to find out about it. Paul Broward thinks he's clever, but not clever enough for that. He knows how to buy information, but he wouldn't have enough money to buy it from me. He doesn't deserve to get that baby. I'd do anything to make certain he never gets him."

"Oh, Hester, I'm so glad I had you to talk to about this. It'll make it so much easier not to say anything to anyone else."

Continuing to grin, Hester nodded. "Of course. We all need someone to talk to. I knew that from the moment I read in the paper what Paul Broward was doing to your father and you. It filled me with such . . . such emotion! I knew something had to be done, and that I could probably do it."

"And you have! What a difference you've made in my life. In Pop's and Jimmy's life."

"Not as much as I can make. But that will come about, dear Poke." She sighed and rose from the sofa. "But now Daddy and I have to get home again. With all that's happened today, I forgot to tell you we're going away for a while. Every once in a while, he has to check into a sanitarium and go through a series of tests to make sure he's doing well."

The news shattered Poke. "Oh, no! I was hoping—"

"Oh, we won't be gone forever. Maybe little more than just a few days, maybe up to six weeks. And I'll make you a little bet, dear Poke, that by the time we come back, everything will have changed. Something tells me that your father won't have a reason to keep running for very much longer. As far as I'm concerned, the sooner that happens, the better." Then she got her father and left.

CHAPTER
▪▪ EIGHT

THREE MORNINGS LATER—
SQUIRREL SPRINGS, WEST VIRGINIA

"It's right here, like I thought. We're close to the state park, Daddy," said Hester. Through winter-stripped trees lining the three-lane roadway, she spied white brick walls licked pink by the rising sun. "We used to go there all the time, remember? Cacapon. The beach was so nice—never crowded, and the lake so clean and cold. And we could sleep in our old Winnebago. I used to think we were so rich to be able to go on two-week vacations like that, with swimming for me and Momma, and fishing for you—and we cooked the fish on a campstove—and that castle we used to visit, remember?"

Lester, strapped into his bucket seat next to Hester's, grumbled. His irritation didn't surprise her—he'd been strapped in for several hours and forced to sleep there while she'd driven through the night. She'd have liked to make more stops, but the long time it took to prepare the van for travel precluded that. On short notice, she'd had to buy a small auxiliary generator to run appliances when the van was stopped. Then she'd bought a portable refrigerator, stocked it with food for a week and enough insulin to last a couple of months, if necessary. To heat food and make coffee and tea, she'd bought a small microwave oven. How she coveted Dr. Broward's wonderfully equipped vehicle!

But Hester was good at making do, and she'd improvised as she'd had to all her life. A sleeping bag and air mattress on the floor made a decent bed for her; an empty crate served as a frame for an old oversize sofa cushion on which her father could sleep swaddled in a down quilt. His toileting took up little space—ostomies and indwelling catheters had their advantages. Her own needs had to be satisfied at gas stations and full service rest stops. Even off the road in some woods, if need be. If she couldn't accomplish her mission quickly, laundry would cause some problems. Some RV stops had laundromats, but most campgrounds would not. She would have to make stops in more well-developed towns.

As she drove into the small hospital's parking lot, she saw a large bright blue Ram van parked in the visitor's section up against the old four-story building. "They're still here, Daddy," she said. The license plate made her giggle. "We have a friend from Pennsylvania here."

Lester grumbled and drooled.

"I know you're uncomfortable now. But we're going to be treated in style real soon. They don't get too much business here this time of year. And they must have had lots of snow—there are dirty snowbanks walling in the whole parking lot. They'll be thrilled to admit us and keep us overnight when they see our insurance card. And we'll get a whole new supply of dressings and a couple of those plastic bedside care trays and stuff. They'll come in handy even when we get home."

She drove around the building to the emergency room entrance—white-lettered black glass double doors at ground level—and parked in a handicapped slot. Bright in the mid-February morning's icy breath, an ambulance, its tailgate thrown wide, sputtered and puffed at the end of the entry ramp. Wisps of exhaust rose and tripped up courses of frosted brick and tiers of square blank windows, and merged with the fog that now clung to the uppermost branches of ancient oaks.

Hester kissed her father, wiped the drool from his downcurved lips, and disengaged herself from her seat belt, as she opened the driver-side door. While preparing her shot of insulin in the rear of the van, she spoke gently to him as she would to a baby awaiting its morning bottle. "Now, now, I know what I'm doing. It worked with Dr. Broward and it'll work here. And I'll make sure they come right away and get you, too. I'll give them your chart, with all the notes and orders, and they'll know exactly what to do for you while I'm 'sick.' We'll get a few good meals while we're here. And, tomorrow morning we'll be on our way, and they'll never know what happened to poor little Jimmy Broward."

She hummed to herself as she prepared to carry out her plan. She averted her thoughts from Poke, whom she'd come to like and pity more than she'd wanted to, and focused her resolve on doing to Paul Broward's family what he had done to hers: poisoning their blood. Innocent people would suffer. That could not be helped. Her father had been innocent. Hester herself had been innocent.

She'd thought, until she'd read the article on the front page of the Philadelphia *Inquirer*, that the last innocent to suffer would be Dr. Liz Broward. The lawyer had no other heirs, she'd been certain. But, the headline read, "Broward Grandson Kidnapped." Had Hester missed something? She'd thought she'd known everything there was to know about the Main Line family.

The subhead read, "Missing, Son of Doctor Struck Down by Strange Malady," and the article had gone on to explain how the doctor had "never regained consciousness." That much had pleased Hester. She'd known what the malady was that for the second time in two months had stricken the woman. It had worked perfectly. No one suspected carbon monoxide poisoning in the second more concentrated dose, because in the first dose, the symptoms were vague and no one had tested for the gas. And she knew that death could occur long before the skin and mucous membranes blushed cherry red, a sure sign in corpses. So if, as must have happened, Doctor Broward had grown steadily more fatigued a second time before collapsing and going into a coma, CO tests might be neglected again. Apparently, Paul Broward himself had interfered in the medical testing. A hospital spokesperson told the investigating reporter that he'd had his daughter transferred to a private facility "up north" before they'd completed tests. Evidently no one at the unnamed private facility had discovered the truth, either before or after she'd died.

To the lawyer, her death seemed less important than getting his grandson back. *What a cruel, wicked man! Caring about only his family name and fortune! Here it was in the article, just as Poke had said. Broward believed what he wanted to—that James had "brainwashed" his daughter to believe his paternity claim so he could get his hands on the Broward fortune.*

"It's sad to have to do it like this," said Hester to Lester as she got her equipment together. "But at least we won't let the little boy suffer. I'll poison his blood all at once, and it will be over. And don't you think that doing it with insulin instead of carbon monoxide has a poetic kind of justice in it, Daddy?"

Lester grunted.

Hester kissed and fondled him for a moment, then, exposing one mammoth thigh, plunged the narrow needle in just above the elastic band of her thigh-high hose.

Lester let out a shriek. His face exploded in panic. As she started to the emergency room entryway, his deep throaty moan followed her.

Hester's stomach had long been empty; the quick-acting insulin did its work. By the time she arrived at the triage desk, clutching her father's chart to her bosom, she was sweating and weak. She managed to clunk his aluminum-clad log on the desk before she sank, breathing hard, to the floor. The startled triage nurse called for help as she tried to make sense of the chart and connect it to the woman propped up by her own mass on the floor.

"Daddy's in the van. Get him. Handicapped," Hester panted.

"Is this his or yours?" asked the nurse, a tall, middle-aged, tough-looking woman of eagle-beaked countenance. She tapped the chart with one long index finger as her squinting eyes bored into the chart summary page.

"His."

"Then this isn't a diabetic thing you're having?"

Hester shook her head.

"Get her into a bed," the nurse said to the two male paramedics who'd dashed to the scene at her call.

As the paramedics strained beneath her weight in half-rolling, half-lifting her onto a collapsed gurney, she said, "Get Daddy, too. He's afraid."

They untelescoped the gurney and began to wheel it toward a green curtained cubicle, puzzlement in the looks they passed to the nurse.

"Diabetic quadruple amputee," the nurse explained as she followed them, chart in hand. "Is he having problems?" she asked Hester.

"He's afraid. 'Cause I'm having an attack of some kind."

"Mhmm. Ever have it before?"

Hester shook her head, just as it hit the pillow. She felt nauseated.

"Don't worry about your father. We'll get him. Let's find out about you first." She instructed the paramedics to get the on-call ER resident who was just finishing work on an earlier emergency. Then she checked Hester's blood pressure and vital signs as she asked her a stream of questions.

Hester knew how to answer and skillfully led the questioner through the health history in such a way as to carry her to a logical diagnosis in light of physical findings and symptoms. By the time Dr. Stanley Bernes arrived by the bedside, Nurse Shirley Petrowski was able to suggest, "I think it's hypoglycemia. Hasn't had a meal in eighteen hours, hasn't slept in twenty-four. She's too nauseated to hold down anything now. Should we start glucose IV?"

"And Compazine, rectally," he concurred, nodding, and made a quick pass of cold instruments, ungentle fingers, bored eyes, and barely attentive ears over Hester's body.

"What we need, young lady," said the young man in a peevish and patronizing tone, "is a good night's sleep and something to eat."

"Oh, yes, Doctor," Hester said, like the good girl he wanted her to be. She nodded her head against the pillow as she extended her arm to receive the needle.

Dr. Bernes tied a flat rubber tourniquet around Hester's arm, probed the inside of her elbow, and shook his head. He knit his brow and pondered the difficulties of finding a vein entrenched between thick mounds of flesh on either side of the joint. "Your weight needs dealing with," he said, clearly piqued, "but fasting is no way to do it." He snapped the tourniquet off and tossed it on the IV tray on the bedside stand. "See what you can do with this, Shirley," he directed the nurse.

With barely more kindness, Nurse Petrowski found and penetrated the vein. When the fast glucose drip had begun, she said, "Dr. Bernes is right, you know. You'd better find a motel room and get some sleep."

At this Hester began to cry.

"Now, that won't do you any good, my dear. No use working yourself into a snit. The glucose will get you stabilized enough to get you on your way as soon as the Compazine wears off."

Indeed the drip was working, and Hester felt better quickly. But she wouldn't allow herself to look better for quite a while, so she threw a crying tantrum that stunned the nurse and the doctor into having her admitted for twenty-four hours, which required that Lester also be admitted. The insurance card in her wallet sealed the arrangement. After all, the calming suppository could impair Hester's coordination and make her an unsafe driver. And, besides, two patients whose diagnoses justified significant fees for two otherwise vacant beds and a slew of diagnostic tests to boot, were gladly welcomed. Father and daughter could share a room, and the daughter, when well enough—which she surely would be by the morrow—would happily give her father his morning care and medication. The staff would

be free to tend to other patients. What luck this bizarre pair
had brought to the underfunded and understaffed hospital
during this slow, even difficult, time of year!

In fact, luck had struck the hospital twice in a single
week, thought Shirley Petrowski as she turned the matter
of Hester and Lester Jones over to admissions. Last week it
had brought Zack Zachary and his son Jimmy through the
automatic sliding black glass doors to her desk, the man
red-eyed and scruffy, the boy in his arms pale-faced and
fevered, full of apparent croup. A sudden storm had dumped
two feet of snow on the roads and parking lot, and fallen
utility lines had forced the hospital onto their emergency
generator for power. The day staff had remained all night,
no one had slept longer than an hour over the past two days.
By some miracle, Zack had driven his van through the snow
on its oversize wheels. As the snow piled up to the south of
Squirrel Springs, his son had lain in a crib inside the van,
a couple of yards from a makeshift humidifier.

The man had emerged out of the black and white night
in a hunting vest and a plaid shirt with snow-caked tall
rubber boots covering his jeans to the knees. He'd stood
there looking oddly messianic with the child in his arms and
snow clinging to his long black hair and embryonic beard.
Shirley had drawn in a sudden breath and summoned Dr.
Bernes from his moment of respite behind a curtained ER
cubicle. Moments later the boy was in pediatric intensive
care, snatched from death by no more than several hours.
His father had sat barely dozing outside the room until
the fever had been stopped in its tracks by the IV fluid
and penicillin, and had begun to creep, however slowly,
down toward 104 degrees Fahrenheit. Only then did he
allow himself to sleep fitfully for a few hours.

He'd awakened at eleven A.M., when at last a relief
nurse arrived to take Shirley's place. A single small path
had been plowed through the parking lot, and the sheriff
was bringing in staff two by two in his four-wheel-drive
military surplus Jeep. The operations had taken all night,

and still were going on. There was no one on staff free to run the hospital plow; all hands were busy running the hospital itself. Jimmy Zachary had been the only emergency patient—at least the only one who had made it into the hospital. Shirley felt there must be others the weather had kept away. The weather itself would cause emergencies as people worried themselves sick, or overexerted themselves clearing driveways or installing tire chains, or went into premature labor.

Shirley had turned down the sheriff's offer for a ride back to her house, a small two-bedroom two-story dwelling set just yards down a paved road off State Route Eleven. "We plowed out your driveway," he'd said.

"Thanks, Rodney. I sure appreciate that. But why go home to no one? Take someone like Barb, that's got a family. I'll catch a nod in the doctor's lounge, and be back here where I'm needed by tonight."

He'd said that made sense in the circumstances. Shirley was the most skilled and versatile nurse on the staff, having been in the Air Force Reserves in the early seventies, where she'd had the autonomy often lacking in civilian nursing, and had frequently carried out medical as well as traditional nursing procedures. She'd worked in a jail outside of Washington, D.C., where she knew more than most of the doctors, young men just out of school and getting advanced training on the taxpayers, at Walter Reed Army Hospital or Bethesda Naval Hospital. Enlistees themselves, they respected her military connection and understood her scorn for the unconnected, not realizing her scorn extended to them for the soft life they'd lived, having escaped not from Appalachian poverty, as she had, but from the draft during the Vietnam War, which they'd spent in medical school. At the County Detention Center her autonomy did not extend very far. Status there depended on politics, and though she was a lieutenant in the Reserves, she had no rank at all in the correctional system. Doctors passing through their temporary military obligations swung more weight than any nurse permanently employed by the county. She had no association with the County Health Department, where she might advance in her profession. And her inclinations were decidedly unlike those nurses'; she had no desire to do good works in ghettos or even in Appalachian mining towns, where her father and brothers had ruined their lungs and rained terror on the women in the family. She wanted to stay as far from that kind of life as possible, and to have as much control over others as she had over herself.

That control had been wrested out of her hands by a rapist who'd brought her down at the door of her own apartment when she returned from her two-to-ten P.M. shift at the jail. She'd felt that the man had followed her from work, and she wasn't sure whether he was a jail guard or a recently discharged inmate. Which he was had hardly mattered. She'd told no one what had happened; still, every man she came in contact with from that night on wore a knowing leer. She would never feel safe or whole again. So she'd returned to West Virginia, whose coal mines still disgusted her, but whose beautiful mountains and rural roads curtained off the truths nestled among them. She had taken the emergency room job in Squirrel Springs ten years ago and had become a fixture of it, as it had become a fixture of her. More than a triage nurse, she ran the entire emergency department, an administrator without a title, doing what the figurehead-appointed administrator had neither talent nor inclination to do. Her keen business sense, her toughness, which edged on callousness, and an intuitive knowledge of human and inhuman natures— deepened by her over fifty years living or working with scoundrels—set her apart from her colleagues. Quietly, with somewhat grudging respect, nurses, doctors, and directors alike allowed her the run of things. Not only in the ER but throughout the hospital, wherever she chose to inject herself.

She had chosen to inject herself in the sudden arrival of the coarse-looking man delivered by the whistling storm and carrying an angelic frail boy through the doors of her domain. At a glance she knew the man was no scoundrel.

And logic told her that he was a fugitive. Why else would he—an obvious outlander—be on the road with a very sick boy on such a night? The boy must have become sick while they were traveling. And a man and a boy alone would not travel this hilly country this time of year, unless the trip were unplanned. Unless they were escaping from someone, somewhere. And a fugitive running for his own skin, one who cared not for this boy, would not have sought aid for him, not even in this relative backwoods community far from the interstate highway. He'd have likely abandoned him on a hospital doorstep, maybe in Maryland if he was running from the north and east, maybe in Richmond, or Fredericksburg, or at the very least Winchester, if he was coming from the south.

So, when the sheriff had left, Shirley immediately went to the pediatric intensive care unit and looked in on the child, whose fever had dropped a full degree and who was breathing easier. She then sat next to the man in the waiting room. "It looks like you got here in time," she said.

He rubbed his eyes and nodded.

"Did you sleep?"

"Yeah. A little. How long will he have to be here?"

She raised her eyebrows. "You aren't thinking of leaving already?"

"I'll stay as long as it takes. Just want to know how long that'll be."

"That's how long, sir. As long as it takes. You aren't from nearby?"

He stiffened and then stood up and went into the ICU to look at the boy. She followed him, catching the sour odor of his breath and wrinkled clothing. He hadn't removed even his boots. Gingerly, he reached into the ventilated crib and touched the boy's head. The child's eyes fluttered open and a small choked-off sound came from him. "Daddy's here, Jimmy," said the man.

"Mommy . . ."

"Not here now."

The eyes closed. The boy was asleep again. The man sighed and walked out of the room.

"Would you like to call his mother?"

"Yes."

"Why don't you? He's not out of danger yet, but she'd want to know where he is. That he's getting care." She grinned. "The best in West Virginia, believe it or not."

He showed no sign of amusement. "I can't. Liz is dead."

"Oh!" said Shirley. "I'm sorry."

"Sure." He sank back into the chair he'd spent the last eighteen hours in. "Not your fault."

"Look—your son is being cared for. He'll probably not wake up again soon. Why don't you get a shower and lie down for a while. We've got lots of empty beds and rooms in peds. That's where he'll go from here."

"Thanks. But I can't afford your rents here. I'll sleep in my van."

"We don't charge much for parents rooming in. Even if your insurance doesn't cover, it won't be a lot. Not much more than a motel with a crib. A van's no place for you now," she said.

"I'm not covered. Neither is he. I already put cash out in advance for three days. I hope it won't be longer than that. I got to get going. Get away from here. And the reason we're in my RV is I don't have money for motels."

She eyed him. Definitely running, she thought. Leaving no paper trail. And trying to change his appearance. That beard was no more than two weeks old. Then there was money—cash enough for three days' hospitalization, including intensive care—yet he was conserving money. Why? She'd seen his van in the lot. Custom built and well maintained, no question. And the boy had designer pajamas on and had been wrapped in a handmade down quilt in Pennsylvania Dutch design. The teddy bear was a Gund. The man was substantial. "From what I can see," she said, "you'll be here more than three days. Even if you head back home, wherever that is, you'll want him well enough to travel." From his license plate, she knew that back home was somewhere in Pennsylvania.

He leaned forward, face in his hands. He groaned. "Just make him well."

"Look," said Shirley, "you could use something to eat. Something hot and fresh, not from your microwave. Let's get a bite from the cafeteria, then you can lie down in one of our doctors' rooms off the lounge. No charge. And the lunch is on my tab."

He looked up, puzzlement creasing his face.

"You're right, City Boy. I *am* a tough old bird. No liberal bleeding heart, either. But you're here on my watch, and I let you in. You might have figured by now that I'm the one who runs things in this hospital, not those good old boys in administration."

For the first time, his eyes crinkled with humor. "Yeah, I figured."

"So, your boy's going to get along fine. I'll see to it in person. Now get on up out of that chair and take time to tend to yourself. That's an order."

"Yes'm," he said, and accepted her offers with a grace that belied his rough exterior.

She was the first to waken, and had showered and changed into a fresh uniform before he emerged from his room and headed straight for the weathered aluminum coffee urn. At Shirley's insistence, this urn was never allowed to run dry, nor its contents turn bitter. Unlike most twenty-four hour employee lounges, this one maintained an aroma of freshness. Food wastes were immediately disposed of. The effluvia of drowsing humans was ventilated out through raised windows, whatever the weather. Resident physicians learned quickly that, whatever emergency wakened them while they were on call, throwing up the window came immediately before throwing open the door. The lounge must never reek of slumber's sulfurs.

On seeing Zack crossing the lounge, Shirley checked the bedroom he'd just vacated. What she saw and sniffed raised her eyebrows in admiration; a chill breath from the lifted window rolled across the newly stripped bed. This man lived cleanly and picked up after himself. He wanted no charity, preferred to earn his own keep.

"When you're done with your coffee, get a shower over there. I assume you have a change of clothes."

"Right. Thanks." He drank the coffee black.

"I called in on Jimmy. His fever's way down. They're going to move him to peds in the morning," she said as he drank.

He smiled. "Thanks, Ms. Petrowski."

"It's 'Miss.' Not ashamed of it. Either that or Lieutenant."

"Oh?"

"Air Force Reserves," she explained.

"Lieutenant fits. Anyway, thanks."

She grinned. "I like you. You're honest. Well, anyway, after you get washed up and dressed, and spend some time with your boy, I've got a job for you. Help you earn your keep here, so you don't have to worry about running your money down."

He set down his mug. "A job? Hey, how long am I going to have to be here? If Jimmy's getting better—"

"Figure a week. Long enough for you to plow out the driveway and help with some janitor work. That's not too low for you, is it?"

He laughed. "No. I've been much lower than that."

Nodding, she said, "Suspected as much. All right, it's into the evening shift. Things get pretty busy about now. I'll be on my ER desk. Check in with me there."

His many talents impressed her. As good in getting along with people as he was in doing hard physical work, he could help as much in transporting patients to X-ray as in running the hospital's balky twenty-year-old snow plow. When the computer in accounting went down, he quickly brought it on-line again. One mention of the problem it was having fetched a diagnosis of the trouble from him. It was not, he said, a bug in the software as they'd thought; it was simply some dirt in the keyboard that had caused the same command to be sent a dozen times over. So he cleaned the data processor's keyboard, as well as all the keyboards at all the terminals throughout the hospital, and threw in a general hardware check of the entire in-house network of PCs and terminals. His services, worth several hundred dollars in themselves, were sure to save unknown future costs as well. So, after meeting with "the good old boys in administration," Shirley handed Zack a refigured bill and a refund of $1,500 in cash. His entire bill for Jimmy's week in the hospital, a week that ended the next morning, would come to $400.00.

She had tried to convince him to stay another three days. For the boy's sake, to finish the ten-day course of penicillin, which in a child still under two years of age couldn't be most effectively given by mouth; and for her own, as she'd come to think that if he stayed for ten days he might decide that Squirrel Springs was as good a place as any to hide from your ghosts. For, as he revealed in bits and pieces of unguarded conversation over the week, ghosts were what he was running from: the ghost of one wife, Maryellen, who'd died four years ago of leukemia; the ghost of Jimmy's mother, Liz, who'd died a month ago from an illness nobody could diagnose. He'd never said he and this Liz—doctor—hadn't married, but he'd also never called her his wife. Clearly, though, he mourned her as though she were, so, as far as Shirley was concerned, the romance between them had been legitimate.

He brushed off all her entreaties to him to stay in Squirrel Springs until the last shot of penicillin had been delivered into Jimmy's gluteal muscle.

"Well, then," she'd said yesterday afternoon, "you'll just have to learn to give him his shot yourself." She'd smiled when he'd blanched at her pronouncement, sure she had sealed her advantage with this argument.

"Can't I give him a jigger of syrup or something? He's just a little kid."

"Exactly. And sick as he's been, you can't take a chance that he'll spit it all out, or bring it back up."

"I always wondered how Maryellen could do it on Poke," he'd said.

"Poke?"

"Yeah, our daughter. She's sixteen."

"Oh. I guess you left her with relatives."

His eyes had flashed, his jaw had worked, making his new beard seem to bristle.

Backtracking quickly to safer ground, she'd said, "Children cry when you jab them, then they forget it."

"Guess so. I can learn to do it. I just can't stay here anymore. It's already been too long."

And you've told on yourself too much, she'd thought. "All right, then, I'll teach you."

"OK." He'd swallowed hard. "When?"

She'd just come off duty, but checked her watch. "He's due at six P.M. Hmnn, it's four now. Come on with me." He'd followed her through the corridors to the cafeteria.

"What are we going here for?" he'd asked.

"You'll see." She'd pushed through a pair of swinging doors that read "Employees only," and entered the kitchen. Curious men and women in snoods and green smocks looked up from stainless-steel food preparation counters. On seeing Shirley, they quickly returned to preparing salads and sandwiches and arranging them on plastic plates, onto which they snapped clear plastic covers.

Zack had stopped just inside, his back catching the return swing of the door, his eyes seizing their momentary questioning glances, which he returned with a shrug.

Shirley had turned and said, "It's OK. You're with me." This statement encompassed the whole of her power to the farthest reaches of this hospital.

He'd nodded and followed her toward the floor-to-ceiling stainless-steel refrigerator. She'd opened the door of one segment and reached in, pulling out a grapefruit. Tossing it to him, she'd led him back out of the kitchen and through a metal rear stairwell door and up a level to a laboratory wing. Down the hall they'd continued to a small room at the end, where she'd turned on a bright fluorescent ceiling light, illuminating several life-size models of human beings lying silent in bed under white sheets pulled up to their necks.

She'd grinned as she saw him step back. "You're going to bruise that poor grapefruit. Don't worry. They're just practice dummies."

"Oh." He'd relaxed his grip on the fruit and come in.

She'd opened a tall white enamel cabinet and reached in and retrieved a syringe and needle. "OK. First on the grapefruit." On that fruit she'd taught him how to pinch up flesh and insert the needle at the proper angle, and aspirate to test for accidental blood vessel penetration. Quick as he was, he had gotten the physical motions down pat in moments. With equal dispatch he'd learned to measure off the buttocks quadrants on the pediatric dummy, and insert the needle in a spot that would avoid hitting the sciatic nerve. And this deft, sure-fingered man had no trouble at all in mixing and drawing into the syringe the aqueous solution of penicillin.

"Straight A's, Zack. Let's have supper and then get to peds for the real test."

The real test, of course, had not gone quite so smoothly. Those broad sure hands had trembled in the nurses' station when mixing the medicine in the vial. They'd dropped the filled syringe, and he'd had to start all over again. And Jimmy had been far less cooperative a subject than had the dummy. His gluteus had squirmed and humped, twisted and pulled away while being measured into quadrants; his legs had kicked; his lungs, having gained back their tenor, had given forth bellows and whoops. He'd known what it was time for, and his father's presence exacerbated rather than calmed his fears. Shirley had had to restrain him while Zack had found his mark and driven the medicine home. And Zack, in Jimmy's eyes, had become not a rescuing hero but an accomplice in injuring his son.

That, of course, was what Shirley had been counting on. That giving a two-year-old an injection without an accomplice was fraught with peril for a parent, would surely be clear now to Zack, would dissuade him from his ideas about taking his son out of the hospital three days early.

But Zack was more stubbornly fixed on his plan than she had anticipated. No, he had said, whatever it took, he was leaving. He would practice again with the next dose tonight. He would wait until Jimmy had gone to sleep when he would sneak in on him and deliver the shot before the child knew what was happening. This idea was not as treacherous as it seemed. She'd known it to work quite well, especially in a child weakened by a bout with pneumonia and thus subject to dozing off. So, tonight she would supervise him one more time. And, damn it, by the time she'd come on duty tomorrow afternoon, he'd be gone from her life forever. And damn it, she was going to miss him! And, no, she wouldn't work another double shift. Now that the weather had cleared up and staffing was back to normal, she could no longer hide her real reasons for spending so much extra time at the hospital. What had she been thinking of, anyway? At fifty-two she couldn't have possibly stumbled on a man who'd changed all her ideas about what men were like and could subsequently change her life. The stress of the past week had gotten to her. That or the picture she held in her head of a moment of epiphany, a picture of an oddly messianic-looking man coming out of a snowy night with his child in his arms, seeking a place to stay. Now she must let them go.

LATER THAT DAY

Hester was in her own milieu in the hospital. She knew how hospitals worked, and how to use their mystique to accomplish her own purposes. She knew of no better place to commit murder undetected. All the tools were available, easy to find, easy to use and destroy. And no time was better than a time like this, in a small backwoods hospital in an off-season for tourists near roads not quickly cleared after storms like last week's. The staff at times like these was bare-bones, particularly on second and third shifts. A city hospital might have access to temporary nursing help

services. Not so a place like this, which instead depended
on dedicated home-folk willing to work extra hours when
needed. And, dedicated, they always took call lights seri-
ously, so if you wanted to get a nurse away from her
desk, you could easily distract her. The unit clerk might
run errands away from the unit, if summoned. Or you
could draw her attention with friendly conversation. Once
disarmed by learning you were a nurse who used to come
to Cacapon as a child, you could get them to talk about
how things worked here.

So Hester soon learned everything she had to know:
where the pediatrics wing was; how many patients were
there; which room a little boy named Jimmy with pneumonia was in.

"Oh, the one that came in with his father that bad night?
Jimmy Zachary. Darling little thing. A few hours longer and
he wouldn't have made it. And now he's going home," said
the short, heavyset nurse making a check of Hester's vital
signs at shift change.

So, James had changed his name. "Home?"

"Well, not home. They're on some kind of vacation, I
heard. In a hurry to get there, and lost a week being sick.
Now, I got to get on with my P.M. meds. You're feeling
OK, now? Your pulse is just fine."

"It passed." Hester grinned to herself. She had gone to the
bathroom and expelled the Compazine suppository before
it had a chance to dissolve, and so had avoided the central nervous system depression that might have slowed
her thinking. After barely a few hours of sleep, she had
wakened completely refreshed. Lester, worn out from the
uncomfortable all-night ride, slept soundly in the bed next
to hers.

"Well, that's just great to hear," twanged the nurse. "And
your daddy seems fine, too. I guess, being a nurse, you take
pretty good care of him. I saw that chart you keep on him.
Sure makes our work easier here."

"I don't want to be a burden. I'm a nurse, and I know
how busy you get. So just go on about your business. Now

that I'm feeling OK, I'm going to take a walk around your place."

The woman's brown curls and wedge-shaped cap jiggled as she nodded. "Don't you just get so excited about how things work in other people's hospitals? I've never been in a big city hospital like in Philadelphia, but if I was there, they probably couldn't keep me from snooping around. Shirley's been in all sorts of hospitals. That's why we're so modern here. She worked in Washington, D.C. You ought to talk to her."

"Shirley?"

"Yeah, the ER triage nurse. But she's more than that. Practically owns this place."

"Maybe I will." Hester knew that would be a bad idea. A nurse who practically owned a hospital would, unlike this local, hospital-trained nurse, hardly be naive enough not to know that Hester was up to no good in her snooping and prying. She stretched and yawned loudly, and slid out of bed. Gathering her shoes from beneath the bed, she slipped them on over her bare feet. "Oh, dear, I don't have a bathrobe," she said sweetly to the nurse, whose white shoes were just disappearing around the door frame.

The nurse popped back in, and surveyed Hester's bulk with knit brow. Then, apparently struck by inspiration, she said, "Hey, I've got an idea. Come with me." As Hester in her untied oxfords shuffled to the door, holding her flowered hospital gown as tightly as possible around her hips, the nurse looked up and down the hall. "All right. This way." She waved Hester on and led her to the linen closet. "We've got some scrub gowns in there. Help yourself, honey." And she hurried on toward the nurses' station with her thermometer tray balanced on one palm.

Giggling to herself, Hester found and donned an extra large scrub gown, then tied her shoes and made her way through the adult medical unit to the stairway leading upstairs to pediatrics. In such a small hospital where strangers stood out, the gown could not possibly serve as disguise. Still, it gave her a feeling of security and warmth. Nevertheless, she wouldn't make herself obvious in her reconnoiter of the wing. She knew that the nurses' station would be placed at the same architectural point there as in the adult wing she was staying in. The layout of the station would also be the same: counter at the front, call lights on a board that was visible from both inside and outside the station, chart rack to the back of the unit clerk's desk, medicine room adjoining the station and accessible from the hall. The room arrangement would probably be different, with a play room for recovering children, and multiple crib nurseries for infants. She wanted to learn where Jimmy's room was and figure out how to get there during the night without being seen by the night nurse. She'd deliver him a shot of insulin. Next time they'd check he'd be gone. They'd never guess what killed him.

Emerging from the stairwell door into the corridor, several yards from the nurses' station, she looked both ways. She could hear second shift activities under way. A meal cart stacked high with brown plastic trays sat halfway down the hall. Three young women in aproned candy-striped dresses tagged along behind a kitchen aide carrying trays into rooms. The girls would be volunteers, helping to feed young patients their evening meals. Obviously, this part of the corridor housed patients old enough to eat table foods. Jimmy Broward would be one of them.

Hester slipped into the corridor and sidled down the hall to a room across from the meal cart. No name plates on the door. The room was unoccupied. Jimmy's room would be two doors down, across the corridor.

Sucking in her breath, she slipped quickly in, pulled the door almost shut, and posted herself, alert to every sound and light change. When traffic receded she stuck her head briefly out, measured the tray service progress. Emergency calls, beeping monitors, lights flashing in the nurses' station distracted staff from routine duties, sent them scurrying to help patients in distress. She smiled to herself. She'd return tonight, her syringe filled with the insulin stored for her father in the medical unit refrigerator, and distract them real good.

Ten minutes later a lone tray remained on the cart. The kitchen aide returned, picked it up, and walked with it to the nurses' station. "Here's the Zachary boy's supper. You know who's giving it to him tonight? I'm out of volunteers."

A nurse with a tall white cap and harried looking sharp features appeared at the counter. "Isn't Zack here yet? Shit! We had three admissions this afternoon, and wall-to-wall surgical preps this P.M. Tomorrow's Dr. Pulliam's operating day."

"I don't know what you want me to do about it. I can't feed him."

"I guess Queen Shirley's still around. She probably knows where Zack is. Wouldn't be surprised if she was with him."

"Yeah. Never saw her act like that about a man since I've been here. You suppose he melted that frigid old pussy?"

The nurse laughed. "Keep in your place, Jeannie. Besides, you know she doesn't have one. Just set the tray down here. They'll probably be along any second. She's probably giving him more lessons. He didn't do too well last time."

"Lessons in what?"

"Giving the boy his nine o'clock penicillin. They're waiting till he's asleep so he can sneak it in on him this time. He's leaving tomorrow morning. And Miss Perfect Nurse has him convinced that he should get the medicine IM till the ten-day course is over. You ask me, she wanted to keep him here long as she could. Why else couldn't he be sent home on the syrup like any other kid?"

The aide shoved the tray to one end of the counter and turned away, grinning. "Don't you have any pity for her? She's got as much a right to love as any other turkey vulture I know."

"Sure. Maybe I can set up a bed for her next to his in the boy's room to give her one last chance tonight." The elevator across the hall from the nurses' station opened. "Oh, oh. Better get going, Jeannie," she said.

The giggling Jeannie hid her gleeful expression behind

her cart as the stocky bearded man in plaid shirt, hunting vest, and blue jeans emerged from the elevator. Smiling above his head was the beaked countenance of the nurse who owned the hospital—and owned along with it the obvious displeasure of some of her dispossessed underlings.

The turn of events took Hester aback a moment. The man was rooming in with his son. She hadn't thought of that. Once he'd gone to bed, she'd have no way to get past him unseen to inject the boy with the insulin. This changed her plans. She would have to take off tomorrow when he did and follow him to his next stop. And the longer she followed him, the less likely he'd be not to notice her. His growth of beard, his change of name made clear that he knew they were after him. No doubt Joyce Price had told him that he'd been charged with kidnapping. He'd be alert to any tail, throw off followers.

So she'd have to stay back out of sight. If she didn't conclude her mission tonight, she would have to get to the Tonto Basin by another route, meet him there, and go through the long awkward process of winning his trust and that of the archaeologists there so she could get a hold on his son.

As she slipped from her hiding place and sneaked down the hallway and downstairs, she vowed to find another solution to her problem.

Another solution! That was it! As Hester had often found, the solution of a problem lay within the problem itself.

On her return to her room, her father was awake and had been set and strapped into his wheelchair. Their diet trays were set on overbed tables. She kissed him gaily on the head and wheeled him close to a spot where she could put both trays together on one bed and feed him as she fed herself.

She outlined her plan to the man: "So you see, Daddy, we'll just have to put a *different solution* in the syringe. And his very own father will give him the medicine. Isn't that just the most ironic thing you ever heard of, Daddy?

His very own father? And all the time, I'll be right here in the bed beside yours, sound asleep, while the poison gets into his blood."

Between supper and nine P.M. were some of the hospital's busiest hours: medicines were prepared, personal care given, and visitors contended with. This gave Hester her chance to distract the staff with false alarms and appear in the unit more or less undisguised, claiming to be a visiting aunt of some poor sick child. Pediatrics' staff knew nothing of her and her father. And she'd leave with the visitors. Down the stairs to her medical unit she'd come, and undress and get into bed. She'd hum to herself and her father in warm anticipation of the events about to unfold upstairs.

Moments after appearing in peds as a visitor, Hester had the staff running in three different directions to check on patients on monitors she'd disconnected and set to screaming. While they tripped over one another and reconnected machines and patients, Hester slipped into the medicine room, found Jimmy's premixed penicillin in the refrigerator, withdrew it into a syringe, replaced it with an equal volume of insulin, put it back into its refrigerator slot, and escaped down the stairs.

"It was easier than I thought," she cooed to Lester as she stroked him gently after cleaning him up for the night. "The perfect solution for our problem."

"Are you ready?" Shirley asked Zack. "He's as sound asleep as he's going to be."

"Yeah. And I'm as ready as I'm going to be."

Her lips curled in a knowing smile. "Well, you'll do just fine, Zack." She walked him down the hall to the medicine room. "OK, now what's the first step?" she asked as she ushered him in.

"Ah, mix the penicillin with sterile water." He went to the shelf where the powdered drug was stored, and reached for a vial of it.

"Not this time," she said.

He shook his head. "Right. He still has some left from yesterday."

"Exactly. There were several doses in the one you mixed last night. Enough to last in your refrigerator till you're done with it. The vial's in the fridge."

He fetched the vial, and looked around. "Can you get me a syringe?" His hands trembled slightly.

"Cold feet?"

"Better 'n your cold heart, Lieutenant Petrowski."

"Doing it yourself was your idea, Zack."

"I know they give some kids syrup. That's got to be good enough."

"Look, you can't take any chances with him. It's not like you're taking him home or will be near medical care if something goes wrong."

He drew a deep breath. "Yeah, I guess you're right. Sorry. I really appreciate your help. I know Liz would, too."

"OK." She got a syringe and gave it to him. "Watch your technique in handling this."

"Don't touch the needle. Don't touch anything the needle touches. Don't touch anything wrong with the needle."

She watched him, nodding him through the steps of unsheathing the apparatus and setting the syringe assembly on the small medicine tray while he sponged off the rubber vial diaphragm with alcohol.

Then he shook the vial and raised it to eye level under the bright fluorescent lamp, upended it, and inserted the needle. He drew back on the syringe, pulling the liquid into it.

Shirley watched the vial contents as they drained.

"Harder than yesterday," he said.

She puckered her brow. "Let me see that."

"Am I doing something wrong?" He withdrew the needle and passed the vial to her.

"No. You're right, that mix looks too viscous. Are you sure you got the right vial?" As she asked, she checked the liquid remaining in the tiny bottle. Then she read the label. It read: Penicillin G Potassium 1,000,000 units. A label notation gave the date of reconstitution and Jimmy's name. She put her hand out again. "Let's have that syringe." Taking it, she held it up to the light. "This isn't right. It's not only too thick, it's too cloudy. Something's contaminated it. We can't use it."

"Oh, Jeez, Shirley, I tried to do it right when I mixed it last night."

"And you did. I watched you. There was nothing wrong with it last night. Damn it, Zack, this isn't going to work, is it? I must have been full of shit to suggest it."

His eyes widened a moment. Then he turned aside.

"Did I say something wrong?" she asked.

"No, it's just . . . the way you said that . . . reminded me of . . . of someone."

Now she drew a breath. "Well, let's just forget the IMs. I'll give him the shot tonight. He'll probably do fine on the syrup for the last few days. And it'll be easier on everyone. I'm sorry I complicated your life."

"You didn't. You made it easier. If I'd've had to pay the hospital bill, I might not make it to Arizona."

"Oh, sure you would. You and Jimmy are going to be fine. Now, you go on about your business while I take care of this shot."

Nodding, and eyeing her sideways, clearly aware his tongue had just slipped, he picked up the contaminated medicine vial and tossed it into the waste can and fled quickly.

Back in the medicine room after she had finished giving Jimmy his shot, she thought about the clunk the vial had made when it landed in the can. She reached in and retrieved it and slipped it into her uniform pocket. Someone must have been responsible for contaminating this medicine in the twenty-four hours since it was mixed. She'd have to look into this, find out who it was and why. Only by chance had she averted what might have been a serious mistake.

She'd make sure that it didn't happen again.

CHAPTER
··NINE

A WEEK LATER,
GLENSIDE, PENNSYLVANIA

Grace Ellen Stanford Broward, disguised as a dowdy matron in navy blue jogging sweats and running shoes, drove the rented Geo Prizm across the Delaware River to Philadelphia, then took Route 611 to Glenside. She parked a few blocks from the high school Jill James attended and looked at her reflection in the rearview mirror.

"No one would know you, Grace!" she said as she saw her surprising spectacles. The sunglasses, bought in Cherry Hill, New Jersey, where she'd also surreptitiously purchased a custom-made wig, hid the arched bridge of her nose, masked her high cheekbones. The brown wig with chignon concealed her perfectly coiffed, gray-streaked honey hair. She looked like so many women her age did today, even some women she socialized with, even when they lunched at fine restaurants. Casual, they proclaimed. Sloppy, was her word for it. Disgraceful, she thought.

"I'm thoroughly dis-Graced!" she said to the mirror, wryly twisting her lips. "Even Paul wouldn't know me." And that was the whole idea; she was about to betray her husband, her husband of forty-two years. Betray him not because she couldn't *handle* him anymore, but because she couldn't lie to herself anymore. She could no longer deflect his sarcasm with humor and deny he meant it to hurt. She could no longer make herself love him—make Liz love him—by denying his bigotry, his pride, his abuse of power and money. Liz, if she could know, would know what Grace knew at last: Paul Broward was all the things others saw and she had refused to see. He bought and sold people: newspaper reporters, politicians, even judges. He would stop at nothing to destroy his clients' enemies, did it within the law, *with* the law. Now he was his own client. And the enemy was his grandson's father. He would destroy him, stopping at nothing, though it meant destroying his daughter, Grace's dear daughter, Liz. He had allowed her to die. But Grace would not allow her to die. Paul had gone too far, even for Grace. She would bring Liz back to life, though it meant betraying her husband. For Liz was not dead. Others believed she was, but her mother, who'd carried her inside her forty years ago, knew the truth. Liz could not be dead. Grace wouldn't allow it.

She sighed, fought back a pang of grief. For Liz? Or for the marriage she was about to destroy? She wasn't sure. Then, her composure recovered, she turned to the mirror again, put the finishing touches on her disguise. To make sure neither her husband nor the agents he'd hired to track Jill James would recognize her, she teased a few hairs from the wig's chignon, and tissued off her lipstick. She donned the tasteless fanny pack she'd bought to match her tacky outfit, and locked all her own fine clothing and her large antique diamond ring in the trunk. She'd almost forgotten to take off the ring. Her right hand felt naked. She wondered if the left hand would feel strange and empty when she took off her wedding ring. She shuddered, then went on her way.

A tall, strong woman, Grace had rounded the high school a few times by the time the teenagers began pouring from the doors. Guessing which door Jill James would exit was futile. But Grace had made several dry runs between the school and the Jameses' home, and she knew which route the girl would take. She'd parked several blocks from a major juncture on that route; now she walked to the corner where the girl would be crossing.

There she was, crossing the street, her books hugged against her, eyes downcast, tread even and resolute.

Grace drew a sharp breath. She saw the young woman's pain and knew where it came from. Other students came by in laughing pairs and groups, reveling in their freedom, but she walked alone. Not simply alone, but banished. Paul knew how to kill without killing. *Look what he's doing to this child! I won't let him do it, not to her, too. I won't!*

Paul had dismissed the girl's worth the moment he'd seen her. The instant he'd heard her name. Poke, Liz had called her, that day in the hospital room. A nickname Paul found offensive, typical of the names men like Zack James gave their offspring. "Poke," he'd sneered to Grace later. "A kind of sack, isn't it? One you hide pigs in."

And once when he'd gone to the house in Glenside to try to claim Jimmy, he'd come home and said, "That Poke hides a pig. A whole family of them. The squalor they live in! You wouldn't believe it, Grace. They took him out, long after his bedtime, and left food lying around, even an open bottle of milk turning sour on the table. Imagine, serving milk in the bottle instead of from a pitcher, in the first place. Salad dressings in their bottles, no cruets. With the dressings dripping and hardening around the neck. I can see him licking them off his fingers like a gorilla. I hate to say this, Grace, you may hate me for it, but Liz is better off where she is than in that man's bed."

And, in that moment, she had begun to hate him, to see him for the monster he was. Dear God, she'd thought, anywhere but where she is, please God! I'll carry her in my arms to Zack's bed if you'll only bring her back.

She hated him even more as she watched this truly beautiful young lady bravely carry her awful pain.

Poke mounted the curb near Grace, and Grace watched her a moment as she passed and went on toward her house a few blocks away. Her neat clothing and glowing skin belied any lack of cleanliness. The perfectly twined plaits that hung from beneath a wrapped red scarf gleamed in the afternoon sun. They bounced against the back of her wool-en peacoat as she walked, making her seem happy from behind. Still there was a rigidness, a stolidness in her step that rejected anyone who might approach. Ostracized, she ostracized others. She was not only hurt; she was afraid.

Grace had expected her to be, so she fell into step behind her for half a block before pulling up beside her. The girl moved aside as if to let her pass, but Grace walked beside her for a while. Poke at first kept her eyes on the ground, kept her pace even. Then she wavered and glanced sidelong at Grace, before quickly looking away.

"Keep walking, Poke," said Grace.

The girl's face filled with fear.

"I'm not going to hurt you. But I must talk with you. And no one must see us. It has to look like we just met on the street and talked as we walked."

The girl glanced at her again. "Who are you?" she asked in a frightened whisper.

"You met me only once. In my daughter's hospital room."

Poke stopped, breath bated, and stared at Grace.

Grace stopped and smiled, hoping to calm her, as she said, "Keep walking, dear."

The girl caught her breath and, after a second, resumed walking somewhat haltingly. "Why . . . don't you look the same?"

"I can't be seen talking to you. My husband has hired detectives to watch your house. So I had to disguise myself. We have to look like strangers. Or acquaintances meeting accidentally on the street."

With a slight shake of the head and knitted brow, the girl asked, "But, why? Why would you want to talk to me?"

"Because Liz would want me to. She'd want you to know that I believe that your father is Jimmy's father."

Poke's face reddened, and she let out a cry and sped up. Grace managed to keep up with her shorter companion by lengthening her stride so she wouldn't seem to be in a hurry.

"No! You're lying!"

"I know it's hard to believe. But if you love Liz . . . your father . . . you have to give me a chance to talk to you."

The girl bit her lip and shook her head. Tears glittered at the corners of her eyes. They were now just a half-block from Poke's house. One of the cars parked on this street, or one just now circling the block contained a private detective. Grace mustn't lose this chance. If she were seen walking beside Poke on her way home from school a second time, she would become a suspected liaison, would be followed herself and unmasked. And Paul would find a way to destroy her, too.

As the two neared the house, Grace said, as calmly and in as low a voice as possible, "Meet me at Beaver College tomorrow afternoon after school. Don't go home first, or you'll be followed. I'll be just inside the door of the administration building. You know where that is?"

The girl hesitated a second, then nodded.

In front of the house now, Grace called out as Poke turned down her driveway to the flagstone path, "How nice to see you again, Poke! Enjoyed the short walk." She waved and casually walked on, picking up her pace as she went, as her hopes rose that Poke would come tomorrow so that Grace could help her father prove his paternity before this kidnapping thing had gone any farther.

It had gone too far already.

She first noticed the woman driving the brown Toyota sedan when the driver yielded to her at a side street so she could cross. Then, after deliberately extending her walk for several blocks beyond the Jameses' house, she circled back toward the school. The campus had cleared of most students, but the warning lights on the school zone sign had not stopped blinking. As she traversed the pavement between the signs, her pace kept her even with the slowed cars on the street. She noticed the car again, and was disconcerted, but didn't want to reveal her concern to the driver. She concealed her momentary pause by removing her glasses, which had become annoying anyway, because they pinched her nose, and wiped the lenses on the inside bottom of her sweat shirt. As the car passed the second school zone sign, she pretended to inspect the glasses, breathed on the lenses, wiped them again, reinspected them. By the time she'd concluded this charade, and put the glasses on again, the car once more was out of sight. Grace couldn't be sure where it turned.

"Oh, for goodness' sake, Grace," she said to herself. "The woman has probably finished some errand and is returning to where she came from." A moment's amusement at how deeply she'd gone into her counterspy role made her laugh. And she realized she hadn't laughed in weeks; this unexpectedly lifted her spirits. How amazing that trying to solve a problem, that acting instead of stewing, could lift you, however briefly, out of your pall. Well, then, she must keep acting, if only for that reason. Whether or not she'd prevail in her mission, she couldn't allow grief to overwhelm her spirit.

Taking a deep, grateful breath, she resumed her walk, striding with a spurt of vigor toward the street where her rented Geo was parked. She could see it at a distance when she once again noticed the Toyota. This time she had no doubt. She was not simply lost in a romantic counterspy role, she was engaged in a duel of wits with her husband, who she knew could—and would—crush her if she failed her mission. Horror washed over her. There was no turning back now. He had all the tools, the people he'd bought over the years, the hired agents, as ruthless as he was and cannier by far than she. She, though wealthy in her own right, had never learned how to use the power that money gave her. The only powers she'd learned to use were her extraordinary intuition and the female wiles she'd manipulated her husband and daughter with. Stunned with how these had backfired, she'd pressed on with them, nevertheless. Now he could turn them against her one last time, lift her on her own lance, dash her to the ground, grind her beneath his feet as he had so many others.

No! It could not happen. This had become a battle between good and evil and good must win out. Grace's powers were good ones, used rightly. They'd made bearable the duties her socially correct marriage imposed on her. They'd sustained Liz through adolescent rebellion, let her make choices never allowed to Grace. They'd preserved the family, Paul's relationship with a daughter he might have estranged. And she'd taught Liz to use the same powers to preserve her father's ties with a grandson he'd surely have disowned. Liz had used the powers with courage. Could Grace do less? *Never!*

She mustered her intuition, then readjusted her glasses to relieve their painful pinch on her nose, squared her shoulders, and walked on past her rental car, not even looking at it as she passed it. The neighborhood had become familiar to her through earlier reconnoitering, so she knew she was about half a mile from a small shopping center with a supermarket and a pharmacy. She hid there and phoned for a taxi.

When it came, she told the driver to take her to the Clairview In-Town Resort Hotel in Downtown Philadelphia. The driver, a young blond man, tried to engage her in conversation, but, distracted by her knowledge that the cab was being followed discreetly by the brown Toyota, she responded in monosyllables, discouraging him. When he left her off at the hotel, she dashed into the lobby, registered under the name of Angela Fortune, and paid in cash for one night. Then she dashed around the corner and downstairs to the shopping arcade. At a dress shop she bought the most acceptable looking jacketed dress she could find for ninety-five dollars, which drained her of nearly half her remaining cash. At a leather accessory shop, she found some stubby leather walking shoes discounted to fifty-eight dollars, and a cheap vinyl purse.

Packages in hand, she went upstairs and back toward the lobby, and saw her pursuer had staked out a spot across from the elevators, where she'd see everyone getting on or off or riding. So she retreated to the arcade, which had a back exit leading to the spa and swimming pool and an attached health club. Though the pool was closed, the health club was not. Her hotel key card gave her entry. A dressing room gave her a place to change into the new clothes and to remove her wig. With no comb—she'd left hers in her purse in the car trunk—she could do little with her poor squashed hair; still she brought it into a semblance of neatness by running her fingers through it several times, then patting it at the sides and pulling out the ends as evenly as possible.

Satisfied she could look no more presentable under the circumstances, she put her spy clothes and fanny pack with her glasses in it, her wig and her hat in the plastic bags from the stores, then, on her way out through the arcade, she bought a tube of lipstick and a face powder compact. When she exited the hotel through the lobby she looked almost but not quite like Grace Broward, whom her pursuer had never met and had no reason to suspect.

By the time she'd retrieved the car from its Glenside parking space, parked it in a Philadelphia parking garage, and come home in another taxi, it was after midnight. Security lights lit her way into the main house, then shut off behind her as she let herself in. Paul would know that she'd entered, and by which door, by the voice-simulated announcement through the system's intercom. He'd doubtless be pacing like a lion, as she had not told him where she'd be going, and she seldom went out alone after dark.

She prepared to face him and his questions as she mounted the sweeping spiral staircase to the second floor of the high-ceilinged, three-story mansion. Somewhat disheveled from her ordeal, still wearing the unbecoming dress and carrying her own dress in the hotel dress shop bag, she rehearsed in her mind the dialogue she'd contrived for the occasion.

"*Where have you been, Grace? I've been going out of my mind.*"

"*I just had to get away.*"

"*That dress*" (with a grimace):—"*Where in the world did you get it!*"

"I went into the city. To lose myself. I bought it on a whim. I thought it would make me feel better."

"How can an ill-fitting dress make you feel better? I'd think it would make you feel cheap. You look like you've slept in it. Your hair—"

"As a matter of fact, I did. I've barely slept in the past month. I got a hotel room and lay down. Actually slept. When I woke up and realized what time it was, I caught a cab. I'm sorry I made you worry."

"I don't understand you, Grace. It's not at all like you."

"You have your work to get things off your mind, Paul. I have nothing but my volunteer work. And I can't bear it these days. Everything's so futile."

"It would probably help if you spent some time at the hospital."

"I simply can't face that anymore. We've lost her, Paul. She's never coming back."

Over and over again as she climbed the stairs and started toward their bedroom, she ran this conversation through her mind, editing the script with each new pass, coming up with new possibilities. Suppose he'd grow angry and accuse her of infidelity? No, that was out of character for him. His ego would no more allow him to believe that than it let him believe Zack James had sired Jimmy.

Suppose he'd guessed her mission? Suppose he'd show her photos of herself in her disguise, leaving the wigmaker's shop, entering the rental car, waiting at the corner for Poke?

Impossible. He'd no more dream her capable of betraying him than she herself could have a month ago.

She'd tried to conjure his every possible response to her erratic behavior, and couldn't imagine any other scenarios. She'd felt sure, as she'd entered the huge crystal-lit foyer, mounted the staircase, quietly but firmly strode down the double-wide hall past her private study, past his, past the suite that once had been Liz's, past the three extra bedroom suites and the large main bathroom, past the back stairway leading up to the third story and down to the kitchen, to the double door at the end of the corridor where she and her husband slept together most nights.

But she hadn't imagined the one possibility that proved true. She was stunned as she entered the open bedroom door and saw by the light behind her before it automatically flickered off, that Paul had fallen sound asleep. Paul didn't care that she hadn't come home, didn't even wonder about it. He had turned off the intercom above the bed so her return, which he'd surely presumed would occur in its own good time, wouldn't disturb him.

She stepped back into the hallway, again triggering the light. She stood there a moment seeing from a distance her husband's sleeping form. How soundly he slept! How soundly he'd always slept! Nothing he'd ever done, no hurt he had caused anyone ever kept him awake. She realized now that he had not even lost a night's sleep over what had happened to Liz, over what he had done to her and was continuing to do to her against what was surely her will if she could express it.

What he had done was evil, what he was doing was evil, he—God help Grace—was evil. Yes, oh yes, she must keep on in her battle against him. She couldn't lose. No matter the cost, she had to keep on and make things right by her Liz.

She retreated down the hall to her study and poured herself a sherry. Then she turned out the lights and went to the large multipaned window, pulled back the draperies and, as she sipped the rich drink, looked down on the sweeping circular driveway through the naked gnarled branches of the ancient maple that centered it. She imagined she could see Liz pulling up in her Mercedes-Benz, parking, looking up at her mother's window and waving up at her. So real was the picture, that she waved back. So real was the picture that she believed it might someday come true.

Grace prepared and disguised herself and got to the Beaver College campus the next afternoon more quickly than she'd expected to. This left her time to worry about whether

Poke would show up. Having decided she wouldn't, Grace wandered the campus desultorily for nearly an hour, and forced herself to return to the administration building a half-hour before Poke could possibly reach it if she came straight from school.

As she pushed open the heavy door, she saw, to her surprise, the girl was already waiting on a bench, her books piled beside her, her head-scarf unwound, draped loosely around her shoulders, her peacoat unbuttoned, revealing a bright blue sweater beneath. Again, the girl's beauty struck her. The small face was a perfect oval, the black hair pulled back in plaits shone with cleanliness and care. She noted for the first time that her eyes were almond shaped. Were her skin not so pale and white, her eyes not so green, she could be mistaken for an oriental.

Poke rose as Grace approached. Without greeting, she spilled out her concern: "If I came home late from school, they might start looking for me. So I cut my last two classes. It took longer to get here than I thought."

Grace lifted her brow. "A good idea. I hope you won't get in trouble in school. I can drive you back. Let you off close to the school. Very good thinking, Poke."

"Yeah. If you're telling me the truth."

"I think you know I am. But let's not talk here. We can walk around the campus while we talk. Here, I'll help you carry those books." She bent to pick up a couple.

"No!" Poke jumped up and pulled her scarf up against her neck. "I'll carry them myself." Without buttoning her coat, she grabbed up the books and hugged them against her in a self-protective gesture.

To get her to open up would take patience, and Grace had no time for patience. Still, she was here, a good sign.

"All right. Then let me get that heavy door," she said as Poke headed toward it. She strode past the girl and pushed it open and held it for her and a pair of students that followed them through.

Capricious March, still a little more than a week off, sent a windy harbinger of itself on this suddenly graying afternoon. Grace's heavy fleece sweats shrugged it off, her wig beneath her wool cap insulated her head. Her disguise, so ridiculous and foreign to her when she'd donned it yesterday, seemed suddenly sensible. She jammed her hands in her pockets. Poke must be cold, yet she would not relinquish her shield of books so she could button her coat or scarf her head. Grace didn't press her. She let her choose the path and direction they'd follow around the campus.

After a few moments of the familiar, stolid forward walk with eyes downcast, Poke seemed to ease her body. She turned her head and said, "What did you want to talk about?"

"About how to help your father prove he's Jimmy's father."

Suddenly stopping and turning, Poke said, "But why? You're married to Mr. Broward. And he's the one that says he isn't. My mother would never have tried to prove Pop was wrong. No matter what he did."

Grace fixed the girl's eyes with her own. "Not even if he was doing something to hurt you?"

Poke's eyes grew wide, then wavered. "He wouldn't of." She started forward again.

"Of course not," said Grace, falling again into step with her. "Your father wouldn't deliberately hurt his children. Liz's father would. He'd do anything to prove he's right. To get what he wants."

Stopping and shaking her head, Poke looked at Grace with disbelief. She shook her head again, swallowed, and began to walk. The headshaking continued for several paces.

"I know it's hard to believe," said Grace at last. "I never believed it myself. I didn't think a father could do what he's doing to Liz. But now I know he can. He'll keep hurting her even though . . . even though she can't feel it now. And, even though she can't feel it, I can, and I have to stop it. Because I know now he's an evil man." She shuddered at hearing herself say it aloud.

Her companion shuddered with her. "Hester said that, also." A worried look crossed her face and she stopped.

"They must have followed Hester, too."

"Hester?"

"Never mind. She's a friend. They must've followed her, though. That's why she stopped visiting. She's smart. She'd've figured out they were following her."

"They would've followed her. They'd follow everyone for a while, at least. To see if they'd lead them to your father. If she's not visiting you anymore, she might've figured it out."

"Anyway, she said Mr. Broward was wicked."

"Poke," said Grace, "with your help, I can stop his wickedness from hurting your father and Jimmy anymore. Then Liz can be at peace, whatever else happens."

Poke shook her head. "She'll never know, though."

"Oh, yes," said Grace, fervently, "I'll reach through and tell her. I'm her mother. I can reach through her darkness even if no one else can."

With a deep inhalation Poke stared at her for a moment. Then she let out her breath and nodded. "Yes. I know what you mean. Momma reaches through to me sometimes. She sent Liz to Pop. She was her friend, not just her doctor."

"Yes, I know."

"Maybe Momma can reach through to her, too."

Grace grasped the girl's shoulders and said, "Oh, my dear Poke, I know she can. She's doing it now." She longed to draw Poke to her for a moment, to kiss her burning cheek, and so kiss Liz. Instead, she let go of her shoulders, and wiped the corner of her own eye.

The two began walking again, circling the perimeter of the parklike campus. Traffic buzzed by on nearby highway 309. The wind had dropped, the clouds had slipped away over the horizon. With a slackened, almost lazy pace, they moved closer together. What had begun as a confrontation had become a communion.

"Here's what we have to do, Poke," said Grace after a few moments of silence. "We can prove your father's paternity only one way. Through a DNA test. You know what that is?"

"Um-hmm. We learned about it in school. If Jimmy's DNA shows it could only come from Pop and Liz, then that would prove it."

"Something like that. Can you get me samples of Jimmy's blood, and your father's?"

"But how? I can't get in touch with Pop without getting him in trouble."

"But you must know where he might be. He surely would let you know somehow that he's all right."

The girl's eyes flashed suspiciously.

"I know you've got every reason to believe I'm here to trick you into telling me where he is. Well, I don't expect you to tell me. But I want you to try to get a message to him about this. Get him to send samples. He can send them directly to me. I don't even need to know where they came from. Mr. Broward trusts me. He'd never open anything addressed to me."

"That wouldn't work. I've never talked to him since he left."

"But you have to have talked to someone who knows where he is. How he is."

Poke kept silent.

"Of course you can't tell me. I don't want you to. Believe me. I'll just wait for a package to come."

"No. There's no way I can tell him what you want. Besides, he knows he can prove he's Jimmy's father. He just was scared to stay here anymore when he knew Mr. Broward was going to take Jimmy away. He knew he could take him, even if he could prove it. He'd find some way to get him from us."

"I see," said Grace. "Yes, he was right about that. Paul has the power to get whatever he wants. I can see why your father did what he did."

"Mrs. Broward," Poke burst out, "can he really still keep Jimmy, even if Pop proves he's Jimmy's father? How can he?"

Grace sighed deeply and shook her head. "If nobody gets in his way in time. The longer your father stays away, the easier it will be for Paul Broward to bring in a whole array of evidence against him, and show how incompetent a parent your father is—"

"No! That's a lie and you know it!"

"I know. That's not the point. Look, Poke, he's gone away and left his sixteen-year-old daughter alone. He took a little toddler in a van to go God knows where. How can you take care of a little boy in a van? You'd have to keep running and hiding. He'd have to be kept inside a moving vehicle for hours, maybe days at a time. How could the little boy play? How could he get a bath? What if he got sick? Don't you s—"

The girl let out a cry and began to run.

Grace ran after her. "Poke, I'm not saying your father did wrong. I'm showing you what Paul would make of it. And he would win. He will win, if we don't stop him."

Poke kept running, shaking her head and crying.

Grace easily caught up to the girl, whose scarf had come undone as she'd run, whose books kept slipping in her arms. "Please, Poke, stop a minute, listen to me."

A notebook spun out of Poke's arms and some papers tore loose and whipped away. Poke began to weep and sniffle as she tried to chase the papers. "No. Go away."

Grace chased down some wheeling pages and picked them up. She retrieved the notebook, picked it up, and firmly clipped the papers between the canvas covers. Then she grabbed the books that were sliding from Poke's grasp and set them firmly on the ground, with the notebook between them. She placed her foot on the top book and grasped Poke's shoulders, holding them fast, shaking them twice.

Poke's eyes and mouth widened. She swallowed.

"Listen to me, Poke, dear child. I can't bear to see your pain. It's like watching my own daughter's pain, as I've had to and not been able to help her. I can help her by helping you. And I know it will hurt you in the short run. But I've told you the truth. That's all. I think you can get your father to send those samples . . ."

Poke shook her head, bit her lip.

". . . and I trust you will get him to. You'll figure out some way to do it. Now, I won't say another word. It's getting late, and if I don't get you back to school within ten minutes, the lady in the brown Toyota will start looking for you." She let go of Poke's shoulders, grasped the trailing red scarf and draped it around the girl's head and neck, then removed her foot from the skewed stack of books. When Poke made no move to pick them up, she did so herself.

"Come on, dear," she said. And Poke followed her quietly back to the car.

Neither spoke again until they were halfway to the school. Then Poke said, "Jimmy got pneumonia. Daddy didn't neglect him. He took him to the hospital. He's better."

Grace's hands trembled on the steering wheel. "Oh, God."

"They must've done blood tests. It's in Squirrel Springs, West Virginia. He was there for a week. But he's been gone from there since last week."

Nodding slowly, she said, "They'd probably have a sample of Jimmy's blood, then."

Poke nodded and straightened herself from a slump. "But I can't get to Pop. I can't. That's the truth. I can't think of any way."

"Well, let's try to think of something." Grace smiled. She turned and looked at Poke, then took her right hand from the wheel and patted the girl's leg. She pulled the car over to the curb a half-block from the school. As Poke got out, she said, "I'll get in touch with you as soon as I can."

"I hope you can get Jimmy's blood."

"Nothing will stand in my way, dear. Take care."

Poke closed the door and turned. Then she turned back and pulled the door open again. "Nothing will stand in my way, either," she said. "I'll think of something. Oh, Mrs. Broward, you're so brave! As brave as Liz. As brave as Pop. And I'll be brave, too. I promise!"

Before Grace could answer, she slammed the door and started toward home. As Grace watched the child walk away in her even, determined stride, she said to herself, "We're winning, Liz! We're winning! I knew I could reach through to you. I'm your mother, and I'll bring you back."

CHAPTER
▪▪ TEN

THE NEXT WEEKEND

"Oh, Hester, I've missed you," said Poke. "There's so much to tell you."

The pleasure flush on the girl's face unnerved Hester. Though she'd read the newspaper every morning since coming home, nothing on Zack James or Jimmy Broward had appeared. She'd watched CNN until her eyes grew bleary—still nothing. At first she'd thought that the backwoods hospital might have tried to hide their horrendous medication error. Possible, but not likely. Not when the patient's father was a fugitive, something they'd be sure to uncover in the "accident's" wake. That would get the hospital off the hook and leave Zack firmly impaled.

No, something else had happened. She'd had to find out, had to visit Poke and see what she might know. For Zack would have gotten in touch with her through this Joyce person. He might have decided not to press charges on this hospital. Then they might have looked the other way and let him go. Then he would have to keep on running. He'd then tell no one, not even Joyce or Poke. But what had he told them to wipe the anguish from Poke's face?

Hester carried Lester in through the door Poke held open, and set him in his usual family room sofa corner.

"How's your father?" Poke asked, when he was settled.

"Oh, a little grumpy. He hates to travel."

"He looks it. Lester, did you miss me?"

Lester grunted.

Picking up on that, Hester said, "I bet that was it. He did cheer up a bit when I said we were coming to see you."

"He passed all the medical tests, I hope."

Hester's brow creased. Then she recalled her pretext for neglecting her visits. "Oh, yes. They went fine. They didn't take as long as I expected. A few days is all."

This brought the first look of worry to Poke's face. "But you've been gone a long time. Is it 'cause they were following you? The detectives?"

Hester had known from her first visit that she would be followed, and she had been, the first few times. But once her visits had become routine and open, the surveillance had ceased. It was clear to her that the detectives had not figured out her relationship to the Browards. They must have thought her and her father simply an odd pair of friends, maybe the only ones Poke had left; for anyone but freaks would avoid her. Hester knew about things like that. And no phone calls to and from Hester, no unexplained mail in her mailbox, could possibly tie her and her father to Zack, or Dr. Broward. No one had followed her to Squirrel Springs.

"Oh, them? They gave up on me a long time ago." She giggled.

Poke looked relieved.

"But what about your father, Poke? I've been thinking about him so much. And your brother."

"Oh, Hester, they're fine. After Jimmy was all better, Pop made the rest of the trip in less than a week. He's at the dig site already."

"You're sure?" asked Hester, trying to sound bright and pleased. "You're not mistaken?"

"Oh, no. Joyce let me know as soon as she heard from Pop two days ago."

"You might have misunderstood her. You said she talks in a kind of code."

Looking puzzled, Poke said, "You almost sound like you hope I'm wrong."

"Oh, no," Hester said, smiling brightly. "I'm so happy for you. But I don't want you to think anything because of wishful thinking. That's happened to me, and then I'd be so disappointed. And being talked to in code can be so confusing."

"I know that. OK, well I'll tell you exactly what she told me, and you'll see it's got to be true. Joyce called and said she was Pop's computer friend from Arizona. You know, they talk by computer on a network. She said she'd sent messages to Pop on the computer, but he'd never answered. You see, as long as Pop doesn't log on and pick up messages from his mailbox, there's no way they could be intercepted. They don't come over the telephone lines to our computer. Oh, boy, how I wish they could!" She walked over to the computer and touched it, as if she could reach her father that way. Then she sighed.

"It sure would be nice," Hester said, nodding sympathetically. "Joyce must be very smart to think of that. She knew no one could check her story about the messages she told you she'd left."

"Oh, she's smart. But she didn't figure it out herself. Pop explained it all when we figured out how we'd communicate. Also, I think when he calls her, he tells her ways to code the messages so I'll understand."

"So, what did your father's 'computer friend' say?" Hester giggled conspiratorily as she asked this. But she hoped the pretend message would tell *Hester* that Zack was covering the fact that Jimmy was dead.

"She said, 'I hope your father's OK.' Then when I said he was on a long trip, she said, 'Speaking of long trips, I have pictures of him and my little boy when he was on a trip to here three years ago. He was holding him on his shoulders. I'll try to remember to send them to you when I get home.' So, you see, Hester, there's no mistake. Not only are they there and OK, but Joyce has pictures of them."

"Hmmnn. I see. It sounds like that's what she meant. But you can't even see the pictures to be sure."

"But, Hester, Joyce wouldn't lie. She must have the pictures. I know Pop sometimes mails things to her. And she said, 'I have pictures.' That has to mean Joyce has them there. And I could tell by her voice how happy she was."

"Oh, Poke, I just wish you could see them. To be sure. Oh, I know how much you want it to be true. But it could mean something else."

"Don't you think I want to see those pictures? Not to prove it's true, but just to see them. I know it's true. I know it!"

Lester keened loudly at her cry.

"Oh, Daddy," said Hester, "don't worry. Of course Poke wants to see those pictures." She patted Lester on the head and kissed him. "He's such a tenderhearted person. Don't you just love him, Poke?"

She sniffed and nodded, as if more concerned with her own needs now.

"Daddy and I can get you the pictures."

"What! How?"

"It's easy. I'll get them from Joyce."

Poke shook her head shortly. "But I can't tell her to give them to you. She'll think you're spying on her."

"Sure you can tell her. Just write a note and tell her I'm a friend. Tell her to call you and say she's someone else and that she should give you some kind of code that I can't possibly know that you can answer yes or no to. If it's yes, it means I'm your friend, and she should give me the picture to take to you."

Poke's eyes flashed from somber brown to green with hope. Her mouth puckered thoughtfully a minute. Then her face fell. "What if they follow you?"

"The detectives? I'll make sure they aren't following me. Besides, why should they suddenly start again?"

After a moment's hesitation Poke said, "Because of Mrs. Broward."

"Mrs. Broward? What would she have to do with it?" Hester grew uneasy.

"A woman in a brown Toyota followed her. She warned me to watch out for her. And I saw her myself. And she drives around here a lot. She was out there just before you came."

"Yes, I know. I saw her. But when did you talk to Mrs. Broward? And why? She's an enemy."

Shaking her head fiercely, Poke said, "No! She's a friend. She's going to help prove that Pop's Jimmy's father. Before it's too late, and Mr. Broward can prove he's a bad father. Like he proved your father was bad and didn't deserve the money."

Lester began wailing disconsolately. Hester shushed him and cradled him and whispered to him, all in vain. He could not be silenced until she had him dressed and back into his seat in the van.

How angry Hester was at Poke! How stupid the child was to believe Mrs. Broward! It would hold everything up. If Jimmy still was alive, she'd already lost more than a week. And she'd lose more until she had a chance to get that picture to prove he was still alive. It could prove to Hester that it was taken before she'd loaded the syringe with insulin and his very own father had injected it into him. She'd be able to tell by the length of Zack's beard when the picture was taken. She had to see that picture as soon as possible.

"And you're not helping a bit, Daddy, behaving the way you just did. Now I'll have to go back again to get that note from Poke and to get her to tell me where this Joyce person lives."

As Lester began to cry again she stopped the van by the curb and reached over and fondled him. "Oh, Daddy, I'm sorry. I really am. You know how I hate to hurt you. If all this weren't so important, I wouldn't care about another week or so. But I can't just put you in this van and drag you across country for a week, if he really is dead already. That wouldn't be fair to you. And you've suffered enough."

After a few minutes of such comforting, Lester sniffled and sulked into silence. Hester sighed and began to drive

again. "Well, this will give us a chance to make sure no
brown Toyota's following us. It hasn't so far. If it doesn't
tomorrow, or any kind of car of any color at all, then we'll
know that Mrs. Broward hasn't learned anything about us.
So, let's just relax and think things out carefully, Daddy.
If we didn't get him with the insulin, we'll just have to get
him some other way. There must be a way."

And Lester began wailing, not in agony but in joy. He
was singing one of his favorite songs from his oldies but
goodies album. She giggled and joined him in song—
"There Must Be a Way" . . . And they sang it all the
way home.

The next day Poke, convinced that Hester was sincere and
that no one was tailing her, gave Hester Joyce's address.
She composed a note and sent it along with a token Joyce
would recognize as authentic—the page of the travel atlas
with the planned cross-country trip mapped out. After all,
if Hester had this, Joyce would reason, she'd already know
where Zack and Jimmy were. What more could Hester learn
from Joyce?

To make absolutely certain she wasn't being followed,
Hester made a few trips over three days to Joyce's
neighborhood, buying some groceries at a nearby supermarket, walking her father to a nearby park, reconnoitering
Joyce's house.

On the fourth day, at dusk, after parents heading home
from work had picked up their children from the nanny, she
parked in the driveway of the small, brick, one-story
house and said to her father, "It's all clear. We'll know by
tomorrow at the latest."

She left him waiting in the van and climbed the front
porch steps. The yellow porch light, which had moments
ago turned off, turned on again. A redheaded woman
opened the door. After a strange look and a long hesitation
she asked, "Yes, what can I do for you?" She looked
as if she'd prefer to close the inner door, but was too
polite.

"Mrs. Price, I have a note for you from Poke," Hester said without opening the storm door.

The woman's eyes opened wide. "I don't know what—"

"It's all right. I'm a friend of hers. The note explains."

"I don't know anyone named Poke." She started to close the inner door.

"Please," Hester said, pulling open the storm door wide enough to hand in the note. "Just take this and read it. I'll wait out here."

Joyce looked through the wedge opened in the inner door. Quickly she opened it wider, snatched the note, and closed and locked the door.

Hester closed the storm door and waited several minutes, imagining this tall, confident-looking woman pacing back and forth inside this warm-looking house, reaching for her telephone then withdrawing her hand, reading the note, studying the itinerary page, rereading the note and the page.

At last the house door opened and Joyce said, "Come back tomorrow night." She shut the door quickly, then turned off the porch light. Hester tramped down the porch stairs in the dark and drove her father home. Another day passed, again delaying her plan to poison Jimmy's blood. But there was no hurry now. If he was still alive, she knew who and where he was. Doing away with him was just a matter of time.

"It might even be an adventure, Daddy," she told Lester as she prepared him for bed. "You and I have never been to Arizona. I bet it's beautiful there. We'll take our time along the way. I'll find interesting things to do. We'll stop at motels so we don't have to sleep in the van. Won't it be grand to see this beautiful country, the land of the free and the home of the brave?"

Lester started moaning loud and waving his flipper toward his face. He wasn't unhappy at all; he was singing "The Star-Spangled Banner."

Father and daughter returned the next evening to Joyce Price's house. The woman, still reserved as she opened the door, said nothing, but handed Hester an envelope. Hester thanked her, then clomped heavily down the porch stairs as the yellow light blinked off. In the van, with the dome light turned on, she opened the envelope.

She gasped. "Oh, Daddy! It's true. I don't know what went wrong, but Jimmy's still alive. We can't let him still be alive. We'll have to go to Arizona. But this time, Daddy, we'll do it right. They're going to be there a long, long time. That nasty, wicked Mr. Broward won't ever stop looking for them."

And once more Lester began to sing "The Star-Spangled Banner."

They took the pictures to Poke the next day and joined her at dinner in a celebration of her father's and brother's safe arrival at the Roosevelt Lake archaeological site. She talked incessantly about her plans to join them next fall. She'd taken her SAT exams in her high school junior year and had excelled. Her grades were just short of all A's in the honors program. She'd applied for entrance to Arizona State University, the school that helped sponsor the Roosevelt Lake digs. On her application she'd included an essay on her interests in Southwestern archaeology, her roots in the Tonto Basin and the San Carlos Apache tribe. She expected an acceptance any day now; she was so sure she'd be accepted she hadn't applied to any other school. Her father had thought that a mistake. "But I know I'll get in! I know I'll see him in August!"

"Oh, Poke, I know it, too," Hester said.

"Maybe even before. If Mrs. Broward gets the blood."

Hester narrowed her eyes. "I don't trust that Broward woman. And what blood does she have to get?"

Poke told her the fantastic story of her meeting with Liz Broward's mother.

Hester laughed at the end of that. "Well, let the old lady go on her wild-goose chase. Probably her husband will catch her—if he's not in on it in the first place, trying to get you to tell him where your father is—and that will end that. And good for them. They don't deserve a grandson!"

"Don't you want her to prove that Pop's Jimmy's father?"
Poke looked angry.

"You know he can prove it himself. And, besides, it was
stupid of you to meet her. I've been thinking about that,
Poke. Did you tell her about me, too?"

The girl's face reddened and fell. Her mouth opened and
closed.

Lester let out a wail.

"Shush, Daddy! You did tell her about me, you little
fool!"

"No . . . I . . . I just said you were my friend that didn't
come to visit anymore."

Hester stood up from the table. She shook her fists at
the trembling girl. "I shouldn't of come at all. How dumb
you turned out to be." She turned to her father, who'd been
propped up and tied into a heavy oak armchair to eat. "I'm
taking you home now, Daddy. Before this stupid baby tells
more about us, and they start following us again."

"But I never . . ." Poke stood up, but fell weakly back
into her chair.

Hester shook her finger at her. "Shut up, stupid baby! I
don't want them following us the rest of our life. But if
they do, if they come up to me and ask where your father
is, I'll tell them exactly where he went. I hope they don't,
because I don't think those wicked people deserve to have a
pretty little baby like Jimmy. But Daddy and I have already
suffered enough."

With that, she unstrapped her father from his chair and
carried him outside and to his wheelchair, as he railed in
his own way at Poke. When she had him in the van, she
said, "You see how many people have to suffer for what
that awful man did to us, Daddy. Poor Poke. Oh, well,
it was dumb of her to take such an awful risk with the
Broward woman. But what's done is done, isn't it? And
it looks like nothing bad's going to happen to us."

Lester responded with a squeak of agreement.

Then Hester giggled. "And wait till Mrs. Broward gets to
the hospital and finds out that no one by the name of Jimmy

Broward was ever there. A wild-goose chase, that's all it'll be. And while she's on it, we'll be on our way across the country. We've got plenty of time to get there. Come on, Daddy, let's sing!"

CHAPTER
▪▪ ELEVEN

ROOSEVELT LAKE

On the first Sunday in March, Shea Passamore woke up at five-thirty A.M. as usual. As usual, she looked out the lakeside window of the double-wide trailer that was lab, office, and home-on-site at the dig. Until last week she'd wakened to a mockingbird's screech or a coyote's howl. Except for the rare occasions when Marla Engels, her university faculty liaison, had stayed overnight with her in the fenced-off dig site, no human beings had shared her space between six each afternoon and eight the next morning.

She'd wanted it that way. Without Doug, her husband, whose post here she'd inherited a year ago when he'd died from a burst brain aneurism, she'd craved no companion. Extraneous voices irritated her like her field intercom's static; they drowned out the only voices she wanted to hear—her inner ones. She needed no one but herself and the man who, try as she would, she couldn't resurrect from his grave, and their neverborn child who'd ruptured her ovaries—assuring she'd never bear another. Those she'd needed and loved she couldn't have, so she wanted no one. Until one day last week.

On that day last week, sleet and snow turned the dig site and its three-mile dirt road access to gritty swamps, the nearest paved road to ice. As always when the weather made passage hazardous, she gave her team the day off, to make up for the many seven-day weeks they put in when weather allowed. They knew—and crew manager Bill Jennings never stopped reminding her —that paying archaeology jobs were rare, and university and government grants hard to come by in these austere times. Dedicated professionals all, they, including Bill, deserved what few breaks she could give them. As chief contractor for this excavation of an intriguing Salado ruin, she made most of the money. As boss, she'd get the credit for breakthroughs that led to solving the mystery: Where did they go, these prehistoric Indians who seemed to have disappeared in the wind, like so much desert sand in a whirling dust devil?

Her crew and she knew she wanted more than simple credit. From the tedious scraping away of earth to reveal buried homes, temples, and ball courts; from painstaking cataloging of tiny bits of bone, shell, potsherds, and obsidian points—all artifacts of several centuries past— she was piecing together her next few decades, her working future. Though genetic immortality shimmered forever beyond reach, she might, through persistent digging into the past, achieve some personal perpetuity. She expected she'd have to do most of that alone. Even—*especially*— on cold, late February days, when sleet clicked against the foggy pane above her tiny, neat desk.

Against the nearby foothills barely seen through her window, a light flashed, catching her eye. She looked up from her log for a moment, then shrugged. Maybe she'd seen a silver reflection from her pen, or a glint of her outside lamp, captured by pelting sleet. She'd heard thunder earlier; the mountains surrounding the Tonto Basin might still harbor lightning in the clouds that obscured them.

With a glance at her own reflection in the pane, she pushed a long, fine strand of blond hair from before her lime green eyes, which she turned again to her notes. She was lost in the work a few minutes later, when the light flashed again closer by. This time she rose and wiped the condensation from the window and pressed her forehead against it, parenthesizing her eyes with cupped hands to block reflections. Her own breath steamed the window, but not before an approaching vehicle's outlines bounced into view.

The vehicle stopped just outside the locked yard gate. She waited a few seconds, expecting the gate to open and let in a van or pickup she could spot as a colleague's. A man debarked and stood between the headlights and the heavy wrought-iron gate, and tried to open it. After a few moments of pacing back and forth, he returned to his vehicle. She presumed he would drive away, but several minutes later, he came out of the van. At first he appeared to be alone, carrying a parcel over one shoulder. Then as he approached the six-foot-tall gate again, the parcel took on life.

Shea gasped and backed away from the window. A *child!*

Perching the child on his shoulder, one-handedly grasping its ankles, the man climbed the gate, gaining toeholds on four broad hinges. *He must be out of his mind!* To drive out here with a child on such a day was itself insane. Tonto Creek, which bisected the dirt road, would have swollen and made passage harder than ever, even for a high clearance off-road vehicle. To climb a gate taller than himself in such cold slippery weather, and with a small child balanced on a squall jacketed shoulder was . . . was . . .

She ejaculated an explosive breath, incredulous. Grabbing her squall jacket from its hook by the trailer door, she tossed it on over her green plaid shirt. She secured it at the neck and tugged on the hood while dashing across the muddy yard. She still wore the thin-soled terrycloth slippers she'd donned that morning, intending to remain inside all day. Jacket and hood askew, she ran the ten yards to the fence, losing one slipper to the cold muck, jettisoned its mate as a worthless encumbrance.

The man had thrown one leg over the gate and was searching for a hinge pin with his boot toe. The child, in precarious tilt on the shoulder, seemed unperturbed.

Shea got to the gate just as the man lost his foothold on the hinge pin and dropped. With acrobatic grace, he landed on both feet without losing his grip on the child. Then he turned and stared at Shea.

"What in God's name are you doing here? And who the hell are you?" she cried. She'd sunk to her ankles in muck; but sheer astonishment would have riveted her there, anyway. The sleet had become a soaking rain that ran in rivulets along the stranger's uncovered long hair onto his shoulders, down his short heavy beard and his jacket front.

He took the snugly snowsuited and booted boy down from his shoulder and stood him on the ground between his legs. "Jimmy got tired hearing me talk about Great-Gramps and where he came from. He hates being stuck in the van all day when we're not on the road, so it was easier just coming straight here, weather or no. I've been in lots worse in that Ram." He gestured with his head to the van.

"Great-Gramps?"

"Yeah, my great-grandfather worked on The Apache Trail when the dam was built."

"Oh."

"I knew about this dig. I keep up on things like that. I want Jimmy to get to know his roots."

Shea loosened her feet from the mud and looked down at them. "His roots. Here?"

"Well, sort of. Great-Gran was an Apache. She set out to find what killed Great-Gramps, and she disappeared, too. When the Basin was flooded. No one knows what happened to them."

Shea was nonplussed. Rainwater trickled down her nose and into her open mouth.

"You're getting soaked," he said. "I didn't expect you to come out and meet me."

"Didn't expect! I didn't expect to see you—anyone—climb that gate. It's there to keep vandals and pot hunters out. And even they aren't likely to break in on a day like this."

"I'm not a vandal or a pot hunter. I'm an amateur archaeologist." He smiled. "Looking for folks. The van's beginning to feel old after a month on the road. Can Jimmy and
I come in?"

She laughed and shook her head. "I can't believe this.
Oh, God. All right. Come into the trailer. But for God's
sake don't let him near any of the specimens. There's so
much for him to get into."

"Right," he said and picked the boy up. He followed
her to the thirty-eight-foot double-wide trailer. It stood lit
up and steaming in the bleak and rocky expanse bordering
this side of the lake, which looked foreboding and black in
such nasty weather.

How inviting her temporary home and office must have
looked from the road! He'd have seen her looking out at
him from its heated interior, known she was waiting for him
to go away. A curious vacationer foolhardy enough to drive
here in this weather would have turned and left. Someone
with ill intentions would know she was a phone call and
helicopter ride away from police help; would guess that she
had a shotgun at hand and knew how to use it. Good guess.
She'd bought it for hunting, not self-defense. And she still
would rather use it against a trespassing mountain cat than
a human intruder. But she wouldn't hesitate to wound—or
kill—an armed trespasser.

But this man had caught her so far off-guard that she
hadn't thought of her gun. Now, it flashed through her
mind, standing in its niche between her desk and filing
cabinet, unloaded, but with deer shot cartridges handy.
This man would know how to use it and had the strength
to overpower her. But, instinctively, she knew he'd meant
what he'd said. He'd come to explore his roots with his son.
Though what had driven him here now, in these conditions,
puzzled and intrigued her.

As they tracked through the sloppy yard, she—her bare
feet alternately clinging and slipping through puddling soil,
he in booted, deliberately shortened strides—she felt him
stop and stoop, then straighten twice. When they arrived

at the trailer, whose door she'd left ajar in her haste, the vinyl entry tiles gleamed slippery and wet.

She entered in gingerly steps, while he stopped outside and removed a boot at a time before coming in.

"Oh, forget that," she said, turning to him. "Mud and dust are facts of life in this business. It'll dry quick enough, and I'll sweep it out. Just set your boy down inside, for God's sake. You don't want him to catch pneumonia."

"Sure don't," he said, knitting his brow as he stood the boy where she'd pointed, and held out her mud-logged slippers. "What about these?"

"Oh, Jesus! You didn't have to pick those up."

He shrugged and grinned. "You didn't have to let me come in. I appreciate it." He continued to hold out the slippers, which resembled a pair of dead catfish.

"I never expected to. I never expected to run out in those, either. Well, toss them in the boot box by the door. And close the door, please, before the whole place floods."

He complied, then stood dripping there, while the boy stood complaisant where set.

Ignoring her own discomfort, which the return to her warm abode intensified, Shea went to the youngster and removed his snow jacket. He let her peel it off, then sat at her command so she could pull off his boots and strip off the pants. What a beautiful child he was, with eyes the color and shape of green olives and soft, light-brown hair! His face glowed red from the cold, and his nose ran slightly. She wiped it with a tissue from her jacket pocket. Then she looked up at his father and said, "He's so unafraid of me, a stranger. That's not always good."

"Right," he said, grinning at her as he took off his jacket and hung it on one of three door hooks.

She stood and nodded and grinned. "Right!"

"Children and dogs know when to be suspicious. Especially when their dad's in the room."

"Ummhm. Children and dogs. And anthropologists. We have a sixth sense." She took off her jacket, hung it next to his, then looked at her feet. "Yuck." Her tiny kitchen was on the wall facing her office, just a few steps away. To keep from dragging the dirt farther into the trailer, she tiptoed across the vinyl tile floor and ducked to retrieve a pail from beneath the sink. She filled it with warm water and tiptoed to her desk. She set the pail on the floor, sat, and slipped her long narrow feet into the soothing water. Sighing with relief, she washed away stinging frostbite and sandy mud. Looking up at him, she continued, "Not that we know enough to stay in out of the rain on a day like this."

When she was clean and dry, she put some pots and pans on the floor by the sink for Jimmy to play with. She turned to his father. "Why now? It doesn't make sense," she said.

He caught her meaning. "Couldn't before. Now I had to." He'd washed at the sink and dried his hair, and now sat on the chair she'd unfolded. His heavy wet jeans clung to his thighs and calves, revealing their thickness as muscle. He wore a flannel plaid shirt beneath a camouflage hunting vest with bulging pockets.

At her question, his eyes flashed from green to brown. *An emotional reflex? Or a physical reaction—a glimmer of reflected color picked up in a movement of his head? Fascinating!*

"Something happened?" she asked.

"Right." He nodded and averted his eyes.

"Your jumping my fence gives me the right to probe, you know," she said, after considering that right a moment.

He stood and went to Jimmy. Bending down and gently touching the toddler's head with his large broad hand, he said, his voice barely cracking, "This kid happened."

Jimmy looked up. "Daddy pay dums." He banged on the pan with a plastic spoon.

The man picked up a spoon and banged the pan. "Bam, bam, goes the drum."

"Bam bam dum," said the boy, and laughed. "Zimmy dance." He bounced up, seeming fully alive for the first time since coming inside. "Patsey dance." He bounded in small circles and burbled against his hand.

The man stomped with him, patting his open mouth with his palm as he sang, in an obvious—though poor—imitation of an Amerindian call and dance.

Jimmy soon tired of this, and, Shea feared, would be ready to get into trouble. She wondered what else she could give him to entertain him. She needn't have, for his father pulled out of one vest pocket a handful of oversize crayons. "You have any paper bags, or something? I left mine in the van."

"I happen to," she said. "Wait a minute." She went through a curtained partition to her lab, and fetched one from the supply she kept for uncataloged specimens.

He tore it along a crease, then spread it on the floor near his son. "Draw Daddy a picture," he said, giving Jimmy the crayons.

Jimmy began scribbling. He gave his first drawing to Shea.

Warmed by this signal of friendship, she said, "That's beautiful, Jimmy. Make me another."

He repeated the exercise several times. Then, apparently having enough of it, went up to his father, climbed up on his lap, and poked and pulled at his vest pockets. "Tanny."

"Nope, it's too close to supper. I'll give you candy afterward."

Shea'd forgotten about eating, though she'd skipped lunch today. She jumped up. "Supper, of course. I'm stocked to the gills. As long as it can go in the microwave, I have it."

"Something hot'd feel good."

"Does he need something special?"

He shook his head. "Anything he can pick up with his fingers."

"That leaves out soup, I guess."

"No. He's got pretty sticky fingers." He grinned and rubbed the boy's hair. "Don't you, Jimmy?"

Jimmy nodded, and continued to pull at his dad's pockets.

Laughing, Shea rooted through the freezer, and picked out a package of mixed vegetables, some chicken breasts, and strawberries. Looking at the man's compact, muscular frame, she decided the Sara Lee brownies had languished long enough. She set them on the sink board, which served as preparation counter, and went about cooking the food. As she did so, she became more and more aware that her offerings must seem paltry to a man built like her visitor, so she cooked up some high calorie foods and garnishes. She set the chicken to simmering on the range top in orange and pineapple juices, heavy with chunks of fruit. She baked her last fresh yam. She set out thick bleu cheese dressing for the salad.

Soon the air swelled luxuriantly with cooking aromas. She was lost in a homey routine she'd almost forgotten. For a year now, she'd cooked (the word was an exaggeration) only for herself, eaten more out of habit than hunger. Lack of company was a blessing. Especially company such as a man and a boy who might waken a pang of grief.

Suddenly, as she sat at the table across from the man with the boy on his lap, that pang overpowered her. Jimmy was about the age her boy would be now. Yes, perverse though it seemed, she'd wanted to know the sex of the child that, conceived ectopically, had burst her ovaries. They had told her, and she'd been distraught at losing her husband's only chance at a son. She blamed herself for it, had not yet forgiven herself.

And this man with the boy on his lap for an instant reminded her of Doug. His long, black hair, his short new beard, his eyes, at least when they were brown, his quiet strength, his gentleness with the boy. She'd seen these things even as he'd landed and turned from the gate. Add a Texas twang to his baritone and—

Shaken a moment, she turned her eyes to her food. He was not Doug. His name was . . . "What is it?"

He looked puzzled.

"Your name."

"Zack."

She nodded. "I'm Shea."

That was as far as they got during the meal, hardly a restful affair. She couldn't imagine thinking the bobbing and weaving entailed in eating with a toddler as being fun. Yet she found herself laughing and enjoying it. Cleaning up afterward was the worst part. The smeared chocolate from brownies made her regret her choice of dessert. But Jimmy's grungy smiles, then his whines and yawns as he rubbed a mixture of food into his eyes with his fists, tenderized her feelings to the point that she took the messy kid in her lap and kissed his sticky hair above the ear.

He responded by kicking himself free and wriggling to the floor. A spate of noisy laughing and banging his pans, whirling like a dervish, then collapsing in a heap followed his escape. When she tried to pick him up so she could wipe his face with a wet washcloth, he shook his head vigorously, stuck his thumb in his mouth, and turned away from her.

"Don't take it personally," Zack said as he calmly finished eating his second brownie. "He's bushed. He's had a long day."

"Why should I take it personally?" she said, the desultory washcloth drooping from her hand. She did.

"I did at first. Before I got to know him. I used to always think he was mad at me when he did stuff like that."

Shea again sat across from him. Picking apart a brownie, she ate small pieces and watched him. His eyes had grown distant, unfocused. On the floor a few feet away, the little boy was fighting sleep.

Shortly, his eyes closed, though he sucked his thumb on and off for a while.

"He should be in bed," she said. "That floor's hard."

"He'll be OK for awhile. I'll take him back to the van soon. OK if I have more coffee before I go?"

"Sure." She got the thermal carafe and poured him the last of it. "I can make more."

"No, thanks. This is fine."

Disappointed, she nodded and sat again. "Zack, I can't help wondering what you meant when you said you had to get to know Jimmy."

He tried to stretch out his legs beneath the table, but didn't have enough room, so he pulled them back and swiveled them to the side. "He was mostly raised by his mother. And even when I had him when she was sick, Poke mostly took care of him. Poke's my daughter."

"And his mother . . . now?"

"She died about a month ago."

Drawing a breath, Shea said, "Oh. Oh, I see. I'm sorry."

"Right," he said, then he drained his cup. "Well, I better take Jimmy to the van. His crib's there. But maybe you can open the gate and I can bring it in and hook in to your power and water for tonight. It'll be a lot nicer than having the generator run all night long."

She pointed to the key on the hook above her desk. "I'll watch Jimmy while you get it hooked up."

While he was gone, she wet a towel with warm water, tiptoed over to the boy, and gently sponged the crumbs from his face. He stirred a bit and sucked louder, but didn't waken, even when she reached up under his chin and around his neck creases. When he was as clean as she could get him, she left him a moment and retrieved from the foot of her cot the beige and blue afghan she'd begun to knit when she was pregnant. Its center square was solid blue, and the wide trim she'd added after her loss was beige. She'd wanted to keep the blue loss at the center, but enclose it, encapsulate it within the wide border that she would periodically add to, to symbolize the ongoing reach of her life. Before Doug had died, it had grown to its present size: smaller than a full-size blanket, but larger than the crib blanket she'd set out to create.

Now she rubbed the thick, spongy wool against her cheek and smelled on it the light scent of apple it had picked up from the soap and shampoo she used. She carried it, still pressed against her, to the little boy on the floor, then swaddled him in it before lifting him onto her shoulder.

When his father returned and took him from her, she sensed he was aware of the tug she felt in her belly at the moment of letting him go. She did not, in fact, let him go altogether. The apple scent she'd wrapped him in remained in her nostrils and clung to her body, as if it were not hers in the first place but his all along.

She took it to bed with her.

Zack found the San Carlos Apache healer, Peter Chavez, where Shea had told him he would be, in his prefabricated house at the base of a mountain in the high desert peopled by his tribe. Shea said she had met him two years ago at a seminar held in the Heard Museum in Phoenix, where she, a physical anthropologist, had attended to learn more about the similarities between Native American and traditional Western medicine. She had seen a confluence between them, she said, especially in psychiatry, and the use of herbal medicines.

"Peter's such an open man," she'd said. "Not all Indians are. They're not happy about folks like me with our digging. Especially when we start dissecting their ancestors' skeletons in the name of science. *Mea culpa,*" she'd added. "I did it for the university. That's what a physical anthropologist is supposed to do."

Zack understood her ambivalence. He had just enough Indian in him to resent the arrogance of those ethnocentric anthropologists who measured the worth of other cultures only against their own, and found their values curious or quaint. Yet, as an amateur genealogist with mostly Caucasian blood, he honored scientific research into the past. It helped you ground yourself, find your way to the future.

His van was one of many on the macadam roads entering the reservation; one of the few obeying fifty-five-mile-per-hour speed limits. Despite what Shea had said about Apache reserve, white men coming here to hunt or fish, to shop in the reservation store for baskets, clothing or other authentic artifacts were welcome. If he'd come on a Sunday in spring or summer, he'd have been treated to a Sunrise Ceremony, marking a woman's entry into adulthood. Poke would like that. Or Liz.

Liz! Oh, Liz!

His vision blurred a moment and he pulled to the side of the road, afraid if he drove on, he'd miss the landmarks Peter Chavez had mentioned.

It is better to trust in the Lord than to put confidence in MAN said a roadside fence sign. The Church of Calvary, welcoming him, he thought, as he saw the cross-topped building down the road. "Sorry," he said, wiping his eyes with the back of his hand. "The Lord done let me down."

"Et me down," mimicked Jimmy.

"You too, fella," said Zack. He pulled off the shoulder and continued toward San Carlos Road, the reservation's main street, with its edifices dedicated to both God and man: The Church of the Nazerene, a jail and courthouse, The Bureau of Indian Affairs Building, The San Carlos Cafe. In a dirt lot adjacent to the hospital, a woman sold greasy burritos from a picnic cooler, a man sold peridot necklaces from his pickup tailgate. A sign by the lot proclaimed, *Swap Meet Every Saturday*. Obviously these enterprising merchants knew hungry people looking for authentic bargains could come by here any day.

"This would be about where we turn, Jimmy," said Zack, as they passed the schoolyard on his right, across from the low-slung hospital building. He turned right onto an unpaved road. In the distance he saw a water tank inscribed: SAN CARLOS APACHE TRIBE UTILITY AUTHORITY. He followed the rough road past tufa stone buildings and houses, past two cholla cactus patches to another dirt road, and turned left. Prefabricated post–World War II houses were set in clearings beside the unnamed street where Peter Chavez lived in the fifth house on the right.

Peter came to his door as Zack pulled his bright blue Ram up behind the pickup parked in front of the house. When Zack carried Jimmy across the herb-planted front yard, the healer opened his screen door and greeted them warmly.

Zack jerked his brow on seeing that the fifty-five-year-old Chavez was clothed in jeans and a heavy plaid shirt, much like his own. He wore his hair, which was long, thick, and black with steel-gray strands running through it, pulled back in a heavy ponytail, much as Zack did. A headband paid tribute to his Apache background. The high cheekbones of his broad, ruddy face and the ivory-set deep dark irises left no doubt about his roots. There would be no flash of green in his eyes, no heavy beard on his face to signal a mix had taken place three generations before. Peter was pure-blooded Apache. Only his higher education outside the reservation set him apart from those who had never left it.

"Come in, Zack," he said, as he offered a strong, squat hand. He drew Zack inside. "Lucy will feed us, then take the boy off our hands, so you and I can talk."

Lucy, a slim, attractive woman wearing jeans and a multicolor hand-knit sweater, fed them their midday meal, a stew of lean meat, acorns, and a mix of familiar and unfamiliar vegetables. It reminded Zack of Poke's stews, except for the lack of thickening, and was surprisingly un-Indian to his mind, as it wasn't accompanied by cornbread or frybread.

The hands that prepared and served this tasty meal clearly did other things. Broad, with long, thick-knuckled fingers, they bore scars, healed nicks and earth-colored abrasions. When Lucy rolled up her sleeves to wash dishes, he saw muscular, sinewy arms. Her sweater tightened and rippled at the shoulders as she lifted Jimmy, borrowed high chair and all, and set him near the counter by the sinkboard. There she set a small pan of cool water so he could wash plastic dishes while she washed the brown and orange stoneware plates. "We're prepared for visits from grandchildren," she explained with a twinkle in her nearly black eyes. "While you talk, I'll take him to visit our daughter and her children down the road."

"Hey, Jimmy," said Zack. "How 'bout that. Some friends to play with. Like at Joyce's house."

Jimmy said, "Doyce," and clattered the dishes in the pan as he kicked the rustic wood cabinets beneath the counter. "See Doyce."

Zack realized suddenly that the boy had had no one to play with since he'd left the hospital, with its twice-a-day play hours.

"We'll see Anna and her twins," said Lucy. "They're just your age and have lots of toys. And a big yard to play in, with statues in it." She finished her dishes, and helped Jimmy dry his, then lifted him down. "Does he use the potty?" she asked Zack.

"He can. But lately . . . well, on the road it's hard, so I just use disposable diapers. They're in the van." He started to the door, feeling he was doing something wrong.

Peter, following him and holding open the door, said, "There are times to accommodate, Zack. Your ways have their place and time. Even here, for the short time you'll be here."

"An open man," Shea had said.

Zack nodded, and swallowed the knot in his throat.

When he returned with Jimmy's restocked diaper bag, Lucy proudly announced about the waist-down naked boy, "We did it, Daddy. We used the potty." Then she took the bag and chased him with a clean diaper as he giggled and dodged her till she captured him. At last she had him dressed for outdoors and the crisp late-February afternoon. The speed of his joyful going left Zack breathless.

"Well," Peter said, "let's go back to my study, where we can talk."

"Right," said Zack, as he followed him through the house to a small room furnished with Mexican leather and wood chairs and carved wood tables. In niches along the walls stood colorful pottery and alabaster sculptures of Indian male heads, whole figures, women and children. Big heavy pieces they were, but fluidly carved, the brown grain working as part of the image.

"Lucy did those."

Zack, a skilled graphic artist, was drawn to one head, a stunning life-size old man's face, the facial wrinkles so finely carved they might have been formed from parchment.

Five different textures delineated hair from skin, hair deco-
rations from both, smooth eye surfaces from facial lines. He
could not keep his hand from running over it. Then, fingers
singed by a memory, he jerked his hand back. *Stone cold
dead! Yet this stone feels alive.* He looked up at Peter.

Peter nodded slowly. "That is the one you need."

Zack shook his head shortly. "Oh, no, it's just . . ."

"Come sit down, Zack. Tell me why you need that one."
He motioned him to a chair, and sat in the one across from
him. "You can see it from here." He nodded toward the
head as Zack sat.

So compelling was the pull of the work, that he might
not have been able to escape it, even with his back turned
toward it. It suffused him, like sexual desire. No . . . like
desire at the moment of fulfillment.

Both men sat silent for a while, one able to speak but
knowing the wisdom of silence, the other momentarily
spent by emotions he dare not mention. At last Zack said,
"Liz . . ." then dropped his head into his spread hands.

Peter sat silent while he wept. Several minutes passed.

Then Zack told Peter everything about what had brought
him here with Jimmy.

"You seek your ancestors. But you need a safe place from
which to search, Zack."

"There's no safe place, Peter. Not with that man after
me."

"Everyone has a safe place. You've heard of the happy
hunting grounds?"

"The Indian idea of heaven. Yes."

Peter nodded, then shook his head. "It doesn't equate
with heaven exactly. It's a belief that we have a safe place
to be in. But we aren't rewarded by being sent there.
We're there already. It's simply part of the familiar, with
all powers still intact. So we've nothing to fear."

"I'm in a safe place for the moment. Paul Broward won't
find me here."

"For the moment, maybe. But this place is not your safe
place. That's something you have to find for yourself.

I can't give it to you, I can only tell you—from what you've told me—that that's what you're looking for, and that's what you must find before you can find your Indian ancestors."

Riddles! Zack didn't need riddles, he needed answers. He stood and turned away from Peter and from the tug of the sculpture.

Peter laughed. "You've also got white man ways that stand between you and your ancestors."

He turned to face Peter, who had risen. "No way, Peter. The only thing that stands between me and my ancestors is information. And I use my white man ways to find the information."

The healer spread his hands and smiled. "Yes, to find information about your white ancestors. But you need to use Apache ways to find your Apache ancestors."

"That's why I came to you, Peter. Shea said you were open. Not secretive like so many Indians. And you start telling me about finding my safe place, and that this isn't it. Wait. You're saying that before I try to find more about my grandmother's parents, I have to go back and face Paul Broward, is that it? Turn myself in?"

Peter shook his head slowly. "No. That sounds like a white man way to me. I didn't tell you what you *should* do. I told you what you told me you *needed* to do. That's all an Apache healer can tell you. And, if you're willing to listen to your own thoughts coming back through my lips, then I may be able to help you."

"Hey! What makes you think I came here because you're a healer? Shea told you why I came—to find my roots. For Jimmy, too. I was going to come before all this happened, with Liz. Even before, with Maryellen. Waiting to have enough time and money. Never did. Never had the chance. Now I had to go somewhere, a safe place, like you say, so I made it here. Fine. It's as safe a place as I can find right now—either here or on the dig site. But I'm not sick and I don't need a healer. I need someone with a way to get me answers. To find where my great-grandmother disappeared to when she was looking for my great-grandfather."

Peter nodded. "Shea told me what you told her, yes."
He sighed. "Well, here we are speaking the same language
and hearing different things, then. Whatever you say, I
listen as a healer. Healers can be wrong. But not out of
stubbornness." He grinned.

"You think I'm being stubborn."

"Maybe, in some ways. But that's for you to decide."
More riddles!

"But stubbornness met by stubbornness helps no one. I'll
give way to yours"—he held up his hand to stay Zack's
retort, and continued—"You may find your safe place only
after finding your roots. Maybe I didn't listen hard enough
before." He walked over to Zack and grasped him by the
shoulder. "I'll do what I can to help." Then he glanced at
the alabaster head in its wall niche. "Meanwhile, you need
him, so you must have him."

Zack drew a breath as he turned to look at the sculpture.
It hadn't lost its magnetic pull on him. He pressed the hand
on his shoulder, then shrugged to free himself, so he could
go to the piece, touch it again. He ran his fingers along the
surface, feeling the different textures, channels gouged into
the face as if worn there by tears from a million sadnesses,
thin lines suggesting filaments of hair, roughened spots like
sueded hide forming the headdress. Alive, as stone should
never be.

He lifted it, felt its satisfying heft. Yes, he needed it. It
had been made for him. And, yet—He turned and looked
at Peter. "Why are you giving it to me?"

"I'm not," he said, "It's not mine to give." Then he
chanted something in Apache. "Stone, this is a man; man,
this is a stone. Take what you need and get rid of the rest,"
he translated.

Another riddle. Yet Zack wasn't bothered. He figured
he'd know the answer to all of them in good time.

The earth in the Basin had resumed its sandy color and
texture two days after Zack had left with Jimmy for the

San Carlos Reservation. Having referred him to Peter, Shea immediately wished she'd said nothing. If he'd headed off to the reservation on his own, he'd have returned that night put off and discouraged; his attempts to break through the centuries-old distrust between Indians and whites would certainly fail. The man's strength and vulnerability, enhanced by his almost holy assumption of motherhood, had won her immediate trust. But they shared a common culture; not so he and the Apache. His blood contained seven drops like hers for every one like theirs. The women he'd loved, from all he'd told her during his first full day here, were the kind of women she was: independent, medically oriented, and humanistic. And they were wise and good mothers, as she'd trusted herself to become when starting out on that course.

When he'd come over the gate with the boy on his shoulder, she'd had, for an instant, a vision: Doug had come back with their son. In the afternoon and evening that had followed, she'd forgotten the sudden flash. No mystic, she dismissed it as a long denied grief pang, a sign that she at last knew they *would not* come back *ever again.*

More important, she knew now how empty she'd been, and that the emptiness couldn't be filled, as she'd thought, by her work. She'd been running away. Like Zack. From grief. And they'd both been seeking refuge in the same place: in the past, in their roots. The only difference was in the distance each chose to run from the present. He looked to a recent past to rescue him from the meaninglessness implied by loved ones' deaths; she would go back millennia to find an eternal past intimating immortality.

Through Peter he might find his way to his past all too soon, all too close by. Peter would welcome him, teach him Apache ways, win him over from Shea.

The thought, coming on top of her referral to the healer, left her stunned. She knew Peter would put Zack up as long as he needed to be put up, and she wanted to put him up here, near her. She wanted to heal him while healing herself.

When Zack and Jimmy did not return by late afternoon of the second day, she'd said to herself, "Easy come, easy go." It had been a bad idea in the first place, having a child at the dig site, near a lake in a desert valley frequented by rattlesnakes and wildcats coming down from the hills after coyotes. Where you could hear the screams of their two A.M. kills, and find the next day the silent mangled carcasses they'd left in their wake.

And what about having the man himself on the site? Bill Jennings, her fifty-eight-year-old crew manager, had frowned when he'd returned to work and seen the van parked next to the trailer "sucking up the juice you're charged for, Shea. What the hell's the guy with the beard doing here?"

"He's an amateur archaeologist, among other things," she'd said, deciding not to claim he was a visiting relative. It was a decision she'd later regret, as it would have explained the unexplainable to others, if not to herself.

Jennings's sun- and wind-wizened skin had seemed to crackle. "Amateurs belong in noncontract jobs. What if they find out at ASU? Jesus Christ, you want him messing up?"

"Your job's not in jeopardy, Bill. Even if he does hang around here for a while, which I doubt. He's more interested in finding his Apache roots."

"An Apache. Shit!" To Bill, any Indian more recent than the Salado was not to be trusted. Canal builders dead six hundred years, they and their civilization held no threat to him. Not all archaeologists were openminded about cultures different than their own. Bill was one whose reasons for digging in the past included a desire to prove the superiority of his own.

Shea again had said, "He's no threat. He's got a kid with him. Less than two years old."

"Great! Now we'll be baby-sitters, too." He'd grabbed his tools and headed across the five-acre site to the stacked stones that looked like the walls of a temple mound had begun to emerge.

She sucked in a breath. He'd said it before, not knowing she'd overheard him, following her and Doug's announcement of her pregnancy, just a week before she lost the baby.

Bill's resentment was nothing new. It began several years before, when Doug and Shea married, a de facto replacement of Bill, the senior employee in a struggling archaeological consulting business. Until laws were passed making compulsory the archaeological study of all redevelopment projects before construction began, few significant jobs existed for professionals. Doug saw the changes and opportunities coming and was among the first in Arizona to move from consulting into contracting. Bill, who'd previously helped manage volunteers, saw himself as the natural eventual full partner. Doug had encouraged him by giving him a small share of the business and naming him treasurer, a nominal title as all day-to-day money management was handled by the firm's accountant.

Still, the shares and appointment made Bill feel powerful, a feeling he expressed in a gruff football-coach manner on the job. By the time Doug married Shea, Doug had seen management problems rising out of Bill's personality. Volunteers became difficult to recruit, and the professionals he hired stayed mainly out of respect for Doug, a man whose business offered them the only paying jobs outside of academia.

He kept Bill on out of genuine devotion to the man who'd stuck with him while things were tough. He meant to move him into some less people-sensitive job eventually, but he couldn't figure out how to do that without seeming to demote him. He and Shea came to the conclusion that after their marriage, she would become site lab manager, and he would spend the time left over from chasing new contracts in tacitly overseeing Bill.

Naturally paranoid, Bill felt the silent scrutiny and believed it was Shea's idea. He was openly hostile toward her, a woman, and an anthropologist who, in his opinion, had no business taking away a job from a real archaeologist. Management jobs belonged to men. A woman would get pregnant and turn the place into a fucking day care center. Shea's pregnancy proved that. He'd lost no time in saying it to his crew, half of whom were women. And he said it often enough in the week before she lost the pregnancy, and almost her life, so that she overheard him.

As he'd walked head down toward the temple mound walls two mornings before, the pain of his words returned, reminding her of what she'd lost and might be on the edge of recovering in some small part through Zack and Jimmy. It was almost as if those cruel, thoughtless words themselves were a curse. That they alone presaged another loss.

Still, she, not Bill, had been the one to send Zack to see Peter Chavez. And Peter would take him in. What was that Robert Frost line? Something like home being the place where people had to take you in when you had to go there. More poetic than that, but it was close. Shea knew that for some reason she had to take Zack in. The trouble was, Zack didn't have to go to her. He had to go to Peter. *Easy come, easy go.*

Now, as she sat at her desk with her log and gazed at the dusk chasing red tails of sunset over the mountains, she shivered. Bill and the crew had left an hour ago, locking the iron gate behind them. Though she was glad to see them go, its grating clank and the rumbles of their receding vehicles no longer signaled a night of respite. She would force herself to transcribe their notes to her log, check their small piles of points and shards against the lists on the collecting bags to ready them for cataloging.

They were nothing much; most collections unearthed in a day of backbreaking troweling and sifting and mind-numbing tedium were nothing much. Another few inches of wall had been uncovered, another few square yards had undergone their scrutiny; and when it was all done, the total of all their findings would be analyzed, the artifacts put on display or archived, the site itself mapped and graphically reproduced on paper, then covered over. Even if something stunning and different emerged to become a permanent attraction, like the nearby Tonto cliff dwellings that were part of the National Park system, it would likely have to be simulated in plaster castings and placed elsewhere, for this project was being done at this particular time, because the level of Roosevelt Lake had been lowered for an eight-year Reclamation Service repair of the Theodore Roosevelt Dam. When the repairs were complete, the site would be flooded, raising the level of the lake about seventy feet.

Shea sighed as the last of the sunset flickered off. She methodically performed her own tedious chores and set aside for tomorrow the dry, dull cataloging of minutiae. The last light had drained from the sky. She was alone on her strip of desert. Seen from a distant mountain, her lighted trailer and its reflection in the lake would twinkle like tiny twin stars.

As she'd done the past two nights, she left the outside lights on all night. Before she went to sleep, she picked up the blue and beige afghan and resumed her knitting. She was adding a new blue border around the beige. The blanket, smelling of apple and the elusive scent of the boy who'd slept in it, begged to be expanded. Even if the boy and his father no longer had to go to her, she had to take them in. If they passed through her life again, she would be ready to warm and shelter them.

Three nights in the Chavezes' modest home, with no generator rumbling in his ears, had taken the kinks out of Zack's muscles and mind. Jimmy, seasoned by his month on the road, by exposure to new sights and sounds and people every hour, not just every day, quickly adjusted to the Chavez house and activities. Lucy gave him stones to bang together in his "watching place," screened off safely from the chips flying from her work, but close enough to watch as, masked against dusk and goggled to protect her own eyes, she chiseled a new statue out of green alabaster. The cacophony struck by hammer and chisel, the strength wielded by her sinewy arms as she delivered each blow,

belied their precise, elegant outcomes. Zack understood
that as only an artist could. She mastered her medium by
becoming a part of it, knowing what was under its skin and
how to uncover it.

When finished with her morning's work in the lean-to
studio behind the house, Lucy prepared lunch for Zack and
Jimmy, and Peter when he was present. She then took the
boy to visit her grandchildren.

Today, Peter had gone to visit a woman whose age—
maybe one hundred, nobody knew for sure—had given her
secret memories, along with the wisdom of how and to
whom to dispense them. All Apache were storytellers, but
only enlightened members of Peter's generation and their
offspring wrote memoirs, kept diaries or records. And of
all storytellers on the San Carlos Reservation, this woman
was the most revered. Peter's visit to her today was his
third. On the first he'd joined her in conversation about
the days of the dam building; his purpose was to loosen
her memories of that time. On his second visit, yesterday,
he had told her about his guest, whose Apache blood was
so diluted he no longer knew the ways to his ancestors; his
purpose on this visit was to disarm her, for she'd otherwise
feel Zack had lost any right to know his ancestors. Peter
was trying to teach him Apache ways, felt he was worthy
of such teachings, asked for her help.

She'd told him that she would consider his request; he
must return today to get her decision.

A bare half hour after Lucy's departure with Jimmy
for the afternoon, Peter returned. Waiting anxiously in the
small living room, Zack heard his host trudging to the front
door. The footfalls told him that Peter was alone.

Zack stood. He would not let his expectancy drain away
completely. The footfalls did not drag with bad news.

"Ah," said Peter, looking up at his apprehensive guest.
"You've eaten?"

"Yes. Lucy took Jimmy."

"Umhmm. As I thought. Well, I'm hungry. I've waited
for food longer than you've waited for your answer."

He meant he'd gone off without breakfast and hadn't eaten lunch.

"Lucy left you something."

Peter did not need to be told; he was on his way to the kitchen where he warmed up thick, savory soup with boiled meat while Zack looked on. It was an Apache way Zack had learned over the past three days: patience. Peter did not mean to tease him, keep him on tenterhooks. His hunger for food was simply more compelling than Zack's hunger for the news he carried, which wouldn't change in the time it took Peter to eat.

And it took him forty-five minutes, for he had his prayer to say, which was similar to the invocation he'd made over the sculpture the other day: "Food, this is a man; man, this is food. Take what you need and get rid of the rest." And, to acknowledge its full meaning, he had to eat slowly and avoid eating more than he needed out of his excessive hunger.

When he finished at last, he leaned back in his high-backed wooden chair and smiled. "Well, you want to know what Storytelling Woman said."

"Ah, um, right," said Zack, trying to project his new, more patient ways.

Peter nodded. He pushed his soup bowl back. "She cannot decide in her house. It's too new, she said, and hasn't absorbed the powers."

Sighing, Zack said, "How long will it take to absorb them?"

"Until she is as old again as she is."

"Jesus Christ, Peter! How can I wait a hundred years? That's ridiculous, even with your kind of patience, which'll take me a hundred years to absorb."

Peter stood up and removed the bowl and spoon from the table and carried it to the sink. Turning on the water, he turned to look over his shoulder at Zack. "And you haven't yet absorbed the patience to hear all of what she said."

Chagrined, Zack looked at him a moment. "Right."

Peter nodded and finished washing his dish and spoon

and set them in the drainer to dry. He dried his hands on a towel. "Let's go to Lucy's studio," he said.

Another delay! The patience lessons came hard. Well, between riddles and delays, his hurriedness would get him nowhere. *Follow him; listen to what he says; keep your mouth shut for a while, Zack!* he told himself. He followed Peter through the house and out to the lean-to shelter where Lucy's latest sculpture was taking shape.

Peter strode to the green rock. He touched the jagged piece, which measured about eighteen inches tall by nearly a foot in diameter. "This rock is as old as the earth, and holds all its powers. Storytelling Woman's house is made of wood and metal, like our house here. The wood and the metal came from the earth, but the white men who took them stripped away all their powers and tossed them back to the earth. But Lucy is not stripping away the rock's powers. She is releasing them so others can absorb them, take what they need, and get rid of the rest."

Zack's mouth grew dry. The prayer, the stone he'd been given, his response to it began to make sense.

Peter studied him a moment, nodded, and led him back inside the house. He sat in a chair in the living room and motioned Zack to take another. "Indians know the earth's power. It gives us life. The earth is a woman, like all life givers. The sun renews and releases its power each morning as it rises. Storytelling Woman must go up on the eastern face of the mountain before dawn tomorrow morning and learn what the powers tell her to do. Then she will be able to decide."

"Before dawn! An old woman like that?"

"She's gone up before, many times. She knows the trails, every tree, where the clearing is to wait for the sunrise. From the time she lived in a wickiup as a child, she's made her way up the mountain with her questions and problems. And the sun rose, and spoke with the powers of her ancestors."

Zack shook his head vehemently and he grasped the arms of his chair. "No! It's too cold. There are hungry cats up

there. How can you let her? Forget it. I'll find my Apache
roots some other way. Tell her I've changed my mind. I
won't have her on my conscience."

"Zack, oh Zack, what a sad thing your conscience is."
Peter's head wagged. "Why should you stop an old woman
from doing what she needs to do?"

"I can when she's doing it for me." He stood up. "If I'd
known . . ."

Still shaking his head, Peter stood up and went to him.
"She's doing it for the ancestors, not for you. Among them
are ancestors of yours, whose memories she carries. Now
that you've sought them out, she has no choice but to go
to them. She's not afraid. She has her safe place."

"Safe!"

"Yes. Now, let it be. You've entered in on the Apache
way. Tomorrow afternoon, we'll go to Storytelling Woman.
She'll know what to tell you."

Storytelling Woman was not at her house when Peter
took Zack there in his four-year-old four-wheel-drive Toyota
pickup truck. Peter let himself in through the unlocked door
of the tiny prefab house that sat a half mile down a cragged,
narrow dirt road. Chickens in an overgrown yard pecked
at pebbles and scattered grain, undisturbed by the human
intrusions. Three fat gray and tan cats curled and uncurled
in a sunlit spot, stretched their claws, yawned and curled
up again.

Inside, the two-room house was sparsely furnished and
neat. A handwoven rug covered much of the wooden floor
of the larger room. A woodburning stove and a refrigerator
from the 1940s stood side by side at one end. The air inside
the house was chilly and smelled sour of burned uncured
pine logs.

Peter went into the second room, where Storytelling
Woman's empty bed stood against a wall that was covered
with ancient oilcloth. The handwoven blanket was rolled at
the bottom. Instead of a mattress, a thickly padded board
rested on the narrow bed's slats. It bore the impressions of

someone heavier than Zack had imagined her to be.

"She hasn't come back," Peter said.

"Maybe she's somewhere outside."

"No. The house says she hasn't come back. We have to go up on the mountain to talk to her."

"You . . . you mean you think she's not coming down?"

"I think that. But she hasn't yet gone to her ancestors."

"She's alive. That's what you're saying?"

"She took her dog. If she were with the ancestors, the dog would have come back. Come on. To reach her will take about an hour."

The climb, made easy by the well-worn switchback trail, took less than that. As they hiked it, Peter told Zack why Storytelling Woman wouldn't have feared wild animals in these hills. "She had a pact with them. They weren't food for each other. And she never raised food for herself that she wouldn't share with them. She lived through many droughts and floods, and had a small herd of sheep for many years. When deer were short, the wildcats would come after sheep. She never denied them. When she and her dog grew too old to keep the sheep, her children and grandchildren provided carcasses during dry years."

A turkey hunter, Zack said, "They have that sense, wild animals. They know if you're out to hunt them." He told Peter the story of a certain wild Tom who eluded him for a few seasons, going so far as to walk up close enough to tease him before flying away. "I finally got him, though."

"You respected him. He had powers. I hope you thanked him after you shot him. Before you ate him."

"I didn't exactly thank him. He did have powers, though, I guess. It was nearly a year after Maryellen died, and I hadn't been able to . . . to get my life back together. Getting him kind of helped me."

Peter nodded as they rounded a switchback and neared the east face about three-quarters of a mile up the mountain. "He knew to share his powers. You needed them." He rounded a ridge to a clearing. A dog barked out of Zack's sight. "There she is. Come on."

The old brown sheepdog stood next to the woman, who lay on a blanket surrounded by a circle of small boulders. Though the sky was bright, the sun had swung around to the other side of the mountain. But as Peter and Zack approached Storytelling Woman, Zack realized that the boulders, which had absorbed the morning sun, were still giving back its heat. *Keeping what they needed and getting rid of the rest?*

She looked up at Peter when he reached her and bent to touch her face. She didn't seem surprised to see him. He spoke to her in Apache. Zack heard his name among the unfamiliar syllables. Her eyes in their craggy caverns turned to him and studied him. As old as they were, they were clear, with neither rings around the iris nor the haze of cataracts in the wide pupils.

But her face was so old it had become ageless. She opened her mouth to speak, and he was amazed to see all her visible teeth intact, though some were worn with deep brown ridges. She had no trouble saying, "Zack," in a strong voice that gave no hint she was fading. Then she pushed herself up into a sitting position, and spoke to the dog. He sat behind her to keep her propped up. The long, colorful, canvaslike dress she wore covered her from neck to ankles; its sleeves reached to the wrists. Long, thin gray hair wound in plaits covered her scalp. Left uncovered were only her face, her hands—lizard skin stretched on thin sticks—and her time-cobbled feet, both thick soled, but one thin like her hands, one fat and swollen, discolored. She had hurt herself, then. Well, they would be able to carry her down all right, Zack thought, relieved.

He took a step toward her. Peter extended an arm, stopped him. Storytelling Woman was speaking. After a few chanted lines, Peter translated: *"The memories of ancestors held by women in the tribe can be passed on only to their daughters."*

"The Apache," said Peter, "are matrilineal. Possessions go from mother to daughter."

"She's decided not to tell me."

"No. Not quite. You have a daughter."

"But—"

Storytelling Woman had begun to chant again: *"A widow conceived a daughter. The seed took root though the land was dry. On the dry land, the woman gave birth to a child with no father. But on that day, a flood was let loose by the father's white kin, washing away his name, which was etched in the dry land. The widow, searching for the father's name, ran to the flood and embraced it. A flood too soon was carried away in a basket that took nine months to weave. It is full of memories that only a daughter may know, even though a father's memories are woven into the basket, and even though a father leads her to it."*

"Peter, what does it mean?"

"Shhh. She's got more to say."

"The floodwaters now recede for a short time, so white men may seek old memories and try to understand them. But the ancestors will not release the memories to white men. They will not know what they find and will lose it again to the flood. The memories can only be known to a woman with Apache blood."

Storytelling Woman's voice trailed off as she drew a breath. She reached back and touched her dog, who barked and stood up. The dog stood as she eased herself down onto her back. Then he whined and went to sniff her swollen foot. He looked at Peter and barked.

Peter spoke to the woman. After she answered, he turned to Zack and said, "That's all she has to tell you. She wants us to go now."

"Go! What about her foot? Shouldn't we carry her down so you can treat it?"

"She doesn't want me to treat it. She wants to remain here with her ancestors." He touched Zack's shoulder. "Come on, Zack."

"You'll leave her here? Alone? What happens at night? It's already getting chilly. Those boulders won't help for long."

"This is her safe place, Zack. It's where she wants to be.

Why should we carry her away? For what?"

Zack clenched his fists by his sides. He stared at the woman, who had closed her eyes. "Safe! How can it be safe when she's already been badly hurt? And not even covered."

"You may cover her, then, if you want to."

"Yes! Yes I will." He stepped forward between two boulders. The dog stepped away, off the blanket, to let him lift its edges and wrap them around her. Gently, he lifted the foot of the blanket and draped it loosely over the swollen foot. "Thank you, Storytelling Woman. I'll take the memories to Poke. She's almost a woman now, and she has Apache blood."

Peter translated. Zack touched the ageless face as the eyes opened again. Storytelling Woman smiled. Her lips were dry. They would tell no more stories, Zack knew. He stood and stepped back behind the circle of boulders. Their heat, he noticed, had dissipated.

"Tonight, the dog will keep her warm with his body. When it's time for us to come for her, he'll come to her house."

"Peter, I don't understand—"

"You will." He took Zack's shoulder and turned him, and they descended the mountain in silence. When they reached the plateau where the houses were, Peter said, "She had a pact with the animals, but not with the rattlesnakes."

Zack gasped.

"They emerge this time of year. She would have seen it basking on the boulder. She may have decided to allow it to strike. She may have tried to keep it from striking her dog. She's a very old woman, Zack." He took Zack by the arm. "Let's get back to the Toyota. Lucy will have our supper for us when we get home."

Shea locked the gate behind her on this first Sunday morning in March and left for Globe in her old green Ford pickup. Though snow still capped some of the taller mountains and flurried even below the timberline, the basin captured and held the sweet warmth of spring. The rainy winter had released the germination of a million wildflowers: bright yellow daisies, red and orange poppies, and purple lupine on waving stalks. They festooned the hills and carpeted patches of earth that had remained dry and brown through the previous spring.

They wakened her senses. Over the past year, she'd hated to go into the old mining town to shop for her household supplies. She'd make excuses, stretch a two-week cache of food to cover three, ask one of her crew to shop for her and pick up a few things on the way into work. They were glad to help, because they knew her work often began before they arrived in the mornings and continued after they left. They knew the work was her refuge, and the shopping, which forced her out of her sanctuary, was painful, sometimes almost impossible for her to face. For the first few months after Doug's death, going into the supermarket sometimes overwhelmed her. The shelves of food seemed to be tipping toward her. Dizziness engulfed her. She became confused, disoriented. Maybe she managed to choose among items and load some into her basket; then she would panic, leave the partially filled cart in the aisle and run out. One day, having run back to her truck and gotten in, she sat helpless in the seat, unable to turn the key in the ignition. Then she couldn't get out of the cab. She sat there, immobile, for hours. A state highway patrolman saw her and sensed her trouble. He drove her back to the dig site and had his partner follow them in her pickup.

When she told Michelle, her lab assistant, the next day, the woman insisted on coming in every other Sunday to accompany her to the store. After a few months, she was able to go alone again, but still she hated it, put it off as long as possible.

Now she had run out of food a week early, partly because she'd fed Zack and Jimmy for two days last week, and partly because she herself had recovered her healthy appetite since they'd been there. Now her appetite for the smells and sights of coming spring also returned. By now, she was sure Zack and Jimmy would never come back again, at least not to stay for long, but that didn't matter. Their mere passing through had released her, as the rains had released the wildflowers.

In Globe at the Safeway, she replenished her stock of frozen and vacuum-packed microwavable meals, bought a small sack of baking potatoes, some lettuce, cucumbers, carrots, tomatoes, green peppers, and scallions. For a few days she would have fresh salads. Eventually, her love of these would bring her back to Globe, even if she could wait for the other things.

With the replenished supplies in five heavy brown bags under the tarp in the pickup bed, she drove back to Roosevelt Lake. She parked close to her trailer door and turned back the tarp. Taking the frozen foods in first, she immediately arranged them in her freezer, mentally indexing them for quick retrieval when she'd need them.

The lack of packaging standards among food producers irked her. Despite her organizing skills, she never got everything in place in the freezer on the first try. Why ice cream makers like Dreyers insisted on packing their products in tall, top-heavy cylindrical tubs, she did not know. On the upper shelf, where it could stand, it stacked poorly; on the bottom shelf she had to lay it on its side. It hogged both depth and width, creating a squeeze. At last she decided on her usual solution, which she hated as much as she loved this particular brand of chocolate chip dessert. She got a square plastic container from an overhead cabinet and transferred the ice cream to that with a thick aluminum paddle. She left, as always, a serving in the bottom of the carton, as a treat to sustain her through the balance of her grocery stashing.

With the carton in one hand, spatula in the other, she turned toward the door. The large figure backlit there jolted her.

"Where do you want these things?" He stepped inside.

"Zack! Dear God! Where did you come from? You could have knocked."

He set the two grocery bags on her desk. "You left the door open. Besides, my hands were full."

"Where's Jimmy?" She ran to the door. The dust-covered bright blue Ram was standing beside the pickup.

"Still strapped in his car seat. Don't worry. Finish your ice cream. I'll put these things away for you."

She looked at the carton in her hand. "I'll put them away, Zack. You go get Jimmy. He can have the ice cream. Right from the carton. I'll bet he'll love it that way."

He grinned. "Right," he said, that day, the first Sunday in March.

CHAPTER
■ ■ TWELVE

SQUIRREL SPRINGS, WEST VIRGINIA

On the first Monday in March, the analysis of the contaminated vial's contents came back from the lab. *"Insulin! Dear God!"* said Shirley Petrowski aloud. *"Enough to kill ten men!"* The paper in her hand trembled as she read the report. *"Insulin!"* It was worse than she could have imagined. She must find out who was responsible for this horrible mistake. What if she hadn't caught it? What if Zack had injected his son with insulin?

She left her emergency room post and hurried to peds. Bursting into the nursing unit she snapped at the head nurse, who was giving morning report to her staff, "Where's your February roster?"

The nurse, her tall white cap jolted by her head's sudden motion, opened her mouth. Nothing came out.

"Your February roster! Please get it this moment."

"I . . . ah . . . sure, Shirley." The four staff nurses peeled away from their semicircle around Charge Nurse Elaine Wilkins. Elaine opened her desk drawer and pulled out four weekly time sheets.

Shirley grabbed them from her hand.

"This week's is on the bulletin b—"

"Never mind this week. I want to know who was on and who was in charge on February tenth and eleventh." She pulled the sheet with those dates and flung the others

on the desk. She found the dates she was looking for and
looked up.

"You were in charge afternoons, Elaine. I want you to
phone all the others and tell them to come in at four P.M.
today. We'll meet in the DON's office." She faced the staff
nurses. "Rubins, Crandall, and Johnson, you were on those
dates, too. Be there this afternoon. Tracy's office at four."

"But, Shirley," Rose Crandall began. "I—"

"This is vital! No excuses. Every one of you must be
there. Anyone who isn't will have no job tomorrow."

"But you're not DON. You can't fire—"

Shirley whirled toward the speaker, a young dark-haired
nurse with a nose that lent her a know-it-all look. "If you
wish to find out what I can and can't do in this hospital, I
suggest you defy my orders."

The other staff, except for Charge Nurse Elaine, looked
down at the fronts of their uniforms and made muffled
sounds. The nose of the nurse who had spoken glowed.
Her mouth puckered with either embarrassment or anger.

"I'll see you people at four. Don't be late."

All who worked on the two days when the medication
might have been tampered with or accidentally mixed up
appeared in Director of Nursing Tracy's office on time.
The nine squeezed with Shirley and Gen Tracy into the
office, which comfortably held only five. All chairs had
been removed to allow the group to pack in and stand
compressed against the walls. Shirley had briefed Gen on
the accident and the lab report. The young black DON had
turned gray-skinned and gone mute. During the meeting she
stood helpless and voiceless by the window overlooking the
parking lot, while Shirley, facing the women and the single
male staff nurse, drilled them with the horrifying details.

She questioned them one by one: Who from each shift
cared for Jimmy Zachary? Who even went into his room?
Who handled medication for anyone? Whose patient was on
insulin? They all shook their heads at the last question.

Elaine said, "I can check, Shirley. But we haven't had a
diabetic in weeks. In fact, you know our census was low

that week because of the weather. It's been low since fall."

"No diabetics? You're sure?"

"Positive. The Sanders child from Hedgesville was the last one we had. That was in October, I think. Yes, I'm sure. We had the Halloween party and she dressed like Snow White."

Shirley bit her molars hard together. "Then you must have had some insulin in the fridge. Left over from then."

"Not on my unit!" said Elaine, vehemently. "You know that's not done. Just to prevent mistakes. Shit, Shirley—"

Shirley shot her a glance. "It's not *supposed* to be done."

"It simply *isn't*. Not on any unit I've ever been in charge of. Neither is having a child Jimmy's age get IM penicillin when he's going to be discharged and having his father mix and give it."

Gen Tracy looked up. "What?"

Elaine smirked. "Shirley taught Jimmy's father to give the penicillin IM, so he could give it after he left. We usually switch them to oral syrup when they're out of danger. It's much easier for the parents. And what didn't make sense at all was that Jimmy and his father were going across country—or somewhere or other—in a van. He'd be handling that kid and giving him the shot *in a van!*"

The gathered nurses passed glances and murmurs among themselves.

Gen raised her long, arched brow. "Wait. I know who you're talking about now. That man who worked on the computers."

"Yes," said Shirley. "That's right. In fact, he did quite a bit to help during and after the storm. And it was *because* I knew he would be on the road that I felt precautions were in order. The lessons on giving the shot kept him here a few days longer, gave the boy a better chance. I did that deliberately, to keep him here."

"Yeah," said Elaine, smirking again, "she did all she could to keep him here."

Shirley's face flared.

Gen, mindful of Shirley's standing with administration, sprang to her defense. "I concur with what Shirley did in the circumstances. And it has nothing to do with the insulin incident."

Elaine flushed. Her smirk rolled off her face like melting wax.

Shirley quickly regained her composure. She'd known at the time of the near accident that she'd been overzealous with Jimmy, but that was past. The insulin incident, as Gen called it, was the issue to deal with now. Elaine's obvious professional jealousy could be safely ignored, then used later, should Shirley need to use it. She'd handled such envy before; in fact, she relished the chance to go at it. Now she said, "When you leave this meeting, Elaine, we'll go back to your unit together and have a good look through the fridge. The rest of you may leave for now." She turned to Gen. "Thank you for letting us use your office, Gen. If you have any ideas on how to proceed with this investigation, I'll be grateful."

The nurses, except for Elaine, pushed out the door in a whispering clump. They hung around the corridor till Shirley and Elaine stepped out of the office, then quickly dispersed, choking on nervous giggles.

Gen called to Shirley as she left. When Shirley turned, she said, "There may have been some diabetics in one of the other services, Shirley. I'll check and let you know what I find."

Shirley nodded and led Elaine back to pediatrics. The unit refrigerator contained no insulin; that proved nothing, of course, but it did bring obvious relief to the charge nurse's face. At her sigh, Shirley said, "You've nothing to worry about, Elaine. I wouldn't plant it there to embarrass you. What possible ax would I have to grind with you? On the other hand, I can't imagine your having one to grind with me, either."

Elaine's face blanched, then turned crimson. She fled. Shirley allowed herself a moment of satisfaction. Then she frowned to herself. Something Gen had said nagged at the back of her mind. There had been at least one diabetic in-house during that time. She couldn't put her finger on it, but it seems one had come in through the ER around then. She'd check back through her notes.

But not tonight. She needed a good night's sleep before she could deal with this. She could find no evidence of staff medication error, or even poor handling. In spite of her rising distaste for Elaine Wilkins's behavior, she was pleased at the woman's handling of the unit. All staff members used good care and technique routinely. They were, by and large, dedicated professionals. This should have made her feel better; instead, it made her feel worse. If this had been no accident, then it might have been deliberate tampering. Who in the world would tamper with a toddler's medicine? Surely none of the staff. And why? In light of what happened at the meeting, the thought that Elaine might have done so to bring Shirley down crossed her mind. Never had she imagined the woman resented her so. But, no. Such a thought was bizarre, impossible. Clearly, Shirley needed to go home and to bed.

"Shirley, can I talk to you a second?" His voice caught her by surprise on her way into the ER the next morning. She turned and waited for him to catch up.

The sheriff slammed the door of his Jeep and loped the few yards to her side.

"What's up, Rodney?" she asked as the sliding doors parted for them. She hadn't seen him since the morning he'd offered to take her home after her triple shift. Shirley noticed when Rodney was absent. A compassionate and rumpled man, he was always there when you needed him. He did kind things, like having her driveway shoveled out so she could go home that morning, even though she'd decided to sleep at the hospital. He'd never force kindness on you, or get angry when you turned down his offers. Rodney was the only man she trusted. She'd known him almost all her life, and he never had betrayed her trust.

"Got something here to show you." He held out a covered clipboard with papers inside.

"Sure. Let's go to my desk."

He looked at her, his face creasing. "Not the triage desk, Shirley. It's more or less private." He sounded concerned.

"OK. Let me tell them where they can reach me." She leaned into the clerical cubicles. "I'll be in my private office with the sheriff," she said to the clerk. "If a patient comes in, just buzz me."

The clerk nodded. Shirley led Rodney around the bend to her office. "Coffee?" she said, pointing to the readied pot as he sat.

"No, thanks. Had mine. Go on if you want some."

"No. I'm fine, too." She sat across the desk from him. "What've you got there?"

He opened the vinyl cover and exposed the top paper clipped onto the board. Turning it, he slid it across her desk, then nodded at her and sat back in the leather chair.

Pulling the clipboard close, Shirley looked at the page and gasped.

"That came in several weeks ago, Shirl. We were tied up with the storm, so I just glanced at it and set it aside. Didn't look like anyone I knew. You know 'im?"

For a moment she considered lying, but she'd already given herself away with her first reaction to the FBI wanted notice. "I . . . recognize him, yes." She swallowed hard. "But I didn't know he was—"

"Wanted for kidnapping?"

"Rodney—"

"Shirley, I got to tell the FBI he was here."

"Why? What difference does it make? He's been gone more than three weeks. How will it help them to know he was here? It wasn't as if we helped him get away."

"We have to report it. He's a kidnapper, Shirley. He's got an innocent kid with him. If he was here, it's a link in a chain."

She leaned forward. "That man is no kidnapper. I saw the way he treated that boy. And the way the boy responded to him. If he'd meant to harm him, he'd never have brought him here."

Rodney shook his head. "I checked the background on this, Shirl. He took him from his grandparents. Claims he's his father, but he isn't."

"Grandparents!"

"The old man's a wealthy lawyer. The boy's mother went into a coma. Never came out—"

"Died! Zack said she'd died. Name was Liz."

Rodney knit his brow. "Liz Broward. Maybe she died. Anyway, she wasn't competent. Old Man Broward claimed custody. When he went to get the boy from James—that's your friend Zack's last name—the guy just skipped town."

Shirley shook her head, nonplussed. "But he's the father. Why wouldn't he have custody?"

"That's just it. He isn't the father. The mother wasn't married, never recorded the father's name or identity. When this guy stepped up when the woman first got sick and claimed he was the father, it was pretty obvious he was after the Broward fortune. When she went into the coma and Broward claimed custody, he grabbed the kid and ran. He wants that kid alive and well or no Broward money. It's pretty simple. Straightforward."

Shirley shook her head and clamped her jaw. Straightforward was not the way it sounded to her. Something about it was wrong. Was Jimmy's mother in a coma or dead? How did Zack manage to get hold of the boy in the first place, if he wasn't the father? The boy called him Daddy. The boy and man were intimate as only people who'd known each other for a long time could be. But then, if they were father and son, why couldn't Zack prove it? And why hadn't the mother, Liz Broward, just recorded it? Straightforward? Not on Shirley's life was this thing straightforward!

"That man is not after money. He's not a kidnapper, Rodney."

Rodney sighed and shook his head. He reached for the clipboard.

Shirley stopped his hand. "I want this sheet if you don't

mind." She released the clip and pulled it out.

"Course." He retrieved the board from her after she took out the notice. He stood up. "I'll have to say he was here. They'll probably come to question you."

She snorted. "I can handle their questions. The same way I would've before you showed me this. I know guilty men when I see them. I know when a father loves a boy and when he doesn't."

The sheriff studied her a second. "Shirley, you know fathers don't always love their children."

Stiffening, she said, "You bet I do. And I know just as well when they don't. And this man does."

"I'm going to have to tell them everything that went on here," he said, his massive Adam's apple bobbing.

"Whatever does that mean?" She clenched her fists despite her attempts to sound casual.

"How do you think it's going to look?"

On guard, she frowned. He must have heard about the insulin. "I . . ."

"They're going to wonder some about how you let that man work off his hospital bill doing chores and computer repairs. About how you used your suasion on the board to let him do it. When he'd already prepaid in cash, you got most of his money back. Didn't you suspect the cash in the first place?"

"I knew he was running. That was clear. But a man doesn't just run from other men. Sometimes he runs from himself."

Again the sheriff shook his head.

The man has a doubting disease, she thought.

"Something's come over you, Shirl. What went on between you and that man?" he asked at last.

She froze, unable to speak for a moment. Ramrod stiff she said, "Nothing ever could, ever would go on between me and any man alive, and you know that. Nothing! Not as long as I could stop it."

"I don't want to hurt you, but I know what happened with your father and brothers when you were little. And I know you left this state and got yourself together. We were proud and happy to have you come back. And this hospital wouldn't be the first-rate one it is without you. We're proud of you for that."

She was moved, as always, by this heartfelt praise. No one but Rodney ever acknowledged her contribution in words.

But . . . she heard the but coming . . .

"But a woman reaches an age where a storm comes and she sure would like someone to come and help dig her out. And she might want someone to take her in out of it."

"You've got no call to talk to me like that, Rodney!"

Despite her angry retort, he went on. "This is a small town, Shirley. Things like you did for that man get around. Nothing would bring more pleasure to some of those wagging tongues than to wag for some FBI agents. You better be prepared to do some explaining."

He left her standing with her mouth wide open and the FBI wanted sheet in her hand.

She was still standing there when Gen Tracy stuck her head in the door.

"Can I come in?" the nursing director asked.

Immediately recomposing herself, Shirley nodded. Gen came in with a paper in her long, neatly manicured ebony hand. She glanced at the page Shirley already held. Shirley quickly set it on her desk, facedown. "I just have a minute. I have to get to triage."

"It'll just take a second," said the tall, slim woman. Gen never moved quickly. Her motions echoed the languid regional drawl of her speech. "I checked on diabetics in on the tenth and eleventh," she said, extending the paper. "We only had one. On medical. Seems he came in through ER, Shirley. On your shift."

Brow furrowed, Shirley reached for the paper. "Lester Jones? I sure don't remember."

"Well, maybe you can check. Here's the staff that took care of him." She pointed to a short list of nurses. "And, Shirley, I hope you treat them a little more gently than you did the girls in peds. I can't see how they could even be involved in this whole mess, anyway."

"Probably not. But someone made a mistake. Either accidentally or on purpose. And that boy could've died."

Gen's face reacted more sharply to that. "What do you mean, or on purpose? You think someone wanted to kill that child?"

"I can't imagine someone wanting to. But there are lots of crazy people around. One of them could be in this hospital."

Shuddering, Gen said, "You can't be serious."

"You explain it then, Gen. It was either an accident or a deliberate tampering. We have to find out what it was in either case."

Gen fixed her black eyes on Shirley. "I hope you keep this inside these walls, Shirley. I couldn't help noticing the sheriff leaving just now."

With an upward curled lip, Shirley said, "Now you know me better than that. No one in this hospital can afford to try to live down something like this." No local lips would waggle on about this matter, she felt sure. Still, "Rodney came about something else," she added. "Some sort of FBI investigation about a patient. They may come around asking questions. But they'll probably just talk to me."

"Well, that sure sounds interesting. We haven't had so much excitement around here in years."

"Anyway, as far as the other's concerned, I'll investigate myself." She tapped the page in her hand. "This isn't much to go on, but it's all I've got for now. Thanks, Gen." She walked out with the DON, fully recovered from her encounter with Rodney, and went to her triage desk, just as a new patient came in.

At the shift's end, she went directly to the medical unit to talk with the evening staff nurse who, records showed, cared for Lester Jones.

Kitty Colson looked up as Shirley came into the unit office. Her light brown curls jiggled ceaselessly beneath her cap, as if she were always giggling. Her perpetual happiness sometimes irritated Shirley, as she felt that only the most naive could believe the world was such a cheerful place. But patients seemed to love and trust the woman, and that was good on a unit where so many patients suffered from metabolic conditions that required lifelong management. Only when the management didn't hold well did they arrive in the hospital.

"Hi, Shirley," Kitty said, joyfully.

After the disrespect she'd had to endure in the past twenty-four hours, Shirley welcomed the greeting. "Do you have a minute, Kitty?"

The wedge-shaped cap stood at attention as Kitty said, "Sure."

"Do you remember a diabetic patient that came in several weeks ago—a Lester Jones?"

"Gosh, Shirley, I have millions of diabetic patients. That name sure doesn't sound familiar. I know most of the folks from around here."

"He came in through ER. On my shift. And I know most of the patients from around here, too, and I can't even remember someone coming in, in diabetic emergency. I . . ."

It wasn't the man who'd come in through ER. I never even saw the man. He'd been out in the parking lot in a van. They'd admitted the woman for hypoglycemic emergency.

"You remember something?" Kitty asked.

"Yes. The woman. I sent her up. Her father wasn't in trouble, she was. But he was a quadruple amputee—"

"Oh, them! Sure I remember. Hester and Lester. Now, they were an odd couple if I ever saw one."

"You treated them, then."

"You might say that. Actually, Hester was a nurse. She took care of everything: ostomy, meds, everything. All I did was the routine vitals."

"She gave him his insulin, then."

"Oh, yes. I was glad to have the help. We were short staffed. So I just let her fend for herself." She hesitated, then she said, "I don't mean I ignored them or anything. I checked in all the usual times."

"I'm sure you did."

"Half the time she wasn't there. One time I was just getting ready to feed old Lester because she'd wandered off at suppertime and we were short of volunteers. But, before I had time to get to it, there she was, back again, talking to him oh so sweet and lovey."

"Wandered off? Where did she go?"

"Oh, I don't know. She knew her way around hospitals, being a nurse. She made herself at home."

Idiot! Letting a patient go off the unit!

"Asked all sorts of questions."

Dear God! And I suppose you answered them. How could anyone, even this naive girl who'd never been west or east of Lake Cacapon, be quite so stupid. Still, Shirley held her peace, nodded her on.

"Even seemed to know about some of the patients, though I can't figure out how, seeing how she wasn't from around here."

"What other patients?"

Kitty knit her brow, then her face lit. "Oh, yeah, I bet I know where she was at suppertime."

"What patients did she know?"

"Why . . . why, it was that little boy with pneumonia. I told her she ought to ask you about him, since you—"

"Go on, Kitty," said Shirley, through clenched teeth.

"Didn't she ask you? I was sure she had because—"

"No! I never saw her after she left the ER. What makes you think she did?"

"Oh. Well, like I said, she was talking all lovey to her daddy when she was feeding him, and she said something about the little boy's daddy going to give him the medicine that night."

Shirley gasped. "How did she know?"

"Like I said, I figured she'd taken my advice and talked to you. She'd wandered off after I said it. You sure you didn't see her? She was wearing a scrub gown, because she didn't have her robe."

"I suppose you gave her the gown." Her sarcasm was lost

on the young nurse, whom everyone thought of as sweet and nice, but who obviously hadn't a brain in her head. A loose tongue, in her case, was made even more dangerous by loose screws above.

"Oh, no. I had my hands full. I let her get it from the linen closet herself."

"I see. Thank you, Kitty."

"Sure, Shirley."

"Oh, and before you come on duty tomorrow, I want to talk with you again. Please come to me in my office."

Shirley walked slowly off the unit, controlling herself, containing herself. She had to learn more, but what she had already heard spawned feelings of horror she hadn't felt since the night she'd been raped at her apartment door.

In two days, by the first Thursday in March, she'd had Kitty fired and had learned enough to frighten her even more: On the evening of the insulin incident, according to an embarrassed black kitchen aide, peds Charge Nurse Elaine Wilkins and the aide had discussed Jimmy's father's medication lessons just before Zack arrived with Shirley to give the child his dinner tray; and peds, according to a chastened Elaine herself, on that very same evening had suffered a spate of patient monitor disconnections that had sent all staff running down the hall, leaving the nursing unit unattended; none of the staff recalled seeing anyone resembling Hester's description, but one recalled that a visitor complained of a tall, heavy woman emerging from the nurses' station, who ignored his requests to get a nurse for his little girl.

All of these findings added up to confirm Shirley's horrifying suspicions; all of these findings plus one intuitive hunch: Hester's hypoglycemia was itself induced by a shot of insulin. She had set the entire plot up before coming to the hospital. Somehow she planned—for whatever crazed reason—to kill little Jimmy. And Shirley herself, along with the loose-lipped, careless, resentful nursing staff helped her fall upon an insidious way to do it without going near the boy.

She took a deep, shuddering breath and thanked a god she didn't believe in for also letting her stop the plot from succeeding—*or at least from not* yet *succeeding! It still might. For somehow Hester Jones knew that Zack and Jimmy had been here in this hospital. That meant someone had told her. Someone who trusted her or was in league with her.*

Shirley stood in the hospital, wondering, tapping her square white teeth with a pen. Hester would not have known when she left the hospital that her plot had failed. She would have gone home, thinking it had succeeded. So, Jimmy, wherever he was, would be safe for a while. Zack had let slip to Shirley that he was going to Arizona. Did Hester know that? Quite likely. Like Zack, she'd come in a van, fully supplied for a long trip that she'd talked to Kitty about continuing.

Suppose it took her a few weeks to learn her plot failed. Yes, that would be as long as she could wait when nothing showed up in the newspapers. As a nurse she would figure a fatal medication error would be hidden as long as possible, and she would quite likely think that Zack, a fugitive charged with kidnapping, might go along with a cover-up of the boy's death, for fear that he'd be accused of murder. He wouldn't, of course. He wasn't that kind of man; but Hester probably didn't know that.

After a while, the murderer herself would grow curious. Shirley had known murderers at the jail. The urge to revisit the crime scene was not simply a cliché, a canard. The murderer could only revel in her crime when the world knew about it.

If somebody innocent told Hester that Zack had been here, that someone would know he'd gotten off safely. And if that innocent person trusted Hester, Hester would have gone back to her or him and found out the truth. And if that person was not *innocent—no, that hardly seemed likely. The woman was crazy. Acting alone. Shirley was sure.*

And Zack and Jimmy were in peril. Hester would track him down.

Shirley nodded to herself as she walked down the hall, her large nose ceiling-ward cocked. She knew now that the FBI was not Zack's greatest threat. She would handle them when they came. Meanwhile, as clever Hester had probably intuited, the judgment errors that had led to a near-fatal accident would stay guarded by an unspoken pact among the administration and staff. From the lowliest to the most exalted—and that included Shirley—the cost in reputation and power to the small community would be too great if the story got out. It would be a long time before tongues waggled as loosely as before. Kitty, poor idiot, was too naive to understand the reasons she'd been let go. However, the others knew, and they once more snapped to when Shirley passed by. The reasons for her command of respect in this hospital grew clearer as she'd unraveled this plot. If nothing else, she'd proven that no one here had made a medication error and that the tampering hadn't been an inside job, despite the internal carelessness that let it happen.

Shirley wasn't satisfied with that alone. She must stop Hester. Without letting anyone know where Zack was headed with the boy she *knew*—no matter what anyone said—was his son. She would start at the cashier's office.

Once she had Hester's address and phone number, she'd figure out a pretext for calling her. Or calling on her personally. The second might be better. Catching her off guard, warning her that she was being watched, might scare her off permanently. Yes, Hester was very clever, however mad. She must believe without a doubt that Shirley knew, without a doubt, what Hester had tried. There was no proof, Shirley would tell her. It all could be proven wrong, but Hester was being watched, so she'd better be careful. Yes, that, she decided, was the best tack to take. The next day was the first Friday in March, and Shirley had the weekend off. By Saturday evening she would be in Philadelphia. She would call on Hester on Sunday.

But on the first Friday in March she changed her plans.

The woman approached the triage desk from the administrative wing at ten A.M. "Miss Petrowski?"

Shirley looked up into calm gray eyes. "Yes?" The woman, about sixty, with perfectly coiffed honey and silver hair and wearing a fine peach wool suit with a silk peach and white blouse, nodded as if satisfied that Shirley was the one she was looking for.

"They told me to speak with you," she said, unguardedly, gesturing her head toward the administrative wing.

"How can I help you?"

The woman looked about the room, which bustled with activity. "Have you a private office?" Though her manner and motions were calm, she projected an air of urgency, much like a skilled surgeon preparing to operate on an emergency case.

Shirley responded as she would have to the surgeon; she called for relief at her post and led the woman back to her office. When the two had sat down across the desk from each other, Shirley nodded to her.

"I've come about my grandson."

"I'm sorry, I—"

"My grandson, Jimmy Broward. He was here four weeks ago."

Shirley tightened her jaws. She swallowed. "We had no Jimmy Broward here."

"No. He came in under another name, I'm sure. They told me they had a Jimmy Zachary in. That you'd had him admitted."

Shirley shook her head, not in denial, but puzzlement. Why was this woman, if she was who she said she was, so open about her purpose?

"Forgive me," the woman said, as if reading Shirley's thoughts, "I'm Grace Broward. My daughter, Liz, is Jimmy's mother."

Is! Then Rodney may have been right. The boy's mother might still be alive, not dead as Zack said. But Zack would not have lied.

"Exactly what do you want to know, Mrs. Broward?"

"Then he was here."

"I thought you already determined that."

"Yes. To my satisfaction. I wanted to determine it to yours."

"He was here. Now, what's your concern?"

Grace Broward nodded and sat back in her chair. She was a beautiful woman, long limbed, elegant, who looked younger than her age, the way wealthy women often did. "How was he, Miss Petrowski? When he left?"

The woman's question was so emotionally loaded, that Shirley didn't hesitate. "Why, fine, Mrs. Broward. Your grandson had a close call. He was very sick when he came in and . . . but when he left he was fine."

Grace Broward sighed. "Good. Very good. Thank God for that."

"He was well cared for here and when he left. Otherwise, we wouldn't have let his father take off with him in a van. That man gave him the best of care. Seldom left his side when he was here. But you didn't come all the way from Philadelphia to . . ." Shirley caught herself. Since Zack himself had appeared, she had never been so instantly and completely disarmed.

"No. That wasn't my only reason. But it's good to hear it from someone who was there."

"You heard it from someone who wasn't?"

"Zack keeps in touch with his daughter, Poke."

Thoroughly mystified, Shirley shook her head again.

"Miss Petrowski, you seem to know more than you're saying. Where I'd come from, for example. You couldn't have learned it from Zack. He wouldn't've told you where he'd come from either."

Nodding, Shirley opened her top desk drawer and pulled out the FBI report. After Grace had read it, Shirley said, "I saw that for the first time on Monday. Our sheriff brought it over. He's reporting that Zack and Jimmy were here."

Sliding it back to her, Grace asked, "What will you tell them?"

"I don't have anything to tell. He was here, but I don't know where he went from here. So if that's what you—"

She shook her head. "No. That's not what I want from

you. As long as I know Jimmy's fine. Or was when he left here."

Shirley stood up, thoroughly bewildered. She paced her small office for a while. Then she stopped and looked down at Grace Broward, who remained calm and lovely through it all. "Mrs. Broward, you must know how confused I am. I not only know that Zack James is a fugitive from the FBI, but that he's been charged by your husband. I also know that Zack thinks—really *believes*—that your daughter is dead. But you talked about her in the present tense. And Rodney—the sheriff—said she's in a coma. Which is it?"

Grace drew a deep breath and bowed her head. Contemplating—what? At last she raised her head, and motioned Shirley to sit down. Strange, how she seemed to have wrested control. In Shirley's own office, from the wrong side of the desk. Still, Shirley felt unthreatened.

"Liz isn't dead," Grace began. "Her father, my husband"—she winced when she said it—"is a very powerful man. He fed the news of her illness to a reporter he, er, ah, owns. Warned him against saying Liz had died. But his wording had better imply it. He also implied to anyone he wanted to imply it to that Liz was permanently gone. That's why Zack ran off with Jimmy. He knew Paul was demanding custody, would get it. The kidnapping charge came later, after he'd run."

Horrified, Shirley was speechless.

"As to why he made the charges, let me tell you from the beginning." Grace then outlined the story, ending with Liz's forced transfer to a private institution owned by a corporation that retained Paul's firm.

"He got their agreement to keep her there in a locked wing under twenty-four-hour guard. Actually, it wasn't simply an agreement. He has knowledge and documentation about some of their practices that they wouldn't want revealed. Liz isn't the only patient from a prominent family in their locked wing."

"Oh, Mrs. Broward—"

"Yes. Horrifying, isn't it?"

Shirley stiffened. "And you've known about this place since—?"

"Only since he had Liz moved there."

Relieved, she relaxed.

Taking another deep breath and nodding, Grace said, "Yes. You wonder how I could stay with a man who'd do these kinds of things. You're right to wonder. The answer is, I let myself believe that Paul's arrogance and prejudice weren't all that bad. He was a basically good man who just knew more than I about using power. So I handled my power base, the family. He let me handle that, as long as he got what he wanted. When I got in his way, he punished me. Subtly, not physically, of course. I can't explain."

"You don't have to." Shirley knew what she meant. She recalled her early life with a physically abusive father and a mother who never could leave him. "Please don't try." She reached across the desk and grasped Grace's hand.

Grace's gray eyes glittered. She bit her lower lip, then pursed both lips together. With a deep sigh, she fought back emotion, withdrew her hand from Shirley's. Her lips quivered into a smile. "Thank you."

Straightening herself, Shirley said, "You haven't told me why you're here, Mrs. Broward."

"Yes. When Poke told me Jimmy had been here, I guessed you'd have done blood tests and you'd have kept a blood sample in your lab."

"Yes."

"I'd like some tests run on it."

For the first time, Shirley felt uneasy. "For what? Everything pertinent was checked."

"Probably not this."

"Well, I could get you the report easily enough. Let me call the record room." She reached for the phone.

"Miss Petrowski, I don't want the report. I want the specimen. At least enough to send to a genetic lab."

"A genetic lab?" She took her hand from the receiver.

"Yes. I want to prove Zack James is Jimmy's father.

Now, before he builds a case against his own fitness as a father."

"He's proven his fitness. I'll be thrilled to testify for him if it comes to that."

Grace smiled and shook her head. "Thank you for that. For Liz, too. But the last thing you'd want is to face Paul Broward's cross-examination."

"Why should that scare me? I'll stick to the facts, and—"

"You don't know my husband. He's ruthless. He'll twist things to imply you slept with Zack. He'll find witnesses happy to support him. People here in your hospital."

The blood drained from Shirley's face.

"I'm sorry. I didn't mean to sound crude. That's the way he works."

"No. That's all right. I mean, it wasn't crude. I . . . I know what you mean. I'm fifty-two, unmarried, and not always loved by the staff here, who think I'm a frustrated old bag."

Grace's mouth fell open. After a few seconds she said, "I don't believe that at all."

Snorting, Shirley tilted her head back, feeling her beaked nose burning. "Then you're as naive as I was when I gallantly volunteered my testimony, Grace."

"You're astute, Shirley. You get my point. So, now that we're on a first-name basis, may I have the specimen?"

"I'll arrange it. But you'll need to get your daughter's. And Zack's." She brightened. "Maybe his daughter can get him to send it from Arizona."

Grace lifted a brow.

"Yes, he slipped once. Mentioned that was where he was heading. That doesn't help much, though. It's a big state, with most of the population centered around Phoenix and Tucson. There're lots of places to hide there in a van. But don't worry, I won't spill it to the FBI."

"Thank you, Shirley. I need to trust you. There's no one I *can* trust. The FBI aren't the only ones looking for Zack. He's not even top priority with them. But he is to Paul. He's got private detectives working round the clock. I've had to be clever to evade them. It hasn't been easy."

"I admire your courage, Grace."

"Thank you. It's come . . . late in life." She looked rue-
ful.

Filling her lungs with air, Shirley said, "It came when
you needed it. And now you're going to need it even more.
Because you're not the only one who knows that Jimmy
was here. Somebody else knows it, too. And she tried to
kill him."

Grace blanched. Her knuckles whitened as she grasped
the edge of the desk. She never let go throughout Shirley's
story.

"Dear, dear God!" she said when Shirley finished. "Oh,
dear, dear God! I'm sure no one but Poke knew Jimmy was
here. No one else could've told the woman. But how? She'd
have been seen if they'd met. They watch that poor child's
every move. They tried to follow me."

"Familiarity breeds contempt," said Shirley.

"What do you mean?"

"Suppose Hester visited Poke openly. Not once, but regularly. That would have done two things: gained the girl's
trust, and thrown off suspicion that she was some sort of
messenger."

"But why, for God's sake? Why would she want to
hurt . . . kill . . . a little boy?"

"I don't know, Grace. She's probably killed someone
before. Maybe a child. She's crazy, and crazy people do the
same crazy things over and over again. They're determined.
That's what scares me. She left here thinking she'd succeeded. When she finds out she didn't . . ." She shuddered.
"Hester, if only I could read that warped mind of yours!"

At that, Grace looked up, clearly stunned. "Hester! Yes.
You're right! A Hester did visit Poke. Then suddenly
stopped. Poke told me. My God! I've got to get back
to Poke before Hester does. I have to keep her away
from that madwoman. A serial killer. My God!" She
stood up. "I can't lose a minute. Poke might be next."

Shirley rose, too. "Be careful, Grace. Don't waste a second, but be careful."

On the second Sunday in March, Grace Broward slipped into a restaurant rest room and donned her now faded navy blue sweat suit, her wig, and fanny pack. She picked up her rented car where she'd bought a space for three months and drove to Glenside. She hadn't time to set up secret meetings with Poke. Though she'd made her trip to West Virginia within a day, despite the long car ride from and to the Martinsburg airport, she hadn't got back to Bryn Mawr till nearly midnight. She'd gone straight to her study and slept on her daybed; for the first time since marrying Paul, she no longer shared his bed. The distance kept her from blurting out her hatred. The distance, and her mission to stop him from destroying his family. Liz would regain consciousness one day. Grace never doubted that. She would get well, and when she did, she would know her mother had found the courage to stand up to her father's wickedness. *To betray him then leave him, after all those years.*

But now there was a greater threat to their family than Paul: a woman with a crippled father and a twisted mind, a crazed killer, who'd picked Jimmy as her next victim and was determined to kill him. She'd left Squirrel Springs thinking she'd succeeded. Now she'd be wondering why Jimmy's death hadn't been in the news, like everything else about the Browards.

Grace caught her breath. *Yes! The Browards were prominent. Powerful, thus hated. That could have something to do with it. Families like theirs had been targeted by killers before. Jimmy was a Broward heir, the only one left after Liz. Did this Hester want to destroy the Browards? It was crazy, but it might explain not only* why *Hester chose Jimmy, but* how. *She'd read the kidnapping story. It had set her off for some reason. And it helped her track Jimmy down. Everything she'd have needed to track down a stranger had been there: names, addresses, photos.*

Galvanized by this thought, Grace screeched her car into

a parking space near Poke's school. Then she got hold of herself. She had to look casual, her old calm unhurried self as she walked to the Jameses' house.

She took, as before, an indirect route. They'd see her go into the house, but wouldn't know where she'd come from. And she wouldn't let them follow her afterward. Her mind raced as she reprised her past artful dodges. She'd never been under such pressure before. Was she skilled enough, confident enough to throw off followers now? No one must know where Jimmy was.

She passed the house before feigning an "Aha!" expression. Then she turned back, and walked casually up the walk and across the flagstone path, and mounted the porch.

The Sunday *Inquirer* lay by the doorstep. After ringing the doorbell, she bent and picked it up. When, after a long delay, Poke finally opened the door, Grace said loudly and cheerily, "Papergirl calling!" and handed the paper to the stupefied young woman. Loudly, gaily, she said, "I was walking and suddenly thought I'd stop in." Then she dropped her voice and whispered, "I have to talk to you. It's important. Smile as if you're glad to see me. Call me Aunt Hilda."

Poke did as she was told, though Grace doubted her wavering voice carried to the nearby parked car.

After entering, Grace said, "Can you make me brunch, Poke?" She kept her voice calm, so she wouldn't alarm the girl.

Poke nodded.

As Poke made French toast and coffee and set out syrup, milk, and sugar, Grace watched from the family room, which was small and cluttered with furniture but clean and neat. The kitchen, also small, sparkled. There was no sign of the squalor Paul had described to her after spying through the windows. "You keep house beautifully," she said, as if she could make up for the slander Poke had never heard. A way to feel less guilty about what Paul had done, a way, maybe, to calm herself till she could learn what she had to.

The young woman, who'd said nothing since Grace arrived, nodded, silent still. She set up the brunch in the kitchen, and gestured for Grace to come sit. She passed a plate of toast to Grace, who took two slices, and watched from above her empty plate as she ate and drank some coffee.

"Coffee's perfect. Just the way I like it."

"Mrs. Broward, you said it was important."

"It is, Poke. I talked to a nurse who took care of Jimmy in the hospital. She said he was well and happy when he left with your father. I wanted to tell you that."

"Oh," said Poke, brightening and relaxing a little. She took some French toast for herself. "That's nice. But I already knew he was fine."

"You've heard from your father?" Grace took a deep breath.

"I can't tell you how I know, exactly. But he sent me a picture from . . . from where he is."

"A picture! Wonderful!"

"Did you get the blood from the hospital?"

"Better than that. The nurse sent it to a genetic lab for tests. They'll send me the results soon."

"Then I guess you want Pop's blood, too. I haven't got it. Still can't figure out how."

"We'll both keep thinking. But I wanted to tell you about your dad and brother."

"Right. Thanks."

"Oh . . . and you were upset when I left about being deserted by your friend . . . Hester, was it? Has she started visiting again? You were afraid she was being followed."

Poke stiffened and set down her fork.

Grace said, "Oh, no! Someone *did* follow her!"

Mutely, the girl shook her head.

"Something happened! What was it?" Grace set her fork down and reached across the small table for Poke's hand.

She drew it away. Tears leapt to the edges of her eyelids. She struggled to hold them back.

At last, she said, "She was mad at me for telling you

about her. She said I was a stupid baby to trust you. Said . . . said if they followed her, she'd tell them where Pop went." She gripped the table's edge and implored, "You didn't tell them about her. Say you didn't!"

Shaking her head, Grace said, "No, dear, I didn't." She bit her lip.

Poke's tears ran freely. "She said her daddy'd suffered enough from what Mr. Broward did. You didn't deserve a sweet little baby like Jimmy—"

Grace swallowed. "When did she say that, Poke?" Her tongue stuck to the roof of her mouth.

"When she brought the picture. Almost two weeks ago."

"The picture? Of your father?"

She sniffed up her tears and nodded. "And Jimmy, on his shoulders."

Grace breathed deeply. "May I see the picture?" At her hesitation, she went on, "Poke, please trust me. Jimmy's my grandson. I want to see him."

She stared at Grace a few seconds more, then rose and ran into the family room. She opened a drawer, shuffled through some papers, and pulled out the Polaroid print. She handed it to Grace, who had followed her, still trying to remain calm, just a concerned grandmother, not a spy.

Yes! Oh, dear God, it was her grandson! He was well as he sat on his bearded father's shoulders. Well and smiling. Grace wept.

When she'd regained some composure, she sighed and handed the picture back to Poke, who clutched it against her chest. Weak-kneed, she looked around the room for a place to sit, then sat on the corner of the sofa.

Poke stared at her.

"Should I sit someplace else?"

"No . . . it's OK." Then Poke swiveled out the desk chair, and sat on it, still clutching the picture.

Grace asked, "When did you first meet Hester, Poke?"

"She came with a basket of fruit. Condolences. For . . . for Liz."

"For Liz? How did she know Liz?"

"She was her doctor. Hester felt sad, and she knew how I felt, because of, well, she knew Pop had to go away because of Mr. Broward, and Mr. Broward had made her and her daddy suffer, too."

The second time Poke had mentioned that.

"What did she mean? Did she tell you?"

Poke told her about Lester Jones as Hester had told her. Unbelieving at first, Grace slowly comprehended. *She'd guessed right: oh horror of horrors! Hester was after Jimmy because he was Paul's grandson!*

The girl finished her story of Hester's first visit. "And then she said it was too bad Liz had to suffer, but she had Mr. Broward's poison in her blood."

Poison in her blood! Paul's poison! And Jimmy would have it, too! Revenge . . . Hester was avenging her father. It all made sense. Too much sense.

"I told her it wasn't true, that Liz was nothing like her father. And she said that was true. That's why she was so sad and brought me the fruit, because Liz had told her all about me and Pop and Jimmy."

But, Liz had told no one about Zack. The woman had read the kidnap story that Paul had managed as Grace had once managed him. How well he had managed it! Hester inferred Liz had died because she'd expected her to . . . because she had somehow . . . Oh, God! It all fit together now! Carbon monoxide—undetectable in blood tests unless you were looking for it. Liz's symptoms, the same as Lester's, except she didn't have diabetes. Carbon monoxide! A poison in the blood.

Grace's blood drained from her face. Poke stared at her.

"Mrs. Broward, what's wrong?"

Shaking her head, Grace said, "It's awful. What he did. To them. To Liz, Jimmy, all of us. We have to stop it, get to Jimmy before . . ." She looked up at Poke. How much should she tell her?

"Do you think they found Hester? Do you think she told them?"

"No. I know they didn't. They don't know about that picture, or they'd've found your father. He's contacted you since, hasn't he?"

"Yes. He talked to someone who knew about my great-grandmother. He'll tell me what she said when I get there in the fall."

"Not till fall . . . that's too late! We have to reach him right away."

"Why? What's the matter? You've found out something bad!"

Grace fixed Poke's eyes with her own. "Poke, do you trust me? No matter what Hester said?"

Her head shook. "I don't know."

"You must. You have to trust someone. Your father . . . there's more than one person after him. And he's always in danger. Not just from the FBI. If Hester . . . should tell someone where he is, if there's even a chance . . . Poke, you have to trust me."

Again, the lovely head shook, not with a no, but with uncertainty.

"You trusted Hester, and she turned on you. Can you trust *anybody* else? The person you get your father's messages from? *Anybody?*"

"Yes. I'd trust her."

"Then get a message to her."

"I can't. If I call her, they'll find out."

"But how does she reach you?"

"From a phone booth. Never the same one. And she uses a kind of code. I told Hester that."

"But, Poke, why didn't you just call *her* from a phone booth? No one would know."

"They follow me. Someone could listen. If I called from the booth in school, they might have some kid or teacher listen in. My friends all blew me off when Pop went away."

"Oh, Poke!" Grace stood up and crossed the room. She grasped the girl's shoulders and pulled her to her feet. "You poor, dear child! They've terrorized you. All of them!" She pulled Poke toward her, embraced her. "They'd have

stopped at nothing to break you down. I won't let them!
No, it's just too much."

Poke broke down in Grace's arms and wept uncontrol-
lably. Grace embraced her, supported her through the outburst, absorbing her pain as her sweatshirt absorbed her
tears. Weak at the end, the girl allowed her weight to rest
on Grace, who bore it until her arms and legs ached.

Poke regained her composure and gently disengaged from
Grace's arms. Her face quivered as she stared at the woman
for several moments. "I *do* trust you, Mrs. Broward. Liz
sent you here, I know it. I know you're not like her father,
because if you were like that, she wouldn't have been like
she was."

"Then, tell me the name of the person you exchange
messages with. It's important. I must get a message to
your father. Today."

Poke's eyes grew wide with fear again. "But Joyce never
calls him. She waits for him to call her from a pay phone.
Oh, Mrs. Broward, something bad is happening. Who else
is after Pop? Why? Tell me!"

*Why must she pile another hurt on this child? Why
couldn't she find in her repertoire of lies to protect loved
ones, one that would cover this case? Why? Because she'd
asked Poke to trust her. And now she had to trust Poke.*

"Yes. I'll tell you. I have to. I want you to be brave,
Poke. Braver than you've been up till now, and I've never
met anyone braver."

The young woman's throat rippled. "Tell me. Please. I'm
not a child!"

"No. You're not. Please sit down next to me while I tell
you. We need each other, you and I." She led Poke to the
sofa and sat with her arm around her shoulder. As softly
as she could, she said, "Hester is after Jimmy, not your
father. I didn't know why until you told me. I only know
she followed him to the hospital in West Virginia and tried
to kill him."

Poke gasped.

"She failed, because of a very caring nurse. I won't

go into more detail now. But she failed. She came back home thinking she'd succeeded. But nothing showed up in the news, so she came to visit you again, probably to find out."

"I told her about Joyce!"

"You had no reason not to. Don't blame yourself. She's a very clever woman, and she's insane. The picture probably made her angry."

"She knows where Pop is, Mrs. Broward. Oh, God!"

"There's no question she's on her way there. And that's not your fault, either. You must remember that."

"She could be there already! She could get there in less than a week."

"Maybe. But she'd have her father with her. That would slow her down. Especially if she knew there was no hurry, that your father was at his final destination in Arizona."

Poke stiffened. "How did you know?"

"The nurse at the hospital. Your father let that much slip out, but not the exact spot there. Anyway, I think that Hester would take a few weeks crossing the country in her van with her father. She wouldn't want to slip again, so she'd plan things out very carefully."

"But why does she want to kill Jimmy?"

Grace explained that she was avenging her father. "She tried to kill Liz, and she thinks she succeeded. She didn't know about Jimmy till she read about him in the paper."

Poke bolted up, then turned and stared down at Grace. "Liz! You mean she's alive!"

Filling her lungs with as much air as they could hold, Grace said, "Alive, yes. But still in a coma."

"But Mr. Broward said she was dead!"

Shaking her head, Grace explained how her husband left that impression.

"Joyce said he told her she was dead. She told us he was coming here to take Jimmy."

"Joyce Price! Jimmy's nanny. She's the one who's been helping you. Oh, thank God for Joyce!"

"Where is she? Where's Liz? Will she get better?"

Grace explained that her daughter was under lock and
key in the hospital she'd been moved to. She theorized
that Hester had poisoned her with carbon monoxide. She
said she hoped that Liz would recover. *A mother's hope.
Liz couldn't be gone forever.*

When she'd laid all this out for Poke, she rose and
embraced her again. "I'll call Joyce from home. She must
find some way to reach your father. Meanwhile, I can't take
any chances that Hester will get to Jimmy first. It would be
better to let the FBI do it, if it comes to that. So, here's what
I'm going to do. As soon as I've spoken to Joyce, I'll catch
a plane and go to Arizona. You'll have to tell me where
your father is."

"It's a place called Roosevelt Lake. He was going to go
there with Liz. Some archaeologists are doing research at
the lake. I got some of their magazines with maps of the
place. But you can't just fly there and get off the plane and
take a taxi. You have to have a Jeep or something, an RV
like Pop's, 'cause there's a dirt road you have to take."

"I can rent one."

"You have to know how to drive one," Poke said as she
ran to the desk where she'd gotten the photo, and pulled
out a page with a diagram.

Grace looked at it and nodded. "I can rent a driver, too.
Don't worry, dear. I'm a seasoned detective by now." She
smiled. She studied the map and committed it to memory,
then handed it back. "I'm not going to let this fall into the
wrong hands."

No sign of a brown Toyota, or any other suspect vehicle
complicated Grace's return to her rented car. The gods were
on her side, no doubt. Not for her sake alone; they'd have
Jimmy and Poke, those besieged innocents at heart. She was
only a tool in their rescue. She offered herself to them, those
gods, to take her if they wished, but only after she'd done
what they'd sent her to do.

They answered swiftly, as gods often do.

Still having detected no tail, she arrived at her rented

parking garage space. Sunday had emptied many of the monthly rental slots around her. Still, the garage screamed and screeched and squealed with entering and leaving vehicles. These sounds always made her uneasy, especially as she crossed the dank cement floor and walked to the elevator, a trip she would have to make three times: going to the rest room two tiers down at ground level to change her clothes, then returning to put her disguise in the trunk, then leaving again to catch a taxi below. She fully expected that on one of these trips the screech would be of tires bearing down upon her, and the scream echoing off the walls would be hers as they struck her. And that would be the last sound she'd hear.

She shuddered as a sudden March wind whipped up from the street below and over the parapet. A newspaper on the floor lifted and hopped, and let free a flapping page, which chased her and curled about her ankles. She kicked it loose and ran from it, as if it were a living thing; and, as if it were a living thing, it took up the chase again, and again caught her, this time wrapping itself around her thighs.

She batted it off with the shopping bag containing her clothing, and, in inexplicable panic, knocked it to the floor and stomped it, tearing it and leaving smudged prints of her running shoe treads on the shreds that blew away. *Clues,* she thought, *for anyone following me.*

But, of course, no one was following her. She'd become too skilled at evading pursuit, even preventing it altogether. She stopped, took hold of her breathing, lost it in an escaping giggle, and recovered it again.

Slowly she walked to the elevator, arriving there at the same time as a man who'd approached from the opposite end of the garage.

As the door slid open, he got in ahead of her and held it open. She nodded her thanks, and sighed as it closed and the car started moving *upward*!

"Oh!" she said.

He smiled. "Someone up there must have called it before I pressed G."

"Of course." But hadn't she seen the down arrow glowing above the portal before she'd gotten on? She must have just assumed . . . She glanced at the electronic panel now. G was not lit up. Five, two tiers above the one where she'd parked the car, was. Only he could have pressed its call button.

No, not necessarily. Someone could have pressed it before it stopped for them, then gotten off. That happened sometimes. She'd known of people pressing every button, just for fun, usually children out to frustrate adults. But even adults change their minds and get off before they'd planned, or press the wrong button by mistake or . . . The car stopped at five, and a man was waiting there. He smiled. And kept waiting. The door began to close again. The man in the car pressed the "door open" button.

"Please get off here," he said to Grace.

"I'm going down," she said.

The waiting man stepped into the car. He grasped her arm. "Please come with me. I don't want to hurt you."

She tried to pull her arm free, and to swing her heavy shopping bag at him. The bag slid harmlessly off his nylon jacket. The knees of the man behind her caught her own, propelled her forward. "It won't help you to make a fuss," said the man in the nylon jacket, as he pulled her into the path of a moving car and spun her loose.

The car screeched to a halt inches from her. She imagined her own final scream, the scream of the nightmare she always had in parking garages.

But her scream was caught by a wad of cloth, thrown between her teeth like a bit as she opened her mouth. She felt a hard knot tighten at the base of her skull, another at her wrists, which had been wrenched behind her back. The car's driver threw open his door and then instantly opened the rear door as her two captors lifted her and tossed her into a large padded interior.

Quickly, they climbed in, one through each door, and trapped her between them. The doors clunked closed, the car slid smoothly away. In the opaque black glass of the side windows, she saw her reflection. The trussed-up woman she saw there from her twisted position looked still defiant, still held in her hands the torn shopping bag from Woodward and Lothrop. The fanny pack had ridden up to the center of her back and dug into her bound wrists and her spine. The pain in them left her breathless. Tears came in spite of her will.

The man in the nylon jacket, to her right, nodded to the other, whose blue wool coat rubbed her cheek. The second reached back and released her wrists. She wrenched her arms free, only to have each man grab one.

"Relax, Mrs. Broward. You won't be hurt. Your husband instructed us not to hurt you."

Paul knew. He had known all along, since the first night she'd come in so late. Of course. He had been in no hurry. He'd expected her to learn something useful, given enough time. Well, now he'd become the lesser of two evils. She would have to tell him where Zack was.

"Mmff!" The gag muffled her attempt to say she wanted to talk to Paul. She tried to get her arms loose so she could pull it away. The men held her tight, blocking her attempts at kicking with their large hard legs. She bit into the gag and tried to call out.

"It's no use. No one will hear or see you," the man on her left said, with more exasperation than anger, as he tried to push up her sweatshirt sleeve.

"Forget it," the other man said. "There's an easier way." With that, he pulled open the snaps that closed the front of her shirt, then pulled the shirt off one shoulder. She expected him to tear the shirt off altogether, leaving her exposed, perhaps to keep her from bolting when they'd reached their destination. It wouldn't work. If she had to run completely naked down the street, she would.

But he stopped when he'd exposed one shoulder, then said to his partner, "Pull the arms behind her again. I'll take care of the rest."

Moments later she felt a sting in her shoulder, then a slight aching sensation. And several moments after that, she lost consciousness.

■   ■   ■

When the light from a high window seared her eyes and brought with it a throbbing headache, she sat up. Her skin exuded a familiar smell. She lifted one arm to her nose and sniffed it. She'd been cleansed and creamed with something that reminded her of baby lotion.

Her eye fell upon the wrist. Bruised. She touched it. Very tender. Puzzled at first, she remembered something about being forcibly restrained. *Drugged! By men in a car. How had she got there? Where was she now?*

She lifted her eyes, looked around her. Something in her surroundings seemed familiar. She remembered the pale green walls, the windows high, near the ceiling, the soft sounds of breathing, broken by occasional moans.

She uncovered her legs, found them naked to the bottom edge of the gown she was wearing. A wisp of her graying pubic hair showed between them. She tugged the gown down, and knew where she was, and where the soft breathing sounds came from.

She was not alone. There was another bed in the room, with a curtain pulled around it. Shakily, she got out of bed. She held her head in her hand as she crossed the room, reached for the curtain. Its hooks rattled as she drew it back. A soft moan floated toward her as the woman in the bed turned her head, seemed to look at her.

She stepped forward and grasped the bed rail. "Liz," she said. "Dear, dear Liz." Then she leaned over and stroked her daughter's lovely hair.

"You're in there somewhere, I know. And I'll stay with you until you come out again."

Did she smile? Or was the tiny flicker at the corner of her mouth an involuntary twitch.

No! It was a smile! Grace knew. This was the daughter she'd carried inside her. She knew everything about her every cell. She lowered the bed rail and leaned over and kissed her daughter's forehead.

Again the corner of Liz's mouth flickered before she closed her eyes and moaned once more.

CHAPTER
▪▪ THIRTEEN

ROOSEVELT LAKE—A FEW DAYS LATER

Not Shea, but Zack, had broken through Bill Jennings's resistance to his camping on the dig site. For a few days the older man mumbled under his breath each morning when he arrived and saw the van parked next to the trailer. But, as Zack never threatened his authority, and as he spent few daylight hours on the site, Bill began to accept his presence.

Most mornings, Zack took off with Jimmy in the van to show him the sights within a few hours' drive: The Tonto National Monument, with its cliff dwellings still partially intact, so Jimmy could place his hand over a handprint left centuries ago in a drying mud wall; the petrified forests to the northeast to let him touch wood that had turned to stone; the red rock hills of Sedona, to the northwest, so he could have a picnic in the Coconino National Forest overlooking Oak Creek Canyon. And every few days, he returned to the San Carlos Reservation so Jimmy could play with Lucy and Peter's grandchildren. On those times he stayed overnight.

And Shea found herself pining for his return, as she had the first time, as if he had gone forever.

He'd come back somehow changed that first time, the first Sunday in March, but he'd said little about his experiences at the reservation. He had shown her the sculptured head, and she'd exclaimed, "A Lucy McCoy! How wonderful! Have you any idea how much that piece is worth?"

He'd shrugged. "A few hundred, I guess."

"Hundred! Thousands is more like it." She'd allowed her fingers to play over the piece, to gather in from the different textures and delicately chiseled lines the full effect of its power. "It's the most moving Lucy McCoy sculpture I've ever seen. But all of her stuff is moving. That's what makes her work so powerful," she'd said. "You're a lucky man, Zack. What a wonderful treasure you have to pass down to your children."

"Yeah, right," he'd said thoughtfully; then questioningly, "That's what it means." He'd said no more after that.

The next time he returned at sunset from his two-day stay at the reservation, and to her relief and pleasure he came directly to the trailer with Jimmy. She quickly augmented the dinner she'd begun to cook for herself. *It feels like they've come home here!* she thought.

Later that evening, after putting Jimmy to bed in his van, he returned to the trailer with his baby-minder monitor in hand. "OK if I come in for awhile?"

"Sure it's OK."

He hung the monitor over the doorknob and closed the door. "Just keep on with your work," he said. "I just want to watch a real professional archaeologist at work. Just 'cause you folks won't let me do any actual digging here doesn't mean I can't learn how it's done."

She closed her log book and pushed it aside. "No way. I'll give you a couple of books on method and a copy of one of Doug's monographs. You'll find those boring enough without watching me."

"Watching you work wouldn't bore me. It's a good way to learn."

She felt her face burn. "No. Not tonight, anyway. I'd rather finish tomorrow. Why don't we just have something relaxing?"

"You're sure you don't want me to leave?"

"Positive. I need a break, too. And company. You and Jimmy have spoiled me. I used to think I wanted to be alone. After Doug died. Now, somehow, I . . . well, when the two of you go off and there's no one to stand guard at night—"

"You ought to go off this place sometime yourself," he said. "You have a house somewhere?"

"In Phoenix. But it's no less lonely than here." She rose and went to the refrigerator. "You have your choice, Zack. Chardonnay or Chardonnay."

He grinned and sat on the folding chair and leaned back. "Your pick."

She poured them each a small water glassful, apologizing for her lack of barware. They sat and sipped for a while. Then he said, "I'm glad we've made you less lonesome. I get pretty lonesome, too. Especially after Jimmy and I watch Liz's picture. We do that almost every night before he goes to sleep. I don't want him to ever forget her."

"Oh, Zack!" She reached across the narrow space between them and touched the back of his left hand, which rested on his thigh.

He looked at her; then, lifting her hand in his, pressed it gently before placing it back in her lap. His gesture said, *Not too close; not too soon.* But it did not say, *No! Not ever!*

He broke the pregnant silence that followed by saying, "I wish I could tell Liz about what happened the first time on the reservation."

Shea, still weak with emotion, said nothing.

"She'd know that I needed to talk to someone, Shea. Since you know Peter and Lucy, and sent me to them, well, Liz wouldn't be mad at me for telling you instead." His eyes probed hers for understanding.

"I don't think she would. I'm sure she loved you too much."

"And Jimmy. I've got to share these things with someone that cares about Jimmy. And that understands Peter, too. Like you do."

She laughed. "Me? I'm a long way from understanding that man. He's always talking in riddles."

"Well, you know what he meant about the head."

"Lucy's sculpture? I know that it moved me. Like a living head almost."

"Right. I felt that part, too. And Peter said I should take what I need and get rid of the rest."

"Oh, yes. His favorite incantation. He learned it from his mother. He told us that at the seminar at the Heard Museum, the first time I met him. But I never was sure of what it meant."

"Well, you said something about the head that sounded like what it meant to me."

"I did?" She knit her brow, trying to recall.

"You said it was powerful, and it was a treasure I could pass along to my kids." He drained his glass and held it out for her to pour more. She emptied the Chardonnay bottle, then got a second from the refrigerator and handed it to him, along with a corkscrew.

Holding the bottle between his strong thighs, he stripped off the plastic cork cover, then skillfully punctured and twisted out the cork.

As he handed her back the bottle, she said, "Yes, I guess it could mean that. It would to you, wouldn't it, in that case. But, overall, in a general sense, I think it has a deeper meaning. Something that covers everything in life." She finished filling his glass, handed it back to him, then filled her own again.

"It sure does. But each time, you have to figure it out separately. For yourself."

"Well, that's what riddles are about, I guess. What other ones did he tell you?" Her face was growing warm from the wine's effect, as well as from his presence. She wanted to keep him there as long as possible. It may not yet be time to touch him as she had before, let alone as she wanted to— not on the hand alone, but on the thigh it rested on. Her own thighs imagined his touch, between them. She shifted, allowed them to part slightly.

"The one about safe places. I guess you know about that."

"It's as old as the Bible, Zack. The Lord God is within you, or something like that. Part of every mythology you want to study. It's Peter's way of saying that you aren't safe anywhere, until you feel safe in yourself. Remember, I told you I saw a confluence between Peter's way of healing and modern psychiatry."

"Right. You sure know your riddles, Shea."

"Try another on me."

"I'll tell you about Storytelling Woman's riddles. She's not a psychiatrist, just a storyteller."

"I don't know about her."

"I'll start at the beginning, then." And he told her about Peter's request that the ancient storyteller search her memory for knowledge of Zack's Apache roots, about her trip to the mountainside before dawn to ask her ancestors for advice, about Peter's and Zack's journey to her side, only to find her bitten by a rattlesnake, dying. "And we left her there," said Zack, shaking his head in wonderment. "But I covered her, so she wouldn't be cold."

"She was ready, Zack. That's no riddle. When it comes to keeping people who are ready to die alive, we're the ones with the riddles."

He looked up at her, his eyes glittering, changing from brown to green, back again to brown. "That's no riddle to me. Maryellen was ready, and I held her in my arms to keep her warm. It's Liz that wasn't ready. They took her from me. They . . ." He stopped short, in obvious pain.

She waited for him to go on, explain what he meant. He'd never told her exactly how Liz had died, or of what. Had someone murdered her, done something horrible to her? Was that why he'd fled his Pennsylvania home? She neither moved nor spoke. Nor did he for many moments. He finished his second glass of wine, then seemed steadied.

"Here's what Storytelling Woman told me," he went on at last.

Shea listened intently to the story of the white father whose daughter was conceived by the Apache woman, an obvious reference to Zack's great-grandparents. There seemed no riddle in that. The story seemed much like the one he had told her before the first time he went to the reservation.

"It all made sense to me until the very last thing she said."

"Me too, so far. Go on."

"These were the exact words Peter used when he translated: *'then, a flood too soon was carried away in a basket that took nine months to weave. It is full of memories that only a daughter may know, even though a father's memories are woven into the basket, and even though a father leads her to it.'*"

Shea rose and stood, unable to speak for a minute. Her hands began to tremble and she ran to the sink to put her glass of wine down.

Zack rose. "Shea! What's the matter?"

"Nothing." She shook her head.

"Hey, c'mon. What did I say?" He placed his hands on her shoulders. "Is it the riddle? Did you hear it before?"

"Never!" She turned her head to look at him. "No. I didn't *hear* it. I *lived* it. Something like it, anyway."

He looked puzzled, hurt.

"It's not your fault, Zack. You didn't know. I never told you that part."

He dropped his hands from her shoulders. She turned around completely. "That riddle . . . what it means is that the widow had a miscarriage. A flood too soon, is her water breaking too early. Probably the baby was born dead because of it. Maybe from infection or something. Who knows? Anyway, the basket that took nine months to weave, well that speaks for itself, doesn't it? Her uterus. The rest, about the father's memories being woven in, well that fits, too. And the whole basket was lost then. Something only a woman would understand and could tell you about. What it feels like to lose your uterus."

"Oh, Shea. I'm sorry. I didn't know."

"It's not your fault. Not your fault at all."

"Dear person." He drew her into his arms and held her.
She held herself stiff for a moment, then allowed him to
draw her close. "I'm sorry."

"I didn't tell you. I never told anyone after it happened.
Never talked about it, even to Doug. It was his son I lost.
Then, he was gone, too."

"All this time, you never talked about it. You have to
talk about it, Shea."

"His son, then all of our sons and daughters, grandsons,
granddaughters. We were the end of the line, Zack. Nothing
left but each other. Then he was gone, too."

"Tell me," he said, still holding her.

She did—all of it, the excitement on feeling she was pregnant, the joy on having the feeling confirmed; the search
for the bigger house in Phoenix, where they'd planned to
redecorate the former owner's office and use it as a nursery; the anxiety of the first three months, always the most
tenuous; their passage with no signal of trouble, followed
by their announcement to others; Bill's unkind remarks
behind her back. Then the sudden pain tearing through
her pelvis, waking her, making her scream; the gush of
blood, the nausea, Doug lifting her, carrying her dripping
bright blood and clots all over the floors, to the car, where
she continued to bleed, feeling the warm blood and tissue
seeping out, her heat fleeing with it, her cold self sticking
in it, feeling her consciousness fade along with the pain.

Waking up in the intensive care room, being told to
cough, and being afraid to because coughing might hurt
the baby. Feeling the tightness across her abdomen, under
a large dressing they kept on checking. Seeing the plastic
blood bag hanging above her, realizing its tube was attached
to a needle in her arm; falling asleep for a long time; seeing
Doug, his beard pitch black against the stark white of his
face, hearing him say it was all right. She was all right. That
was all that counted. Finding out her baby was dead, all her
children and grandchildren were dead forever, she was the

end of the line. Wanting to be dead herself, if dying would come in the night, quietly. She hadn't the courage to kill herself.

Then moving into the new house, and using the office as an office, and deciding that Doug was enough to live for, that maybe, when she got over all this, they would adopt a son, for it was a son they'd lost; then losing Doug . . . everything else, everyone else that counted having gone before him.

And, still a coward, going on living; then finding that work counted, must go on, that maybe there was something there in the past that would explain why things like this happened, that would say life was worth living. And not finding it there, either.

She spilled it out into Zack's ear, spilled her tears out onto his beard and shoulders, a beard like Doug's, shoulders like Doug's, a chest like his, moving in even breaths against her breasts, arms like his, encircling her, cradling her, firm thighs pressed against hers, as his would in readying her for love, his own readiness bulging against her pelvis.

When her tears stopped, he said to her, "I'm sorry, so sorry." And he took his arms from around her and placed his hands, large like Doug's, on her face and tilted it up and looked into her lime green eyes with his dark green ones. His fingers played along her drying tear streaks, from the corners of her eyes to the corners of her mouth. She tasted the salt they chased across her lips.

He kissed her mouth. "Dear person."

Words Doug never used, words no one had ever said to her before. His own words of love.

Then he kissed her again, and as he still held her face, his eyes became brown. A switch flicking, changing the mood, losing it. He stepped back, dropped his hands from her face. "Good night, Shea," he said. And he left.

The ache of grief, of emptiness had gone, replaced by an ache she'd almost forgotten, the ache of sexual longing.

For the next two days Shea worried that what had passed between Zack and her would frighten him off. Yet he said nothing. She breathed easier, not simply because it signaled his reciprocal emotions, but because, since he'd come, he'd helped the dig go more smoothly. Though she had made clear to him that he could not take part in the dig as a volunteer, he helped the crew in other ways, running errands to Punkin Center, the nearest place to pick up such things as a carton of cigarettes for Bill, who, while working hard, managed to get away far enough from the dig to smoke more than a pack a day and still avoid contaminating the field with his brand-new ashes and modern day artifacts. On three occasions Zack served the crew a beef barbecue cooked on his Coleman and dressed with his spicy and succulent homemade sauce. For people forced to eat meals from brown bags packed with little imagination at home or white bags packed with even less by fast-food employees with smiles and cute caps and smocks, Zack seemed an angel.

If he was an angel, he was a bedeviled one. By grief, Shea reasoned, or by those who had taken his Liz away from him; for he handled his child as though he thought he would lose him. The adventures he took him on, the tales he told him, would surely fly right over the head of a twenty-month-old. Yet he crammed them into him, as he walked holding his hand, carried him on his shoulder, talked incessantly to him about Poke, Joyce, Peter, and Lucy. And about the boy's mother. Now, every evening at the boy's bedtime, he'd rise from his folding chair, and after offering to help Shea with the dishes—an offer she consistently refused—he'd say, "C'mon, Jimmy. It's time to go watch Mommy's pictures."

For two days after that stunning intimate outburst of hers, he didn't return after Jimmy was in bed. On the third evening he'd shown up again with Jimmy's electronic monitor, and he read and took notes on one of the books she had given him on archaeology methods, while she logged the daily work. He'd asked her another of his questions about how this site was to be preserved. When she told him it wouldn't be, because it would be flooded in another several years, he'd seemed surprised and troubled. "Don't worry. As I showed you, we've got everything mapped in detail. What we uncovered, what we found there, how deep we went. We'll continue to photograph the entire site, every worthwhile find. And we'll archive the artifacts and display anything really exciting and different." She'd already shown him examples of photographs of other sites. "We'll cast and re-create the whole thing and set it up elsewhere if it's unique. And we'll write a complete monograph, in any case. So boring recordwise, at least, it'll never be lost to posterity."

"Hmmm?" he said, and tapped his teeth with his pencil. He then went back to his van.

The next afternoon at Jimmy's nap time he came over carrying in both arms a full-size computer complete with fourteen-inch monitor set on top of the central processing unit. He said he had something to show her, and she hurriedly cleared her desk so he could set the heavy unit down. She was not completely ignorant of computers—she'd used a word processor for years, and had run some statistical analyses while doing research for her Ph.D. She'd also seen graphics programs illustrating dissections of human anatomy and the differences between remains of various races.

But she had no idea of how to create such programs and use them to analyze archaeological finds. So when he booted up the computer and called up a program to do just that, she was astonished. He demonstrated how she could use this to graphically reproduce her entire excavation.

"Look," he said, as on the screen he produced an image of a room in an uncovered section of a temple mound, "here's the way it would look if it was empty. Say, you'd carted off all the potsherds and points. But then, say, you wanted to show that a large pot from here had been reconstructed from sherds and it was painted in a special design. You'd do this." Then he keyed in a few strokes, and a large round rebuilt pot, complete with cracks and missing pieces and a sawtooth design in orange and black belting its belly appeared at the edge of the room.

"Wonderful!" she said.

"And, maybe you had some theories about how the room was used. You could put in people using it. There's no limit. It sure beats a monograph. Like the dull one I worked up this demo from."

She clapped her hands and laughed.

"And," he said, "suppose someday someone develops a theory that could apply to this site. You can sift back through this whole thing and test the theory on it. And if you decide sometime to re-create the site for a museum someplace, you haven't lost the chance. Someday you may be the renowned Shea Passamore, with all her most important works enshrined in the Passamore Museum. Like they do for presidents."

This took her aback. After a brief hesitation, she said, "That's not what I want anymore, Zack. You helped me overcome that."

He nodded and said, "You overcame it yourself, Shea. It didn't have to be me. It could've been anyone. All it took was enough time passing." He turned to the computer again and exited his program, then shut the computer off.

She wanted to protest that it wasn't just the passage of time for her, it was Zack who'd reignited her sexuality. But she said nothing; for it was his own sexual needs he'd been talking about. The swelling against her pelvis, his tender pressure against her thighs—those could have happened with anyone for him. And she couldn't answer them for him. He wouldn't allow her. For him, not enough time had passed.

"Well, I better get back to Jimmy," he said, unplugging and lifting the two stacked pieces of equipment. "He just made a squeak that means he'll be getting up soon."

He and Jimmy ate their dinner in their own van that night, and the next day they left early for the reservation. This time Shea was sure they would not come back. Zack would not risk exposing himself to her need again.

She was wrong. Two days later he returned, and as though nothing had passed between them, he brought Jimmy over at dinnertime again.

Tonight, as on the night they'd shown up and come in out of the rain, Shea and Zack talked over the table as Jimmy slept on the floor. "I've had something on my mind to tell you about, Shea. When I came here, you said that because you let me in that night, you had a right to probe."

"Zack, I . . ."

"No. You were right. But you didn't probe. At least, not very much. And I know my being here isn't exactly looked kindly on by your folks."

"At first, maybe, Zack. But now even Bill asks about you and Jimmy when you're off to the reservation." She smiled. "Looks like he thinks you're one of the folks."

He tilted his head and raised his brow skeptically. "A long way from that. But anyway, after what happened the other night, I guess I owe you an explanation."

"You owe me nothing. It's the other way around."

"Then, let's say I'll feel better if I get some things off my chest. About why I really came here. It wasn't just to find my roots. Oh, I was going to come with Liz, and I did, in a way. She's, well, sort of here with me. I guess she'll always be. As long as I let her be. And I will, all the rest of my life."

"Yes."

"Well, that's off the point. I came here because of that dirt road, and being far away from cities and newspapers and TV."

"To get away from your grief, Zack. The way I did. Till you're ready to talk about it."

He shook his head. "I'm not like you, Shea. It's not just grief I'm running from. I'm a fugitive."

"What?" she said. "Who's chasing you?"

"The FBI."

She gasped.

"I didn't do anything wrong or dishonest. I just don't want to lose Jimmy."

"Oh, Zack! How could you possibly lose him? No matter what you did."

"I could lose him, all right. He could be taken away from me tomorrow. Snap of the fingers." Then he told her what had happened with Paul Broward.

She sat stock-still throughout his narrative. Now she understood things she'd silently wondered about before: why he never contacted his daughter, why he wouldn't travel to Phoenix or Flagstaff or even to Globe, but only to more remote spots, where the crowds wouldn't come for another month or so.

When he had finished the story, he said, "So now you know. You're harboring a fugitive from justice."

"*Justice!* Is that what you call it? *In*justice is what I call it!"

"Yeah, I guess you could call it that. But it doesn't change things. And it's not fair to you for me to stay here. I guess I'll move on. Peter said I can stay a couple of months on the reservation, till I decide where to go next. Nobody's likely to find me there. Till I'm ready to be found."

"I guess," she said, after a long pause, "it's your safe place, Zack, for now. Till you're ready to find the one inside you."

"Right," he said. He rose, then, and stooped and picked up his sleeping son, who was once more wrapped in Shea's growing blanket on the floor.

She opened the trailer door. A thin gust whipped in, teasing up a corner of the blanket. She caught the flapping edge, and secured it around the little boy. She kissed his forehead. "Oh, Zack, I'm going to miss this little kid."

"Thanks for taking us in without asking, Shea."

She nodded and brushed away a tear. "Keep the afghan for him. I don't need it anymore."

He nodded. "I'll tell him you made it." He made a move to kiss her, but stopped short. She knew why. He turned and stepped down the trailer stairs.

"Zack!" she said, as he walked toward his van.

He turned toward her.

"When you find that safe place inside you, will you let me know?"

"You can bet I will," he said. Then he and his son disappeared into the van.

Two hours later, from her bed cubicle where she lay in the dark, expectant, not trying to sleep, undoubting that he would return, she heard his tapping on the trailer door. Without covering her thin flowered flannel nightshirt, which dipped open at the top and clung to her breasts, and would reveal, when the yellow outside light fell upon her, flushed chest and erect straining nipple tips, she went and opened the door.

He said, after hesitating and stepping back, "I, ah, hope I didn't wake you up."

With an ironic curl on her lip, she answered, "You did. Long ago."

He shook his head, "Shea . . . I . . . I just had to give you this. I finished it up tonight, so you could use it." He held out a computer diskette. "It's the program I showed you before."

"Oh." Abashed, she swallowed and took it with a trembling, cold hand. "But I don't know how to use it. I don't even have a computer here."

"I know. But you can use it on any IBM compatible with a lot of memory. It's self-extracting. Just put it in the A drive and type 'Ruins.' And it has a read me and tutorial with it and it's menu-driven. Once you've unzipped it and loaded it, it'll take you through step-by-step, so—"

"Yes. I don't know what you mean by self-extracting . . . but, yes. I appreciate it."

"I . . . ah, guess I should have waited till tomorrow morning to give it to you. But, well, I'm taking off early, and . . ."

"You could have waited. But you didn't. I'm tired, Zack. Have to get to sleep. Good luck in your travels. Good night." She slammed the door on his response.

A few moments later, regret washed away her anger. She knew he hadn't meant to make her a fool; that she had done for herself. Could she allow him to leave, thinking her graceless as well as a fool? But she'd cast that die already, hadn't she? Whatever she'd do now could only make things worse. She was further damned in his eyes if she should open the door again and run after him; she was damned further still—in her own eyes as well as his— if she should allow him to go carrying forever in his mind the vision of the termagant, scolding him for waking her to give her a gift created only for her.

Now she stared at that gift in her hands and knew it was a gift of love. Shame overcame her. How, she wondered, had she allowed herself to behave like a woman scorned? She would have to go to him and thank him, apologize to him. A man like him, who would never scorn her, would need no explanations or excuses, only a simple apology, thanks, and maybe a good-bye kiss.

But not right this minute. Put the diskette away in a safe place, a metal box. Have a glass of wine to calm the nerves, warm and steady the hands. Take a few minutes to plan the exact words, rehearse the apologetic smile. And yes, offer some excuse after all—a dream interrupted—that would explain the sexual arousal.

There, now, she was ready at last, almost an hour later. This time she put on her heavy gray velour robe and the tattered terry cloth slippers turned brown by the mud despite several washings since the night of his arrival.

Wrapping and hugging herself against the chill, windy night, she crossed the sandy patch to his van. Flickering light, like that of a television left on in the dark, came from within. In spite of the cold, he'd left the side gate slightly ajar. After hesitating a few seconds, she slid it a little further open and looked in. He was sitting, his back to her, absorbed in his computer. With one hand he operated a small device, which apparently made the image on the computer screen change.

She pushed the gate open wider, and grasped a pull bar and pulled herself up into the van. She had been in it only twice before, knew its layout, that Jimmy's crib and Zack's

pull-down bed lay just beyond the curtain beside the table
the computer was set upon now. The computer had not been
out on those other times. In fact, until he'd brought it over
to demonstrate his program, she hadn't known he had one
in the van.

Now, suddenly aware she'd come in, he turned. "Shea?"
He sounded more curious than surprised.

"I came to apologize for my rudeness. I was having a . . .
a disturbing dream and . . ."

"Right. That's OK."

She tittered uncomfortably, "And, now I guess I'm being
rude again, just coming in, and, well, the gate was a little
open, and you seemed so absorbed in that program you're
working on."

"Sure. No need to apologize. I'm not working. I did this
one a few years ago. I run it about every night."

She stepped forward so she could better see the screen.
On it was the full-color image of a woman's face. The image
shifted and changed as he pressed buttons on the device in
his hands, a mouse, she realized now. The eyes, amethyst-
colored, moved, their corners crinkled as she smiled. The
nose revealed its high-bridged profile as the head turned.
Highlights shifted across the honey-colored hair. A range
of expressions flickered across the face, conveying to Shea
all possible emotions. She was as moved by watching this
display as she had been by running her fingers over Lucy's
head sculpture.

"That's the way she looked when I made the program
for her. Actually, I made it for myself, but she used it to
catch a murderer. I didn't even know it, then." He did
something with the mouse and the image changed slightly, showing a filling out of the face, a slight change in
hairstyle. "This is how she looked about a month ago.
I can change it anytime I want, to bring it up to date.
Even years from now I can make it look like she would
then."

Shea was about to ask, "Who is she?" Then suddenly she
took a step back.

"I watch *her picture almost every night."* Watch *not* look at! *Liz! He was keeping her alive, would continue to keep her alive, even changing, growing older along with him. She would always be with him, and with her his grief. Shea was—not now or ever would be—a match for such grief, or a weapon against it.*

"I see," she said. "It's an incredible program, Zack." She took a deep breath. "Well, I just wanted to say I was sorry for slamming the door on you before. And to thank you for the Ruins program. I'll think of you every time I use it."

He set the mouse down on the table. "Good. I sure hope you do."

"Oh, I will. And good luck, Zack. Find that safe place, wherever it is. And take care of that wonderful little boy."

"Sure will," he said.

"And, do you mind if . . . if I kiss you good-bye tonight? Since you're getting off early in the morning?"

He grinned. "I was actually planning to do that before. But you didn't seem in the right frame of mind."

"Right," she said. And she threw her arms around him and held him a moment before kissing him on the cheek above the beard line. With Liz looking on, she dared not do more than that.

CHAPTER
▪▪ FOURTEEN

THE NEXT MORNING

Zack had wanted to leave before dawn, to avoid seeing Shea again. Saying good-bye to her last night had been harder than he'd expected. His gratitude to her for taking him and Jimmy in despite grumbling from her chief employee could easily become more. And though his body clearly was ready for more, his mind and soul wouldn't have it. Too much had happened, he'd already caused too much pain—pain and death. If he had never met Liz, never loved her, she'd be alive today. Poke wouldn't have been kidnapped and terrorized three years ago, Liz wouldn't have had to risk her life to save her. In fact, she wouldn't have been able to risk her life to trap Poke's crazy kidnapper, if Zack hadn't come up with the Liz picture program. He'd done that selfishly, to keep her with him during separations. Now, every time he ran that program he thought of how it nearly killed her then, how it kept her almost, but not quite, alive now.

He didn't want to get close enough to another woman to hurt her, not just now, not *ever*. And Shea was the kind of woman you got close to. She couldn't hide her emotions. Her supple expressive face always gave her away. As she'd come out of her grief and told Zack her story, she'd grown beautiful. Her green eyes, once shadowed by passing clouds, had cleared. Her always clean apple-smelling blond hair seemed to bounce on her shoulders with a newfound happiness. Though she still wore her gold wedding band, she'd stopped using her husband's college ring as a scarf band. Instead she tied her colorful scarf Western style at the neck of the neat yellow, blue or green shirts that she always wore with color-matched jeans. And now she was all too ready to let him get close. All too vulnerable to the hurt he could bring her just by being himself under any circumstances, let alone as a harbored fugitive.

So if he could have set off this Saturday morning without saying good-bye again, or seeing and saying good-bye to Bill and his crew, he'd have left at dawn's first light. But that light came late and chill because of a sudden fierce four A.M. rainstorm. He dared not negotiate the narrow dirt road between the site and Route 188. If he and the crew should cross paths in this mess, they might get mired trying to pass one another, especially crossing Tonto Creek. Then he'd have to backtrack in reverse. Too risky. He wouldn't want to try that even without Jimmy in the van.

So he waited till the rain stopped and the sun burned off the fog from the lake and dig site, though not from surrounding mountains. Shea insisted on giving them a hot breakfast, but she seemed changed and diffident, as though she was doing it only to be polite to him and kind to Jimmy. The crew arrived late, and one-by-one. "Passable, but dicey," Bill reported of conditions. "Creek's a little swollen, but you should make it in that Ram with no trouble."

The Ram had been custom-fitted with four-wheel-drive and oversize wheels to handle risky maneuvers on hunting trips. Zack saw no reason to stay longer. It was already after ten. Saying his last good-byes, he strapped Jimmy in his car seat, and headed through the gate and away.

Unlike the thick mud he'd churned through on the sleety evening when he'd arrived, this layer was thin and sandy. As usual in quick desert storms, the water had run off swiftly. He anticipated more runoff as he neared the creek; its banks would spill some his way. But even in spots where this happened, he had little trouble. As quickly as the runoff, the worry tightening his jaw and shoulder muscles evaporated. He couldn't wait to get back to Peter, to commune with him for hours, to gather more insights from his riddles. The last time on the reservation he'd told Peter Shea's reaction to Storytelling Woman's story. Peter had nodded and said, "She listened with her own ears, Zack. To your ears it says something else."

"I don't think it means anything about a lost uterus. Even a miscarriage. Why would it mean that? My grandmother was born, wasn't she?"

"You're proof enough of that." A grin split his broad face. "But was she born of your great-great-grandmother?"

"Who else could she be born of?"

"Remember your Shakespeare. A scene from Macbeth, a prediction that 'no man born of woman' could kill him. But he was killed in a duel by a man who was born by caesarean section, certain that he could not lose."

"Ah, right! Macduff. So you think that's what Storytelling Woman meant."

Again Peter grinned. "Storytelling Woman never read Shakespeare. She didn't go to the university and get a Ph.D. like I did. She's never been off the res. No, Zack, you won't get the answer from me. You'll have to find it for yourself."

Now Zack recalled Shea's saying the Roosevelt Lake dig site would soon be flooded. Just as the Tonto Basin was first flooded when the dam was built. That was right after his great-great-grandfather, Iliad, died in a construction accident. And that was when Iliad's Apache wife had gone looking for him. *A flood had come too soon for her to find a trace of him! That was what Storytelling Woman had meant!*

Zack laughed now and sped up the Ram. He'd talk about that with Peter when he reached the reservation. Now the only thing he hadn't figured out was the part about the basket. Well, that would come, too. If he'd spend enough time with his Apache friends, join in ceremonies, learn the language, all the answers would come. He'd find his roots, and his daughter's. And his son's.

He grinned at Jimmy and said, "We're on our way, son. Off to live on the res with Peter and Lucy. After lunch you can play with Tom and Tony at Anna's house. How 'bout that!"

"Pay Tom. Pay Tony," said Jimmy, as he rocked in his seat and kicked joyfully.

"And we'll have real beds to sleep in. No more van for a while. A safe place to stay."

"Say pay."

Zack laughed. "Right. Your own say pay, Jimmy. At last." He looked away from the road for a moment. Jimmy's joyful eagerness brought tears to his eyes. When he turned to look back at the road, the tears blurred his vision. He slowed down, knowing he'd soon be approaching the creek, and wiped his eyes with the back of his hand. Then he stopped.

"Jesus Christ! What the hell's that up there!" He lifted his foot from the brake and moved forward slowly. "A van's stuck in the creek. Stay here, Jimmy. I'll go see if I can help." He turned off the ignition, and handed Jimmy the keys, a favorite toy, to play with. "Don't drive off without me now," he said, in his standard joke.

"Tees dive ot."

"Right. Be right back." He patted his hunting vest pocket to make sure he had his extra set of keys, then he jumped down from the van and strode to the creek's edge. Swollen, the creek was barely more than two van lengths wide at this point. The vehicle was lodged midway between the two banks. A massive woman over six feet tall stood in front of it, the hem of her tentlike dress eddying in the water.

"Oh, mister, please come help me," she said. Tears splashed over her round doughy face, which was encircled by frizzled wet brown curls. "Daddy's inside, and he's scared."

Zack waded up to her. Icy water sloshed over his calves at his boot tops. He wished he'd worn his rubber hunting boots. "Your father sure drove himself into a fix, ma'am. I'd be scared, too, if I was him."

"Oh, it wasn't Daddy that drove, it was me."

"Oh." Zack didn't want to criticize a woman in distress, though he wondered how she could be so stupid as to take a van with a dropped running board through the turgid rocky creek. "Well, I guess we'll have to get you out. And it'd be best if you back out. There's nothing down this road for you to go to."

"But I promised Daddy we'd go to the Roosevelt Lake dig."

Zack's mouth fell open. Then, "You want to go to the dig? What for? It's not open to the public."

"Oh, Daddy's not the public. He's Lester Jones. The famous archaeologist from Pennsylvania."

Well, that might be different. "Does Shea know he's coming?"

"Oh, no. Nobody knows. It's a surprise."

Zack was sure Shea didn't need any more surprises. "Well, I guess I'll let her decide, then. Look, why don't we just go back in my van, and I'll let you talk to her."

"I can't leave Daddy here alone. He's scared."

"Tell him to come along."

"But, he can't get out. The wheelchair lift can't work with us stuck here."

"Jesus! He's in a wheelchair? What a mess!" said Zack.

Lips pursed, the woman shook her Medusa curls. "He's not in a wheelchair now. He's strapped in the bucket seat."

"Right," said Zack, embarrassed to have sounded ignorant about such matters. He sighed heavily. "Well, I guess we'll have to get you unstuck, then." He sloshed to the slightly tilted down passenger side of the vehicle, a handsome well-made gray Chevy van, and knelt where the running board split for the wheelchair lift to descend through. Beneath the eddies he made out several small rocks. Working his hand under the running board he discovered it was jammed against rocks in two places.

He stood and looked at the woman's oddly grinning face. "Best thing to do would be take the running board off."

"Oh, my. That's hard. I don't have the right tools."

"Lucky I do. Wait here." He waded ashore and sloshed to his van. Hearing Jimmy beginning to fuss inside, he stuck his head in the cockpit. "Hang in awhile, son. I'll try to make it fast."

But Jimmy began to cry. He threw to the seat the keys he was playing with, and kicked furiously. The keys fell to the floor and slid under the seat.

"Shit!" said Zack under his breath. He climbed in and searched for the keys. They had slipped out of reach. "Shit!" He said it full voice this time, knowing that Jimmy would never hear it above his own caterwauling. Exasperated, he backed out of the cabin and went back to the edge of the creek. "Look," he said to the woman, "I've got my kid in the van, and he's getting upset. I'll take him back to the dig site so Shea can take care of him. Then, I'll come back and get you out, OK?"

"Oh my. I didn't mean to cause so much trouble."

"It's OK. I'll be back as soon as I can." As he returned to the Ram he muttered to himself, "Shea's gonna really love this! Bill, too."

But, much to his surprise, Shea laughed and seemed happy to have Jimmy with her again. And of Lester Jones she said, "Never heard of him. But it should be interesting to talk with him. Bring 'em on."

When he brought 'em on, it was already late afternoon, as—in order to avoid further jams either coming or going—both runners had to come off and be stowed on the Chevy's roof rack. And when, at last, Lester Jones was lowered to the sandy dig site yard in his wheelchair, Zack saw the source of the howls and moans that had issued from that van as he'd removed the boards. For several moments he couldn't take his eyes off the half-man. He felt sick. Excusing himself with a mumble, he climbed back into his own van and changed from his clammy jeans and boots into fresh ones, and went to the trailer. Shea shushed him as he entered, and pointed to Jimmy napping on his sleeping spot on the floor. She told him not to pick him up, as an afternoon nap interrupted meant an evening and night of crankiness in a child that age.

"You stay here with him, Zack," she said. "I'll go meet the famous Lester Jones."

He tried to forewarn her, but she put two hushing fingers over her lips and bounded out eagerly. She returned white-faced and grim a half-hour later. "Dear God! That poor man."

"Yeah," said Zack. "Whatever happened to him? Did she say?"

"An accident at a dig at a construction site back east. They were working on the Pennsylvania Turnpike, when they uncovered signs of a prehistoric culture. They let Lester's outfit sift through everything. On the last day, a construction crane moving girders dropped its load on him. Dear God! The *last day!* Not only did it crush all his limbs, it damn near decapitated him. Luckily, if that's what you want to call it, he got off with losing most of his sight and speech. And Hester's a rehab nurse, so she was able to bring back a lot of his motion. God, she loves that old man."

"Jesus!" said Zack, shaking his head.

"Yeah. He's not really famous, you know. Just famous to her." She looked wistful.

Zack empathized with that.

"And besides all that, the guy's a diabetic," Shea went on.

"Boy, that lady's got her hands full," he said. "He's one full-time job."

"Exactly. She had to quit her hospital job to take care of him. They live on a settlement of a suit against the construction company."

"I hope it was millions," he said.

Shea drew a breath and shook her head. "That's what makes it even worse. The company got a lawyer that got them off easy. Made it seem as if Lester wasn't careful enough or something. How can they do that, Zack!" It was a statement of outrage, not a question.

It left him shaking his head.

"Well, there's no way I'm going to disappoint that woman and her father. She promised him an archaeological adventure out West, even though all he can see is light and darkness. She says he loves music and stories, and she wants him to be able to touch things with his stump when she tells him about it. He can still smell, and she wants him to be able to smell the dust and feel the sun on his face, and imagine how all of this looks. So, naturally, I'm going to let her stay awhile."

"God, Shea," he said.

"It won't be long. A few days is all, then they'll be on their way to another site."

"Right. I guess it won't be that bad."

Jimmy stirred, startling Zack, who had almost forgotten he was there.

Shea walked over to the boy and bent to kiss him. Then she looked up at Zack. "I know you want to move on, Zack, but could you just stay while they're here? You know I'm not worried about the law."

He didn't hesitate. "Sure, Shea. No problem. If you want."

She stood up. "Thanks. It's just that I'll need to put in some extra supplies. And, well, I'd feel better going into the Safeway at Globe tomorrow if you went with me."

At that he did hesitate. "I'll sleep on that part," he said at last.

In the morning, he still was uncertain. He'd assiduously avoided driving the Ram into any town important enough to get routine FBI wanted notices. By now, the notice on him would be nationwide. And though out-of-state license plates were common in tourist spots like Sedona—which he'd passed through while heading to Oak Creek Canyon—Globe saw far fewer of them. He would stand out. He explained this to Shea over breakfast in her trailer, while Jimmy, who'd eaten earlier, was being entertained in Hester's Chevy van with Lester's taped music.

Disappointment clouded her supple face.

"I'll help you carry stuff in, Shea."

"I know. No, that's OK."

Clearly it wasn't. "You don't have to get extra stuff. I've got some things. And Hester would've come prepared. With Lester being diabetic."

"That's the trouble. She isn't prepared. She came clear across country, and ran short of some things. Stuff you can't find in Punkin Center." She grinned. "Unless we could feed him canned chili and potato chips."

"Right," he said, and chuckled.

She grew serious. "Zack, have you ever heard of agoraphobia?"

"Yeah. You panic about going out anywhere."

"I had a bout with it. Mostly got over it. Had to force myself to go into Globe." She explained what happened in the supermarket, how she'd had to be rescued and brought home by a highway patrolman.

From anyone else her tale might have smacked of blackmail. From her, it was a sincere plea for help.

"I just can't take the van, Shea. You know that."

"I know. You don't have to. I'll drive the pickup."

"But Jimmy can't go in the pickup. Where would we put him?"

"We can leave him with Hester. She's already fallen in love with him. You saw how they got along last night. And he's fascinated with Lester. He kisses and hugs him like a toy."

Zack smiled. "Yeah. Only a kid would. Right?"

"Right." She shuddered slightly. "Completely unprejudiced. It'll take *me* a while . . ."

"I thought you did forensic anthropology a few years ago."

With an ironic curl of the lip, she said, "On old bones. And I admit being in on autopsies on recently dead bodies. But, this man's alive."

"Right. And he can sing along on those tapes and be happy. Which is all Jimmy cares about. Look, the guy has feelings. And a daughter, weird as she is, that loves him."

As he spoke, keening sounds floated over from the Chevy, with Jimmy's piping as counterpoint to Hester's high-pitched soprano singing. Shea listened awhile. Then she brightened. "They're all having fun, aren't they, Zack?"

"Yeah." Then after a pause he said, "OK. I'll go shopping with you in your pickup. Let's get a list of what Hester needs and ask her to baby-sit for three or four hours."

"Oh, my!" said Hester to that suggestion. She grabbed up a squealing, laughing and kicking Jimmy and hugged him. "I'll keep him for the rest of his life, if you want. Take your time. Take all the time you want."

CHAPTER
▪▪ FIFTEEN

SQUIRREL SPRINGS, WEST VIRGINIA

Shirley had known something was wrong when Grace Broward hadn't called her by Monday, as promised. She'd been sure something was wrong when her own calls to Grace's private line were answered by voice mail and weren't returned by Wednesday.

Never did she doubt Grace's integrity; what she doubted was Grace's ability to do what she'd set out to do: get to Zack James in time to save him from her husband, the FBI, or Hester Jones. As intuitive as Grace was, she wasn't streetwise. How could she be, sheltered as she'd been all her life? Yet Shirley had been so struck with admiration for Grace that she couldn't and wouldn't stand in her way. The woman had to redeem herself. She felt responsible for her husband's evil. She wasn't, of course. Only Paul Broward could be blamed. But Grace had to do what she had to do, and Shirley had no right to interfere till she'd given her time to do it.

But when calls to Hester also went unanswered all week, she'd decided there was no time to spare. Even encumbered by a blind quadruple amputee with an ostomy and diabetes, the obsessed madwoman wouldn't dally long. Shirley had to act. Last Sunday, an FBI agent had stopped at her home. As they'd sat facing each other on matching tweedy loveseats in her modest living room, she'd told the tall, young, brown-haired woman that all she knew about Zack James was that he'd brought in his child through the emergency room in horrible weather, that he'd paid for all services in cash in advance, that he'd used an assumed name, which might seem suspicious, but that she was sure he intended the child no harm.

"We've no doubt of that, Miss Petrowski," agent Lynne Timchuck had answered. "The question is his motive for absconding with someone else's child."

"Jimmy *is* his child. He acted like a father. Jimmy acted like Zack was his father."

"Again, that's not the point. Our job is to find him and bring him back to Philadelphia so we can learn the truth. It's how justice is done. You're sure you don't know where he went from here?"

"Positive. Why would he tell me? If he was running away, he wouldn't leave a trail with me, would he?"

"No. Not deliberately, at least." Timchuck had stood up and smiled. "Well, I appreciate your cooperation. You'll call us if you remember anything else? Or if something else comes up?" She'd handed Shirley her business card.

"Sure will," Shirley had said, glancing at the card before setting it down on the pine coffee table between them. Then she'd risen and shown Timchuck out into the suddenly gusty March day. As the agent had gotten into her blue Taurus sedan, she'd waved.

Shirley had been glad she liked the woman; for something in that nasty chill wind made her think that Grace was in trouble on the second Sunday in March, and she'd wanted someone she liked to turn to.

So today, the following Thursday, she phoned Timchuck and told her everything Grace had told her the Friday before. And, deciding that both she and the hospital could survive the scandal of a devastating security breach more easily than she could survive knowing she'd turned her back on Zack and Jimmy, she told her about Hester Jones and the insulin.

"You've known this since when?" Timchuck said, after a brief hesitation.

"I know I should have told you Sunday. But I thought Grace Broward could get word to Zack quickly through his daughter. Neither of us knew exactly where he was."

"Just what do you know about that?"

"Arizona somewhere. That's not much help."

"With him, probably not. He was trying not to leave a paper trail. But this Jones woman might. From your description, she'd have trouble not being noticed." Timchuck sighed.

Shirley tightened her jaw. "I should've seen that."

"Well, don't be too hard on yourself, Shirley. You aren't in an easy spot. From what you say, your livelihood might be in jeopardy. I admire your courage in coming forward at all. Believe it or not, more people wouldn't than would."

Shirley believed it, yet she still didn't feel she'd shown the grit she should have, could have. Yet the agent's seeing her plight moved her. "Don't waste your empathy on me, Timchuck. Just try to make up the time I cost you."

"You bet I will."

"Let me know when . . . it's all over, will you, Lynne?"

"You bet."

Shirley hung up and cried.

GLENSIDE, PENNSYLVANIA

Poke had known something was wrong when Joyce called her and reported in familiar cryptics that Pop and Jimmy were touring Arizona's wilderness from their safe, comfortable haven at Roosevelt Lake. As Joyce gaily continued, explaining how they were figuring out Indian riddles, the girl became more and more agitated. She'd expected that by now, three days after Grace Broward's visit, that Joyce was calling to tell her that all would be well, her father was forewarned about Hester and also knew that Liz was alive.

"Did you tell him about Hester?" Poke had cried.

"Ah, you mean about the, ah, pictures?"

"No! Did she come to tell you about Hester?"

Sounding troubled and shaken, Joyce had said, "Who, Poke? What do you mean?"

"She didn't! She didn't even come!"

"Please calm down, dear—"

"She lied, Joyce. Mrs. Broward lied. She knows where Pop is. She told her husband, I bet. They'll find him and take Jimmy away."

"Oh, God! Poke, don't say any more."

"It doesn't matter. She tricked me. She lied about Hester. She even lied about Liz. She told me she was alive."

A gasp and a long silence had followed. Then Joyce had said, "All right, dear, just tell me, then. Try to be calm. Exactly what did Mrs. Broward say?"

Between tumbling tears and rubbings of face and eyes, Poke had stammered out the story of Grace Broward's visit and her frightening and horrifying words. "She lied. She said awful things about Hester. She just wanted to trick me into telling her where Pop and Jimmy were. Now they'll find them and take Jimmy away."

"No, Poke," Joyce had said Wednesday. "I know Grace Broward. What she told you must be true. Something must have happened to her. Someone must have stopped her from coming here. Who is this Hester, Poke? Where does she live?"

"I . . . she's Hester Jones. I don't know where she lives. I don't know very much about her, except Paul Broward kept her father from getting the money, and blamed the accident on Lester."

"Lester who? What accident? No. With a name like Jones, we'll never find it in the phone book, if that's her real name. So there's no way to find if she's in town. Whatever this is all about, talking about it to me now, over the phone, won't help. As long as the cat's now out of the bag to whoever's listening, I might as well come right over there so we can talk and decide what to do next. And, Poke, don't let anyone in the door but me."

When Joyce had never shown up, Poke knew that something had gone wrong. Still, she hadn't dared answer the doorbell or even go outside. And when on Thursday afternoon, a tall brown-haired young woman came up on the porch and knocked, and when she went to the rear door and knocked, and when she called out Poke's name, her nickname—how would anyone Poke herself didn't recognize know that she was called Poke?—Poke sneaked up the stairs and hid where she couldn't be seen from the window. And when the telephone rang on Thursday night and Friday morning, Poke picked up the receiver and waited till the caller said, "Hello? Is this Poke? Please listen carefully. I'm calling about your father," Poke hung up as the woman said, "This is Lynne Timchuck, F—"

Poke couldn't trust anyone. She was scared. Her father and brother were in danger, and she didn't even know how to tell them. For not even Joyce had the Roosevelt dig phone number. Her father didn't want anyone to be able to reach him or to trace his calls to Joyce. He spoke to her only from a phone booth, as Joyce spoke to her. Phone booths could be traced, of course, given plenty of time.

Poke shuddered as she realized how long she and Joyce had spoken on Wednesday: long enough for the call to be traced; long enough for the clever detectives Paul Broward had hired to send someone to the telephone booth, then follow Joyce when she left.

By Saturday, Poke knew that had happened, it was what was wrong; and she could do nothing about it, nothing about anything. But then she remembered something Grace Broward had said. Though she didn't trust her, didn't trust anyone at all, she knew there was one thing she could do. And she did it.

CARLETON PRIVATE MEDICAL CENTER AND SANATORIUM

Grace wasn't sure how many days had passed. Much of the time she'd been drugged. She knew no way to avoid it. The drugs were mixed in the liquids she was given, and she had to drink, as the foods, whether salty tasting or not, were loaded with something that made her terribly thirsty. If she refused to eat or drink, a pair of rough nurses would come into the room after dinner and forcibly inject her with something far stronger. So she woozily drifted through the days and nights, losing track, not only of which was which, but also of how many there were.

Still, during her lucid hours, she had her daughter nearby, and she knew that Liz was getting better. Sometimes, when the therapist was exercising Liz's limbs, Liz would make a sound like a small complaint of pain. If Grace would reach out then and touch her, Liz's eyes would turn toward her. These were not random eye movements; they were deliberate, directed. Grace knew she could touch and comfort her daughter. So, all else aside, she was glad she was there and regretted not coming before.

Also, in her lucid moments, Grace would ask to get a message to her husband. "Tell him it's important," she'd whisper out of her daughter's earshot. "He has to hurry. Our grandson's in terrible danger."

But Paul never came, and lightheaded as she was, Grace lost most of her sense of urgency, even though she knew something was wrong.

"It can wait," Paul said when given her messages. "Let her worry awhile."

She's simply upset that she can't handle me anymore, he thought. Well, he was handling matters now, the way he did best, by manipulating the law and its agents and agencies. He knew that the longer Zack James kept Jimmy on the run in that uncomfortable van, without his baths, probably in stinking diapers, eating poorly prepared, inappropriate food in unsanitary conditions, the more he'd be seen as unworthy of custody. Besides, Paul knew that Zack wasn't Jimmy's father, whatever Liz's ridiculous claim. The boy had none of the swarthiness of that unwholesome man: his skin had the honey glow that his real father, Eric, had. His eyes could have come only from Eric. And Paul knew, when the time came to speak up, Eric would do so. So, though Jimmy might be facing some difficulties now, which Grace finally had concluded were dangers, in the long run they'd fade in the light of the life he could live as a Broward, with Paul's patrimony.

So let Grace suffer, that interfering, perfidious woman. She had bolted so easily to the other side. And so easily she'd deserted his bed. There was more to this than he knew. Probably she had a lover somewhere. Her daughter had gotten her propensities for such behavior somewhere. Let her stew now in her own false-heartedness. He'd take care of her lover, too, in good time. Meanwhile, he couldn't bear to look at her.

Even under the influence of the drugs they were giving her, Grace knew something was wrong, terribly wrong, when they took her, strapped into a wheelchair, to the room across the hall, and showed her the new patient sleeping in the bed, and she saw it was Joyce Price. Something was terribly wrong, and for the first time in her life, Grace could do nothing about it. Nothing at all.

CHAPTER
▪▪ SIXTEEN

MEANWHILE—ROOSEVELT LAKE

"Isn't he a sweet little boy, Daddy?" said Hester to Lester. "What a shame we have to make him suffer."

Lester whined.

"And his father's such a nice man, too. I wish we didn't have to make him suffer, too. I wish we didn't have to poison his blood, too. But he's an innocent victim. Like we are. They made us suffer, didn't they? Even though it wasn't our fault at all."

He agreed with a long, wavering moan. Jimmy imitated his noise and laughed and hugged him, and Lester moaned even louder as tears ran down his cheeks.

"Essa ky. Essa sad."

Hester giggled. How cute he was, with his dear baby talk. How smart for someone not yet two. "Yes, honey, poor Lester's so sad. He loves you and doesn't want to hurt you." She picked up the boy and hugged him.

"But all we can do now is get the whole thing over with. At least they made it easy for us. Come on, Hester'll put you in your crib in your van and you can watch Hester work. You like to watch Hester work, don't you?"

"Essa oot." He began to kick at her abdomen, trying to free himself as she carried him to the Ram. When she put him in his crib, surprise flashed across his tiny face. "No! Dimmy no nappy."

"No, no nappy, honey. Just watch Hester work. She's going to get her tools now."

Past Lester keening in his wheelchair, she hurried back to her van. She couldn't bear hearing the little boy cry, so she returned with her electric drill as fast as she could. As she drilled from the inside of the van through the floor and into the exhaust pipe, the noise quieted the child. Soon, he was jumping up and down in his crib, imitating the noise.

"How dear!" she said, and glowed at the pleasure she brought him. The drill rasped and wobbled as it drove through the pipe wall. Then she widened and flanged the hole by sledgehammering an auger through the drill bore.

"Bam, bam, dum," said Jimmy. "Essa pay dum."

Hester giggled and hammered the floor a few times, even though the opening was wide enough to let in enough exhaust to kill both father and son on their first long trip. "Soon you'll be visiting your ancestors on the reservation, won't you, Jimmy?"

"Bam, bam, dum," he said, and chortled. "Dimmy do bam, Essa."

"Oh, not with the hammer. It's too heavy. You could hurt yourself. Hester will take her tools home to her van, and then get you something else to play with. What do you like to play with, Jimmy?"

"Pay Daddy tees."

"Daddy's tees?" She couldn't make out what he was saying.

"Tees, tees." He jumped up and down in his crib and waved his hand. "Tees unna teet. Pay Daddy tees. Unhnn teet."

"Oh, darn! I don't know what you're saying, Jimmy."

"Essa tarry Dimmy." He held out his arms to be picked up.

He seemed to know just what he wanted, and Hester wanted to please him while she could, so she lifted him out of the crib. "Where should Hester carry you, Jimmy?"

He didn't answer her, but kicked himself down out of her arms and toddled off to the front of the van. "Unna teet," he said, dropping to the floor and shimmying himself as close as he could behind the passenger seat. He reached under it and flung his arms from side to side. He grunted and fussed impatiently. "Dimmy tan't eets. Essa eets."

"Ah," said Hester. "You sure make your wants clear. There's something under the seat you want Hester to reach."

He grunted and kept flinging his arm around beneath the bucket seat. "Essa eets. Dimmy pay tees."

She grasped his legs and pulled him away from the seat. "Well, if you want me to reach whatever it is, you'll have to get out of the way. Let's get you back into your crib to keep you out of trouble while I get it for you. Hester'll have to go outside and in through the passenger door. She's much too big to crawl in that little space."

She took him kicking and complaining back to his crib, where he jumped with mixed tears and joy while she went out through the side gate and opened up the front door. She put her head down so she could see beneath the seat. When she saw the keys on the floor, she said, "Oh, my! Daddy must have dropped his keys."

"Daddy tees! Essa eets Daddy tees. Dimmy pay tees."

"Oh, sweetie, how lucky! But Hester's fat old arm can't get under there." She'd seen a broom in the van, got it, and nudged the keys out with it.

When she'd retrieved them she jingled them at him.

Jimmy jumped and cried, "Daddy tees. Div Dimmy, div Dimmy."

"Oh, now, Jimmy, Hester'll give you the keys." As she walked around and reentered through the side gate, she opened the key ring and found and removed the Chrysler key. "But Hester wants one for herself. It's her reward for reaching them for you." She snapped the key ring shut and handed the jangling bunch to the boy.

Grabbing them, Jimmy said, "Dimmy pay dive." He sat down and pushed the keys against the crib footboard and made a dithering sound.

"Oh, yes, you drive with your keys. And Hester's going to drive with hers. We're so lucky, aren't we? We found

Daddy's lost keys. Well, Hester's going to sweep out the mess in the van so no one'll know she made that little hole in the floor." After she swept, she admired her work. "It doesn't even show through that flap Hester cut in the mat."

Jimmy had stopped playing his driving game and was banging the keys against the mattress.

"Oh, what pretty music, Jimmy. Sing Hester a song." She began to sing "Jack and Jill." He mimicked her, jumping and giggling and shaking and rattling the keys.

She grabbed him and hugged and kissed him, with many wet smacks. He struggled out of her arms, saying, "Dimmy dive, drrrrrr."

She giggled. "OK, now you just play in your crib, while Hester fixes up the exhaust outlet valve a little. Then she's going to start the engine and close the doors. Not for long, only a few minutes or so. How lucky we are to be able to test things out before your father gets back. Just to be sure everything works."

He held up the keys to her. "Daddy tees. Dimmy pay. Dimmy dive."

So terribly moved was Hester that she grabbed him and hugged him one more time. "Say good-bye to Hester, sweetie. It's only a test, and you'll probably wake up before Hester goes, but just in case, tell Hester you love her as much as she loves you."

Jimmy looked up into Hester's face. He jabbed the bunch of keys into her nose and giggled. "Dimmy dive Essa nose," he said.

She put him down, finished the necessary details, then turned on the van engine for the very few minutes it took for him to fall asleep on top of his keys.

The test worked to her satisfaction. Then she went to her own van to make lunch for herself and Lester. In the yard outside between the vans and the trailer, she served a fine picnic for them both. "We'll leave first thing tomorrow morning, Daddy," she said. "No need to hang around longer. Zack and Jimmy want to go see their ancestors on the reservation. Didn't Zack tell us that? We sure don't want to hold them back anymore."

Lester mumbled agreement.

"What a beautiful Sunday this turned out to be."

"There's another storm brewing to the southwest," said Shea when she saw Hester clearing away picnic things. "The mountains out there'll wash away if this weather keeps up." She hopped down from the green pickup truck driver's seat. Then, looking around, she asked, "Where's Jimmy?"

"Oh, my. He's taking his nap in his crib."

Zack came around from the passenger side of the truck and started to draw the tarp off the bed. "At one-thirty? What'd you do to him?"

Hester stiffened. A mean look crossed her face, making Shea uneasy. "I can take care of children. I'm a nurse!"

"I was only kidding, Hester," said Zack. "I meant you must have worn him out with games. He usually doesn't go down till after two."

Hester's expression changed again. She looked like a clown who'd played a trick on someone. She giggled. "Oh, I guess it was the last game we played. He dropped off, just like that. A few minutes earlier he was jumping and singing."

Zack grinned. "Right. That's my boy. I'm sure glad you knew what he needed." He finished removing the tarp and inspected the bags and cartons.

Feeling easier, Shea took the carton containing the supplies Hester had asked for. She lifted the heavy box easily. "Now you sit still, Hester. You've had your hands full this morning. Just tell me where to put things. We'll settle accounts later."

Hester rose. "I don't want you to go to more trouble."

"No trouble. Zack's putting my stuff away. I need to get the driving cricks out of my bones. You just stay with your father." Lester was making sad howling noises and seemed to want attention.

"Well, that's nice. You won't have trouble finding the pantry shelf and fridge. You know how tight it is living in

a van. Specially with the wheelchair lift and all. Best way
in is through the side gate. It's open."

Shea nodded and trudged to the Chevy. She slid the
large carton in before grasping a rail on the chair lift to
pull herself in. The portable refrigerator, she could see at a
glance, was an afterthought, not built in, as she would have
expected. As she loaded in the fresh meats, margarine, a
quart each of skim milk and orange juice, and a carton of
cottage cheese, she saw from the energy use label inside
the door that it was this year's model. Well, maybe it was
a replacement for an older model. The van itself was three
or four years old, though it looked like new. She arranged
the items according to her ideas of efficiency, leaving the
shallow tray containing vials of insulin within easy reach,
though there was hardly enough room to make a difference;
then she turned to look for the pantry shelf. There were
two shelves, one serving as a medicine cabinet, containing
boxes of gauze and adhesive tape, over-the-counter pills;
the other holding a single can of soup and a thick album.
Both shelves had slats across the front to keep things from
spilling off them during jostling rides. *She sure let supplies
run low! No wonder she asked me to shop.*

As Shea placed the goods on the shelf, she wondered how
Hester managed baths. Unlike Zack's van, this one had no
shower, only a large bottle of water with a drawing cock, set
upside-down on a jerrybuilt frame, and a pail underneath.
That would do for washing Lester, who was scrupulously
clean despite his tendency to drool. Hester could heat the
water on the butane cooking stove. But to bathe herself,
she must have had to stop at motels.

*Well, of course! Why wouldn't she? And there were
outhouses or portable johns at most RV sites. Shea had
one here that the crew used and that both Zack and Hester
had taken advantage of. Why was Shea looking for trouble?
Zack, not Hester, after all, was the one on the lam.*

She still had one item—a small tinned ham—left after
loading the small shelf. By taking out the album, she could
easily fit that in; and the album could rest on the floor or

the fold-down counter till the space was freed up again. She lifted out the album, which was bulkier than it had appeared, and which slipped to the floor, opening as it struck, tearing its pages loose and scattering them. "Oh, shit! What a mess!" She felt terrible.

After placing the ham on the shelf, she sighed, lifted the countertop onto its retractable legs and picked up the strewn, tattered pages; then she picked up the torn cover, and set all the pieces on the counter. This was obviously a scrapbook, probably a well-thumbed collection of memoirs and exploits of Lester Jones. How could she ever apologize to Hester?

She'd try to put them in order at least. Then later she'd use her own mounting materials to repair the damage. She looked at a page of family snapshots. One shot was of Lester with all his limbs, wearing work clothes, carrying an armload of tools to a truck. A good-looking man, and plainly strong and healthy. She placed that photograph page at the front of the book, and picked up one bearing a folded newspaper article. Unfolding it, she saw that the date noted at the top placed it at several years ago. A Philadelphia *Inquirer* article.

As she started to read it, she heard from outside the scrunching of wheels and large feet crossing sand. "Damn!" Abashed at being caught having messed up Hester's beloved scrapbook, she picked all the pages from the counter and quickly tossed them into the empty grocery box. She would take them to the trailer and repair the damage tonight, then return the book in good order tomorrow. She would even repair the torn cover, which appeared to have been damaged before she dropped it. That would more than redeem her for her carelessness, she thought. Then, she could apologize with aplomb.

When Hester peeked into the van, Shea laughed uncomfortably and said, "I got everything in. Be out in a sec so you can bring your father in, if you want."

"Oh, I just wanted to get the stereo. He wants some music."

"Ah, I saw it just behind the seat. Get it for you." She set the box down out of Hester's sight and fetched her the portable tape player.

Taking it, Hester said, "I'll get his tapes from the console up front."

Shea drew a quick breath, and as the woman rounded the van and entered on the driver's side, she pushed the carton to the edge with her foot, lowered herself to the ground, and secured the box, tilted it toward her to hide its contents, and took it quickly to the trailer.

Zack, who had loaded all the groceries into their proper storage slots, was about to leave. "I thought I got it all," he said when she brought in the box. "What did I miss?"

"Nothing. Oh, Zack, I dropped a scrapbook of theirs, and tore it all to hell. I just have to put it back together. I'll work on it tonight."

"Oh. OK. I'll go check on Jimmy, then."

She put the carton down on her desk. "I'll go with you. I can't believe he's sleeping."

"Yeah," he said as they went toward the Ram. "Well, at least she left the side gate open so she could hear if he woke up."

"She can't hear him now. Not with Lester's sing-along over by the Chevy." She laughed and shook her head. "They are a pair, those two."

"Well, no need to worry, as long as he's in that crib. One thing he hasn't figured out yet is how to climb out. Keeps him out of trouble. I just don't want him to wake up and start crying because we can't hear him soon enough to stave off a bad mood." He climbed in through the side gate, and reached down his strong hand to help Shea up.

The two tiptoed the few steps back to the curtained-off crib. The child didn't stir. "Never saw him sleep so soundly," Zack whispered. "Must have been absolutely zonked."

"Ummhmm," said Shea. "Hester probably didn't even realize she was tiring him. People who've never been around kids don't know when they're overdoing it."

Bending forward, Zack said, "What's he lying on?" He ran his hand along the boy's side, just beneath his waist, and pulled out a small bunch of keys. "Oh, right," he said, "I forgot all about these. He tossed them down yesterday. I used the spare to get back from the creek. They must have slid out from under the seat, and he found them. Funny I didn't see them before."

Shea laughed. "He's good at that. One day he ran off with my wooden spoon and hid it. He remembered where. Then he got it and was playing with it outside. Right under your nose, too!"

He grinned. "Smart boy." Then, sorting through the keys, he said, "Wonder what happened to the ignition."

"Must have come loose."

"Boy, I better get a new ring. Didn't know that could come open. But it must've, and Hester saw when he found them and refastened the ring."

"Sounds logical. At least she knew that much about child care. You can ask her and thank her."

Zack nodded and ran his hand gently over his son's small head. Sometimes this would make Jimmy turn his face the other way; this time his breathing never changed. "Well, looks like he's going to overdo the sleeping, too. Probably be up all night." He sighed.

"Well, no sense in your staying here watching him. Bring the monitor over to the trailer. Maybe I can start fixing up that scrapbook. Might be interesting."

"For you, maybe," he said. "Not my idea of fun. I'd rather go shopping." He grinned ironically.

"I guess this whole day hasn't been your idea of fun. I'm sorry. You've been a good sport, Zack." *He* was *a good sport, and the day with him had stirred feelings for him again. One day he'd work through his grief, and, when he did, maybe . . .*

"Matter of fact, it was a break, Shea. It's the first time I've been away from Jimmy except on the res. The first time I've been to a real live town without having to look over my shoulder. And the first time I've ever gone somewhere with you. It was fun. You're good company."

She said nothing—*could* say nothing.

"Say," he said, "I was going to show you how to enter your data into the Ruins program tonight. Since Jimmy's going to be up all night, why don't I bring the PC over and give you a lesson while he's sleeping?"

"Great idea! I'll go clear the desk. I can work on the scrapbook tonight." It would be better than lying awake again all night thinking about him and Jimmy watching the pictures of their beloved Liz shimmer and flicker across the screen.

Shea had acted guilty when Hester had suddenly come into the van. Now Hester knew why. She'd found the scrapbook and was looking through it. She'd dropped a page with some family pictures mounted on it, but she must have taken the rest.

"Curiosity, Daddy. She's the kind that sticks her nose in everyone's business. Always asking questions. I can tell. Well, curiosity kills the cat. She's going to figure out I was making up some things, and she'll wonder why I have all those articles about Dr. Broward and Zack James. She might think the FBI sent me. We'll have to leave. What a shame! There's no time left. And we can't take any chances, Daddy. I don't want Jimmy waking up and saying things that could make them figure out about things. He's so smart and dear, and he just might say, 'Essa eets Daddy tees' and give it all away."

She sighed and shook her head. As Lester, sitting just outside the Chevy van, keened and rocked with the music. Hester watched from the driver's seat while first Shea, then Zack, exited the Ram. Shea was carrying some small object; Zack carried a computer.

"Now where did he get that from? I didn't see that while we were there. Oh, well, that means they'll be busy for a while. It's a good time for us to do it. Now you just keep sitting there singing while I get the insulin ready." She opened the console between the bucket seats and took out the two cc syringe she'd used in West Virginia. The massive dose it would deliver would mean a fast, painless death for Jimmy; she didn't want to hurt him, after all. And she needn't use a sterile needle. No infection could hurt a dead boy.

Still, it bothered her, a nurse, so concerned with proper technique and her patient's well-being, to employ a dirty instrument. She tossed the syringe in the waste container, and went to the back of the van through the side gate. "Don't worry, Daddy," she called. "We have plenty of insulin and syringes left to get us back home, even if we take our time. And what will be the hurry? We'll have taken care of them all, at last."

From the small refrigerator, she removed a vial of fast-acting insulin; from the box of injection supplies on the medicine shelf, she removed a slim plastic syringe and needle set. She set up a tiny tray, complete with alcohol swabs, then unsheathed the thin, short needle, swabbed the rubber diaphragm on the vial, inverted the bottle, and jabbed the needle in. With utmost care to do it as scrupulously as she would for her father, she filled the syringe to capacity—double the dose usual for her father—and, after withdrawing it, resheathed the needle.

Her massive hand covered the tray, so no one could see what she carried to the Ram where Jimmy lay, still overcome by the carbon monoxide. Still, Hester took no chances. She swung wide to beyond the view of the trailer window that overlooked the yard from Shea's desk. On the way, she cut the telephone line sweeping down from the pole above. Now, if they should see her passing between the vans and entering the Ram, she could always say she was checking on Jimmy. That would be another delay, though. She'd been delayed too often already. She had to finish and get out of here before they knew what was happening.

As her huge, strong legs propelled her easily through the side gate, she knew she hadn't been seen. The drawn curtain just a few steps away hung limp, as though no little boy lay breathing behind it, so still and quietly he slept, with none of the sleeping toddler's characteristic squeaks and snorts, twists and head bobs. Hester herself felt breathless in the face of such stillness in him. She moved forward stealthily, slowly, and lifted one edge of the curtain.

What a dear little thing! she thought, and could not hold back the tiniest "Oh!" her tiny voice had ever uttered. For a few moments afterward she stood motionless. Then she pulled back the entire curtain and reached for the little boy's arm.

"Zack! I heard him squeak. He's waking up."

Zack sighed. "That's great. He'll be back on schedule by tonight. It's only two-thirty."

"You stay here and save all that data you just put in. I'll run over and get him."

He nodded as she ran out the door, across the yard, and up into the Ram. The curtain had been pulled aside, and Hester was leaning forward over the crib.

"Hester! What are you doing here?"

The woman straightened and whirled. Shea saw the syringe in her hand. "Dear God, Hester! What . . ."

"You stole the scrapbook! It's too late now." She lunged at Shea, grabbing her arm with one hand, stabbing her biceps with the syringe in the other.

Shea felt the shock of injected fluid and grabbed at her upper arm. At the same instant, Hester grasped her shoulders and pushed her backward. She tumbled out of the van, and struck her head on the ground as she landed. Dazed, she watched helplessly as Hester jumped out of the van, Jimmy in her arms. By the time Zack reacted to the commotion and ran to Shea's aid, Hester had Jimmy in the Chevy. Shea tried to warn him, but she couldn't speak.

Hester snatched her father from the wheelchair, ensconced him in his seat, and started her engine.

"Shea!" said Zack. "What happened? Jesus! What was that yelling about?"

The Chevy torqued and plowed across the yard and through the gate.

Shea could say only, "Jimmy . . ."

"I'll get him later. What happened to you?"

"Jimmy . . . she . . ."

The Chevy van disappeared up the dirt road in a blur of dust.

Zack said, "She hurt you. Why? How?" He looked around, picked something up from the ground. Through her haze, Shea saw it was the syringe.

She felt her upper arm.

"Jesus! She gave you some kind of shot!"

"No . . . not important. Jimmy. She took him."

"What!" He whirled and vaulted into the van. "Oh, no! Oh, God!" He leapt out. Looked at Shea, then at the syringe.

Her head was beginning to clear. She struggled dizzily to her feet. "I'll be OK. Go after her, Zack."

"It's insulin," he said, staring at printing on the syringe. "She gave you insulin."

"She was going to give it to Jimmy! You have to stop her. I'll call police." She started toward the trailer, beginning to feel a little woozy. She staggered.

He grasped her as she lost her balance.

"I'll be OK. I'll get them to send up a copter. Go after them. Stop them, Zack."

He swept her up in his arms, ran her into the trailer, and set her down on the floor. He yanked a can of Coke from the refrigerator, snapped it open, and poured it into her mouth as she gulped it down. "OK, go now," she gasped out. "I'll call and get them to send up a copter. Hurry!" Then he took a second can, opened it, set it beside her, and ran out.

Within minutes, the sugar in the Cokes restored her blood sugar, as the caffeine worked to reverse the shock of her fall. She picked up the phone. *Dead! Dear God, Hester had cut the line!*

The shock of her helplessness set her head spinning again. She'd have to drive a good twenty minutes to reach Punkin Center and a phone. And she was still too woozy and unsteady, didn't know how much insulin she'd received, and how much sugar she would need to be safe. She sat

down at the desk in front of the computer and watched
the cursor blink at the right of the symbol, C>\RUINS.
After a few desultory moments, she shook her head and
went to get another Coke. "Why?" she asked aloud. "Why
did Hester want to kill Jimmy?"

"You stole the scrapbook. It's too late now."

"Scrapbook! Yes. There's something in there." She
grabbed her folding table and set it up, then got the box
of disheveled pages and dumped them onto the table. She
snatched up the papers as they landed in a heap. Reading
the newspaper articles out of chronology at first, she had
trouble making sense out of them; but one stunning fact
quickly became clear: Hester knew Zack had run off with
Jimmy and had come after him.

With dry mouth and trembling hand, Shea put the articles
in order, read through them again. From the earliest article
about Lester's product liability suit she learned that Hester
had lied. He was neither an archaeologist nor the victim of
a construction accident. But he had lost a large settlement
due to the clever manipulation of a car maker's lawyer. And
the lawyer was Paul Broward, Jimmy's grandfather.

It still didn't make sense, didn't explain why Hester
would kill Jimmy. She read the article again, then looked
for a thread that would tie all the articles together. There
was the suicide of a nurse. Let's see, the nurse's name was
in one of the articles about the trial. She'd been Lester's
nurse and had given damning testimony that he'd neglected
his own care.

But how did that fit in? She'd killed herself, yes, but what
did that mean?

Shea wrung her hands and, still dizzy, paced the small
trailer a few seconds. She returned and forced herself
to concentrate on the next article. Something about Liz
Broward winning an award for humanitarian service. Then
an ad for a health fair, with Dr. Broward's name highlighted
as a participating doctor giving exams in a mobile van, the
service that had won her the award. Then several articles
dealing with the same strange illness that hit her twice,

finally striking her down. Headlining these articles were reports of Paul Broward's charges against Zack; pictures of him and his children and Liz accompanied all of these. It still didn't hang together. Shea had to read through them again. She'd finished another Coke, gotten a fourth. An overfull feeling assailed her stomach, forcing her to belch after every swallow to relieve a mild nausea that could have come from either the insulin reaction or its cure.

Either way, she must leap obstacles to her concentration. She turned her mind back to its search for common threads in the stories.

One jumped out at her then. Carbon monoxide poisoning, slow and insidious in Lester Jones, quick and deadly in the nurse who had treated him and then spoiled his case. *Suicide? No! It was murder! A vengeful act, planned and executed by Hester.* The tie there was clear, but what about the tie to Jimmy? He had no part in ruining Lester.

She shook her head again. Carbon monoxide poisoning, slow and cumulative, insidious, with vague ambiguous symptoms, a mystery . . . mysterious disease struck Liz Broward down. *Of course! It was there in the headline: PROMINENT ATTORNEY'S HEIR KIDNAPPED—JIMMY BROWARD ONLY CHILD OF STRICKEN DOCTOR. And Liz had been Paul Broward's only child! Stricken by the same thing that struck Lester: slow, insidious carbon monoxide poisoning. Hester was doing to Broward what he had done to her . . . ruining, taking away his dearest possessions, in his case the children who carried on the thing he most cherished, his family name.*

Shea recognized the wave of nausea passing over her now as sheer revulsion. As she swallowed the burning bile it sent up her throat, she felt galvanized, alert. The insulin meant for Jimmy had been a desperation measure. When Hester found that Shea had the scrapbook, she'd known she'd be figured out. *You stole the scrapbook. It's too late now!* There was no time for carbon monoxide. She had to act quickly, leave immediately, figure out a way to cover her tracks, leave no witnesses.

The keys! Jimmy sound asleep in the Ram, hours before his nap! "Zack! No! She's fixed the exhaust system. She thinks the insulin will kill me. Please, Zack, get out of that van. Open the windows! Please, Zack!"

But she knew that he wouldn't open the windows and allow the thick dust of the road to fill his eyes and choke his lungs. She had to go after him, try to find him before the gas made him lose control of the wheel on a narrow mountain road. And she had to get to a phone.

Zack saw one discarded running board barring the road on one side of the creek. When he had pulled it free of the rocks and tossed it aside, he spied the other on the far bank. He waded across and dragged it away. Five minutes lost. He churned the Ram across the creek and bounced it along the remaining rough road to the second unpaved road leading to route 188. From here he knew Hester would have to pass Punkin Center, then probably, if she expected to get away, would head to the Beeline Highway, which would let her bypass the major towns and cities and be concealed in the heavy Sunday afternoon traffic. A copter would have a hard time picking her out of that, and Chevy vans like hers were common, so the Highway Patrol would have to spot her Pennsylvania license. She would have to keep moving to avoid that, and that would give Jimmy a chance. She didn't dare speed enough to attract a patrol's attention. He had that, and Shea's call for help, to keep his hope alive as he turned north on 188 and picked up speed.

After a few miles, his head began to pound and the hills in the distance began to waver against the sky. The few small buildings in Punkin Center seemed blurred as he passed them. He must be hyperventilating. His breaths came faster and faster, and didn't seem to bring him enough air. His heart pounded. He couldn't let this terrible fear overcome him. Not when Jimmy needed him. He had to keep going, on around the bends, up grades twisting past ridges, down others descending in curves before rising again. In a few miles more he'd come to Jake's Corner, then be heading south on Highway 87. He'd pull off at the first patrol he saw, or speed so they'd be sure to see him, and tell them he was the one whose child had been kidnapped. They would call and set up a roadblock, and soon he'd have Jimmy back again. It didn't matter, he thought, as he careened around a bend, that Paul Broward would try to get him. It didn't matter, even if he took him away. All that mattered was getting him away from Hester, who was crazy and wanted to kill him.

Coming out of the bend, Zack's hands slipped off the steering wheel. He felt the road fall out from beneath the van, felt a jolt and a wrenching impact. Then there was something like pain, and then there was nothing.

She turned south on Route 87. Lester's terrified keening assailed her nerves. Nothing she said would calm him. She could not stop, could not take him out of his seat. In his crate bed lay the little boy. He would likely remain unconscious for a while. But if he should wake, there was nothing to keep him from climbing out and wandering the back of the van. She would have to stop at a rest stop within another hour and give him the insulin. Though she couldn't be sure, she thought she may have heard him make a noise a few minutes back. Was he passing from druggedness to more natural sleep? Would Lester's noises or the lulling motion of the van affect him more?

"Shut up, Daddy!"

Lester wailed.

"Please, Daddy! Don't worry. We'll get you another wheelchair. Don't you see, we just didn't have enough time to take it."

He wailed again, and rocked in his seat.

"Shut up!" she screamed. And then, when he continued his hollering, she flung her hand off the wheel and, back-handed, slapped his face.

His screech tore through the van; then he began to sob.

"Oh, Daddy, I didn't mean to hurt you. But we're going to get in terrible trouble if we don't get rid of Jimmy so we can go home. I'm doing it all for you. Don't you see?"

His sobs slackened off.

"That's better, Daddy," she said, taking her eyes off the road for a moment.

As she turned them back, stopped traffic just ahead forced her to brake suddenly. A thud from behind made her turn. She could see nothing in front of the crate Jimmy slept in. He must have struck the side, then fallen back onto the mattress. She looked back at the road, and saw traffic was being turned onto both shoulders and was creeping back toward the north. Maybe an accident ahead. They'd gone barely a mile since picking up the Beeline. Now they'd have to turn back. Highway patrolmen were talking to drivers in both southbound lanes, and motioning them onto their respective shoulders.

"What's wrong, Officer?" Hester asked, when she arrived at the roadblock.

The tall gray-haired man leaned a brown uniformed arm though her window opening and bent his head in, looking curiously at Lester and Hester. "Rockslide to the south."

"Oh, my! How do I get to Phoenix?"

"Suggest you go back to 188, then pick up 88 to Globe. You got a map? I'll mark it for you."

She nodded and took the Arizona road map from the console. Lester was sniveling and drooling. After handing the map to the patrolman, she wiped her father's face. She saw the red marks her knuckles had left on his cheek. They shocked her; never had she struck her dear daddy before; never had his eyes looked so hurt or scared when she reached up to touch him.

"Ma'am?"

She turned to look at the officer.

"Here's the way you go, by the lake. Here's where you pick up 88 toward Globe, and just past the Tonto National Monument turnoff here is where you get the road back to Phoenix." He handed her the marked map and said, "Your, ah, passenger going to be all right?"

"Oh, yes. He'll be fine." Then, turning to Lester, she said, "Won't you, Daddy?"

Lester grunted.

"I'll just put a tape on his stereo as soon as I can stop and get it."

"Is it in the back? I can get it for you if you tell me—"

"Oh, no. There's too much traffic behind me. That's all right." Before he'd pulled his arm clear of the window, she began to power it up.

He jumped back, as she pulled off to the right shoulder and began driving back with the creeping wrong-way traffic . . .

The sudden increase in oncoming traffic startled Shea as she passed through Punkin Center. Several drivers honked at her or blinked their lights, warning of trouble ahead. But she could not turn back until she caught up with Zack; she hoped that would happen before it was too late.

A few minutes later, she came on the scene where he'd bounced to the right off the road and plowed into a tangle of desert brush and low mesquite branches. Two cars had pulled up and stopped, facing south, and several men and women gathered in a gaggle near the van. A man was tugging on the tailgate. The side gate was blocked by a boulder, and both driver and passenger doors were entangled in the brush. Shea turned off the road and screeched to a stop so close to the spectators that they hollered and jumped aside. She knew that the tailgate was locked. To attempt moving the boulder would be futile; tearing away the brush would cost too much time. She had a tire iron from her tool chest in her hand as she leapt from the pickup cabin.

"Out of the way!" she cried to the man tugging at the gate. He ducked to the side as she swung the iron at the rear windows, then she dashed through the flying glass shards and grasped and released the door latch and pulled the gate down.

She scrambled, and as she shoved past the crib and

fold-down sleeper that crowded the rear, she swung the iron wildly, knocking out the curtained side windows and shredding the curtains away. Still, the air barely moved.

Zack sat, head lolling to the side, in his bucket seat. Bright red blood trickled from somewhere on his head— she could not tell from where, but the rate of the trickle gave her hope. It was not gushing from an artery, nor was it stopping on its own.

"He's still alive! We've got to get him out of here fast, into the air. He needs air!" She turned to the man she'd shoved aside. "Help me! And hurry. It's carbon monoxide. He needs air."

"Jesus!" said the man.

Shea squeezed herself over the back of the passenger seat, and unfastened Zack's seat belt, then released the seat back and leaned on him till he lay nearly flat. She saw that the blood came from a cut in the corner of his mouth. He was breathing very slowly, very shallowly, but he *was* breathing. His body was completely relaxed.

She instructed the man, who was now at Zack's head, "Just grab him under the shoulders and pull him out as fast as you can. Don't worry about bumping him on things. Just get him the hell out into the air."

The man responded instantly. Shea scrabbled over the seat, followed the man, and called out for more help in lowering Zack onto the ground. "Anyone have a phone?" Shea fell to her knees next to Zack. She felt for his carotid pulse. The beat, thready, weak, rapid, reinforced her fears. He needed more than fresh air to prevent brain damage; he needed one hundred percent oxygen soon.

A woman nodded and started back to a car.

"Call for a medevac copter. Tell them it's CO poisoning. Get an operator, tell her you're a mile north of Punkin Creek."

The woman nodded and turned toward her car.

"Hurry. He has to have oxygen quickly."

The woman ran to the car.

"How do you know it's CO?" said the man who'd pulled

Zack out. "He hasn't turned red all over."

"Thank God he hasn't. He'd be gone."

"But how do you know?"

"The van has a leak. He didn't know."

"Shouldn't I give him mouth to mouth?"

"It wouldn't do any good." She stood up. "We've done all we can till the copter comes with oxygen; meanwhile . . ." She was facing north, looking over the man's broad shoulder, noticing in the back of her mind the extraordinarily long line of traffic snaking and chugging southward. Suddenly an oncoming Chevy van caught her eye. The van slowed a moment as the driver surveyed the accident scene. The clownlike face peering through the window cracked into a broad smile. Then the Chevy moved on.

Shea ducked slightly and stepped into the man's shadow. "Dear God, it's her! She's heading back!"

"Everyone's heading back," said the man. "There's a rockslide south on the Beeline. This traffic's going to last all night."

He continued to talk, but Shea ran and vaulted into her pickup and started it. The slow-and-go traffic pattern past the crash let her merge inconspicuously into the southbound line, several cars behind Hester. Hester wouldn't have seen Shea or her pickup truck; both were screened by a growing circle of onlookers and hopeful Samaritans. But she would have noticed the Ram, and the man on the ground; and she would assume her mission had succeeded, that Shea lay dying of an insulin overdose on the ground where Hester had left her, that Zack was either dead or dying on the roadside. The odd satisfaction in the woman's split-faced smile told Shea that.

Hester could relax now, assured she would return safely to Philadelphia with no one the wiser about the string of murders she'd committed. And, certain she wouldn't be followed, she could administer her coup de grace, Jimmy's murder. Her total triumph lay in that.

And Shea's only hope of denying that triumph lay in keeping her in sight while staying out of Hester's line of

vision, and following her as far as she had to. The long line
of impatient drivers who'd been detoured onto the two-lane
undivided highway, likely unfamiliar with the road, both
helped and hindered her task. While Shea tried to keep her
place in the creeping queue, a pickup truck bearing beer-
drinking teenagers slalomed around her, careening onto the
left road shoulder, which jutted out and fell off over the
west shore of the lake in the basin far below. It rocked at
the edge, then corrected, then barely missed an oncoming
car as it recovered the road. Shaken, Shea pulled onto the
right shoulder for a second. The Chevy van disappeared
from view behind the mountains at a bend ahead, and Shea
lost her place to several cars before a polite driver allowed
her back into line.

For several miles she occasionally caught sight of the
van, some twenty cars ahead of her. It came into view again
just before Shea hit the spot where Route 88 branched off
to the south, to Globe. The Apache Trail formed a rugged
mountainous branch to the west. Beyond this branch was a
turnoff leading to the Tonto National Monument.

Unremarkably, all the cars ahead of Shea headed toward
Globe. Only after she herself had begun her turn did she
notice out of the corner of her eye that Hester's van was
lumbering up the road toward the Monument. She braked
and screeched off onto the right shoulder. *Hester could be
thinking only one thing. She thought no one was following her. She'd head for the monument grounds. There,
surrounded by unsuspecting park visitors, she would get
out her insulin and syringe, and, after injecting Jimmy,
she would descend from her van with that clownish smile
on her face, go to the public toilets, and dispose of the used
syringe.*

Shea sucked in a breath. She backed up her truck to the
turnoff, where she took the road to the Tonto National
Monument. Stopping at the berm of the hill just before it
entered the parking lot, she pulled to the side of the road
and parked. She would have to approach Hester unseen,
attracting neither her attention nor that of any visitors. To

do otherwise could push the powerful gargantuan woman into a desperate act too soon. Shea's timing would have to be perfect; she would have to snatch Jimmy and run into the visitors' center before Hester had time for anything except escape.

Keeping low and off to the side, Shea crept over the berm to the parking lot. What she saw made her hopes plummet. Hester's van alone was parked in the lot. A sign on a yellow wood traffic barrier in the driveway as it passed the cashier's booth warned potential visitors of the rockslide and resultant traffic jams between here and Phoenix. The visitors' center was closed, employees sent home.

And Hester was getting out of her van.

Howls emanated from the passenger side of the van. Hester passed in front of the vehicle and opened the passenger door. She released Lester's seat and shoulder belt and lifted him out. Shea could see his red-streaked face as she laid him, wrapped in a blanket on the ground, then knelt beside him. "Shh, Daddy, shh! Now calm down. I know it's been an awful long ride. And I know you can't sit on the picnic benches, and you're tired of being strapped in the car. And I'm sorry I hit you before. It's the first time I ever did something like that. But it's almost over. This is a perfect spot, you know. Everything's worked out just right. I won't even have to use the insulin. I won't have to do *anything* at all. Just leave him here." She leaned back on her heels and studied the monument's mountain walls, where a trail snaked up among tall bristling saguaro cactuses, small clumps of evilly barbed cholla, and spiny, long-branched ocotillo. In a cave on that mountainside, three hundred fifty feet above the parking lot, prehistoric cliff dwellers had built their remarkable, remarkably preserved shelters. Hester was staring at the walls just inside the mouth of the cave. "Right up there's where I'll put him. Then you can have your bed back, Daddy."

Lester keened sorrowfully.

A chill ran through Shea.

"Would you like to watch, Daddy?" She stood and looked

around, her wide round eyes sweeping in Shea's direction, freezing Shea to the spot for an instant, then swinging away toward a small group of boulders. "Ah, there! I can prop you up there, with the blanket around you." She lifted him and carried him to the spot and secured him there. "How's that? Can you see to the top?"

He grunted, as if he could, though of course he was almost totally blind.

She kissed him. "Don't you look sweet there? Oh, Daddy, I do love you so."

He made a happy sound.

"It won't take long, now, so you just sit still and be quiet. When I get back down, I'll get some water from the johnnie, and wash up your darling little face. You'll feel much better then. We'll find a nice motel in Globe, so you can get a good night's sleep before we start home."

Lester nodded his head. She kissed him again, then went to the van and opened the side gate.

Shea didn't move, barely breathed, as she scanned the mountainside, planned an approach to the cave that would get her to the entrance shortly after Hester, yet allow her to avoid detection. As long as she could remain out of Hester's field of vision, she had a good chance of making it to a hiding spot near the cave. Then, the instant Hester left and started down, Shea would slip into the cave and rescue Jimmy.

Now, at the side gate, Hester appeared, carrying Jimmy across her forearms, as if she were making an offering of him. She came down from the high van floor in two easy steps, took the child to her father, lowered him to within the reach of the old man's flipper. "Say good-bye, now, Daddy."

With a lullaby croon, Lester touched his flipper to Jimmy's face.

Hester stood. "He almost woke up in there. Moved his head, made a squeak or two. But then he was sound asleep again. I didn't expect him to sleep this long. Maybe I ran the engine a little too long for just a test. But I wanted to be sure it would work pretty fast. I was hoping we could leave and never have to do anything to him ourselves. He's so dear. I want to remember him just like he is, Daddy." She lowered her lips to his forehead.

The little boy squirmed slightly, and brushed his forehead with his arm.

"Oh dear. I'll have to hurry." Adjusting the load and pulling him closer to her chest, she crossed the parking lot to the mountain's steep slope and began loping up the established trail.

When she'd reached a turn in the trail that took her up facing away from the parking lot, Shea bolted from behind her cover of plantings and rounded the lot. She avoided passing close enough to Lester that her movements would alarm him. She had reached the bottom of the slope by the time Hester arrived at a trail switchback overlooking the lot. As Hester turned to look down at her father and yodel to him about her progress, Shea ducked behind a saguaro. Luck was with her. Her outfit, green jeans and yellow and green plaid shirt, camouflaged her, as she dodged between cactus and low sere scrub. Rain surfeited undergrowth held down off-trail pebbles she might have kicked free in a normal spring. She kept low, and pushed the rocky terrain out from beneath her feet, clambered up another ten yards to a footing just below an established trail crossing.

Hester, on a stretch several yards above her, stopped and turned again. Again, she halloed to her father.

He responded with a series of excited yelps.

"I'm almost there, Daddy."

She was, Shea agreed. The trail, a round-trip tourist trek of about half an hour, was a ten-minute stroll up, a five-minute lope down for Hester. If Shea could keep to the trail, it wouldn't be much more for her—she jogged four or five miles a day. But now she must climb on all fours over jagged rocks, among plants with vicious thorns and grasses hiding rattlesnakes. She couldn't spring out into the open; she must stay below Hester, stay hidden.

Hester raised Jimmy aloft in both hands and held him

poised there, shimmering in the slanting rays of the low late-afternoon sun. More imposing than the tallest giant saguaro beside the trail, she might have been a priestess, seeking supplication from the vengeful god who'd driven her to sacrifice a beloved in his name.

Below, the truncated blind god burbled a blessing on her act. Then Hester turned and crossed the final few yards of trail. She ducked into the cave, remained there barely a minute.

Shea scrambled around the slope toward the north, just out of view of the trail and the lot below. When Hester emerged, Shea could hear but not see her.

Shea stood, breathless, still, her back pressed against a sheer section to the north. She listened as Hester's large feet crunched quickly down the sandy path. She heard Lester's increasingly urgent cries floating up from below. As they grew more high-pitched, more demanding, the footfalls came faster. Soon Shea could make her move, scrabble down to the ruin several yards to the south. *If only Jimmy would sleep just a little while longer!*

But, from the cave below came a small sound, amplified and reverberating many times by concave walls. Jimmy's wakening noises pricked Shea's ears. She couldn't wait longer. Grabbing rocks and vegetation she propelled herself toward the ledge below the cave opening. Just as she reached out a hand to purchase hold on the trail, her foot dislodged a small rock. The rock bounced and ricocheted down the slope; Shea forfeited footing and handhold, and skidded downward.

She slammed into a boulder, glanced off of it into brief freefall over a cliff, then bumped for several yards, smashing finally into a thick, nasty patch of cholla. Wind knocked out of her, she lay scratched and bleeding for a few seconds. She knew she'd been hurt, but she felt no pain.

The scrunch of Hester's treads grew urgent, shifted toward Shea, picked up speed. Shea kicked herself free of the cactus, wrenching some of its tenacious fingers from their joints. They clung to her clothes and her hair, as she ran to recover the trail. Herself now a bristling weapon, she plunged down the grade toward her pursuer, flailing her arms. Hester raised her arms too late to shield her face; but her elbow deflected and tossed aside Shea's hurtling body.

Shea spilled face first into a boulder. She heard a loud crunch, and tasted blood's metal, bit into the gritty pumice of rock and shattered bone. Through a lightning flash of red fire and blue ice, she saw the shadow of Hester's monstrous shoe plunge toward her.

She rolled aside and caught the raised leg, brought the woman down. As her foe toppled heavily down the slope, Shea struggled to her knees. Blood dripped and ran onto the backs of her hands and through her fingers. Her face began to throb, and with each throb, a shadow beat across her eyes. From below she could hear Hester's harsh breathing. The woman was coming at her again. Shea pushed herself erect onto her knees, then, as she tried to stand, she saw Hester's legs, like two towering tree trunks rising from the burls of her knees, blocking out the wavering light from above.

One leg raised itself and crashed into Shea's mouth, spinning her backward to the ground. The other then chopped into her ribs; one by one, taking turns, the feet on the bottom of those legs cracked each limb. Then they walked away down the path. Before she lost consciousness, Shea heard Hester say, "She shouldn't have stolen the scrapbook, Daddy. But you see, it's all working out all right anyway. They'll think she came up here with that sweet little boy when the park was closed and the rangers weren't around. Then she went off the trail, and it says on those signs that you shouldn't, and both of them fell down and got killed."

Jimmy woke up slowly. He uncurled from the spot on the hard ground, then lifted his head. He looked at the wall in front of him, and knew he was not in his crib. There were no rails or bars, and no curtain for Daddy to sleep behind. Daddy wasn't here, but Daddy had been here

with him. He remembered the smell of this place. It smelled
cool and dusty.

He sat up. On two sides there were walls with little baby
doors that went into other rooms. One wall had no doors
at all, and the last one had a big person door going to the
sky. He got up and went to the big person door. Ahead and
above he saw the sky; below was a little house and a road
and some tiny little hills.

"No. Dimmy fa. Get hoot."

That's what Daddy had told him when he'd hugged him
tight and pointed out the door to the outside. "You have to
hold Daddy's hand when we go out there to climb back
down the mountain."

Daddy wasn't here with his hand. But there was a hand
here he knew he could hold. In one of the other walls, one
with the little baby doors. Jimmy turned and walked away
from the big outside door and walked back into the room,
to the side the gold sun was shining on.

"A long time ago, when the wall was brand new and
soft, like the Play-Doh you play with at Joyce's, a little
boy just like you put his hand there," Daddy had said. "His
handprint's still there. And you can fit your hand right in
it, and shake hands with a little boy from a long time
ago." Then Daddy had taken Jimmy's hand at the wrist,
and placed his hand on the print.

"An," Jimmy'd said. "Dimmy sake an."

"That little boy was an Indian, like Daddy's great-
grandmother, like Peter and Lucy. Except he wasn't an
Apache. But that doesn't matter. Way back, we all came
from the same roots. We once lived in this cave, way back.
It's like coming home, and finding them waiting for us in
our own safe place."

Jimmy'd repeated the words: "Say pay."

And now he could smell the wall's cool earth smell. He
toddled up to the opening and found the handprint. "Dimmy
sake an." He touched it. "Say pay."

He sat down by the wall and sighed. He was beginning
to feel hungry. He stuck his thumb in his mouth and waited

for Daddy to come back to take his hand and lead him down the mountain to the place where they'd had the picnic. He would not go down himself. With his thumb in his mouth and his saliva trickling down around his hand, he said, "No. Dimmy fa, get hoot."

Then, from outside the big door to the sky, came a noise like the time he'd tried to climb up on the table and pulled everything off, and it all fell onto the kitchen floor around him. Mommy had grown very angry and her voice had rat-ta-tatted out of her and scared him. And he'd put his hands up to his ears and gone to hide. And Mommy had come in with her not-angry soft voice and picked him up and held him until he was comforted.

Then another time he'd heard a noise like it when he was at Daddy's house and the television was on, and a bunch of people in the picture were playing peekaboo, and when they found each other they pointed big sticks at each other and made scary ratta-tats that had sparks coming out and knocked each other down. Poke came in and saw Jimmy with his hands up to his ears and a scared look on his face, and turned off the television. And she'd picked him up and held him until he was comforted.

Now the noise coming in through the door to the sky grew louder and more frightening than the angry ratta-tat-tat of Mommy's voice, and the stick and fire ratta-tat-tats of the television, and Poke was not here to turn them off, and Mommy was not here to pick him up, and he didn't know where Daddy was. And his hands were not big enough to keep the sound out of his ears, and the sounds were not just out in the sky anymore, but were coming from the wall beside him, and the walls across from him and behind him, and he was terrified. He closed his eyes and held his ears and rolled himself into a ball and cried.

On Saturday afternoon, Poke remembered something Grace Broward had said. Though she didn't trust her, didn't trust anyone at all, she knew there was one thing she could do, and she did it: She called the FBI and told

Lynne Timchuck, the agent handling what had become an urgent case, where her father was staying.

Timchuck said, "I've been trying to call you for three days, Poke. Since learning about Hester Jones, we've traced her movements to Tucson. She spent Thursday night with her father in a Motel Six there. Then she stopped at an ostrich festival in Chandler on Friday. She must have camped out in her van somewhere north of there Friday night. So she's closing in on your father. Thank God you called. We can warn him. What's the phone number there?"

Poke didn't know. "All I know is that ASU has something to do with the dig."

"We'll call. I'll get back to you."

But when Timchuck called back, she said, "Contract Archaeology's office is closed till Monday, Poke. We'll have to fly out ourselves. I'll keep in touch."

"Take me along!"

"What?"

"Please! I want to go. You can't just leave me here wondering what's happening to Jimmy and Pop."

"I . . . I don't think . . ."

"I can help you. I'm not scared. I won't get in your way. When Pop sees me, he'll know everything's OK."

After a brief pause, Lynne Timchuck said, "Yes. That makes sense. All right. I'll pick you up at seven tomorrow morning. We'll be taking a private jet that should get us to the closest military air base, probably Luke, just after noon their time. They'll have a copter waiting. From there we'll head toward the lake. Meanwhile, we'll alert the Highway Patrol to watch out for Hester's van, so they can head her off. At least, we should get to the dig site before she can do anything."

But when they arrived at Luke Air Force Base, no one reported seeing Hester's van. They would have to fly to the dig site and hope that when they'd set down at about two-thirty, they would bring Zack's and Jimmy's desperate flight from his seen and unseen pursuers to an end.

But no one was at the site, and the open trailer door,

and the telephone hanging dead from the wall, and the
scrapbook pages lying on a card table in the trailer, told
them not only that Hester had been there, but why. And
the insulin syringe on the ground, and the wheelchair sitting
next to the tracks spinning tires had gouged into the sandy
yard and the road running from it, told them they might
have come too late, and Hester had left no witnesses.

The copter clattered aloft. Agent Timchuck shouted into
her microphone, asking for aid in tracking Hester, who
might be dangerous, and might have a kidnapped child
with her now. If she should be seen by patrols, she should
be allowed to continue, under surveillance if possible, and
a roadblock should be set up to net her.

"Stay low over the road down there," she shouted to
the pilot.

"Which way?"

"What's most likely? If someone was chasing you?"

"I'd stay off the road altogether. Get myself into the
mountains out east, and park there."

"Then head to the mountains. The patrol will have to
watch the roads."

The pilot nodded. They rose and chopped off to the
east, lowering from time to time to check the dirt roads
that wound off toward Indian reservations and abandoned
mining towns.

Then Timchuck sat forward. "Wait!"

"I hear it," said the pilot of the announcement spitting
through their headphones.

"Great! That was a half hour before we left the site!"
said Timchuck. She turned to Poke. "The patrol saw her
at a roadblock on Highway 87, just above a rockslide.
They turned traffic back to 188, the road we decided not
to follow. They didn't see a child, but her father, I guess
it was, was howling and moaning in the seat next to her,
and she seemed upset."

"Maybe she doesn't have Jimmy!" said Poke.

"Maybe not. But they're setting up a roadblock on 88,
north of Globe."

"Well, let's head back west," said the pilot, lifting and banking his craft into a sweeping turn.

"Tell them to look for Pop," said Poke. "He might've been chasing her."

"Good idea." Timchuck repeated it to her radio contact. A few minutes later, word came back that a van of the Ram's description had run off the road on 188, and the driver had been medevaced to a hospital in Globe with carbon monoxide poisoning. He was getting hyperbaric oxygen and was expected to recover, thanks to a woman who had come on the accident, told witnesses what had overcome him, then dashed away. No child was with him, or with the unidentified woman.

"Then Hester must have him!"

Timchuck reached over and took Poke's hand. "We'll get her before she can hurt him. I promise you, Poke."

"Someone is helping him."

"I can see the roadblock on 188 below," said the pilot. "They're stopping cars, so she mustn't've come through yet."

"Then we can follow the line back to 87. She's got to be somewhere between here and there," said Timchuck.

"Roger!" He hung down low and swept quickly along the fifteen-mile stretch, then swept back to the 88 junction.

Poke strained her eyes, going and coming, growing dizzy and breathless with the effort. Among the hundreds of vehicles lurching toward the roadblock, she saw none resembling Hester's gray Chevy van.

"I bet she turned off somewhere to wait for things to clear," said the pilot.

"Where?" said Lynne Timchuck.

"Toward the Tonto Monument. She could hang out there till traffic cleared." He swung wide of the road toward the lake, then turned and cut west between the mountain peaks rising near the junction of 188 and 88. They passed over a parking lot, empty but for a single vehicle near the entrance.

Poke cried out, "That's her!"

She saw Hester lifting a wrapped person from the ground near the van.

Lynne Timchuck leaned over Poke's lap and looked to where she was pointing. "Is that the baby she's carrying?"

"It's Lester! Stop her. She's putting him in the van."

"Drop down, Captain," Timchuck ordered the pilot, who hadn't waited for instructions.

"There's someone lying on the side of the mountain. Not moving," he said, as he lowered the copter past the west face.

"Jimmy?"

"An adult. Just below the ruins in that cave directly to our right."

Poke's eyes found the ruins, saw a tiny shadow moving inside, as if running from the helicopter's shadow.

"Stop! Let me out! Jimmy's in there. He'll fall out!"

"Jesus, I can't just stop here. We'll all get killed. And that woman's got the guy in the car. Got to go down there and block her." He flew quickly to the parking lot and landed across the driveway, blocking the van.

Jumping to the ground, Poke raced to the mountainside. A skilled hiker and climber, she ignored the trail and scrabbled up the side, finding footholds and handholds among rocks and vegetation. She passed the woman lying unconscious and bleeding on her back just off the trail. "Thank you for helping Jimmy!" she panted as she dashed by. "We'll help you, too."

The cave was just a few yards above her. She longed to call out to Jimmy, to let him know she was coming; but she daren't risk drawing him to the ledge.

She pulled herself up onto the trail that led directly into the ruins. Then she cried out at last, "Jimmy! Oh, Jimmy! Poke's here, don't be scared. Poke's going to take you home."

"Po," said Jimmy as she stepped into the ancient cliff dwelling.

She took a deep breath and held out her arms. Slowly she approached him.

He toddled a few steps toward her, then stopped. "Po sake an," he said, and started back to the wall he'd been curled up against when she'd come.

She dropped her hands to her sides, though they ached to clutch him to her. It had been so long since he'd seen her. Maybe he thought her a stranger; maybe she scared him. She followed him to the window in the old smoke-streaked earth wall. There he turned and looked at her.

"Po sake an."

"What do you want Poke to do?"

He came to her and took her right hand and led her to the wall. Then he placed her hand on the wall at the window's edge. "Sake an."

A cool, shallow depression in the wall met her inquisitive touch. When she lifted her hand and discovered the print beneath it, she knew that her brother and she could no more be unlinked from each other than they could from the past they had touched and become a conscious part of. Then she picked him up and carried him down the mountainside.

EPILOGUE

LATE AUGUST—
GLENSIDE, PENNSYLVANIA

Zack stood at the window and watched the moving van
pull away in the late afternoon drizzle. The voices of Jimmy
and Poke at play in her room upstairs echoed through
the nearly empty house. They would sleep here one more
night, on the floor in sleeping bags, then pack the last of
their clothes and utensils into the Ram, and start across
the country to Arizona State University, in Tempe.

Yesterday, a hot muggy day, he had said good-bye to Liz,
in her small narrow room at the neuropsychiatric institute.
She had said good-bye to him, in her way. A parrotlike
repetition of his words: "Good-bye, Liz," followed by the
odd look in her dull violet eyes, a look that lay somewhere
between fear and searching. What she was searching for
was the meaning of the moment just past; what she feared
was the totally unknown, the moment to come, which would
disappear, unconnected with either the past or the present.

For Liz had no memory, no memor*ies*. The slate of her
mind had been wiped blank, then the slate itself rendered
useless.

"Good-bye, Liz," he'd said again, whispering, taking her
into his arms, kissing her on the high cheekbone, the one
firmness left on her face.

"Bye, Liz."

Stone-cold dead: her voice, her mind. He should have left well enough alone, made do with remembered warm living kisses.

He'd left then, walked out into the suffocating August afternoon. Grief, like none he'd ever known, hammered inside his head, choked him. Then he'd gone home, helped Poke pack the last few boxes, tried to eat the McDonalds take-out, tried to enjoy watching Jimmy push fries and a cheeseburger into his mouth and smear sauce over his face.

Later, while Poke readied Jimmy for bed, Zack turned on his computer and called up the subdirectory holding the program he'd run almost every night when he'd thought Liz was dead. He hadn't run it since, believing she wasn't. Now he realized that, appearances notwithstanding, she was. He had turned to the program again last night, because he'd thought that running it would help once again to bring her to life as he'd known her when they'd loved each other.

But his fingers had frozen over his keyboard. He could not invoke the program. Now, for several moments, he stared at the cursor blinking on the command line after the symbol C:\DRAWLIZ. Then he brought his fingers to the keys and typed in, ERASE *.*. For another minute he studied what he had done. He lifted his fingers from the keyboard and stared at the ENTER key. At last he pushed it.

The question, Are you sure? y/n, begged him from the screen to reconsider.

He pushed y, for yes, then ENTER again, and his hard disk whirled, and returned him to the DRAWLIZ subdirectory, but he knew that the subdirectory was empty, its contents completely erased. He could recover them from a backup disk if he wanted; but he wouldn't. Instead, he would one day reformat the backup, rendering its memory, its memor*ies*, unrecoverable.

Now he shut down his computer, unplugged it, and carried it to his van.

Afterward, he returned to the house. It echoed with incongruous laughter, and a bathed and sweet-smelling Jimmy rushed down the stairs into his arms. Warm, living kisses fell on his cheeks, and Liz came alive again in his mind.

MEANWHILE—BRYN MAWR

Grace Ellen Stanford Broward stood by the den window and pulled aside the heavy red velvet drapery and looked out the window into the past reflected in the darkening August sky. Maybe, if Grace stared long enough at the centuries old maple tree centering the broad turnaround driveway, Liz would drive up and park her gold Mercedes-Benz, as she had so often those Wednesday nights she'd come with Jimmy for dinner. She would smile as she entered the high-ceilinged foyer and stood in the sparkle of the massive crystal chandelier. Jimmy would run to his grandfather, chortling, "Gampa."

Paul would stoop. His long, freckled, sinewy arms would flex around Jimmy, gather him up against his tan sport shirtfront. Soon Paul would be chuckling and nuzzling the boy. He'd toss him up onto his shoulders, and gallop him through the high-ceilinged rooms into the kitchen where their housekeeper, Mary, had his dinner waiting.

Grace, with her usual humor and aplomb, would have defused Paul's irritation over Liz's lateness, the house calls she made in her van. As the man and boy laughed in the kitchen, Liz would follow her into this comfortable den, and Grace would pour sherry for them both. Liz would sit on the sofa of aged, brass-studded maroon leather, Grace would sit in the matching chair across from her, and mother and daughter would bask in the warmth of quiet conversation, the glow of deep mahogany wall panels and molding, the richness of floor-to-ceiling bookcases crammed full with leather-bound books and family memorabilia, and the luxury of deep crimson carpet.

But stare as she would through this window, tears running down her face, Grace could not stop this August Wednesday night from falling. She could not beat back the nights that had already fallen, one after another, over the past four years. The past could not be manipulated, not even by Grace Ellen Stanford Broward.

Still, she came downstairs to this window every evening at dusk. This window onto her past kept her in this house, made giving up her now very separate place in it impossible. It had become her home, her life, her motherhood, her marriage, all of which lived only in the manipulated past, none of which had survived her manipulation. She'd watched as her daughter had returned to consciousness in the room where they were held prisoner together. On first learning that Liz was memoryless, she reacted with joy and relief. Now she need never learn the truth about what her father had done. Grace would teach her only the good things. She could now go back to the beginning, undo her mistakes, reintroduce her to the kind of life a fine woman like Liz deserved. Grace would do this by leaving this burdensome estate, divorcing Paul, taking Liz with her to a new home. Of course she would set up the home for Zack and Jimmy and Poke. They were what Liz wanted. It would be a much nicer house than the one in Glenside, of course, in a better part of town. Perhaps Chestnut Hill. There were many fine houses there. And Liz would want to continue in her medical practice. Probably her skills would remain intact, though she might need to go back to medical school, go through an internship again. But surely her partners would help her along. However long it took, Grace would do whatever she must. Whatever she could to undo her terrible mistakes of the past.

But Liz *had* no past; and her present could not be manipulated into the future, for her future never came. Therefore, *Grace* had no present but her own to work with, and her own was too horrible to bear. Yet she would go every day to visit Liz, and see that her daughter looked the same, and she could still say things; whatever Grace told her to say, she repeated. A few brief words, perhaps, but surely Liz knew their meaning. And when Grace said good-bye and waved to her, Liz said good-bye and waved back. Yes, tomorrow she'd remember the things Grace had told her today. And one day, Grace would look out this window, and see Liz coming toward her across the driveway. And she would smile and wave, and Grace would smile and wave back.

But tonight, Grace once again drew the red velvet drapery against the black.

A WEEK LATER—PHOENIX

"In here," Shea directed the movers. Into the room that had twice been an office, the tall, slim man and the short, burly one carried the twin bed spring and mattress, and set them on their metal frame. She appraised the bed's fit and look, and shook her head. No, Jimmy's first regular bed should go up against the wall. He should have only one side open, with plenty of play space around it. He'd soon bury the bright blue carpet under the brand-new toys she'd heaped onto the long, low, built-in shelves. Ignoring twinges in her newly knit limbs, she pushed the bed sideways on its casters against the long wall next to the door.

Last week, Bill Jenkins had helped her move the heavy oak office furniture across the house into the Arizona room. The south-facing solarium merged indoors and outdoors and used thrifty passive solar energy, once Doug's passion. Now the room gave up its openness to Zack's favorite pieces of bulky family room furniture: a desk, a swivel office chair, a brown vinyl recliner, and a sofa that was much too long for the room. She had the movers set them all in the middle. Zack could arrange them later. He'd said he'd given away or sold most of his furniture, but he'd still sent more than could be merged with hers. Well, who was she to mess with family treasures and heirlooms? She'd gladly trip over them as long as it took her and Zack to decide which of their memories they needed, which to get rid of.

Houses and furniture, she thought, held memories. All physical things held memories. Her body, which had changed, constantly remembered what it had been just five months before. Even as its scars lost their redness, they held their aches, their tenderness. Even though its long bones had knit, the muscles supporting them railed at her when she used them.

Her face and mouth clung hardest to their memories. Her upper front jawbone knew that the crowned and filled posts embedded there weren't the teeth Hester had kicked out, though her smiles might fool the public. Every bite radiated through her head. The dentist said that feeling might last for years. Eventually, though, it should fade.

Her lower lip, first repaired by an emergency room resident, contorted and twisted whenever she spoke or ate, as it fought to find its old shape. An off-center droop made it hard to drink liquids without losing drops down her chin. She'd need plastic surgery next month, to straighten the droop, resynchronize the corners of her smiles. Last week, the plastic surgeon had not only told but shown her how handy he was.

He sat her in front of a computer camera gig, and snapped her "before" picture. Then, in front of her eyes, he operated an electronic scalpel, cutting bloodlessly through the scars, allowing the misaligned edges of the cuts to fall into the right place again, lacing the edges together intradermally and finishing off the top with black silk sutures.

"Now," he said, "here you are five days later. We've taken out the silk stitches." He zipped a wand across the screen. "Still a little sore and tight. The intradermals've absorbed. Going to hurt a little for a while. But the worst will be over. Want to see how the scar fades?"

Whether she did or not, he flipped her face forward through several weeks, then months. A year later the scar, except for a thin, pale pink loop at the center of her lip, had disappeared into her lip line. "With lipstick, no one'll notice."

She'd nodded and held back her tears, but this man who noticed every tiny facial detail, saw hers quiver.

"Now, don't be nervous," he said. "I know it's hard to believe, you've been through so much, but we'll make you your old self again."

But it wasn't her own computerized future face that upset her; it was Zack's computerized vision of Liz's past, the face he and Jimmy had watched every night. She was frightened at having her image boxed and played with this way. "Please! I don't want to see anymore."

"All right," said the doctor, switching off the machine.

Shaken, she'd left his office. And shaken she'd remained, until Zack called that night and told her that he'd erased the Liz program from his hard disk's memory.

Now she stood among his physical memories: his desk, his sofa, his recliner. The movers had left. She touched her face, traced its lines, so new to her fingers they didn't recognize her. They knew the truth, though. She'd never be her old self again. These scars could be hidden, but never erased; her pains would fade, but always be remembered, in a passing twinge, like grief, in a sudden ache, like loneliness.

The doorbell chimed. Her hand fell away from her face, where Zack's and Jimmy's remembered touches still lingered. Then she smiled and ran toward new touchings she'd only imagined: kisses of the man who loved her and of the son they would raise together.